W9-AUK-592

Breana's Full Circle

To Valinda Happy reading
E Cottrell

J. ELAINE COTTRELL

ARCHWAY
PUBLISHING

Copyright © 2015 J. Elaine Cottrell.

All rights reserved. No part of this book may be used or reproduced by any means, graphic, electronic, or mechanical, including photocopying, recording, taping or by any information storage retrieval system without the written permission of the author except in the case of brief quotations embodied in critical articles and reviews.

This book is a work of fiction. Names, characters, places, and incidents either are products of the author's imagination or are used fictitiously. Any resemblance to actual events or locales or persons living or dead, is entirely coincidental.

Archway Publishing books may be ordered through booksellers or by contacting:

Archway Publishing
1663 Liberty Drive
Bloomington, IN 47403
www.archwaypublishing.com
1 (888) 242-5904

Because of the dynamic nature of the Internet, any web addresses or links contained in this book may have changed since publication and may no longer be valid. The views expressed in this work are solely those of the author and do not necessarily reflect the views of the publisher, and the publisher hereby disclaims any responsibility for them.

Any people depicted in stock imagery provided by Thinkstock are models, and such images are being used for illustrative purposes only. Certain stock imagery © Thinkstock.

ISBN: 978-1-4808-2305-1 (sc)
ISBN: 978-1-4808-2306-8 (hc)
ISBN: 978-1-4808-2307-5 (e)

Library of Congress Control Number: 2015918336

Print information available on the last page.

Archway Publishing rev. date: 12/11/2015

Dedication

For my family who is my inspiration for everything
I do, because I love you all so much.

Prologue
St. Albans, New York
September 1943

The leaves had started to change from green to bright yellow. Some were golden brown and had fallen to the ground. Pedestrians covered their heads with knitted hats, and pulled their coats around them attempting protection against the chilly air as they moved briskly along the streets. The whistle from the Long Island Rail Road train signaled six o'clock am, and the streets came alive as people bustled through their daily routine. Oh yes, life continues marching forward, even as World War II raged on, and the two day riot in Harlem was slowly becoming a distant memory... babies need birthing, children need rearing, and people need to work and rest...that's life!

The aroma of coffee and fresh bagels from a café, near the local fire station filled the frosty morning air. Firefighters assembled inside the Station for their daily briefing. They sat around the table and talked, drank coffee, and discussed the weather.

Captain Maxwell took off his hat. He passed his hand over his curly red hair and brushed it backward, revealing the freckles on the fair skin across his forehead.

"I hope we have a better winter than what we had last year?" he said to one of the firemen, sitting across the room. "Saints preserve us. What a time it was, aye Billy Boy! You remember, don't ya?

"I sure do. I had to cancel my vacation and come in to work that day. Boy was Mary angry; she screamed like a banshee, when I told her the trip to Florida was off."

"Oh yeah! I had to pull my men in from vacation and days off to keep up with the demand," said Maxwell. "Just thinking of that bitter cold and horrid snow storm is enough to shiver mi timbers." Maxwell lifted his cup and proceeded drinking.

"Mm—good coffee," he said as he drained the last drop and sat the cup on the table.

He started walking out of the fire house. On his way outside, Billy shouted, "Hey Maxwell, come to think of it, I should hold you responsible for everything that's gone wrong in mi marriage; after all, it all began that day you called me into work. Tis on the couch I slept many o' nights, I tell ya!"

"William O'Connor! That's blarney, and you know it! Mary ain't no fool, is she? If you got troubles in yo marriage, blame it on that coffee o' yours yo always carry in ya flask!"

"Aye! That's hitting below the belt Maxwell McGovern. You got a sharp tongue, and coming from one who claims to be my friend no-less. What would ya be saying then if ya were my enemy?"

Maxwell laughed out loud, "Billy, yo know I don't mean anything by it. What's the matter with yo?"

Maxwell walked outside, chuckling. His breath created puffs of smoke into the cold morning air. He lit a cigarette, and he walked to the side of the building.

"Jesus, Mary and Joseph!" he cried out. "Fellas, come out here an' see this!"

Billy was the first to reach outside, adjusting his coat as he walked out.

"What is it Chief?" He asked as he hurried to Maxwell's side.

Maxwell was standing over a baby carriage. Billy quickly walked over and looked inside. He saw a baby lying fast asleep. She was dressed in a pink snow suite and covered with a pink blanket.

"Oh sweet Jesus!" he exclaimed, "I wonder how long this poor little thing has been lyin' here?"

"It had to be since early morning," Maxwell responded, "I felt the carriage, and the top of it is dry. If it had been overnight, it would have been wet with dew."

They took the carriage inside the fire house. The movement and voices woke the child. Maxwell picked up the baby, and she started crying. He held her over his shoulder and walked back and forth. He shook her gently as he sang, 'When Irish Eyes are smiling.'

Billy sat at the far end of the table, listening. Maxwell hit a false note, and Billy said,

"Jesus Christ Maxwell; what sort of howling is that to the wee one? Your gray eyes may be smiling, but that singing o' yours is worse than the bawling o' the young lass!"

"Ya think ya can do better then, Billy boy? Let's see ya bring ya pipe over here and soothe her then. How 'bout it?"

Maxwell looked inside the carriage, and he found a clothing bag. He opened up the bag and inside was some baby clothes, an envelope, and a pink feeding bottle filled with apple juice. He picked up the bottle and started feeding the baby, and she drank it all. When he opened the envelope, he found a key chain and a note inside. The key chain had letters on one side which read HHN, and the Rolls-Royce logo on the other side. He read the contents of the note.

'This is Breana, my baby. She is eight months old. I can no longer take care of her. Please find her a good home. I have nothing of value to give her, except this key chain.'

All the firefighters gathered around her. They made funny faces and weird sounds in an effort to calm her down, but she cried more. While the group of men entertained the child, Chief Maxwell called the police. A short time later, two police officers arrived. The officers questioned everyone that was on the premises, and within close proximity of the fire station. Unfortunately, no one claimed to know the child nor to whom she belonged. The officers contacted the 'Children's Aid Society.'

* * *

Almost mid-morning, a white station wagon drove up in front of the fire station.

A woman of average height and medium frame got out of the station wagon. Her auburn hair was cut to shoulder length, and her bangs lay against taut ivory skin on her face. She wore a blue coat that complimented the color of her eyes, and purple plum lipstick graced her thin lips. Her high top black boots and a calf length coat were just right for the morning weather. She walked up to the building, and Maxwell met her by the door.

"Good morning! I'm Elsie Tucker from the Foundling Hospital," she said.

"Top o' the day to you Miss Tucker! I'm Maxwell McGovern." He said as they shook hands. "What a shame it is to bring such a bonnie lass out on a morning like this."

"Thank you Mr. Maxwell, but that's okay; when duty calls I do obey. My main office down town received a call from the Children's Aid Society. They said someone had abandoned a baby on your premises. Since my home is not too far away, my supervisor called me. I got the call just as I was getting ready to leave for the office."

"I do appreciate ya getting here so fast. Where's ya office?"

"It's at the Foundling Hospital on Avenue of the Americas in Manhattan."

"Oh yea, I've heard of the place." He looked at the baby. "She's been crying up a storm, she has...since I found her."

Mrs. Tucker walked over to the carriage and looked inside.

"Well, who have we here?" she said, as she picked up the baby.

"We found this note among her belongings," said Maxwell.

He touched Breana's cheek and said, "Who could have done this to such a wee one? And a pretty one she is."

"Indeed, she is beautiful," said Elsie.

She read the note; then, she looked at the key chain.

"This might be important. I'll save it for her."

"A good thing it is that you're doing, looking after these poor unfortunate waifs, like you do, Miss Tucker."

"We do try, Mr. Maxwell, with the help of good citizens such as you."

"I cannot begin to imagine how anyone could just put down an innocent baby and walk away, just like that." said Maxwell in a disparaging tone.

"Mr. Maxwell, you would be surprised. Some of these mothers see this as their only alternative, and they carry that burden with them for the rest of their lives. The mother is just as much a victim as the child sometimes."

"And even so, they keep on doing it. Why?"

Mrs. Tucker began to bundle the baby up for departure; she said, "There are several reasons that could contribute to the situation. Immigration status, poverty, and poor housing conditions are the main factors. Sometimes the best thing for the child is to be placed with a family who is capable of providing proper care."

Maxwell scratched his head. "I can understand the reasons for wanting to give the child up, but why this way?"

"Because it's done without any questions asked." Elsie replied.

She picked up the bag with the clothes and started walking toward the station wagon. Maxwell followed behind her with the carriage. She positioned Breana in the car and said goodbye.

* * *

It was almost noon when Elsie reached her office with Breana. The place was buzzing with activity as the other workers tackled their caseloads. Breana was fast asleep as Elsie walked towards her desk. Before she sat down, another worker noticed the beautiful baby.

"Oh my goodness!" she said in a high pitched motherese. "Who is this?"

"Hi Connie, she was left outside a fire station in St Albans this morning. Isn't she beautiful?"

"Oh yes she is! Was there a note or anything?" Breana began to wake up by the noisy environment.

"Yeah, her name is Breana," Elsie Tucker said, as she showed Connie the note.

She then placed the key chain next to the typewriter. Breana began fidgeting which quickly turned into crying.

"Here, I'll get her changed and fed; while you get her papers started."

"Thanks Connie."

As Connie took Breana away, Elsie proceeded to start her file. She typed in the case number and the date. When she came upon 'Child's Name', she paused. She looked up at the ceiling and took a deep breath. *'Breana...Doe?'* She thought; she unconsciously picked up the key chain and began twirling it around her index finger. Looking at the key chain, she read, *Rolls Royce*.

"Royce, Breana Royce."

She was pleased with the name and started typing as she said aloud - "BRE-ANA ROYCE!" The baby's complexion was very fair and her hair was dark and straight. Mrs. Tucker typed, *Race* Caucasian...*Sex*...Female. "I think that'll do for now, what she really needs is a good home" she said as she walked over to the filing cabinets. She selected three files; after reviewing all three, she made her choice and soon Breana became a part of the foster care system.

Chapter One

Over the years, the agency frequently moved Briana from one foster home to another.

She suffered many abuses and neglect at the hands of her foster parents and her peers. When she was only four years old, her then foster mother, Jean Simmons, was a recovering alcoholic. She treated Breana fairly well, and Breana liked her. Breana had a favorite book, *Jewels of the Caribbean*. In this book, a family played together, built sand castles on the beach, and the father took his family sailing and fishing.

Jean frequently read this book to Breana. She listened attentively and longed to be a part of that family and go sailing on the ocean.

One evening, Jean sat with Breana on the couch in the living room. Breana had just brought the book for Jean to read to her. Suddenly, there was a knock at the front door. Jean handed the book back to Breana, and she went to answer the door.

She started to open the door. Then immediately she started bracing against it—attempting to close it again.

"Jean!" shouted a voice from the other side of the door. "Jean, open this door before I tear it down with my bare hands!"

The shouting prolonged, and Jean continued to brace against the door. A man Breana did not recognized pushed his way into the house. Jean shouted,

"What in hell do you want with me? Get out of my house, or I'll call the police!"

"The police, Jean!" said the sandy haired man wearing dark glasses, and a red plaid shirt. His sleeves were rolled up to his elbows. "We all know how that works!" he continued to say. "You belong to me! I have the right to come and go as I please! Now why don't you just be a good girl and make it easy on yourself. I can make your life a living hell if I want, and you can't do a damn thing about it!"

He removed the dark glasses from his face. His eyes were as red as crimson, and his face was chafed by the sun. He staggered towards Jean, ignoring Breana's presence.

"Breana!" Jean shouted, "Go to your room, and lock your door now! And don't come out unless I call you!"

Breana was terrified. She ran into her room, clutching the book in her arms, and she closed the door behind her. She could hear them arguing and yelling at each other.

Then, she heard them scuffling, and they hit the floor with a big bang. Jean started screaming.

"Get away from me! Get away from me!"

Then her voice got muffled, and the sounds that followed were indescribable by the four year old. When the scuffling stopped, Breana peeked through the crevice of the door.

She saw her foster mother lying on the floor, crying. Her orange pants were lying on the floor next to her, and her cream colored blouse was ripped down the front and at the sleeves. She had scratches and bruises all over her body. The room was in disarray, and the coffee table was split in half. She watched the intruder walk toward the door. As he reached the door, he stopped, zipped up his blue jeans, and turned around as he shouted at Jean. "You are my wife! I only took what I had coming to me!"

"One of these days you'll get what's *really* coming to you!" she shouted back.

"I hope I'll be there, so I can spit in your face, you son of a bitch! You're an animal!"

He looked at her smugly, and he said, "Thank you Ma'am. It has always been a pleasure. Till the next time, ciao baby."

He lit a cigarette and walked out, slamming the door behind him. Breana sat down behind her bedroom door. She was trembling. Assuming the man was gone, she cracked the door just enough to look out. She watched Jean as she got up and limped into the bathroom. She heard the water running for a long time. After a while, Jean came out, carrying a full bottle of liquor. She sat down at the table, and started drinking.

After she finished drinking, she started searching the cabinets. As she fumbled around, she knocked things over without stopping to pick them up.

She found another bottle under the kitchen sink. She took a glass and walked back to the kitchen table. She sat down and continued to pour and drink.

* * *

Breana had not eaten since she had breakfast. It was getting dark outside and past her usual dinner time. She left her room and started to walk into the kitchen in the dark. When she turned the light on, she saw Jean sitting with her head down on the table. Her brown hair was disheveled, and her arm was wrapped around a half-empty bottle of vodka. She lifted her head as Breana walked into the room. Her lips were swollen, and her face was black and blue around the eyes. Breana was horrified by the sight of her. Through bloodshot eyes, she looked at Breana.

"What are you staring at you little wench?" She screamed, "I told you to stay in the room until I called you! I sure as hell did not call you!"

Breana was startled and shaken by Jean's cruel words. Her eyes bulged and she trembled in fear.

"I don't know why I even bother!" Jean said before taking another swig of liquor.

"You can't even follow simple directions! That's why your own mother didn't want you! I'm going to call that woman to come and take you out of here. I can't put up with you anymore! You don't know how to listen. I don't need any of this shit! I have my own problems!" she said, with slurred speech and put her head down on the table.

Those words cut through Breana's heart like sharp blades. Scared and confused, she ran back to her room and sat in a corner. She clutched her book tightly to her chest. She felt alone with no one to comfort her. She cried, but there was no one to hear; no one to care.

It got darker outside. A dingy yellow nightgown with a large chocolate stain on the front lay crumbled on the bed. She held it up and looked at it; then she put it on and climbed into bed. Since there was no one to read to her that night, she opened the book to her favorite story and looked at the pictures. While hunger pangs gripped at her stomach, she started singing a song she had learned at a former foster home. "By the Sea, by the Sea, by the Beautiful Sea…"

Sleep was approaching, and her voice was fading. She repeated the song over and over until she drifted off to sleep. Jean got up from the table and went into her bedroom carrying the liquor with her. She poured herself another drink, took a big gulp, and sat the glass down on the nightstand. She then reached into the drawer for a pack of cigarettes. She took one of the cigarettes; she lit it and lay in bed as she smoked. She took the glass and drank some more. Attempting to replace the glass, she misjudged the distance, and the drink fell to the floor. She kept puffing the cigarette until she fell asleep. The cigarette fell from her hand to the floor where the drink had spilled. A fire started and soon, the whole house was filled with smoke.

Breana was awakened by the smell of smoke, as it seeped under her door. Fortunately, the window to her room was cracked open. She jumped off the bed and ran to the open window.

"Help, help me! Fire!" she cried.

The neighbors heard her from the open window, and someone called for the fire department.

When the fire fighters arrived and worked their way into the house, they found Breana still clutching her book. She was unconscious and lying on the floor. One of the fire fighters brought her outside and tried to resuscitate her. She was revived and taken to the hospital by ambulance.

The fire was brought under control, but unfortunately, Jean perished. Breana was sent to another foster home. She was traumatized by the ordeal, and for many months she did not speak. Because of this, she endured ridicule from the neighborhood children.

They knocked stones together as they yelled, "Hey dummy, or hey dumb – dumb!"

They pinched her just to see if she could cry.

"Dummy has no feelings," they shouted.

She stayed in therapy for many months. By the time Breana turned five years old, Mrs. Tucker had been the only constant person in her life. One day, she paid a routine visit to Breana. Upon her arrival, Breana was sitting on a couch by the window in the living room. She saw the white station wagon stop in front of her house.

"Mrs. Tucker," she shouted.

Then she ran to the door to meet her. Mrs. Tucker reached for her and hugged her tightly.

"Oh, Breana it's so good to hear your voice again."

Breana looked up at her. "I love you Mrs. Tucker, and I missed you."

"I love you too Breana; I'm so pleased to hear you say that."

She was elated to hear someone say, 'I love you' to her.

As she grew older, her complexion got darker, and waves in her long black hair rippled down her back. She was gorgeous. Nevertheless, she did not have many friends; because, she moved around so often, she was always losing the few she did make. She struggled with the feeling of abandonment and despair. Even so, she found some comfort in finding a quiet place where she could read and sometimes daydream.

* * *

By age eleven, Breana had become so accustomed to moving from one home to another, she considered it a way of life. Early one morning, Mrs. Tucker visited.

"Breana, how are you?"

"I'm fine Mrs. Tucker. Why are you here so early?"

"Well, there have been some changes. You won't be able to live here anymore, so I've come to get you. I'm sorry I wasn't able to prepare you for this, but something came up, and I have to move quickly."

Breana knew the routine. She went to her room and packed her suitcase.

"Any place might be better than here. I'd like to live with people who'll give me more than clothes and food," she mumbled. When she finished packing, she went into the living room where Mrs. Tucker waited for her.

"I'm ready Mrs. Tucker," she said, flatly.

Breana was quiet during the entire trip. She stared blankly out the window. The beautiful scenery went unnoticed. Mrs. Tucker tried to cheer her up.

"I'm sure you'll love it there." She said, "Mrs. White is very nice, and there's a park just down the street from the house."

Breana struggled to maintain her composure. In a soft tone, she said,

"Yes Ma'am."

Tears rolled down her cheeks as she gazed through the car window. After they had driven for a while, they arrived at Mrs. White's house. It was made of red bricks with the wood-works painted in white. It was located at the corner of Highland Avenue in Jamaica Estates. On the inside, frilly white crisscross curtains draped to perfection in front of two large bay windows. The lawn was beautifully manicured, and a tall pine tree grew on the front lawn.

A Bougainvillea plant grew at the base of the pine tree, twined around the trunk, and lavishly covered to the top with bright magenta colored flowers. Breana was fascinated by its beauty.

When Mrs. Tucker rang the doorbell, a woman of medium stature opened the door. Her platinum hair was brushed, neatly braided, and wrapped around the top of her head. She wore a white apron tied around a paisley green dress. In a voice as smooth as honey, she said, "Come in Mrs. Tucker I've been expecting you." Mrs. Tucker stepped into the foyer.

"Mrs. White, this is Breana Royce. Breana, this is Mrs. White. She'll be looking after you. I've known her for many years, and I would trust her with my own child. I've been waiting to place you with her for a long time."

The house was warm and had a sweet fragrance like apple cinnamon. As Mrs. White reached out to welcome her, Breana noticed her complexion was fair with a few age spots on the back of her hands. Her skin was as soft as velvet.

"I'm glad you're here Breana. I've been hearing so much about you. It's nice to finally meet you. You're just as beautiful as I heard."

"Thank you, Ma'am," Breana said softly.

"Come, I'll show you to your room. It's upstairs."

Breana followed her upstairs into the room. She was pleased with this room; because, from there she could see what had already become her favorite tree. Beautiful magenta flowers started from the base almost to the top of the tree. While she unpacked and put her belongings away, Mrs. Tucker went up to the room.

"Breana, I'm leaving. I came to say goodbye. Everything will be fine now."

She cradled Breana's face with her hands. Looking her in the eyes, she said,

"Now I'm sure that you'll be getting the care I have always wanted for you."

Breana gave her a little smile when she heard that. Mrs. Tucker said,

"If you need me for anything at all, you know I'll be here for you."

She hugged Breana, and she turned to leave the room. Just before Elsie walked out, Breana called out to her.

"Mrs. Tucker?"

Elsie turned around, "Yes Breana."

"Thank you for everything that you did for me."

"You're quite welcome my dear."

She watched Elsie walked away. She sat on the bed, and feelings of being deserted started to surface. She thought of all that had happened in her life, and she broke down and cried.

"Oh God, what did I do? Why does no one want me? Even my own mother never wanted me. The girls at school have mothers. They laugh at me; because, my mother walked away. If I was good enough, maybe they would like me," she said softly to herself.

She cried herself to sleep. By the time she woke up, it seemed to her that she was only in the room for a short time, but it was late. She slept past dinnertime.

Mrs. White went upstairs to the room and knocked on the door.

"Breana, are you alright?"

"I'm sorry, Ma'am. I must have fallen asleep. I hope I didn't keep you waiting."

"That's alright child. I know that you had a rough day, but you have to eat."

"I'll be right down Ma'am."

"All right dear, there's no rush."

Breana went to the bathroom. She looked in the mirror, and she cleaned her face. 'At least she sounds like she's concerned about me,' she thought. After she finished in the bathroom, she went downstairs.

"Come, sit down dear." Mrs. White said, "I have already eaten while you were resting; however, I'll have a cup of tea with you. I know it's late, so I fixed you something light."

Breana walked over to the table and sat down. She lifted the cover from the food.

On the plate, there was a ham sandwich with lettuce and tomato and a glass of milk.

While Breana ate, Mrs. White kept the conversation light, telling her about the neighborhood and the parks nearby. She ate half of the sandwich and drank half of the milk, and she started to clear the table.

"Oh, don't bother dear" said Mrs. White, "I'll take care of it later. Come sit with me in the den." They both walked into the den and sat on the sofa. "So, tell me about yourself.

All I know about you is what I heard from Mrs. Tucker."

Breana hung her head down. She did not speak.

"Did I say something wrong dear? I didn't mean to make you uncomfortable,"

"No Ma'am, you didn't. It's just that I really don't have anything to say about myself. No one ever asked me before."

She remained shy and quiet around Mrs. White. During their first week together, she only spoke when she was spoken to, but Mrs. White did not give up. One night after dinner, Breana was sitting at the kitchen table picking at her dessert. Mrs. White was washing the dinner dishes. How was the school you attended? Did you have many friends?" she asked Breana, hoping she would open up to her. Breana had a blank look on her face as she responded,

"They laughed at me."

Mrs. White was confused. She put the last plate in the dish rack and turned around as she dried her hands off on her apron.

"Who laughed at you?"

"All the kids…" Tears trickled down Breana's face, as her eyes locked on her cake. "…at school, they laugh at me and call me names. They say I came out of a pumpkin patch. They called me dummy, and even said that my own mother didn't want me."

Mrs. White listened attentively, and her heart ached for the child. She took Breana by the hand and said, "Come with me. I want you to see something."

She walked her into the living room and stood in front of a mirrored wall.

"Look in that mirror, so you can see what I see," said Mrs. White, "The person you described does not exist. When I look at you, I see a beautiful child who will soon become a stunning young woman. You are a good person. Those people who said those things to you are wrong."

Mrs. White told her that a good person does not hurt other people, so the ones who treated her poorly—they are the ones who need adjusting. They did those things to hurt her because they saw something good in her.

"You are a challenge to them," she said, "If they can get you to doubt yourself that cuts their battle to measure up to you by half. Do not make them win. Believe in yourself. You are Breana; you are beautiful; you are smart, and you are worthy of everything good. Now stand up straight, chin up and say after me, I'm Breana; I'm beautiful; I'm smart, and I'm worthy of good things."

When Breana repeated the statement, Mrs. White said, "Now promise me you will always remember that."

"Yes Ma'am, I promise."

Well,   Breana had a comfortable night's sleep, and she was up with the sun the next morning. "I'll let you take today to get yourself together; then tomorrow, we'll go to the school and have you registered. This way you won't miss too many days." Mrs. White said.

"Yes Ma'am." She said, smiling.

However, she was concerned with how she would be accepted by her peers. *'It might be different kids with the same attitude.'* That thought breezed through her mind.

The first few days of school went smoothly. Then it became evident that she would only speak when she was spoken to. She kept to herself. Eventually, it became known that she was a foster child, and her troubles began.

"You have no parents. No one wants you around," they shouted at her on the playground. They called her names like, 'Orphan'. They threw spitballs at her and tied her long locks of hair to the back of her chair. This went on for weeks, yet she never fought back until one day in the lunch room. Breana picked up her lunch tray and started walking to her seat when one of the girls stuck her foot out and tripped her. She fell face down on the floor, and bit her tongue. It started to bleed, and no one helped her.

Finally, she got to her feet and picked up a carton of milk that had fallen from her tray. She calmly opened it as the other kids looked on. She walked over to the girl that tripped her and she poured it over the girl's head. The girl's blonde hair was saturated. The milk flooded over her pale face, and her blue eyes saw red. The milk trickled down her chest and onto her purple colored blouse. She grabbed Breana by the collar and started punching her, and for the first time Breana fought back. Breana kicked this girl in the shin. She attempted to bend over to grab hold of her leg, but Breana blocked her with a swift kick to her backside. She fell to the floor, and in a minute the pale faced girl was purple. All the children in the cafeteria started uproariously chanting, "Fight! Fight! Fight! Fight!"

Mr. Eubanks was a teacher assigned to the cafeteria that day. He was so enthralled with a magazine he was looking through that he failed to notice the girls until it was too late. He rushed toward them shouting "Stop it! Stop it!"

The children shouted. "She started it! She started it!" as they pointed to Breana.

She said nothing in her defense. Mr. Eubanks took her to the principal's office. Principal Rowe, apparently in his late fifties, sat behind a large mahogany desk. Locks of brown curly hair tousled over his forehead and lay softly against his narrow face. His mustache was neatly trimmed; he had a way of playing with his thinly shaped beard, which adorned his chin like a goatee, when he disapproved of something. Mr. Eubanks knocked on the door. Mr. Rowe looked over his gold round rim eyeglasses. "Come in." he said, sighing at the interruption.

Mr. Eubanks opened the door and pushed Breana in the room then he followed her in. The small mousy man stood behind her. His torso was narrow, and his dark hair was prominently parted to one side and combed over. "I've got a troublemaker here for you Mr. Rowe," he said in a gruff voice trying to sound intimidating.

"What kind of trouble did SHE make Mr. Eubanks?" asked Mr. Rowe, with a hard accent straight out of the Bronx.

"She was fighting in the cafeteria, Sir."

"With whom was she fighting?"

"She was fighting with some—other girl in the cafeteria."

"Then why isn't her opponent here, too?"

"Well, everybody said she started the whole thing, Sir."

Mr. Rowe started playing with his beard. He thumbed the desk top with his fingers and leaned backward in his chair.

"Mr. Eubanks…," he said, "you may go back to your post now; I'm sure I'll be able to handle this big bad agitator that you shoved into my office."

Disgruntled by the tone of Mr. Rowe's admonishment, Mr. Eubanks turned swiftly and walked out of the room. "I get no respect…no matter what I do," he said, as he tramped down the hall.

Mr. Rowe motioned to Breana to sit on a chair on the opposite side of his desk.

"Well Breana, this behavior is not in line with your character; tell me what happened?"

Breana said nothing. Her robust cheeks now wet with tears. Blood from her injured tongue spilled on the front of her white blouse. She hung her head and fondled with the hem of her blue and black plaid skirt. Her white tights were torn from the knees down to her legs, and her black patent leather shoes were scuffed all over.

"Breana, I cannot help you if you do not speak to me," said Mr. Rowe. "Don't be afraid. I won't bite. I promise," he said, in an effort to lighten up the situation.

"I didn't start it as they said. The girl tripped me and I fell. I tried to defend myself, and they all turned on me. Why bother saying anything. I know that no one cares. Every day after class, I walk the halls, scared! Look at me! I'm the one who's bleeding, yet no one seems to care!" Breana was shaking.

"Now wait a minute, Breana, calm down. Don't assume that no one cares. I've noticed that you've been withdrawn, but I never knew why. I was waiting for the opportunity to present itself for me to find out."

He paused for a response; she gave none. "If you ever need to talk, I'm here for you. I'll have the nurse examine you and call someone to come and get you. The next time something like this happens, do not retaliate. You come to me, and let me take care of it, deal?"

Breana hesitated, holding her eyes to the floor; she managed to whimper, "Yes, Sir."

"You are excused from class for the rest of the day. You can wait here for your guardian to come and take you home."

As time went by, she adjusted fairly well. She made some friends, while others continued to harass her. In spite of it all, she flourished academically.

She was now 14 years old, and graduation from middle school was just around the corner. As she was getting ready for school one morning, Mrs. White called out to her from another room, "Breana!" she said, "The money to pay for your cap and gown is on the table! You have to take it in today!"

"Yes, Ma'am, I'll remember."

"I can't believe it's graduation time already." Mrs. White mumbled beneath her breath.

Breana walked out of the room. Just before she started descending the stairs, Mrs. White came out of her room.

"Well, 'Miss Soon To Be Graduate,' don't you look polished this morning in that fresh uniform. You were eleven when you came to live with me. Now you're getting ready to go to high school. And didn't I tell you what a beautiful young lady you would be?"

"Did you really mean it when you said I was beautiful?"

"Of course I did, and I still do. I wouldn't have said it otherwise. And you get prettier every day. Now run along before you miss the bus, and don't forget the money."

"Yes, Ma'am, I won't forget."

Graduation day finally came. Breana and Mrs. White were in the kitchen. "I think you should have a nice breakfast. Lunch time might be a little hurried," Mrs. White suggested. Nonetheless, Breana sat motionless, deep in her thoughts. Mrs. White sat down next to her. "A Saturday afternoon in June is a pleasing time for graduation, especially for someone who is graduating at the top of her class, so why the long face?"

"Nothing," Breana answered, flatly.

"Don't say it's nothing honey. Something is bothering you. What is it?"

"It's just that sometimes I get tired of not having a family with a mom and dad like everyone else. This is supposed to be one of the happiest days of my life, yet I feel so alone."

Just as Breana was wallowing in self-pity, she quickly realized how she may have sounded. She turned to look at Mrs. White, and she began to apologize fiercely.

"Oh, Mrs. White, I didn't mean…"

Mrs. White stopped her. She said, "Never mind honey; I know

what you're saying. I want you to have that too. Someday God will give you the desire of your heart." She gave her a reassuring hug.

"I just don't understand; why can't someone adopt me?"

Mrs. White said, "Being part of a family is important, and I would like to see you have that. However, your circumstances do not make you less important. It makes you unique, so you go and accept your honors in your name. That name will be on everybody's tongue long after the graduation."

"Hmm, I guess so." Breana said half-heartedly, "Would you help me with my hair?"

"Well certainly my dear. I'd be delighted."

She was dressed in a scarlet gown trimmed with fine ivory lace down the front; scooped neckline in front and finished in a V at the back; a high waistline finished with a satin bow in front. Her shoes complimented her dress, and her hair was tied in a ponytail with a scarlet ribbon.

"Oh Breana, you look fabulous, wait right here."

Mrs. White left the room then quickly returned. "The only thing missing...is this."

She slipped a corsage on Breana's wrist.

"This is beautiful. I love it," Breana said admiring the corsage. "You're the best, Mrs. White." They embraced each other, and they left for the graduation ceremony.

Breana was taken by surprise when they arrived. Many of the students, who were never close to Breana, complimented her on how beautiful she looked. During the commencement, each time Breana's name was called for an award or certificate, Mrs. White stood up and cheered like a proud parent as Breana walked to the podium for the acceptance.

"On the ride home...Mrs. White said, "Breana, someday when this society is awakened to the knowledge of God's love and acceptance, you will be in your proper place of honor. You deserved to be valedictorian today, but don't worry; your day will come."

"A teenager?" Henry asked in a voice one octave higher. His eyes narrowed as he looked at Penny. "How would you feel about that?" he asked.

"Well, I was reading an article in the paper. It said that it's difficult to find parents for older children, and it got me really thinking. At this point, it may be wise to consider an older child; especially, since we're planning to live outside the country for a while. What do you think?"

"Well, I never thought of an older child." *Teenagers can be trouble,* he thought, but seeing the hope and longing on his wife's face, he figured that he'd take the chance.

"All I need is a child to love, and I would love a teenager just as easy as I would love a baby," he said.

"Good, I'll get in touch with Mrs. Tucker and let her know of our decision. We'll go to the house in Connecticut; since its closer to New York, we can get the paperwork started."

"That's a good idea. We need to be in Connecticut to close the house before we leave for Jamaica anyway."

It was a beautiful summer afternoon. Breana was enjoying her favorite pass time on the porch as she leafed through her most recently acquired book.

Mrs. Tucker drove up. Breana began to feel anxious. Mrs. Tucker's visits had become bittersweet over the years. Breana never knew if her visits meant that she would be uprooted from yet another home. She ran down the driveway to meet her.

"How are you, Breana?" Elsie asked.

"I'm fine, thank you Mrs. Tucker! I'm glad to see you!"

"I'm glad to see you too!"

"So how come you're here today, Mrs. Tucker?"

"I'm here because I have news that I hope will make you happy. I spoke to Mrs. White on the phone, but I wanted to tell you in person. Let's go inside."

Breana followed her inside and sat beside her on the sofa in the living room.

"I have a couple who wants to adopt an older child, and I think you'd be perfect for them."

The smile disappeared from Breana's face, and Mrs. Tucker was puzzled.

"What's wrong? I thought you would be delighted. You've been praying to be adopted for so long. You're no longer interested?"

"That's not it. I'm still interested in being adopted. It's just that I've been with Mrs. White for so long; I would hate to leave her. I would miss her very much, and I wouldn't be seeing you anymore either."

"I can imagine how you would feel that way, but you have to think of your future.

It's time you get out of the system. You deserve a family of your own.

Being a teenager, your age group is not easily placed. This couple has impeccable references. They have no children, and they've been trying to adopt for a long time."

"What are their names?"

"Henry and Penelope Noble; they're very nice people. He is a former attorney, and is an Ambassador for the United States. They currently live in Stone Mountain, Georgia, and his wife volunteers in the community."

"So why haven't they been able to adopt?" Breana asked.

"Because they were hoping to adopt a child between newborn to one year, but now, they've decided to adopt an older child. They really want to be parents, and this is what you've hoped for all these years. This is your chance."

"How do I leave Mrs. White, after all she has done for me?"

"I'm sure she wants what's best for you. You can thank her by being the best that you can be wherever you are. I'm going to give you some time to think about it. I will check back tomorrow, so we can talk about it some more; whatever you decide."

She told Breana that the Nobles were spending time in Connecticut where they also have a home. If she wanted to meet them, she could give them a call.

"Thank you, Mrs. Tucker. I know you're right, and I really want to be adopted. It's just that I'll miss you and Mrs. White so much."

"We'll miss you too, but we want what's best for you, and I believe that this couple will be good parents. You may never have this chance again."

Elsie said goodbye and left. Breana sat quietly in the den, and Mrs. White joined her. Breana started to cry. Mrs. White saw her tears and asked, "Are you alright dear? I know Mrs. Tucker spoke to you about the adoption."

"I have always wanted to be adopted, but I love you and if they take me away, I may never see you again. Why can't you adopt me?"

"I wish I could my dear. It would be my greatest pleasure. However, I would be considered a single parent, and the agency frowns on that. They'd rather have a two parent adoption. Mrs. Tucker seems to think that this couple would make the ideal parents for you. I have known her a long time, and I trust her judgment."

"I know, I trust her too, but I hate to leave you."

"I would miss you terribly if you go, but if I encourage you to stay…it would be very selfish on my part. The truth is, as much as I would like you to stay, you need stability, and you will never get that in foster care. If this couple is as responsible as Mrs. Tucker seems to think. Saying yes would be a good choice. You will always be in my heart."

"She said they are staying in Connecticut, so I should think about it; she will talk about it tomorrow; then give them a call."

"Well that sounds great; isn't it?"

"I'm so tired of just waiting for somebody to pick me up, and take me someplace else to live. I have stayed here so long it felt like home. Now I'm expected to move again?"

"That is exactly the point I was making Breana. Your only chance of stability is through adoption, and it is what this couple is offering you."

"I'm going to miss you so much, but since you and Mrs. Tucker think it's for the best, then I guess I should meet with them.

"I would like you to meet them too, Mrs. White."

"That's very considerate of you, honey. I would like to meet them too."

"Do you think I should call her today, since I've already made up my mind?"

"It couldn't hurt. This way, she can call the Nobles and they could plan on being here.

Breana called Elsie with the news that she had made up her mind. Elsie knew that the Nobles were well able to provide her with a wholesome life. "I'll speak to Mr. & Mrs. Noble and find out when they can be here to meet you," she said.

She finished talking to Elsie, and she hung up the phone. She went to her room with the feeling of uncertainty nagging at the pit of her stomach. Mrs. White was heart-broken for her. She put some of Breana's favorite cookies and two glasses of milk on a tray. Then she went upstairs and knocked on her door. Breana opened the door and went to sit on the bed.

"I brought you a snack; milk and cookies."

"Thanks", she said softly.

"I'm feeling a little blue myself, so I thought I might share with you. I'm going to tell you how I feel. Then, you tell me how you feel. I knew this day would come, but nothing could prepare me for how I feel right now."

"Alright"

"I love you, but I know that staying here with me would not be the best. It may have been better than other homes you have been before, but the best would be a permanent home with two parents to love and care for you. If it's the Lord's will, you and I will see each other again. This world is not as big as it seems. I know our paths will cross again."

"I feel so sad," said Breana. "This is the first home where I've been comfortable, and you made me feel like I matter. You taught me to love myself even if no one else does."

The following morning Elsie called to say the Nobles would be in town in two days. They were delighted with the prospect of the adoption, and they wanted to meet Breana and possibly spend the day with her.

* * *

Breana woke up before sunrise. She did her chores, then showered and washed her hair. She wore a modest tan color dress, accessorized with a black belt and black shoes. She combed and brushed her hair and let it fall around her shoulders. She stood in front of the mirror and looked at her reflection.

"I'm Breana; I'm a good person, and I'm going to be alright," she said.

She went to find Mrs. White who was sitting in the living room. When she saw Breana, she was very pleased with her appearance.

"You look marvelous Breana. The Nobles will just fall in love. I'm sure of it."

Around ten o'clock, Elsie and the Nobles drove up to Mrs. White's house.

Mrs. White answered the door. "Good morning Mrs. Tucker; come on in."

"Good morning, Mrs. White. Let me introduce Mr. & Mrs. Noble."

Henry walked into the room, and his presence demanded attention. It's no surprise he is a diplomat. His red hair with traces of silver, parted, and combed over in a cowlick style. When he looked at you, his eyes seem to discover the secrets of your soul. Due to his frequent trips to the tropics, his skin was deeply tanned. He was dressed in a dark brown suit, a light tan shirt, and a pair of highly buffed brown shoes.

"This is Mrs. White," said Mrs. Tucker, "She has been taking care of Breana for almost four years."

"It's a pleasure to meet you both." said Mrs. White.

"The pleasure is all ours ma'am," said Henry, "We've heard of the wonderful job you did in raising Breana. You are a special person."

"It's very easy to treat Breana right as you will find out. She is a beautiful person inside and out. She has been a comfort to me these past years." She said, "Please make yourselves comfortable while I go get her." She found Breana sitting in her room.

"I'm too nervous to go down there. What if they don't like me? I would rather not hear it in person. Can't you show them my picture first?"

"Are you joking? Who in his right mind could look at you and not like you?" said Mrs. White.

Breana entered the room, her long black hair bounced up and down as she walked down the stairs. She had perfectly arched eyebrows, and long lashes that swept over her brown almond shaped eyes. Henry looked at her strangely for a moment.

"Good morning, Breana, come in. We've been waiting for you." said Mrs. Tucker.

"Mrs. and Mrs. Noble, this is Breana."

Lost in his thoughts, Henry rejoined with, "Good morning, Breana. It's a pleasure to meet you."

"Good morning, Sir; it's nice to meet you too," Breana said shyly.

Penny stepped up closer to her and said, "Breana, it's a pleasure to meet you."

"Thank you Ma'am."

She looked Penny over and immediately, she recognized the kindness in Penny's eyes.

They all spent the day at Mrs. White's house. Elsie watched the interaction between Breana and the Nobles intensely.

As the hours went by, Breana was more relaxed. She spoke more freely, smiled a few times, and played hostess to the visitors.

The Nobles were very impressed with her. They hoped with all their hearts that the adoption would go through. They would be spending three weeks in Connecticut, and requested that Breana spend some time with them there.

Elsie agreed to drive her to Connecticut as soon as possible. She agreed to have Breana stay with the Nobles on a trial basis. When the Nobles left, Breana expressed to Mrs. White.

"They seemed nice, and I think they really like me."

"I was watching the interaction between all of you," said Elsie, "If all goes well, you might be able to stay in Atlanta with them until the adoption is final."

Even though she was apprehensive at the thought of leaving Mrs. White, she believed that the Nobles might be right for her. She stayed up most of the night thinking of her upcoming trip to Connecticut. The day Breana was supposed to leave for Connecticut; she woke up early in the morning. She packed her suitcase, and she took all her belongings and cleaned up the room. She brought her suitcase downstairs, and she put it by the door and went back upstairs to make sure nothing she owned was left behind.

"I usually have to take everything I own when I leave," she said.

She went back down stairs to the kitchen and joined Mrs. White for breakfast. They both ate very little and almost in silence. Mrs. White looked through the window at the bougainvillea tree.

"I remember the first day you came here to live with me. You were so fascinated by that tree. Every time I look at that tree, I'll think of you Breana."

Breana was silent; she had her head down trying to hide her

tears. She fidgeted with the spoon in the bowl of cereal on the table in front of her. Suddenly, they heard the sound of a car in the drive way. Breana looked through the window, and she saw Mrs. Tucker's car.

"She's here" she said to Mrs. White as they both looked sadly at each other. Mrs. Tucker started up the driveway, and Mrs. White went to the door to meet her.

"Good morning Elsie. Breana and I were just finishing breakfast! Would you like some coffee?"

"No, thank you. I've already had breakfast."

"Breana is in the kitchen. I'll get her," Mrs. White said as she hesitantly walked away.

When she reached the kitchen, Breana was still sitting at the table, staring at her favorite tree, with tears trickling down her face. Mrs. White attempted to change her sad demeanor to a cheerful one.

"Come on now, don't you do that, or we'll both cry up a storm," she said as she walked over to the table.

"I'm not crying." She said, shifting her head to the side.

"Remember all the talks we had?' said Mrs. White, "I was preparing you for this day; because, I knew it would come. I thank God for the time we had together. I prayed that this will not be the last time we'll see each other; we will see each other again someday, don't you fret."

"You are the closest I ever came to having a mother, Mrs. White, thank you. I will never forget you. I wish I could keep in touch with you, but I know we can't."

"God bless you my child. If I had a daughter, I would want her to be just like you.

I will always think of you fondly, and you will be in my prayers always."

"Good bye, Mrs. White," she said. They hugged, and she went to join Elsie.

Elsie was waiting in the living room. "Good morning, Mrs. Tucker," she said, walking into the living room.

"Good morning Breana. You look beautiful, are you ready to go? We have a long drive."

"Yes ma'am, I'm ready."

Breana picked up her suitcase and they both walked outside. Mrs. White watched as the car drove away. As the tears rolled down her cheeks, she closed the door and went to sit by the window, gazing at the bougainvillea tree. Breana watched until the house was out of sight.

A week and a half later, Mrs. Tucker paid the Nobles a visit while Breana was with them in Connecticut. From her observation and from her conversations with Breana, she found out that although Breana missed Mrs. White, she was getting along very well with her new family. In every aspect, Mrs. Tucker's report was good. It was favorable for Breana to go to Georgia for the continuation of her pre-adoption period.

* * *

By the end of July, with the summer holiday almost over; it was time for the Nobles to go back to Georgia, but not without Breana. They decided to have a talk with Elsie to see if she could speed up the process for them. Penny went to see Elsie.

"Mrs. Tucker, we'll have to leave for home soon; we would like to take Breana home with us, if possible. This way she'll have time to get familiar with her surroundings before she starts school."

"Well, that would certainly help to ease the anxiety of a new home and new school all at once. I think we could accommodate that," said Mrs. Tucker. "Everything seems to be in order here, and Breana is happy. Of course you know I'll have to arrange visits while she is there until the adoption is final."

"Oh yes, we know that, and you are welcome to visit us anytime, even for a weekend, if you like."

"Elsie laughed, affectionately. She said, "A weekend at your invitation would not be appropriate. Anyway, thank you for the offering and I don't see any reason why Breana can't go with you."

"Thank you, Mrs. Tucker. You will not regret this; I promise you."

Everything was settled; there was nothing to keep them in Connecticut, so they made plans to leave the following day. It was 6:00 o'clock in the evening when they reached the Atlanta Airport. A black limousine drove up shortly after the Nobles' flight arrived. The driver got out of the car, and he walked toward the curb. 'Tall, dark and handsome,' described him accurately. He was well groomed. He stepped on the curb in his navy blue suit, light blue shirt, and black shoes like a soldier reporting for duty.

Henry came through first. "Briggs! There you are, right on time so happy to see you."

"Welcome home, Sir! It's nice to have you and the family home again!" He said with a deep resonance in his voice.

"Thank you Briggs. It's good to be home!" Penny said, "This is Breana, Breana, this is Briggs our chauffer."

"It's nice to meet you Miss Breana!"

"Thank you, Mr. Briggs. It's nice to meet you too."

In addition to being the chauffer for the Noble family, Briggs frequently wheeled the axe behind the woodshed, *good for building muscles*, he'd say. From his appearance, one might say that the wood shed was never empty, and his effort was not wasted.

As they drove on, Breana drifted off to sleep. It was almost nightfall when they finally reached home. As the car drove up to the house, Penny shook Breana gently.

"Wake up sweetheart, we're home," she said.

Breana stretched and rubbed her eyes with the back of her hand in an effort to eliminate the remnant of sleep that was lingering. She opened up her eyes and saw the house. She noticed brown bricks with round white columns in the front. The doors and windows and all the trims were painted in white. There were two white window boxes filled with red Geraniums in full bloom, and high beamed floodlights illuminated all around the house.

Being born and raised in Jamaica, Thelma the house keeper spoke the 'King's English' fluently; however, the Nobles were fascinated with patois. They would pick up a few words here and there, so Thelma would humor them by speaking patois sometimes. When the family arrived, she met them at the door. Breana found her dialect intriguing when she said, "Welcome 'ome everybody, it is good to have you 'ome,"

Thelma's hair was dark and wavy. She had it brushed back and held in place with a hair net. Her complexion was like coffee—heavy on the cream. Penny said, "Thelma this is Breana."

Thelma's smile revealed a space between her upper incisors, and her blue/grey eyes exuded kindness. She looked at Breana. "Welcome Breana, it's very nice to meet you."

Thelma was delighted to have her join the household.

Breana walked in and the splendor of the interior of the house left her breathless.

The furnishings were of dark cherry wood, and the style was from the Victorian age. The floors were hard wood with a plush area rug in the center of the room. A winding staircase led to a long banister which boasted the grandeur of the house. *This is the grandest place I've ever been in'* Breana thought. She slapped her face to make sure she wasn't dreaming.

"It's going to be nice having yu here Breana. Yu very beautiful!" Thelma said

"Thank you, Ma'am."

Thelma started walking. "Come let me show yu to yu room, so yu can get freshened up honey. Yu must be tired from travelin' all aftanoon."

"I'll have to get my things from the car, Miss Thelma."

"No dear. Yu don't have to do dat. Dat is Briggs jab. Besides, ev'ryting yu need fa de night already in yu room," Thelma said,

Breana followed Thelma to the second floor. They reached the top of the stairs and started walking down the corridor.

"Dis firs door is Mista and Mrs. Noble's room, an' dis secan door is your room. Ev'ry-ting yu need fa de nite is laid out fa you."

Breana walked into the room, and was mesmerized by the luxurious decor.

The furnishings were made from dark mahogany wood. A queen sized four poster bed with a canopy covered with lavender lace was at the focal point of the room. The linen on the bed complimented the lace on the canopy over the bed. It was made from Egyptian cotton with fine embroidered finish. An antique porcelain lamp with pink satin shade sat on each nightstand. A Bible and a book, titled 'The Pilgrim's Progress' laid on the night stand on the right side of the bed. A vase of fresh flowers sat on a table in a corner opposite the bed, and an arm chair next to the table. A dresser with an oval shaped mirror facing the foot of the bed. A pink nightgown, a robe, and a new pair of pink slippers were laid out on the bed. The scenery took Breana's breath away. It was all so inviting; she walked over and swept her hand across the bed. The sheets were so soft. "This feels so nice!" she exclaimed.

"Di sheets are made of di finess Egyptian Cotton." said Thelma. She opened up a closet. "Di rest of yu belongins is in 'ere,"

Thelma spoke to her in patois; however Breana understood what was said. She walked over and looked inside the closet.

"All this for me? How did they manage to do all this before we got here? I have never seen so many clothes in my life, and they are all so beautiful!" She said, reaching inside the closet, and touching the garments in excitement.

"Yu will pick di ones yu like. Di rest will go back. Di baatroom is ova deere," Thelma said, as she walked over to the other side of the room. "Yu go get freshened up. I know you must be tyad, so I will bring up a tray fa you."

"There is a bathroom in my room Miss Thelma…Just for me?"

"Yes dear, it is".

Thelma walked out of the room, and Breana sat on the chair opposite the bed and shook her ponytail loose. Her hair tumbled down around her shoulders and covered her face. When she swept the hair away, her face was wet with tears. Just then, Penny walked into the room and saw Breana crying softly.

"What's the matter honey?" Penny's question prompted her to cry even more. Penny enfolded her in her arms.

"Breana, I know you might be feeling uneasy right now, but I promise we will be good to you. You will go to the best schools, and you will never want for anything. It will take some time to adjust, I know," said Penny, fighting back her own tears. "…but all I ask is that you give us a chance."

"Mrs. Noble, that's not why I'm crying; I'm not having second thoughts. It's just that no one has ever provided for me like this before. It made me think of Mrs. White. She always said I deserved everything good before I believed it myself. She taught me to believe in myself."

"Oh Breana, my husband and I already feel as if you are our daughter. The rest is just formality. As far as we are concerned, you are Breana Noble, the daughter of Henry and Penelope Noble, and someday you will see Mrs. White again. I promise you."

She lifted Breana's face, dried it with her handkerchief, and she kissed her forehead.

"Breana Noble, we are your family. We chose you, and we love you, and you can trust us to take care of you."

Breana smiled, "Thank you, you've been so kind. I didn't mean to seem ungrateful. I do appreciate everything you've done for me. I have waited a long time to be adopted. They say it's not easy for teenagers to get adopted, yet here I am. I must have been waiting for you."

"We feel the same way. We are going to be a family, and we are going to be alright. We'll be your parents and you can call us whatever you wish."

Penny was leaving the room, she looked back and said, "I know you must be famished, so make sure to eat something."

Thelma returned to Breana's room with a tray of food and placed it on the table. "Have a little som'ting to eat dear. Yu muss be staavin by now."

"I'm not very hungry Miss Thelma, but I'll try to eat something."

"Yu goin to be very happy here Breana. Di Nobles are good people. I've been with dem fi years now, and they always treat me like family. I'm looking forward to moving with them back to mi country."

"They told me about going to Jamaica. Is that where you're from?"

"Oh yes! It is a beau-u-tiful island; dat is where I met dem. I was de manija of a guest house in Ocho Rios. Dey was visitin' de Island, and dey stayed at di guest house. Dey like how I took care o' de place, so dey asked me if I would come to di States an' werk fi dem; I said yes. Is been many-many years now an' I neva been sorry."

"I can see dat yu tyad, so I will leave an' let yu eat, so yu can get some ress. Good night mi dear, sweet dreams."

"Good night Miss Thelma."

"Just Thelma is fine wit' me, I won't get mad if yu say it."

"Ok then Thelma." Breana responded, with a quick giggle.

Thelma gave a little smile and closed the door behind her.

Chapter Three

I t was a month or so since Breana had been living with the Nobles. One Friday evening, she went into the kitchen where Thelma was working.

"I came to help you with the dishes, Thelma," she said

"Thank yu Breana. Look in dat closet for an apron." Thelma answered, pointing to the broom closet. While they both got busy in the kitchen, Henry and Penny went out on the lanai. Henry read the newspaper, while Penny reclined on a lounge chair next to him, doing needlepoint. The doorbell rang, and Thelma went to answer it.

"May I help you," she said to the woman standing at the door.

"Good evening, I'm looking for the Nobles."

Before she could say her name, Breana recognized her voice and ran to the door, "Mrs. Tucker!" she squealed, "I'm so happy to see you!"

It was such an excitement. They were hugging… and laughing… and smiling …and just rocking from side to side.

Thelma said, "We- e-ll, it is nice to finally meet you, Mrs. Tucker. I've heard a lot about you. Come on in an' mek yuself comfatable. I will get Mr. and Mrs. Noble."

She found the Nobles on the lanai and announced that Mrs. Tucker was visiting. They walked in from the lanai to join her in the house.

"Mrs. Tucker, how nice to see you again," said Henry.

Penny said, "Welcome to our home, Mrs. Tucker. I see you have already met Thelma."

"Yes I have, thank you," she said, looking around the room. "This is lovely. I love Victorian style houses and furnishings."

"Thank you," Penny responded. "The grounds are beautiful this time of year. Maybe Breana could show you the grounds later if you have time."

"I would love that!" Mrs. Tucker replied, "Well, as you know, we have to make periodic visits as part of the pre-adoption phase, so I'm here to see how everybody is adjusting. I can see Breana is beaming from ear to ear."

"Our hearts are beaming with joy because of her. She is a blessing to Henry and me."

They sat and talked for a while; then Breana and Mrs. Tucker went for a walk.

As they walked, she listened to Breana's comments and decided that she was adjusting very well.

Breana asked about Mrs. White and expressed her gratitude to Mrs. Tucker for being in her life over the years.

"I finally have a home with a mother and a father," said Breana, "they are very good to me. I want to stay."

"I'm so glad to hear you say that." Elsie replied, "This is my last visit, and I'm so pleased by what I've seen. What you've just said to me helped me decide that this is the right place for you."

'Thank you Lord, for this is indeed a miracle,' she thought.

"Mrs. White always said this would happen." said Breana.

"Finally, you'll have the home you've always wanted. The Nobles have proven to be very good parents from the start. I'll speak in their behalf at the adoption hearing."

Henry and Penny were ecstatic when Elsie told them that all the formalities were taken care of. No one else had applied for custody or adoption, and no relatives came forward.

"This statement may sound premature, but let me be the first to congratulate you," said Elsie.

"Thank you so much Elsie," Penny said, "you have been wonderful through all of this."

"That goes double for me Elsie. I'm very grateful for all you've done." Henry said as he shook her hand, smiling a mile wide.

"You are quite welcome. I'm glad I could be of service. Well, I enjoy the company, but my work is done here, and I must go."

Breana gave her a long hug. "Thank you for everything Mrs. Tucker. You've been so good to me over the years," she said, "I'll miss seeing you."

Elsie said goodbye and went to her car. She opened the door, and she sat behind the steering wheel and turned the key in the ignition. As the car pulled away from the curb, she looked back at Henry, Penny and Breana standing next to each other and waving goodbye to her.

She smiled and gave her last wave.

"God moves in mysterious ways," she said pensively in a low, soft voice.

As she drove away, she was overcome with emotion and tears streamed down her face. As she softly cried she said, "Hmmm—hmm, who would have thought? Oh God, please let me know that I did the right thing. This is the best way I know. I may have to tell them someday but—" She took one last look, at the complete family, in the rear view mirror and drove away. "This is not the day."

* * *

Early one morning, everyone was still asleep, when the phone rang. Thelma picked up the phone and walked upstairs to Henry's room. She knocked on the door. Mr. Noble, dere is a phone call fa yu. It soun' urgent."

Henry got out of bed, and went quietly to another room, closing the door behind him.

"Hello. Certainly, of course! Yes, I'll hold." he said. He put his hand over the receiver and shouted for Penny. "Oh! Good morning Mr. President. Yes Sir…."

The conversation went on for a while, then he said, "Thank you, Sir." He hung up the phone and walked back to his room. . Penny was awake.

"Sorry I woke you, but it's just as well. We have to talk." Seeing the uneasy look on his face, Penny sat on the bed preparing for the worst; concern written on her face. "What's the matter? Is it Breana? Please don't tell me we weren't approved to adopt her…after all Mrs. Tucker said, I thought—"

Henry, noting the fear in her voice quickly said, "No, no dear! I just spoke to the President, and he is concerned about us going to Jamaica right now. There might be some unrest on the island."

"Unrest! Over what?" asked Penny.

"The people are clamoring for a Referendum Election. Some want independence from England and others don't. According to the President, it seems trouble may be on the horizon."

"The current Ambassador will remain since he is familiar with what's going on. We'll just have to wait and see what happens."

"Oh dear, I'm so sorry about all of this, especially for Breana. She was really looking forward to this move."

"Well darling, we'll just have to make her understand that we are trying to keep her safe.

There are plenty of other beaches that we can take her to visit sometime."

"Yes, I guess you're right."

That morning, at breakfast Henry broke the news to Thelma and Breana.

"We won't be leaving for Jamaica for a while. There might be some conflict on the island, and my assignment has been postponed for a later date," he said.

"Oh dear!" Thelma said, "So what goin' on over deere now, sah?"

"The people want to have a Referendum Election concerning their independence from England. If they do have the election, we would like to wait and see how it turns out."

"Whedda dem have independence or not," Thelma blurted, "De success of Jamaica will depend on di Leadaship, an' dose paliticians neva deliva what dem promise fi do. Dey all alike, an' no paaty is different. Neda Laba nor PNP. Dem fight an' chop yu up an' kill yu same way, an' dem teef!"

Mr. Noble waited with a smile on his face for her to finish ranting in her Patois. He liked listening to her dialect. He was always trying to learn a few words here and there, so he just laughed at the end of her speech.

"Will we go when it gets better Father?" Breana asked.

"We'll go over there one way or the other, as soon as the coast is clear." replied Henry.

"Then I'd rather stay and be safe here."

The adoption was finalized a week later, and the Noble's household was full of laughter and happiness. Breana was registered for school and began looking forward to her first day of her new life. "Finally, a full name, one I know where it comes from." she said

Henry was in the study looking through the newspaper and Penny walked in.

"Henry, there is one thing that could make everything more perfect," she said, hugging him around his neck from behind. "Let's celebrate by having a christening for Breana"

"Good idea, darling; that would be wonderful." He answered, "I bet that would please her very much."

"Let's go find her and see what she thinks."

Breana was curled up in the arm chair in her room reading. The door was open, and she heard their footsteps as they walked toward her room.

"Hi sweetheart!" said Penny with Henry close behind. "Could we talk to you for a minute?"

Breana marked her page, set the book aside and sat up straight in the chair. Her heart was racing. *'Here it comes. I knew it was too good to be true. They're sending me back.'* "Yes, Ma'am" she said, nervously.

Penny sensed her insecurity and quickly got to the point. "Breana, how would you like to get christened?"

"Christened? I never thought I could get christened…I mean… I'd love to, but I never thought I could get christened at my age."

"Well, let's just look at it as a confirmation that you are being raised a Christian and becoming a 'Noble." How would you like to be named after my mother and me? Her name was Margaret, and so is mine."

'Oh my gosh. I thought for sure they were going to send me back. How could I? They really want me.' "I would love it Ma'am, thank you!" she answered as she ran over and wrapped her arms around Penny's waist.

"Hey, what about your old man!" said Henry, standing at the door with his hands in both pockets of his pants and looking at both of them, beaming with satisfaction.

'Finally, my family is complete', he thought. Breana walked over to him and they both hugged each other.

"Okay, then Margaret Breana Royce Noble, you'll be,"

"That's pretty. I like it." Breana replied.

"We'll still call you Breana, of course. That's the name you've had all your life, and I think it's a pretty name."

* * *

Reverend Smith visited the Nobles' house that evening, at

Penny's invitation. Thelma showed him into the study where the family was waiting.

"Good evening, Penny. Good evening, Henry!"

"Good evening, Reverend!" they said in unison.

"May I offer you some refreshment, Reverend Smith?" asked Penny.

"Some cold water would be nice, thank you."

Thelma heard his request and started off to get the water. "Thelma, would you send Breana to us please?" Penny requested.

"Yes, Mrs. Noble."

In a few moments, Breana arrived carrying a tray with drinking glasses and a pitcher of ice cold water. After she sat the tray down on the table, Henry said, "Reverend Smith, this is our daughter Breana."

"Oh, hello Breana; what a lovely young lady you are."

"She is the reason we invited you over. We would like to have her christened on Sunday, and we would like you to perform the ceremony for us."

"It would be an honor to serve. I'm pleased that you've included spiritual guidance for your daughter."

"Thank you Reverend. You know we've never been parents before, and we realize that we'll make mistakes, but if nothing else, she'll be taught to walk in the way of the Lord and treat others with respect."

"That's good to hear Henry, and that is no less than I would expect from you and Penny.

If you give me her full name, I'll have my secretary complete the paperwork."

"Sure, I have it written down for you,"

Penny handed him the paper. He looked it over, read it back to them and said, "This is a beautiful name, very fitting."

"Yes it is; thank you. Reverend, will you stay and have dinner?"

"Oh, I'm afraid I can't. I have some other stops to make. In fact

I must leave now." He started walking towards the door and Henry walked out with him. "I'll see you wonderful folks on Sunday," Reverend Smith said.

As soon as he was gone, Penny started brainstorming for the event.

"There's no time to waste." She said, as she went around the house, looking for Thelma. She found her in the pantry stocking groceries.

"Oh Thelma, there you are," she said, "I've just made the arrangements for Breana to be christened on Sunday, and I would like us to have a celebratory dinner afterward."

"Oh, dat is wonderful."

"We'll have it here at the house with just a few close friends."

"Okay, Mrs. Noble, I will start the preparations right away."

"You go ahead with the menu, and I'll take care of the invitations, by phone of course."

"What can I do to help?" asked Henry.

"Well, she'll need godparents. Can you think of anyone?"

Henry played with his chin for a moment. "You know, it's a pity Hank is out of the country. We made a pledge with each other since we were boys, to be godparents to each other's first child."

"Really! You've never told me; that's admirable, but he can't be here on such short notice! What will we do then?"

"I'll give Hank a call this evening and let him know what's happening. He doesn't have to be here for the ceremony. We'll just give his name to Reverend Smith. You go ahead and do your invitations."

Penny took her telephone book and started calling the prospective guests including Hanks wife, Rita Ives. She accepted the invitation enthusiastically.

"Of course we'll be there. We always enjoy parties at your house, and Savannah has not seen her godparents in a while."

"Okay, Rita, we'll see you then."

When Penny hung up the phone, she went to Henry and said, "Henry, there's something we didn't think of."

"What's that?"

"If we made Hank Breana's godfather, will Rita be her godmother?"

"Oh, perish the thought my dear, we can't have that."

They both stood silent for a minute. Then Henry said, "Our agreement was before Rita came into Hank's life. I'm sure Hank will understand if we choose somebody else as godmother. Hank is a good man, and I want him in Breana's life. We'll just choose another person to be the godmother, that's all."

"In that case, I have the perfect person!" said Penny.

Henry looked at her and said, "Let me guess. I know that in your vocabulary 'perfect' means Thelma, right?"

With a wide smile Penny said, "Oh, *Thelma* you said? Good thinking. Thank you for choosing wisely. I'll tell her for you!"

Henry laughed and said, "Madam, you are a shrewd character. I let you rope me into that one, but there is no other choice I'd rather make. Thelma is right for the job."

Thelma was in the kitchen, planning the menu as she mumbled to herself.

"Now that big ham I was gonna make this Sunday won't be too big after all. It's just the right size for the occasion. I don't have to go shopping, hallelujah!"

"Thelma!" Penny called out as she headed for the kitchen. "Thelma, I have something to tell you."

"Yes, Ma'am?"

"Henry and I discussed it and we want you to be Breana's godmother, if you will."

Thelma looked at her. "Are yu sure about dis? Isn't Mr. Ives going to be her godfather?"

"Yes he is, and yes we're sure."

"Den what will Mrs. Ives say 'bout dat?"

"Don't give Rita another thought. I bet their daughter Savannah would rather this choice if she had the privilege to choose. Life with Rita is no picnic," said Penny.

"Den I accept it as a great hona dat you truss me that much!"

* * *

On Sunday morning, everyone was up early. They had a light breakfast, and then got ready for church. "Breana, I laid out yu clothes on yu bed, and yu mom said she will help yu wit your hair."

"Thanks Thelma!"

Breana wore a white communion dress, and stood in front of the mirror admiring herself. Penny walked in. "Well, sweetheart, don't you look beautiful!"

"Thank you mother. I was waiting for you to come do my hair."

Penny twirled her hair in curls and finished by tying it in a white satin bow.

"It suits you very well, Breana." She said.

"Thank you mother."

Briggs drove the limousine to the front of the house to pick up the family. "Breana, you look like one of the princesses in those fairy tales you've been reading," he said.

Breana thought about what Briggs said and took it to heart more than he'd ever know. *To think that a girl like me could come from years in foster homes to loving parents, a beautiful home and now a real name.*

"Thank you, Mr. Briggs maybe fairy tales do come true after all,"

While they were gone, the preparations for the party were well underway.

"Hey everybody! Listen up ova here! We're going all out on this one. You have no idea how important this is to me. So put a shine on it!" said the Event Planner who was fresh out of Brooklyn and this being his first job.

In the vestibule at the church Henry, Penny and Breana made

their entrance. Penny looked Breana over to assure that not a hair was out of place.

"I hope you'll always feel as beautiful as you look right now," she said.

"Thank you mother," Breana replied.

They walked into the church and took their seats. All of the invited friends, colleagues and guests were in attendance, including Hank's wife…Rita Ives. She waved frantically, hoping to be noticed by the Nobles. Henry saw her and gave a polite smile and nod. It was time for the ceremony to begin. The Minister called the Noble family forward and began to speak.

"About a week ago, Penny and Henry Noble asked me to dedicate their daughter Breana to the Lord. You know, the bible says that every perfect gift comes from above. Children may not always seem perfect, but nothing else can give you as much joy as having them." There were a few "amens" from the congregation as the Pastor continued.

"Mark 10: 16 says, that 'Jesus took the children into His arms, put His hands on them and blessed them.' Oh, what a powerful scripture. He has Breana in His arms, and He also has Penny and Henry in His arms, assuring that all things will work together for good."

Breana was standing between Penny and Henry. Henry took her left hand, Penny held her right. "Breana, you're going to go through some struggles. You may have already been through some, but the Bible says, 'train up a child in the way he should go…'"

"Amen, Pastor Smith, Amen!" Rita interrupted, nodding her head and looking around for someone to notice, and agree.

The Pastor continued. "I believe it is the right thing to raise this young lady in the Word of God. Life is tough, but with your faith, the love and prayers of the Saints, God will see you through. Let us pray not only for Breana, but for Penny and Henry."

Everyone bowed their heads and prayed. Then Pastor Smith

sprinkled her with water he said, "Margaret Breana Royce Noble, I baptize you in the name of the Father and of the Son, and of the Holy Ghost, Amen."

At the end of the service, Rita Ives was among the first guests to arrive at the Nobles house.

Breana was surprised when she met her. Rita was no taller than 5 ft. 2 inches, and she couldn't have weighed more than a hundred and ten pounds soaking wet. She was a little woman with a big, bad attitude. Her hair was fire engine red, and her skin was very fair. Her eyes were blue, and her raspberry red lipstick presented an illusion of volume to her lips. While everyone mingled, she took Breana aside.

"Margaret Breana Royce Noble is a mouthful of names. Come tell me about yourself. Where did you live before you came to be 'Margaret Breana Noble?'"

Breana was too naïve to detect her condescending tone, so she told her everything about her life. After Rita finished grilling the girl, she went to confront Penny concerning her discovery.

"Penny, I'm very sorry, she said, but I'm afraid Savannah and I will have to be excused. I have a terrible headache."

"I'm awfully sorry that you have to leave because of your headache, but can't Savannah stay? I'll make sure she gets home," said Penny.

"No! I mean, she can't. I 'm sorry; she has to come with me now."

From her tone, Penny knew that the problem was not a headache, so she walked her to the door.

"Good evening then, Rita. I hope you feel better. I'll call you later."

"You do that," she said and walked off in an abrupt sort of way saying, "Come on Savannah, we have to leave. This is not the place for us."

Penny heard the comment. She stood there, agape. She watched in dismay as Rita walked vigorously away from the house with Savannah in tow. She thought, '*what on earth is wrong with that woman. Everyone else seems to be having a good time. Oh well, she wouldn't be Rita if her behavior wasn't strange.'*

As Savannah hurried to keep up with Rita, she asked, "Why mother? Everybody is having fun. I thought you were having a good time too. I saw you talking to Breana. It's still early and..."

"That's the problem." She snapped at Savannah. "I talked to Breana, and time has nothing to do with it. The girl is a social climber, and you will have nothing to do with her."

Penny and Breana watched until they got into the car; then Penny slowly closed the door. Breana noticed the strange look on Penny's face and being curious, she asked, "Are you concerned for Mrs. Ives. Her headache sure came on suddenly. She and I had just finished talking when she came over to you and said she was leaving."

"What did you talk about?"

"She just wanted to know where I came from. She said since Savannah and I will be spending time together, she wanted to get to know me."

"What did you tell her?"

"I told her about my life before I came here, that I was raised up in foster care."

So that's it! Penny thought. Breana detected that Penny was upset.

"What...did I do something wrong?"

Penny put her arms around her, forcing a smile as they went back to join the party, "No, my love. You did the right thing. You have nothing to hide."

When everyone was gone, Penny got on the phone. "Rita, I'm calling to find out if you're feeling better."

"No, I'm not feeling better. In fact, I'm feeling betrayed and insulted. However, I don't have time to discuss this over the phone. Perhaps you could come for tea tomorrow? We can talk about it then."

'Betrayed and insulted?' Penny thought. She was confused, but she agreed to see Rita anyway.

"Okay, we'll meet at your house for tea tomorrow" said Penny.

"Is ten o'clock alright for you, Penny?"

"Yes, ten o'clock will be fine."

Later that night, Henry and Penny talked about the afternoon's events.

"I know Rita's strange behavior is not unusual, but what was this afternoon's all about?" Henry asked.

"She questioned Breana about her past and Breana held nothing back. I don't know what Rita is thinking, but she invited me for tea tomorrow at ten. I'm sure I'll find out then."

"When did she have time to question Breana? She barely stayed over ten minutes for Christ sakes."

"You're forgetting who we're talking about. It might have been her sole purpose for coming, so she wasted no time in getting the scoop. I heard her remark as she walked away from the house. She said something about us not being good enough for her anymore."

"Then if that's the way she feels, we have no use for people like her. I say good riddance."

Meanwhile, Breana stood in front of the mirror; she repeated her name in several ways.

She smiled and went to sleep a happy girl, knowing, the whole afternoon was all about her. She had no idea of the storm that was brewing.

* * *

The following day, Penny arrived at Rita's house as scheduled. As she walked up to the door, the butler was there ready to open it.

"Good Morning Mrs. Noble. Please come in. Have a seat. Mrs. Ives will be right down."

Just then, Rita came walking down the stairs. "Penny, you're here! Good. Let's go into the parlor. Nigel! Bring our tea in the parlor!"

"Yes, Mrs. Ives."

"Penny, I love that lime green dress on you. It reflects in those eyes of yours. It's beautiful."

"Thank you Rita, but I'm sure you didn't invite me here to discuss my dress, so what is it? I'm anxious to hear."

At that moment, Nigel brought in the tea. He sat the tray on the table and began pouring. Rita impatiently watched him. As soon as he was finished and walked out of the room, Rita started.

"Penny, I have known you for years, and all I can say is either you have lost your mind, or you have lost your sight. What is the meaning of you picking up that little reject and trying to inflict her on the decent upstanding people in this community? Can't you tell that the girl is colored? And if you can, that means you have plumb lost your senses, if you think this community will accept her. Don't you care what the neighbors think? That child doesn't belong in this society; at least, not to be pampered and spoiled. There is a place for everything and everything must be in its place. She needs to be among her own kind. Where does she get off trying to pass herself on us? She can't fool me. I can spot them just like that," she said, as she snapped her fingers. Penny was speechless as Rita continued raging.

"I was very curious, so I asked her about herself, and she told me everything. It wouldn't be so bad if she was one of us, but did you need to be a mother so badly that you settled for that? You can dress up a monkey and call it a baby, but it's still a monkey."

"Wait just a minute! Penny shouted. Are you referring to my daughter as a monkey?"

"Neither your fancy shindigs, elaborate christening, nor giving her a proper name, nothing and I do mean nothing, will ever make her one of us! Rita yelled.

If you think my Savannah is going to associate with your Miss Margaret Breana Royce Noble. She laughed mockingly. "ROYCE, wherever the hell THAT name came from; it won't be happening, not in my lifetime!" She finished speaking, crossed her arms over her chest, and she kept staring at Penny, angrily waiting her response. Penny's eyes turned ice cold, but her face was on fire. Bible scriptures whipped through her mind, and this allowed Rita's life to be spared. She slowly rose to her feet.

"Well, well, Rita Ives. I've always known you were an evil woman, but I had no idea you had such poisonous venom in you, until now. Don't you worry, because, I would never have my daughter associating with the likes of you. Good day Mrs. Ives, and May God have mercy on you!"

Penny stormed out of Rita's house and got into her car. As she drove away from the house, her eyes were filled with tears. She was so distracted that she almost hit an oncoming car.

"Hey lady—watch where you're goin'!" yelled the driver, blaring the car horn.

Penny was shaken and had to pull over. *Okay, Penny. Calm down. Don't let that woman get to you*, she thought to herself. A knock at her window startled her.

"Are you okay, Ma'am?" asked a concerned passerby.

"Oh, oh, yes, thank you. I'm fine." She drove away before the man could say anything else. When she arrived home, she quietly slipped into the house through the back door and went up to her room. She lay on her bed as images of the confrontation with Rita played over and over in her head. Rita's hateful words sickened her, and she cried some more. Finally, she washed her face, and then went downstairs. She found Breana sitting in the library by a window reading and occasionally looking outside. Penny watched her for a short while.

"Breana," she said, "it's such a nice day. Would you like to go walking around the grounds with me?"

Thelma overheard the conversation and brought out two parasols. She handed one to each of them, curiously eying Penny but said nothing. Penny and Breana started walking down the path towards the grounds. The magnolias were in full bloom, and so was a wide variety of tall flowering trees. There were pine trees with broad-leafed philodendron twined around the trunks and patches of wild flowers, daisies, dandelions and ferns.

"This is beautiful. These trees must have been here a long time," Breana commented.

"Some of these trees are very old. That oak tree over there is over five hundred years old they say," Penny answered, pointing to a large oak tree several feet away.

They came to a shaded pine tree, and sat down on some pine needles under the tree. She suddenly felt an urgent need to share all that was on her mind.

"Breana you are very precious to your father and me, and I want you to always remember that. You are very important because, there is no other person in the world like you. God made each of us and no other human being is better than the other."

"Mrs. White told me the same thing" said Breana.

"Then I'm reinforcing it. You can be a better person because of your character; the way you treat other people; the respect you have for others, and for yourself. When you have good character, the only person that is above you is God. Remember this, my child, God loves us all equally, and he forgives us all our mistakes. Therefore, as God forgives you, you must always be willing to forgive others."

"Yes mother I will,"

Penny continued, "A person that tries to see the good in others is a better person. A secure person works to uplift others. An insecure person tries to tear others down. You must always be comfortable inside your skin."

As Penny continued to speak, she lovingly brushed back a stray lock of hair from Breana's eyes. Breana listened attentively to her mother's advice.

"We must have faith; remember this. Faith does not provide

immunity from troubles and trials. Troubles and trials are a test of faith. So when troubles come, don't give up. Pray for strength to endure."

While her mother spoke to her about trials, troubles, faith and prayer, Breana could not help but wonder about the meaning of the conversation. *'Where is this coming from? Mother is trying to hide that she's upset about something. I know that she was just at Miss Rita's house. What could have happened?'* Breana pondered, but she said nothing

As they returned from their walk, they stopped at the kitchen door before entering the house. "Thank you, mother. This was a good walk. I'll always remember what you said to me."

That night as Henry and Penny retired to their room, Penny laid on her back staring at the ceiling. It was obvious that she was upset. Henry asked her what was wrong. She told him everything that happened at Rita's house.

"I think it's sufficient to say that we've seen the last of them."

"I feel sorry for Savannah because she and Breana were getting along really well before her mother got her sudden headache."

"Or maybe that's what brought on the headache in the first place," said Penny.

"I never knew she was such a bigot," Henry remarked.

"We'll just have to love our daughter through whatever comes her way."

Henry hugged her, drew her closer and muttered, "That we'll do dear. That we'll do."

In the room next door, Breana was on her knees by her bedside praying.

'Thank you Lord for giving me a mother and a father. Thank you for my home, and everyone that lives in it. And Lord, help me to be a better person. Amen.'

* * *

The morning sun was peeking through the shutters of Breana's bedroom window. Lazily, she opened her eyes and turned her face away from the window as if the sun dared to invade her space. She was tired from all the activities of the previous day. She stretched and repositioned herself. However, the smell of fresh cinnamon buns coming from the kitchen was irresistible. She could no longer delay getting up. She threw the covers off and she went into the bathroom. She got dressed and scampered downstairs. As she was halfway down the stairs, Thelma was walking from the kitchen to the breakfast room with a jug of freshly squeezed orange juice.

"Good morning, Thelma." Thelma looked up, "Good morning, Miss Margaret Breana Noble."

She smiled at Thelma. "Breana is easier…I won't get mad if you say it," she teased.

Thelma chuckled, "I just had to hear myself say your name. It sounds good to me.

Breakfast will be ready in a minute, and your parents should be up soon."

Thelma went on to finish her work, and Breana went outside to get the morning paper.

As soon as she came back inside, her parents were on their way down stairs.

"Well, Penny. I see our daughter is an early riser. That's my side of the family. Good morning, my princess," Henry said, grinning from ear to ear.

"Sure Henry, so I won't have to wake you in the mornings anymore?" Penny retorted.

"Good morning, Father. Good morning, Mother. I got the morning paper." Said Breana enter the room.

"I called for the puzzles first!" Penny said, kissing Breana on the forehead.

"Well, since you're the smarter half, I guess I'll take the funnies…Good morning Pumpkin." He said, giving Breana a smile.

Thelma announced that breakfast was ready, and all three went to the table.

"Hot cinnamon buns? Thelma, you spoil me!" said Henry.

"Breakfast looks wonderful, Thelma," Penny said as she took Henry's hand to give thanks for the food.

As they said Amen, Breana said, "I got a whiff of the buns when I was still in bed, I had to come down."

"Well, Miss Noble today is your first day of school under your new name," said Henry.

"For the first time in my life I have a full name. Before, I was always Breana Royce, and I don't even know who Royce is. I'm glad I didn't start school until the adoption became final. This way everybody will know me as Breana Noble from the start."

After finishing her breakfast, she went upstairs and finished getting dressed. She hurried back down stairs as if she was skipping. Briggs got her to school just before the bell.

Breana walked into the classroom. She noticed that Rita's daughter, Savannah was sitting in the front row. They quickly waved as there was no time for conversation.

"Good morning, students, I'm Mrs. Ryan. I will be your teacher for this school year," said the petite woman with straight reddish-brown hair. The short bobbed style reached just below her ears. Her light brown eyes seemed kind as they roved over her class.

She wrote her name on the chalk board, and in a southern accent, she said, "I would like you all to introduce yourselves. I think it's always a good idea to get to know each other since you all will be sharing at least a year out of your lives together."

The students started with the introductions. When it was Breana's turn, their reaction was appalling. "My name is Margaret Breana Noble. I'm called Breana," she barely had the chance to finish her name before one of the students whispered something, and the rest started whispering and giggling, except Savannah. "I will not tolerate this kind of behavior in my classroom," said Mrs. Ryan.

The girl rested one elbow on her desk as she ran her fingers through her flaxen hair. She rolled her blue eyes and looked away as Mrs. Ryan said, "Now Molly, if you have something to say that will benefit the class, you can speak, if not, please be quiet."

Molly whispered, "She just crawled out from under a rock, and all of a sudden she is Miss Margaret Breana Noble."

When Breana heard that statement, all the past teasing she had endured flooded her mind. She sat down and cried, thinking, *nothing will ever change for me. No one will give me a chance, and they don't even know me.*

When Mrs. Ryan suggested that they establish a buddy system, no one wanted to be Breana's buddy. Ironically, the only one that went over and sat next to her was Savannah.

During the lunch break, Breana took her lunch tray and found a seat in a corner at the back of the room, hoping no one would notice her. Savannah walked into the lunchroom later.

After getting her lunch, she scanned the lunchroom, and then focused on the table where Breana was sitting, alone. She walked over to the table.

"May I sit with you, Breana?" she asked.

"Sure," she responded, surprised, but grateful for the company.

Savannah hardly had time to sit down before Molly walked over to their table. "Well, if it isn't Savannah and Miss Margaret Breana Royce Noble. What kind of a name is Royce anyway, and you, Savannah; you are such a hypocrite. Your mother called our parents and told them all about Breana. She said you weren't going to have anything to do with her, yet here you are having lunch together like good buddies.

Just wait until I tell Mrs. Ives," said Molly, as she walked back to be with her friends. Savannah walked briskly behind her. She grabbed Molly's arm and spun her around.

"What has Breana done to deserve this? She asked, "You don't even know her, but you just can't leave her alone."

"Let go of me and go back to your friend!"

"Are you going to tell my mother?" asked Savannah.

"For half of your allowance, I won't tell." said Molly.

Savannah contemplated the thought. "Okay! If that's what you want! You can have it!" replied Savannah. She turned around and walked back to join Breana, but she was gone.

After that incident, Breana tried to avoid Savannah, but Savannah was persistent. When school was over, Savannah saw Breana walking out of the building. She called out to her, but Breana didn't stop. She finally caught up to Breana's side.

"Breana, everyone needs someone and I'm not going to let you push me away. I want us to be friends."

"And what will your mother and Molly have to say about that?"

"You let me worry about that."

When Breana arrived from school, she had a scowl on her face. Penny was in the foyer sorting through the mail as she passed by without saying a word.

"Breana," Penny called. "What's the matter?" Breana stopped and without turning around, she sighed and said, "Nothing mother I'm alright."

Penny walked up to her and gently turned her around. She lifted her chin and the first tears rolled down Breana's cheeks.

"Now, what has happened to make my girl cry?" she asked.

"Mother, I know people can be so awfully mean sometimes," she said, but in my case…it seems like all the time."

Her voice quivered, and before she could say anything more, she began crying inconsolably; burying her face into Penny's waiting arms.

Penny took Breana into the library. Once there, she allowed Breana to express what was on her mind.

She told Penny the things Molly said, and how humiliated she felt. Penny listened intently.

"Breana, it seems to me that Molly is the one who has a problem.

When people mistreat you, they do it because of their own insecurities. They think the faults they find in others, will make their flaws less visible."

She reached up to the shelf and brought down a little book. "Here's a present for you," she said to Breana. "It's a little book of poetry written by my mother's friend. She gave my mother this copy of her work years ago. I've read it over and over, and now I'm giving it to you. You can say it's from your grandmother."

"Oh great! Your mother knew an author?"

"She certainly did, and a very talented author too. In addition to writing poems, she wrote short stories and other literature. According to my mother she was a remarkable lady."

"Have you ever met her?"

"Yes, I remember my mother took me to her house once. She seemed very nice but also sad, and some of her poems don't reflect a happy life at all. When we visited, I was playing with her dogs while she and mother talked. I didn't hear what they talked about, but mother said she was a good person who had been misunderstood, and it was taking a toll on her."

"I can't imagine meeting a published author; thank you mother for the book."

"You're welcome dear. I know how much you love reading, so I thought I would share it with you."

Breana started leafing through the pages, and she came upon this poem. She read it to Penny.

<u>*The Roller Coaster Ride*</u>
Why did I stay so long at the fair?
I came early. I was first at the gate.
It's almost closing time; it's really late.
Why did I stay so long at the fair?
The clown was tense, even surly at times,
with a personality like sucking on limes.

Why did I stay so long at the fair?
I didn't ride the merry go round,
nor the carousel on a pretty little horse.
I was detained on the 'roller coaster ride,'
for this—I have remorse.
Why did I stay so long at the fair?
I stayed because I was needed there,
for the little ones whom I hold so dear.
But, from the roller coaster ride,
as my coach leaned to the side;
I reached out for my own brass ring,
whatever it may bring.

"It sounds to me like she had some personal conflict, but despite her own turmoil, she set aside her wellbeing, and put the welfare of others before her own. That was a selfless thing to do," said Breana, pensively.

"She had quality in her that others failed to recognize. She had inner strength, and no one could break her; she was a survivor. It had to be God," Penny replied.

That evening, the family was at the dinner table. Henry asked, "Well Breana, tell me about your first day at your new school."

Breana drew her breath and made a long sigh. She wanted so much to give him a positive report.

"The students are no different from the ones I'm used to, but I know that the better person is one who is able to forgive others who hurt you, right? So, I'll be the better person. I'll do my best to ignore them. I don't know…there's not much more they can do to hurt me, than they've already done." She said with a sigh.

"That's the spirit Pumpkin! Henry said. And don't let anybody define who you are."

Chapter Four

In the winter of 1960, Breana was now seventeen years old. One cold morning, the Noble family sat around the breakfast table. Breana was hastily eating her scrambled eggs and pancakes.

"Slow down, Pumpkin, you're gonna make yourself choke, eating so fast," Henry said, looking over the newspaper he was reading.

"I have an oral report in English class today, and I don't want to be late," Breana replied between sips of hot cocoa.

"Honey, you'll be fine. The report alone is great, and if you present it the way you did for me last night, I know you'll get an 'A'. Just relax and be yourself," said Penny.

"Thanks, mother. I'll do my best." She looked at her watch; "I've got to go."

She took her last gulp of cocoa, kissed her parents goodbye, and rushed off. Henry and Penny were still sitting at the breakfast table when Penny started coughing. Henry noticed that she hadn't touched her food.

"Honey, don't you think it's time to call Dr. Lloyd about that cough? You've been like this for a couple of days now."

"I told you, it's probably just a cold, nothing to waste his time over; although, I've got such heaviness in my chest since last night and I'm having a hard time breathing. I even woke up in a cold sweat this morning."

Henry set his newspaper aside, leaned over and touched her

forehead. "You're burning up! That does it." he said firmly. "You're going back to bed, and I'm staying home with you."

"I'm so cold," she said as she pulled her robe around her.

"Okay, let's get you upstairs, and I'll call Dr. Lloyd."

He helped her back up the stairs to their room and picked up the phone.

"Hello Austin, good morning. Well, the reason I'm calling is... my wife isn't feeling well this morning, and I was wondering if you would come over and see what's wrong. I'll be here with her; I've taken the day off. Please come as quickly as you can...Okay, see you soon. Thank you Austin."

When Dr. Austin Lloyd arrived, Thelma met him at the door, "Good morning, Doctor," she said, "Thank you for coming so promptly."

"Good morning Thelma. Henry sounded very urgent on the phone. I came as soon as I could."

"I'll take you upstairs. I've never seen Mrs. Noble acting so poorly for as long as I've known her."

They walked upstairs to the master bedroom. "Oh Austin, thank God you're here, she's been sick all night," said Henry as he anxiously escorted him over to the bed. "She's been burning up with fever all morning. I've been trying to give her fluids to prevent her from dehydrating. Sweat is just pouring out of her. Is there anything else we can do for her? I feel so helpless."

"Well, you did the right thing Henry. You called as soon as you found out her condition. I'll do all I can to help her feel better." Dr. Lloyd moved closer to Penny. "Well, good morning, my dear Penny."

"Good morning, Austin. I don't know why Henry is making such a fuss. It's nothing but the flu. It's the season for it you know."

"Well, let's see what we have here. Would you describe your symptoms for me?"

"I have difficulty breathing, and I'm coughing. I'm chilled to the bone. I'm sweating excessively. My body is stiff and aching all over, and I have no appetite."

"Hmmm…" said Austin as he picked up her hand by the wrist. Then he used both hands as he palpated from behind her ears. He checked her eyes, ears and throat. He removed his stethoscope from his white coat pocket. He rubbed the head of the stethoscope in the palm of his hand. "Thank you for doing that. Those things are always so cold, and I'm cold enough as it is," she said, shivering."

"That's why I'm your special doctor," Austin joked, as he placed the stethoscope on her chest. "Any chest pains, Penny?"

"Yes…mostly when I breathe. You think I may have to give up the habit?" she jested in a near feeble voice.

"Now that's one habit you can't afford to break," he said, trying to remain cheerful.

After he finished a systemic assessment, he said, "Penny, I believe you have pneumonia. I will have to get a chest x-ray and a test to be more specific with your treatment."

"Austin, I don't want to go to the hospital. I never cared for hospital stays; I could pick up more germs there than at home."

"Alright…I'll collect a specimen from you now. You can come into my office this afternoon for the x-ray. For now, I want you to take lots of fluids, get out of bed every two hours, and sit up for at least thirty minutes. Drink plenty of Thelma's chicken soup with lots of garlic."

He brought her a specimen cup. He sat her up and instructed her to cough deeply and spit onto the cup.

"Henry, get her to my office for the X-Ray. I wish she would let me send her to the hospital, but she has made up her mind against it. Call me if there are any changes."

"Austin, I really don't feel up to going out today," said Penny. "Is it possible to reschedule for tomorrow?" she pleaded.

"Well, the X-Ray is very important to the diagnosis and

treatment. It's very important that it be completed no later than tomorrow morning."

"I promise I'll be there first thing in the morning with bells on and..." she began coughing again in mid-sentence.

Austin was concerned; he softly patted Penny's hand. "Alright Penny, get some rest now. I'll check on you later."

"Thank you, doctor." Penny replied softly with a pained expression.

Henry watched Penny close her tired eyes and turned her head to the side as if she was drifting off to sleep.

"Thank you, Austin, I'll see you out," said Henry worriedly.

* * *

When Breana got home from school, usually, Penny would be either on the patio painting, or in the den working on her needlepoint.

Breana looked in the usual places for her, but she didn't find her. She walked into the kitchen.

"Thelma, where's Mother?" she asked.

"Your mother isn't feeling well, but don't you worry, it's nothing that my chicken soup won't cure. A few cups of this, and she will be as good as new. Don't worry my dear your mama will be just fine." Thelma encouraged.

"Why didn't Briggs tell me mother is sick? I'll go up to see her now."

She made haste upstairs and knocked on the door. "Come in" said Henry.

She walked in and saw her mother lying on the bed; she was looking very pale.

Henry was wiping her brow with a cool damp towel. He placed the towel in a basin on the table at the side of the bed. Then he gave her sips of water.

"How is she, Father? Why didn't anyone tell me mother is ill?"

"Oh, Breana, don't fret. Dr. Lloyd will have me up and about in no time." Penny responded.

"I hope so. Father let me do that. You take a break." said Breana.

"Okay 'Miss Nightingale', you may have your turn." Henry said smiling at Breana. He handed the glass of water to Breana, and sat in the Queen Ann chair on the other side of the bed.

Mother, are you sure you'll be alright. You look all worn out. Why didn't you tell me you weren't feeling well this morning? I could have stayed home with you." She chided her mother as she took the towel from the basin and started wiping her forehead.

"That's exactly the reason I didn't tell you. I didn't want you to worry at school."

Thelma brought in the chicken soup on a tray and placed it on a bedside table. Henry stood up, "Let me do the honor of feeding my beautiful wife".

Thelma removed the napkin from the tray and placed it under penny's chin. Henry lifted a spoonful of soup and attempted to feed her.

"Honestly you are making such a fuss…" Penny groaned.

"There's no one we'd rather fuss over, right Thelma?" Thelma? Henry repeated. He turned realizing there was no response. Thelma had already left the room unnoticed. She was overwhelmed by seeing Penny in such a weakened state. *'Lawd my God, how could she go dung suh fas? Have mercy pon her Fada.'* Thelma prayed silently.

Penny continued her protest. "Besides, darling, you must be tired. You need to get some rest. You've been fussing over me since last night."

"Stop talking and have your soup," said Henry.

Penny took a sip from the spoon, and she forced a swallow. After two or three more spoonsful, she stopped Henry's hand.

"Darling, please, no more. I can't taste anything. I just can't take anymore right now." Henry put the spoon down and set the dish back on the tray. He took her hands and kissed it. He gently patted the back of her hand and spoke softly. "It's alright my darling. You could have some much later," Penny closed her eyes and slowly drifted off in slumber.

The following morning at breakfast, Breana ate alone. Thelma brought a tray upstairs for her parents. Henry ate very little, and Penny ate nothing. Dr. Lloyd stopped by as promised. Penny's condition was deteriorating. She was drenched in sweat, and she complained of being cold in-spite of being covered under layers of blankets.

Dr. Lloyd arrived with his nurse. She took Penny's vital signs, and the results were alarming. Breana was anxious about her mother's condition. She went to her parents' room to see Penny for their usual morning prayer. Penny was aching, but she insisted on not going to the hospital.

"Having the doctor at home is good enough," she said.

Breana pleaded with her parents to let her stay home from school, but they wouldn't have it.

"You can't possibly stay home until I'm better," said Penny; besides, I have plenty of help, honey. You run along and don't be late."

Breana felt helpless and frustrated, but she had no choice but to do as she was told. On her way to school she prayed for her mother. *'God, please help Mother get better. I need her to get better.'*

As the day progressed, Penny got worse. Her vital signs were deteriorating rapidly; her breathing was raspy and shallow; her skin was pale and clammy, and she was sweating profusely.

"What's happening to her doctor? Is she getting worse?" asked Henry.

"I'm afraid so Henry. If there's anything you need to do for her, do it now."

Henry was confused and distraught. He looked at Dr. Lloyd. "What do you mean Austin?" He asked, "Do *what* now?"

Austin looked at Henry, and his expression said it all. *'Your wife is dying.'* With trembling hands, he picked up the telephone. He dialed the number for the church.

He called Reverend Smith, and he told him of Penny's condition. "Doctor, Austin Lloyd has been called in since yesterday. She hasn't been well for a few days. The prognosis isn't good. I would appreciate it if you would come, please hurry. Thank you Reverend Smith. " he said as he slowly put the phone receiver down.

Penny began to get restless. "Water, please," she whispered feebly.

Henry picked up the glass and gave her a sip of water.

"Thelma...get Thelma please," she said in a weak voice.

Thelma was in the kitchen making pie crust while a fresh batch of soup simmered on the stove. Henry ran to the top of the stairs and shouted, "Thelma, come quickly!" Henry's voice was so urgent that she didn't stop to wash her hands. She ran from the kitchen, while wiping the flour from her hands with her black apron. She hurried up the stairs and into the room.

"Penny is asking for you." Thelma hurried over to the bed. Penny's voice was now very weak as she struggled for every breath.

"Thelma, come close," Penny said.

Thelma approached her, and Penny reached out to hold her hand. "Breana—I want you to promise me you'll take care of Breana. I love that girl so much..."

Thelma was too frightened to answer. She swallowed a lump in her throat as her tears started forming. No words came. She hadn't expected this.

Henry stepped closer. "That's just the fever talking, Thelma. She's going to be alright. She's got to be." He said tightly.

Penny reached out her hands to him, and he quickly sat on the side of the bed. Thelma stepped back with a startled look on her face. She was tortured with trepidation.

Penny reached out her hand, and she held on to Henry. She was barely able to sustain her breath, she whispered in a gasping voice.

"I'll love you, always my darling."

Then slowly, her hand went limp and fell to the bed. Her eyes rolled back, and her eyelids slowly closed, as she breathed her last breath.

"Austin! I think she has fainted! Help her! Quickly Austin!" He stepped aside and Dr. Lloyd hurried to the bedside.

He opened up his pen light, and lifted her eyelids. As he examined her he mumbled to himself. "Eyes dilated, both pupils fixed, and carotid pulse absent." He picked up her hand, and her fingernails were blue. He pressed against her fingernail and mumbled, "No capillary return."

He looked at his watch. It was 11:30 am.

"I'm so sorry, Henry, there's nothing more I can do. I'm afraid she's gone."

Henry hurried over to the bedside. He sat beside her, and held her close to his chest. He rocked her back and forth as he cried, "Oh…no…Penny! Oh, Penny, my darling! How can this be?"

Her cheek rested on his shoulder. White foam exuded from her nostrils and from the corner of her mouth. It dripped from his shoulder down to the back of his grey shirt. As he laid her gently on the bed, Thelma stood by the door, sobbing.

Reverend Smith came walking up the stairs with a bible in his hand. He hastily made his way up the stairs and toward the bedroom. Henry, still sitting on the bed, was unshaven. His eyes were red and puffy. He drew a handkerchief from his pocket; he wiped his eyes and blew his nose.

"It's too late Reverend. She's gone, just like that, she's gone. My beautiful Penny is gone."

"Oh, Henry, I'm so sorry. God rest her soul," said Reverend Smith.

While the nurse prepped Penny for transfer to the morgue, Dr. Lloyd closed her chart. *'Penelope Margaret Noble, deceased at home, at 11:30 am, on January 16th 1960.*

Cause of death: Complication from Viral Pneumonia.' Henry

walked over to the doctor, "Austin, how can this be?" He asked. "How could this happen?"

"Maybe she ignored the early symptoms believing that it would go away. We have no idea why these things happen so suddenly Henry. Her lungs just filled up with fluid, and her heart couldn't sustain the overload, so it gave out," said Dr. Lloyd.

Instantly, Henry thought of how Penny had been coughing frantically for days.

"How will I go on without her? What do I do without her? She was my life."

"I wish I had the answers for you, but it's times like this that I feel like a complete failure, a doctor who couldn't save his friend. I feel your loss Henry. I'm so sorry."

Reverend Smith took Thelma's arm and walked out of the room.

"May I use the phone please?" He asked in a whisper.

"Yes, Reverend," Thelma said as she wiped away her tears. "There's one in the study. I'll take you there."

They walked together down stairs, and she pointed him to the phone. He picked up the receiver and dialed the rectory.

"Hello, this is Reverend Smith. I'm at the Noble's residence. There has been a death in the family. Please ring the bell for Mrs. Penelope Margaret Noble. She has gone to be with the Lord, thank you," he said as he hung up the receiver. He turned to Thelma who was studying a picture of herself and the Nobles when they first met in Jamaica.

"Thelma, shouldn't someone get Breana home, now?" asked Rev. Smith.

"Oh, my Lord! Everything happened so fast; I didn't think to send for her.

How do I tell that poor child that her mother is gone?" She whimpered as she mopped her tear dimmed eyes.

She hurried down stairs and out through the back door; as she moved along she started calling, "Briggs! Briggs, where are you?"

Briggs was by the shed, chopping wood. When he heard the echo of Thelma's voice calling out his name loudly. He responded, "Goodness gracious! Is the house on fire woman?"

"Briggs hurry! Go get Breana! Mrs. Noble is dead!"

Briggs looked confused. He thought that he heard wrong, so he repeated what he heard.

"Did I hear you right; Mrs. Noble is dead!

"You heard me! Her mother is dead!"

Briggs dropped the ax and started running to the car. He drove at top speed to the school. When he arrived at Breana's school, the Principal met him in the front office.

"Breana will be right with you. Thelma called to alert us that you were on your way. I'm so sorry about Mrs. Noble. Please give the family my condolences."

Breana was in the lunch room. As she received the message, she made haste to the office. When she saw Briggs, she immediately walked over to him.

"Briggs, why are you here? Mother has gotten worse hasn't she?"

"Miss Breana, you know your father doesn't discuss anything with me. I was sent to pick you up that's all," Briggs kept his cool.

As soon as they walked out to the car, they heard the first clang of the church bell.

They looked at each other as if they understood for whom the bell had tolled. Hurriedly they got into the car and drove home.

* * *

The car had barely stopped in the drive way when Breana swung the door open and bolted out. She ran into the house and up the stairs. When she reached her parents room, the door was open. She saw Henry sitting at the side of the bed with his face in his hands. She gazed over to the bed, and saw Penny's lifeless body covered up on the bed. "Mother!" she screamed as she threw herself across her mother's body. She cried hysterically.

Henry placed his hand on her shoulder, and lifted her to her feet. He brushed her hair from her face and kissed her on the forehead, while guiding her over to Thelma. Thelma wrapped her arms around Breana and rocked her as they both continued to weep.

Thelma decided to do some housework; the furniture she cleaned just the day before was suddenly too dusty. Staying busy had always put her mind at ease, but not today. The doorbell rang and she realized that she had been cleaning the same spot on the dining room table thinking about all that was happening. To her, it all seemed so surreal. She answered the door and a man stepped into the foyer. He was dressed in a gray suit and solid dark shirt. His sandy colored hair was neatly trimmed. A pair of black rimmed glasses sat on his thin high bridged nose.

"Hello. I'm Raphael, the funeral director of *'Farley's Funeral Services and Crematory Inc.,'* he said to Thelma as he handed her one of his business cards. "Reverend Smith placed a call to us this evening."

"Yes, please come in."

He walked into the great hall. "I'm so very sorry to hear about Mrs. Noble, my condolences to the family."

"Thank you. The family is upstairs. I will let them know you're here."

Broken hearted, she climbed up the stairs thinking, *'Oh Lord; wake me up from this nightmare. This cannot be real.'* However, reality set in when Raphael went to the door and signaled two attendants to come in. They brought in a gurney and proceeded upstairs to transport Penny's remains to the morgue. As they entered the room, Henry ran over to the bed.

"Please, don't take her. Don't take her from me!" He sobbed as he held on tightly to his wife's body.

"Raphael, would you mind giving him a few more minutes to say goodbye?" asked Reverend Smith.

"I certainly understand Reverend. I don't mind at all. Let's go fellas."

They all walked out of the room, giving Henry his last moment alone with Penny.

"I can't thank you enough for giving him this time." Reverend said as he left the room with them. "They were so much in love. If ever a marriage that was made in heaven, it's theirs. They had the perfect example of what a marriage should be. It breaks my heart that she is gone so suddenly. That woman was the salt of the earth. I'm telling you, a light has gone out and there will be a void for a long time."

After they had waited a while, Raphael said, "I'm sorry Reverend, but we have to get going. I have another appointment, and it's getting close to that time."

"I understand. I'll go upstairs and speak to Henry."

He walked upstairs and into the room, he could hear Henry sobbing. He walked over to the bed and rested his hand on Henry's shoulder. "Henry, I'm afraid it's time.

Henry reluctantly stepped away from the bed and walked out of the room. The funeral attendants went in and put Penny on a gurney. As they were leaving, Henry grabbed on to the gurney, and started sobbing uncontrollably. Briggs heard the commotion and went upstairs. It hurt his heart to see Mr. Noble in such despair. He hurried to Henry's side to remove him from the gurney. Only Briggs was able to stay strong, keeping his emotions in check for the sake of everyone else.

The attendants walked slowly downstairs and out through the back door.

The family watched in agony as their beloved Penny left her home for the last time. Henry's knees buckled and he fell backward. Luckily, Briggs was still standing behind him. He broke Henry's fall by quickly holding him under both arms and placed him on a chair. Henry stared straight ahead, blankly with both hands holding the sides of his face, and his mouth opened wide as in a silent scream. Thelma, Briggs and Breana looked on in horror.

"Father! Father what's happening to you?" cried Breana as she tried to move his hands from his face.

"He's not going to respond right now, dear." Dr. Lloyd said as he stepped closer and moved Breana away. "He's in a catatonic state. The shock of Penny's death is too great for him. His brain has put him in a safe place for the moment."

"He can't possibly remain in this state for long. Oh my God, what else is going to happen to this family? Doctor, how long do these conditions last?" ask Thelma.

"Every individual is different. He might snap out of it soon on his own, but in most cases it takes professional help. He will be alright when he gets out of it, don't worry," he said as he proceeded to take Henry's blood pressure. He then placed fingers on the wrist at the base of Henry's thumb. "His pulse is strong; his blood pressure and his breathing are normal. Those are good signs. We'll let him rest for a while, then talk to him. He might surprise us any minute."

"And what if he doesn't doctor, then what?" asked Breana.

"Then we'll get him all the help he needs. Don't worry."

The news spread fast that the bell had sounded for Penelope Margaret Noble. Friends and neighbors started calling to offer their condolences. Breana and Thelma regularly checked on Henry but there was no change. He seemed to not care and wouldn't eat or drink anything. Breana and Thelma were worried and stayed in constant communication with the doctor.

No one who visited came empty handed. By days end, a vast assortment of food graced the kitchen counters and tables. Thelma was having difficulty finding space for it all. She opened the refrigerator and found it almost full to capacity. She shook her head and muttered, "There's no way we'll ever eat all of this. What are we—?"

"We'll donate it to charity." Thelma looked up, startled at seeing Henry. She hadn't heard him enter the kitchen.

"Are you alright Mr. Noble? We've all been so concerned. We tried everything, but the doctor did say you would snap out of it when you were ready." she said still surprised.

"Yes Thelma." he said, sounding a bit embarrassed. "I'm feeling fine. I believe that I'm finally coming to grips with Penny being gone." Even as he recited those words his voice caught in his throat sending a clear message to Thelma that it wasn't quite true. He was just trying to be strong. Thelma seeing the hurt on his face changed the subject back to the food. "I'll call to have someone pick up the food." she said, and started for the phone.

"Thelma."

"Yes Mr. Noble." She turned to face him.

"When you're done with that, we should start making the funeral arrangements." He said with a deep sigh.

Penny was buried in the churchyard with a host of friends and relatives attending. Rita Ives was among them.

It had been the first time she saw any member of the Noble family since the incident at the christening.

After the funeral, she approached Henry. "I feel terrible that I wasn't there for Penny, but no one even bothered to call and let me know she was sick. It's a shame that all our years of friendship have been cast aside, and for what!"

"Not now Rita, I have just buried my wife! Please let us have some privacy!"

"You have time to pamper that little urchin that knows nothing about our way of life and barely had time to know Penny, but you don't have time for me! I thought you were a better man!" Rita replied. Henry walked away with no response.

* * *

Penny's friends and neighbors mourned her passing for many months. They kept her memory alive by talking about the things that made her special. Henry and Breana comforted each other through their grief. They relied on Thelma a great deal. Being Breana's godmother, she became a surrogate mother to her, and a valued friend to Henry.

Breana was out of school for two weeks. She surprised everyone by how strong she appeared to be. She immediately took over where Penny had left off. She made time to volunteer in the community, just as her mother did. She took Penny's strength and compassion and made it her own.

When she returned to school, Molly did not hesitate to annoy and ridicule her.

The girls had a soccer game one morning; after the game, they gathered in the locker room. As soon as Breana walked into the room, Molly started wagging her tongue maliciously.

"Some people are really jinxed. Wherever they go, dark clouds hover overhead.

Mrs. Noble was fine until she opened up her home and her life to a certain type. Now, she's gone because of some kind of disease she picked up. I wonder who the little waif will depend on now."

The other girls started giggling. A voice from behind one of the lockers said, "Maybe this is our chance to be rid of her. Mr. Noble's next wife might ship her off somewhere."

"Yeah, another girl jumped in; maybe back in the gutter where she belongs."

Breana heard it all. Her embarrassment reflected on her face. Savannah heard it too, and she was angry; she said, "You all should be ashamed of yourselves. Kicking a person when she's down is your favorite sport, isn't it Molly?"

"Well, since you feel so sorry for her being down an' all, why don't you go down with her?"

She pushed over one of the lockers in an attempt to hit Savannah and Breana. The girls instinctively jumped out of the way. Molly leaped at Breana and shoved her against the remaining lockers. When Savannah came to her defense, a fight started. The others started shouting and rooting for Molly, "Get her! Hit her in the face!"

Suddenly, the coach walked in. She heard the commotion, and she saw the rumble between the girls.

"Break it up, ladies!" She yelled repeatedly while pulling the girls apart.

The rest of the team began leaving the locker room, laughing and talking about who won the fight. Molly, Breana, and Savannah were sent to the Principal's office, and their parents were called. They were all charged with destruction of property and were facing suspension. However, some of the girls told the story exactly as it happened, and Breana and Savannah were excused.

The parents of the three girls finally arrived at the school. Lee Ann Reynolds, Molly's mother, entered the room and sat beside Rita. Lee Ann was a portly woman with fairly tanned skin, and light brown hair.

"If Molly did those things, she's wrong," said Lee Ann, "I don't know what's wrong with that girl. I swear, ever since her father died, she won't listen to anything I say."

"I agree with you Mrs. Reynolds. That's why I've decided to put her on two weeks suspension." The Principal's secretary buzzed in, informing him of an important phone call from his wife.

"You'll have to excuse me for a moment. I'll be right back," he said as he walked to another room to take the call. As soon as the Principal left the room, Rita began complaining.

"Goodness gracious Lee Ann, I've never heard such nonsense in all my life. Don't you understand what's happening here? If you don't speak up for your child, who will? A mother must be strong enough to defend her own child. Why should Molly be suspended for speaking the truth?"

Rita had always mistaken Lee Ann's amiable temperament for weakness. She continued to instigate.

"If only Savannah was more like Molly and stay with her own kind. She would be better off. I don't believe that Molly is the only one who is responsible for knocking over those lockers. If you lie down with dogs, you'll get up with fleas, and that's exactly what happened here today."

Lee Ann looked at Rita in disbelief that she was condoning Molly's behavior. Rita's rant continued..."And really, Savannah, what were you thinking? Taking up with this girl like that. You're going to be the death of me. When your father comes home, young lady, he's going to give you a talking to."

Henry's face changed to different shades of red. He looked at Rita, and lashed out at her. "You think you can carve out a little piece of society for yourself, and whoever you deem unworthy is an infringement on your rights? Well, if you're looking for isolation Rita, I have a suggestion! Get on your broom, and fly off the face of the earth, you witch!"

Henry's response had Rita flabbergasted. He was oblivious to her bulging eyes and gaping mouth. Henry took hold of Breana's arm and said, "Let's go home sweetheart," they both walked out of the room.

Rita's face was flushed with anger. She was mortified that Henry spoke to her like that, and in public. She started fanning her face with an accordion pleated fan decorated with the picture of a geisha girl. As Henry left the building, he said, "That woman's mind is so warped; I'm surprised that she even used a fan with the face of a geisha on it."

Even after Henry and Breana left, Hurricane Rita was still raging.

"Well!" she said, "I declare…that man has plumb lost his mind. Did you hear the things he said to me?" She was looking at Savannah in embarrassment. Savannah looked away as Rita continued her complaint.

"How dare he speak to me in that manner? Honestly the, way he carries on, one would think the little mongrel is his own flesh and blood. Sometimes I wonder..."

"Come now Rita, stop!" Lee Ann interjected.

She looked at Lee Ann and said, "You heard what he said to me. I didn't hear you stopping him! Can you imagine, so many years I've spent thinking of them as friends, and they choose that little half breed over me? She already killed Penny. He should be fearful for *his* own life, instead of attacking me the innocent one who only has his best interest at heart!"

Lee Ann was annoyed. She rolled her eyes upward, then looking at Rita; she said. "You know, Rita, you shouldn't say those things. You have no proof of the girl's lineage. And what could that child have done to cause Penny's death?"

"I've got all the proof I need. She doesn't look like any pure blood to me. Lee Ann, you can say what you want; because, you don't know her like I do. That girl has been in and out of so many homes, and she mingled with different people; who knows what she might have picked up and passed on to Penny."

As she raved on, she made a feeble attempt to 'educate' Lee Ann. "Some people are just carriers you know. Their bodies are so used to certain conditions; they're immune for goodness sakes. They just pass it on to other unsuspecting victims like Penny. I heard that Penny died of a lung disease. She got it from some kind of virus that she picked up. Where else could she have gotten it? Not from us, that's for sure."

"Rita, people have been dying from pneumonia before we even had a name for it." Lee Ann said.

"Hmmph...it's your privilege to think whatever you want, but I know different. Come on Savannah, let's go."

She walked off with Savannah following slowly behind her. As she walked behind her mother, Savannah talked to herself, "Why me? Why is it that the most embarrassing person I know has to be my mother? I wish I had some place else to go right now except home with her."

Rita walked outside to her car and opened the door. She looked back and saw Savannah dawdling behind. "For heaven's sakes Savannah, put some life in your steps girl. I don't have all day. You're as slow as molasses in January, I declare! I shouldn't even be here. I have an appointment at the beauty parlor, and now you're going to make me late!"

"I'm coming mother," said Savannah through clenched teeth. She quickened her footsteps to the car and got in. Rita drove off, complaining.

"On account of your silliness, taking up with that Breana girl, I'm going to be late for my appointment!"

Molly was very angry that Savannah and Breanna went home without suspension. As she walked out with her mother she muttered, "That Breana, she hasn't heard the last of this."

"What did you say?" asked Lee Ann.

"Nutten,"

"Don't say NUTTEN honey, the word is NOTHING. And I know you said something, so whatever is on your mind, I suggest you drop it right now before you get into more trouble than you're already in."

* * *

One afternoon a few weeks later, while in school, Breana was called to the Principal's office. When she arrived, she was told that her father had called saying that their Driver would be picking her up early that day. She arrived outside at the appointed time expecting Briggs to already be there but he was nowhere to be found. She looked up and down '*Hmm; this is odd for Briggs to be late. I hope he's okay,*' she thought.

Then, a car came around the corner, and pulled up to where Breana was standing. The car stopped and a passenger came out from the back seat with a piece of paper in his hand. He pretended that he needed to find an address. He wanted to know if Breana could help him. As soon as she got close enough to the car, he opened the door, grabbed her and shoved her onto the back seat.

He pulled a pillow case over her head, and he closed the door. Another person helped tie her hands together. As they drove away, the driver reached over to the back seat and punched her in the head, and crashed into a light post in the process. One of the abductors shouted, "My car! You idiot!" The driver nervously reversed the car and sped off.

Breana screamed and struggled as they continued to punch and hit her. When they were a good distance away from the school, the driver stopped the car in a secluded area. They got out of the car, dragging Breana with them. They pushed her down causing her to hit her knee on the pavement. The abductors ignored her cries as she pleaded for them to stop. Just then, the driver picked up a large stick and hit Breana on her head, then said, "Take that bitch!" and laughed harshly. Breana's body went limp. They dumped her into a nearby ravine and took off in a mad rush, almost hitting a pedestrian who was walking his dog along the side of the road.

"Why don't you pay attention to where you're going old man!" shouted the driver.

"What is this world coming to; young kids driving like that? To be so disrespectful, it's a shame before God," the pedestrian lamented as he went on his way.

Briggs drove to the school to pick up Breana. He parked the car in the usual spot. He got out of the car and walked around to the passenger's side and leaned against the car waiting for her to come out. Ah…nothing can mess up a beautiful afternoon like this." He said under his breath. The bell rang, signifying the end of the school day. Students emerged from the building, laughing and chattering in excitement. Briggs waited for Breana, but she didn't show up. He went inside to inquire about what was going on. He reached the Administrative office.

"Excuse me." He said. I'm here to pick-up Breana Noble but I haven't seen her and the other students have already left."

"Breana Noble?" The Secretary asked. "She left early after receiving a phone call from her father. The driver picked her up." Briggs looked at her surprised. I'm the driver; something is wrong here. I have to call home. May I use your phone?"

Thelma, still mourning Penny's passing, answered the phone as jovial as she could muster. Her countenance quickly changed after Briggs explained everything. "Oh my dear Lord!" she said. She dropped the phone and ran to find Henry.

"Mr. Noble we have to go to the school now! I think something has happened to Breana. Briggs was just on the phone!"

"What happened?"

"He didn't say much. He said he has been waiting for Breana, and she didn't come to the car. He said something about Breana leaving school early. The whole thing sounds ridiculous, Sir."

Henry was bewildered. "Ridiculous, to say the least, I think one of us should remain here at the house just in case she shows up. I'll go to the school, and I'll call you as soon as I know anything."

"Oh, please hurry Sir, but drive carefully. Oh, please God, watch over that child," Thelma said as she lifted her apron and wiped her eyes.

When Henry reached the school, Briggs was waiting for him at the door.

"Briggs, I can't lose my daughter. Tell me what happened," Briggs repeated the story. "Wait a minute," the Custodian interrupted, I saw a white Volkswagen Beatle this afternoon near where you normally park, but I didn't think anything was wrong."

"Call the police," Henry demanded. "My daughter is not the kind to wander off when she is expected somewhere else. I suspect foul play, and I want the police on it right away."

"I've already called the police, Mr. Noble." Briggs replied, "They're on the way as we speak. We'll get your daughter back, Sir."

"We have to Briggs, we just have to."

* * *

All the time they were searching, Breana was lying at the bottom of the ravine off Memorial Drive. She was bleeding and unconscious. The police searched the school grounds and nearby fields, and found nothing. Although exhausted, they continued searching all night, but were unsuccessful. People gathered at the Noble's for an all-night vigil. Mr. Noble was distraught, but he remained active in the search for his daughter. He would not rest until she was found, he told them. Thelma stayed busy cooking and feeding the people that stayed at their house. Briggs stayed with the search party.

Early the next morning, miles away from the turmoil at the Noble residence, a young boy was walking his dog near his home. The dog started to act strangely, barking and jerking the leash. He got away from the boy and started running over the road bank and down the ravine.

"Justice, Justice come back here!" he yelled.

The dog kept running and barking, as the boy chased after him. He stopped in his tracks when he saw the bloody pillow case. Justice was shuffling back and forth around the body, and whimpering as if he was hurt.

"Dad! Dad, come quick!" He ran back to his house. His father heard the commotion and ran outside to meet him.

"What's wrong Thomas? You look like you've seen a ghost."

"There's a body in the ravine, Dad!" Thomas said, almost out of breath. "Honest, there is!" His father looked at him for a moment, and decided that his little prankster son was telling the truth.

"Martha! Call the police!" he shouted to his wife.

When the rescue team got there, Breana had no identification. Dried blood had replaced the luster of her black hair, now matted down to her head. Her eyes were swollen shut. Her face and lips were swollen twice the normal size. Her right shoulder was dislocated. Her body was black and blue all over, and her lips were dried and cracked. When the ambulance arrived at the scene, the team leader began to assess the situation.

"Oh man," he said, "This is bad. Her pulse is weak, respiration is shallow, blood pressure is at the lowest and she is severely dehydrated. Let's start 'ringer lactate IV' stat, and get her out of here!" They started the IV, got her on the stretcher and out of the ravine. At the hospital, in the Emergency Room, a battery of medical test were performed.

At the Noble's home, gloom and despair hovered over the household like an Egyptian plague, for no one knew that Breana had been found. Later that morning, Officer Lee was about to call Henry to inform him that they may have found Breana.

Breana's picture was etched in his mind from the night before when he joined the search party. Her face was extremely swollen but there was still some resemblance.

The phone rang at the Nobles residence, and Henry immediately picked it up.

Officer Robert (Randy) Lee said, "We met last night during the search party for your daughter. I'm over at Grady Hospital in Atlanta. An unidentified young female was brought in this morning. I think you might want to come and take a look at her to see if you recognize her."

"Can't she say who she is?"

"No Sir, she's unconscious."

"She hasn't said anything at all since she was brought in?"

"No Sir, she was brought in unconscious and she hasn't woken up since."

"I'll be right there! Briggs! Thelma! That was Officer Lee on the phone. He said there's a Jane Doe who was brought in unconscious to the Grady Hospital this morning. For all we know, it might be Breana. Hurry, Briggs! Let's go!"

"Oh, dear God! How in da world did she get so far from home?" Thelma wailed, "I don't know whether or not I should hope that it's Breana. How could I bear to see her in that condition?"

Thelma went into the kitchen to clean the breakfast dishes. She had made a simple meal of sliced fruit and cereal, but no one had the appetite to eat. As she cleaned the kitchen table, the thought of Breana's condition made her knees buckle. She quickly grabbed a chair to sit down. All she could do at that moment was pray.

Henry and Briggs arrived at the hospital. "Good morning, Officer Lee. Thank you for calling us. Where is she?"

"Come with me to the reception desk. You'll need a pass in order to see her." When they got to room 221, he walked over to the second bed. Henry recognized her right away.

"Oh, my God! My beautiful daughter! Who could have done this to you? You have never hurt anyone in your life. Why would anyone do this to you? " He cried bitterly.

"Officer Lee, would you mind calling my house and let my housekeeper know that Breana is here, and that I will be staying here for the evening."

"I certainly will do that for you, Sir. I'm so sorry for what you and your family are going through. I promise we will get to the bottom of this."

"Thank you, I'm going to stay with her in case she wakes up." He sat by her bedside, and a few minutes later, the doctor walked in.

"Good afternoon, Mr. Noble. I'm Dr. Hardy. Your daughter is badly injured, Sir. She has a fractured spine, her right shoulder is dislocated, and her nose is broken. She also has a concussion, and was badly dehydrated when she was brought in.

However, she is responding to I.V. treatment. She's in traction right now, but in a couple of days we will do a body cast. As for the concussion, we won't know the extent of the damage until the swelling is gone down. Her vital signs are fair as of now, and we're doing all we can for her."

"Doctor, she's been unconscious all this time, how will this affect her recovery?"

"I understand that as her father, you're very concerned, and you need answers, but we have to wait. I can't answer those questions until the swelling has gone down."

"Is there anything I can do for her now?"

"You're doing it, just talk to her. Let her feel your presence. Though she may not be able to respond, she may still be able to hear and feel."

"Would it be alright if I stayed the night? I'd like to be here in case she wakes up. I don't want her to be alone."

"I think that's a good idea. I will arrange for a cot to be brought in for you."

Thelma brought him food, but he had nothing except coffee. The incident made headlines in the news, and it was the talk around town.

* * *

On the third day after the abduction, the police got a break in the case. A call came to the police station from a concerned citizen. "Hello Officer, my name is James Reid. I was reading about that car you are looking for; I saw it Wednesday afternoon. The driver almost knocked me down on the same street where they picked up that girl from the ravine. I saw the driver as clear as day, it was no boy. It was a girl; I would never forget that face, no Sir."

"Can you come in to answer a few questions for us Mr. Reid?"

"Yes, I sure can."

After talking to some of the students and faculty at the school, the investigation led to Molly. When Officer Lee learned of the new revelation, it troubled him greatly. He and Molly's mother, Lee Ann had been dating for a month. He didn't want to think of what would happen to the relationship if he had to arrest her daughter. He still had hope that Molly hadn't taken part in the crime. That Saturday morning, he went to Molly's house. He knocked on the door, but no one answered. He went to the back of the house. Molly and Lee Ann were hanging laundry on the line. Just as he was about to approach them, Lee Ann suddenly turned around.

"Oh, my word, she said, "You startled me!"

"Sorry, Lee Ann, didn't mean to scare you none."

"Good heavens, Randy," she tried to slow her heart down. "You about near gave me a heart attack," she said laughing.

He then acknowledged Molly with a glare and nod, "How are you, Miss Molly?"

Molly made no eye contact. "I'm fine Mr. Lee," she said in a low tone.

"Well, I wasn't expecting you until later. You were missing me that much?" Lee Ann asked, with a flirtatious grin. Officer Lee was too preoccupied with the real reason for his visit; he didn't hear Lee Ann's question, so he did not respond.

"Hmm…I guess I'll take that as a no." Lee Ann mumbled under her breath.

Randy noticed a sheet set with one matching pillowcase hanging on the line. It resembled the one that was found at the crime scene. He immediately felt a sinking feeling in the pit of his stomach.

"Y'all need some help?"

"Well sure, honey," Lee Ann said.

He casually went over to the basket and picked up the pillowcase.

Molly watched his every move. "Where is the match to this?" he asked.

"Funny you should ask," Lee Ann answered. "I took them off the bed for the laundry, and it seems to have disappeared."

He looked at Molly. "Maybe I can help you find the other one," he said.

Molly lost her composure. She was so nervous, she dropped the bags with the clothes pins, scattering them on the ground.

"Good gracious child, must you be so clumsy? Pick them up." Lee Ann said.

She turned her attention back Officer Lee. "Well Randy, what have I done to deserve a man like you…helping out with laundry and such?"

"Just feeling neighborly Miss Lee Ann; we're supposed to be good neighbors, aren't we?" he said, looking at Molly.

Lee Ann carried on about the delicious lunch she was planning for him that afternoon.

Molly was too busy picking up the scattered clothes pins to notice Officer Lee putting the pillow case into his jacket.

"You know Lee Ann, that lunch sure sounds wonderful," he said, "but there's something I need to take care of; I don't know how long it's going to take, but I'll catch up with you later on."

"Well, what time should I expect you?" Lee Ann asked.

"As I said before, I don't know how long it will be."

"Alright, sugar, I understand; I'll see you when you can."

Randy said good bye, regretting what he had to do next. Lee Ann smiled as she watched him leave. When he got back to his office, he confirmed that the pillow case was the exact match to the one procured as evidence from the crime scene. The police went back to Molly's house…with a warrant.

* * *

Lee Ann met Randy at the door. "Well that didn't take too long sugar." The other officers standing behind Randy smiled sheepishly, some snickered. Lee Ann started to react but Randy quickly jumped in.

"Lee Ann, I'm sorry but I'm here on official police business." Lee Ann's brow furrowed in surprise and confusion. Randy continued. "It involves Molly. We need to ask her some questions."

"What for; what's going on?" She prodded.

"That's what where here to find out. Where is she?"

"Upstairs reading—Molly get down here right this minute!" she yelled turning her head toward the stairs. She turned back to look at Randy expectantly, but he said nothing else. The silence was maddening as Molly took her time coming down. "The police need to ask you some questions. I'll be right here." Lee Ann told her as they all took seats in the living room. Lea Ann sat next to Molly on the sofa and the accompanying officers stood around the room watching. Randy sat in the chair right across from Molly.

"Molly you can tell me what you know about the Noble girl's kidnapping now, or I should I take you down to the station for questioning?"

Molly glanced around the room, and then said, "How would I know anything? I wasn't at school. I'm on suspension, and I've never been in that area where they found her," she claimed. Randy studied her face and her body language. *"For being so innocent, she sure is acting guilty"*. He thought. Alright then; we'll go down to the station and have this straightened out.

Molly was taken to the Police Station. James Reid was called to the station for as he claimed, he had seen the driver, 'as clear as day.' When he arrived at the station, he had no doubt in his mind when he said, "That's the girl officer; I would remember her anywhere."

Molly got scared, and she started rambling.

"I didn't push her out of the car. The door opened up by accident, and she fell out. I didn't hit her either; I only drove the car. I only wanted to scare her. She always acted as if she's not afraid of anything. I didn't know this would happen!" She went on and on, proclaiming her innocence.

"Obviously, you didn't accomplish this alone. Who helped you?" Asked the other police officer who was standing by?

"No one!" she snapped at the police officer.

"Listen kid, you better make it easy on yourself. Tell us all you know and do it fast, or things could get really tough around here."

"Alright, you don't have to make threats. It's William, the boy who works for us and his friend. I told them I didn't want her hurt, but they hit her anyway."

"Does William have a last name?"

"Booth, I think. I'm not sure."

"And what's his friend's name?"

"How should I know? He's William's friend, not mine!"

"Listen kid, don't get smart with me. You're in enough trouble as it is. Where can I find William and his friend?"

"I don't know. His friend lives in Macon. Sometimes William stays over there.

"Who owns the car?"

"It's Jimmy's car."

"Who's Jimmy?"

"Jimmy is William's friend. Jimmy Lee. I think. Can I go home now? I've told you everything I know."

"Why, princess, you don't like our company? We don't care much for yours either. Unfortunately, you'll be here for quite some time. You lied to us enough in the last few minutes to earn you a jail sentence." Molly was placed in a holding cell, and the police prepared for a man hunt to find the boys.

Outside, a white pickup truck rolled into the station's parking lot. A confederate flag was painted on the hood, as if it was waving in the wind. The truck came to a stop, and the driver and a passenger, sat as if they were waiting for someone.

After a while, a blue Mercedes entered the parking lot and pulled up beside the truck. The young man from the driver's side of the pick-up hopped out. His pale face looked gaunt, and his blond hair, long and matted.

"Ain't you coming out Will, he's here," he said in a southern drawl.

"Alright! I'm coming!" William snarled as he hopped out of the truck. "I wish I never listened to you in the first place, or I wouldn't be here now in this mess."

"Would you rather wait for the police to come get us and make it worse then?" Jimmy replied.

The driver of the Mercedes swiftly opened the door and stepped out holding a black briefcase in his hand. He reached inside the car and grabbed a gray pinstriped jacket that matched the pants he was wearing. He placed the briefcase on the top of the car and slid his arms into the jacket. The red neck tie with the dark shirt in the background made him look like a man who gets what he wants.

"Come on, fellas! It's now or never!" he said in a commanding voice.

He shook his head as the two young men walked toward him.

"Look at the both of you…looking as disheveled as bums off the street. You didn't know you were coming to the Police Station? They might just take one look at both of you; decide that you are a menace to society; lock you up, and throw away the key."

He rolled his blue eyes at them; then he picked up his briefcase and walked into the Police Station.

"Hello Officer, I'm Joseph Martin, Attorney-at-Law, he said while handing out his business card. "These are my clients, William Booth and Jimmy Lee. They were coerced and blackmailed into committing a crime, and they are here to turn themselves in."

They confessed to their involvement in the kidnapping of Breana Noble. They also implicated Molly as the mastermind that planned the kidnapping. She had borrowed Jimmy's car, and blackmailed both of them into helping her. She was charged with kidnapping, aggravated assault and attempted murder. She was set for arraignment. William and Jimmy agreed to be witnesses for the prosecutor in exchange for a lighter sentence.

* * *

At the hospital, Henry sat by Breana's bedside. He was weary from lack of sleep.

His eyes grew heavy, and he leaned his head down on the bed. Suddenly, he felt a touch on his head. He looked up. "Praise be to God; Pumpkin you're awake; I'll get the nurse." He hurried out into the hallway. "Nurse, come quickly. She's awake!" He shouted as the nurse rushed from the nurse's station.

"What is it Mr. Noble?"

"She's awake. She just touched my head! My baby is awake, get the doctor quickly!"

Her vital signs were checked. They were good. However, her memory was clouded. She could not recall the events that caused her to be hospitalized.

A few days later, the doctors removed the traction and replaced it with a body cast. Her shoulder was mending; her bruises were fading, and her appetite was improving. Nevertheless, she had no feeling in her legs. Henry spent most of his time at the hospital, so Thelma and Briggs brought meals for him and Breana. They tried to make a homely atmosphere by setting up a little table in a corner of the room.

"I knew you'd want lemonade Breana. Briggs has gone to get some ice."

"Thank you, Thelma, Mr. Noble said, "That's very thoughtful and here he comes now."

Briggs walked in the room with a crystal ice bucket filled with ice. He fixed Breana's drink and proceeded to walk towards her.

"Okay, Breana, I'll just set your drink right here on this table; until you're ready."

The drink slipped from his hands and went through the sheet covering Breana's legs.

Breana flinched and jerked her leg back.

"Briggs! How could you spill the drink on the bed like that?" Thelma sternly retorted.

"Wait" Mr. Noble interrupted, "Briggs, go find the nurse or the doctor! Don't you realize what's happening? Breana felt the cold on her legs!"

"Oh my goodness, this is shaping up to be a blessed day!" said Briggs, as he ran to the nurse's station. "Nurse, will you please get Miss Noble's doctor? I think she has feeling in her legs."

"Well! That is good news. Dr. Hardy is with another patient right now. As soon as he's free I'll let him know."

Shortly afterwards, Dr. Hardy entered the room. "May I join the party?" His voice boomed as if he was James Earl Jones. He walked in, and he lifted the covers from Breana's feet.

"I heard there's been some miracle working in here, and somebody is ready to go dancing, huh!"

Henry all excited, "It happened unexpectedly doctor! Her drink spilled on the bed, and she felt it on her legs! Thank you God!"

"Okay Breana, I'm going to give you a little prick. Let me know if you feel anything."

He put his hand at the bottom of her feet pretending to prick her. "Did you feel that?"

"No I didn't, what's going on?"

"Can you feel it now?"

"Yes, I felt it that time. How come I only felt it once?"

"Because I only pricked you once. This is a very good sign of recovery."

Breana's healing progressed, and she was released from the hospital with wheel chair assistance; a nurse to assist with her personal

care, and a physical therapist. In addition, Henry hired a tutor for
her to keep up with her school work. She was determined to walk
again. She did therapy twice a day and each day was better than the
day before. She soon went from chair to walker, from walker to cane.
Finally, she walked on her own. Nevertheless, Thelma's protective
instincts remained active.

"Mr. Noble, she said, I'm not bringing up this subject to cause
any sadness, but I would like to remind you of something."

"Sure Thelma, what is it?"

"Well do you remember when Penny was dying? God rest her
soul. She had asked me to look after Breana, and I promised her
that I would."

"Yes, yes she did. I remember it as if it were yesterday."

"Well then, I would like to make a suggestion concerning her
education. I think the home tutoring is working out just fine, so
maybe we should keep tutoring her at home; this way she will avoid
the troubles she's been having. I'm really worried about her."

"I've been thinking the same thing. I'm glad you feel that way.
I think we should find out what she thinks about it."

Breana had just finished her range of motion exercises. "Hello
sweetheart, are you ready for the Olympics yet?" Henry said looking
pleased with Breana's progress.

"If you're talking about the one for the physically challenged,
I'll win hands down."

"Whichever one you enter my dear, my money is on you. Come
sit down. I want to discuss something with you."

Breana slowly moved closer and sat next to him. "Thelma and I
were discussing the possibility of keeping the home tutoring for you.
How would you like that instead of going back to school?"

"Well, I've already missed so much of school. I guess it wouldn't
make much difference going back now. The only concern I have is
Savannah; it's the only place we get to see each other, I know you'll

just worry about me every time I leave, so it might be the best thing to do."

"Then it's settled; I'll talk to the instructor about extending his time, and we'll arrange with the principal for you to take your exams at the school and possibly graduate with your peers."

"Hmm, I'll never have to endure ridicule, and I'll never be late for class, sounds great to me!"

"Somehow I knew you would see that as a benefit. Thelma will be thrilled."

He started walking through the house calling, "Thelma! Thelma where are you? I swear that woman has never stayed in one place for two seconds. I always have to be searching and calling, Thelma!" he said walking briskly through the house.

"Yes Mr. Noble!"

"Oh, there you are. I wanted to give you the good news. Breana thinks keeping the home tutoring is a splendid idea!"

"I assumed she would Sir, that's great. It's a load off my mind fa sure. I'll do whatever I can to help her adjust."

* * *

Home tutoring proved to be very successful for Breana. She had exceeded the requirement for graduation and received her cap and gown, and tickets to the graduation through the mail, two weeks in advance. It brought home the reality that she would soon face the people who had treated her so badly.

"I do wish I didn't have to face those people. Why did I agree to go to this graduation?" she mumbled as she turned and walked upstairs.

Henry entered the den and saw the box with the cap and gown sitting on a table with tickets next to it. "Oh good, the tickets are here. You're going to the graduation aren't you, Thelma?"

"I wouldn't miss it for anything, Sir."

On graduation day, Breana wore her hair curled and swept up at the sides, and a single strand of pearls around her neck. Her turquoise dress was tailored to fit the body of the young woman she had become. Henry looked at his daughter with pride.

"Well, Margaret Breana Noble, you are a rare beauty. You'll be the most beautiful young lady at graduation."

Everyone made their way to the limousine where Briggs waited, checking his watch every few minutes.

'Come on people; I don't want to have to rush getting there.' He wanted to say out loud.

It was 2:30 pm, when they reached the school. An usher greeted them at the door, "You're late, the ceremony started almost an hour ago," he said.

"That's impossible," Henry protested. "Here are the tickets. The ceremony starts at 3:00 pm." The usher took the tickets and quickly scanned over the contents. He glanced up at Henry.

"Wait here a minute Mr. Noble," he left them standing at the door.

"I knew something would happen to humiliate me. Only now, you and Thelma are right along with me."

Thelma wrinkled her brow as she shook her head briskly. "You don't worry, Breana, those narrow minded fools can't hurt me."

"There's got to be a logical explanation," Henry assumed. Suddenly, the door opened.

"I'm afraid there has been a misunderstanding," said the returning usher. "Somebody sent you the wrong time. I'm extremely sorry. Please follow me." Henry attempted to escort Breana inside.

"No Sir," said the usher. "I have to escort the graduate."

He held his arm for Breana. She walked up beside him and took his arm. Henry and Thelma followed behind. As they walked into the auditorium, Breana stopped.

"Oh my God!" She gasped, struggling to hold back the tears.

The auditorium was decorated with flowers, ribbons, balloons and bows. A large banner stretched across the platform read, *"Welcome back Breana!"* As she made her way down the aisle, the crowd rose to its feet and cheered until she was escorted to her seat on the platform. The principal presented her with a plaque that read, *To Breana Noble, The Most Courageous Student.*

She was overwhelmed by the sudden recognition. She graciously accepted the plaque in shock. She said, "Thank you; I don't know what to say. I did not expect this." Again, the crowd got to its feet and cheered.

She got to see Savannah, although, they didn't speak. Rita Ives would not permit it.

"They could applaud all they want," she said, frowning, "It makes no difference to me. The way they carry on over her, it's like she is some kind of hero. I'm glad she's ok, but it doesn't need all that attention."

Rita claimed that Molly was wrong for what she did, but she was provoked into it, and how she was locked away in reformatory school while the little 'social climber' was being lauded. "Where's the justice in that?" she asked.

Breana was spared from Rita's serpentine tongue. The Nobles had already left and did not hear any of her remarks. In the car, Breana was so overwhelmed by the events of the afternoon. "Father, did you know they were going to do that?" she asked.

"No, but it's been a long time coming. No one has ever apologized for all the terrible things they did to you. It's about time someone showed some courage and did something."

"I second that motion Mr. Noble. It's about time." Thelma said.

"I too, Miss Breana, I feel the same way" Briggs said, "Enjoy your victory!"

"I thank you all for always supporting me. Father, I saw you talking to the Principal. What was that about?"

"He was apologizing for the delay at the door. He said they had to do it that way, so you wouldn't just walk in and spoil the surprise."

"Now I feel guilty for making such a fuss about the whole thing."

Thelma was sitting behind Breana; she leaned forward and rubbed her back.

"After everything that you've been through, who could blame you for thinking the worst?" said Thelma Mr. Noble asked, "How would you say worst in patois Thelma?"

"You would say 'Wus.' yu really getting into the patois business Mr. Noble."

"Yes, but I've noticed that you're speaking it less and less, so I supposed I won't learn too much?"

* * *

After the graduation, Breana was exuberant. She went around the house humming songs and finishing chores that she had been postponing for weeks. Everyone in the household was elated to see her so happy.

On Sunday morning, Thelma was in the kitchen making breakfast. As she took the last batch of pancakes off the griddle, Breana jubilantly walked into the kitchen.

"Thelma! Why don't you go to church with Father and me this morning?"

"Anything that puts a smile like that on your face I'm all for it. Of course I'll go."

"Good! I'll help you with making breakfast, so we won't be late."

At the breakfast table, Breana announced, "Father, I'm learning to cook. I helped Thelma with breakfast."

"Oh no, Thelma, you allowed this girl near fire and food?" he teased. "What did you make?"

"I made the eggs, the toast and the coffee."

"She mastered the kitchen Sir. She's a natural," Thelma answered with pride.

"Father, I invited Thelma to church with us this morning, she said she'll come."

Henry, feigning shock, "How did you manage that? Every time I ask her to go, her answer is the same, 'I'm Seven Day." Henry said in his best Jamaican accent. They all had a good laugh.

They arrived at Pine Grove Baptist Church just before the worship service started. As they were being ushered to their seats, Henry requested that Thelma sit with him and Breana. The seats that Henry requested were unofficially designated 'whites only', nevertheless, the usher shook his head and granted the request. Rita Ives watched in disgust, as the Nobles were seated.

The minister preached this sermon, GOD'S ABUNDANT LOVE, MERCY and GRACE, is extended to all. Rita did not heed the preacher's words, for no sooner than church was over, and they walked out of the building, she was at war. She rushed to catch up to Thelma; she grabbed her by the arm and swung her around.

"What you did today was very disrespectful! How dare you, and in the house of God no less! Why don't you stay with your kind? Henry may not have a problem with commingling, but the rest of us do, and we don't have to put up with it!"

Before Thelma could say anything, Henry came through the door. "What's the matter?" he asked.

"You are the matter!" Rita snapped. "Not only do you inflict that half breed you call your daughter on us, but now we must also endure mingling with your maid as if she's our equal! Whatever you're doing in your house is your business, but you have no right to force it on us!"

"Madam, a lady possesses good character, and I see that you have none. The ladies in my household will not crawl into the gutter for an altercation with you." He crooked his arms for both Thelma and Breana; they each took an arm and they walked away without saying another word, but Rita kept on screaming after them.

Reverend Smith heard the commotion and went to see what

was wrong. As soon as Rita saw him, she shouted at Henry. "I'm the church secretary, and I know you do not pay your tithe. Yes you give, but it should be more. You are a robber; you are the biggest sinner of all, you hypocrite!"

Henry was quiet on the way home, until Breana said, "I wish we didn't have to run into Mrs. Ives. She always manages to spoil things. And why does she call me 'half-breed'?"

"Sweetheart, don't worry about anything that woman said. When people are mean like that, they're experiencing their own misery. Yet, rather than dealing with their own pain, they project it on other people."

When they made it home, Henry went to sit out on the Lanai. Breana brought him a glass of iced tea. He took a sip and set the glass down. He laid back on the recliner. "Ahh, there's nothing like a glass of ice cold tea to quench a hot summer thirst; thank you Pumpkin."

"You're welcome."

They both sat quietly for a while lost in their own thoughts. Henry had his eyes closed. After a while Henry asked. "What's on your mind, Pumpkin?"

"What do you mean?"

"Breana, you've been sighing and squirming in your seat for five minutes. I know you...I know when something's bothering you."

"Oh. Well, there is something I wanted to ask you."

"Alright, I'm listening."

Breana didn't really know how to begin. She had been remembering all that Rita Ives said over the years, but it was what she said at the church that really bothered her. She always thought of her father as an honorable man, one who always did the right thing. The idea that her father was a "robber" made her uncomfortable. It just didn't seem right. Rita Ives just had to be wrong as usual.

"Um, okay...well, it's something Mrs. Ives said today." She said you're not a tithe payer, and you're a robber. What did she mean?"

Henry chuckled a little. "That's according to her perception my dear. Neither Jesus nor his disciples ever collected tithes because they were not Levites; however, they had to pay tithes to the Levites because they had to obey the law of the Old Testament. The Disciples supported the church by making up in their own mind to give when they gathered together on the Lords day. We are to honor the Lord with our substance without expecting a wind fall in return. In my opinion, it is our duty to support the Church without any strings attached. I don't enter my giving as tithes. It's my offering of thanks giving for God's blessings on me."

"So you give because God has already blessed you." Breana stated with understanding.

"Precisely; if you make up in your own mind to give a tenth, then it's a good thing, but no one has the right to exact a tenth from you. It's our duty to support the Ministry with our best, and with a joyful heart. The bible tells us exactly how to support the ministry; you can read it in 2 Corinthians 9:7. The myriad of gimmicks that some of these self-proclaimed Prophets and Apostles conjure to fleece their flock is a shame. If Jesus was still here in the flesh, He would no doubt put a whip to their collective BACKSIDE."

"Father, I've read that scripture before, and it's one of the reasons for my work with the gift baskets. Does that count?"

"Pumpkin, whatever we do for God's people, we do unto God. You see, it's not wrong for the church to accept tithes; however, it's wrong for ministers to hold the church accountable for a covenant that God made with the eleven tribes of Israel."

"I'll say Rita Ives understands far less about giving than I do," said Thelma, after she had listened to the conversation for a while. She had joined them with her own glass of iced tea and had brought sandwiches as well. "That woman claims to pay tithes as if it guarantees her a spot in heaven, even though she is as mean as a rabid dog. Frankly, I feel sorry for her." She said while placing the sandwiches on the side table.

It's simple Thelma. When Roman Emperor Constantine made

Christianity legal, he had to come up with a way to support the Church Leaders. His Pagan Priests were already being paid by tithing, so he made it into law that the Christian Church be supported the same way. That was around 300 A.D., which means the Church survived hundreds of years without tithing. It had nothing to do with Old Testament tithing. There is no need to bring Malachi 3:10 into it."

"Well that was a good thing to do on behalf of the church," Thelma said, "…because the Church needs to have finances just like any other organization."

"Quite right." Henry responded.

On the other side of town, Rita Ives was pursuing her own definition of tithing. She opened her Bible and read, '*Will a man rob God. Yet ye have robbed me, but you say wherein we have robbed thee. Ye have robbed me in tithe and in offering. Ye are cursed with a curse, for ye have robbed me. Even this whole nation. Bring ye all the tithes and offerings into my storehouse, that there may be meat in my house….*" (Malachi 3: 8-10).

Rita wrote a sermon and set in motion. "Reverend, it is important that I speak to you as soon as possible," she said on the phone. "This afternoon will be fine." She said.

Curiosity brought the minister to her house sooner than later. When he arrived, she got straight to the point

"It is of great concern to me that some of us are paying our tithes and others are not, and you have not been saying anything about it, so I wrote this sermon that I would like you to preach next Sunday." He looked at her in disbelief. She continued, "I believe you should make it very clear that—"

"Thank you very much" said the pastor, "but I don't depend on the members to write my sermons for me. Besides, the people are supporting the church. Whoever chooses to do it by free will offering is just as acceptable as those that chose to do it by tithing.

It has to be what they make up in their own mind to give. God loves a cheerful giver."

"But the scripture is for a purpose; you must preach it!" She said emphatically

"If I have to hound anyone to give ten percent, that's not a willing sacrifice, and it's not acceptable in God's sight. Where is the blessing in that?"

"So, you are supporting the likes of Henry Noble who has been robbing God?"

"I don't think God minds very much since Henry is prospering more than those that claim they are paying tithe," Rev. Smith replied.

"May I remind you that I was very instrumental in bringing you to Pine Grove? And I can just as easily have you fired if you are not the right minister for our church?"

"If the right minister means taking orders from you on how to lead my members, then by all means, go right ahead." replied the Pastor.

After that response, Reverend Smith walked away, leaving Rita more miserable and frustrated than ever. In fact she was seething and plotting her next move.

Chapter Five

Breana sat staring out the kitchen window as if in a trance. A grocery list was on the table in front of her, and a slice of apple pie sat half eaten next to a glass of milk. Thelma rushed into the kitchen.

"Breana, the rice girl, the rice!" she shouted. She rushed over to the stove in an attempt to save the meal. The water had boiled out and the burnt smell filled the air.

"Oh my gosh Thelma, I'm so sorry," Breana said while scurrying to help Thelma salvage the rice

"Hurry, give me that pot over there," Thelma emptied the rice into the clean pot. Only the bottom had started to burn. She tasted it. "Thank God, we caught it just in time."

"I'm so sorry Thelma, I was watching it like you asked; and then I decided to make out the grocery list for the gift baskets. I started thinking about mother and the next thing I knew—-"

"Oh, it's okay child don't fret about it. I understand," said Thelma, "There are times when I think about her too. God rest her soul."

Breana finished her grocery list. She was ready to go shopping. Briggs brought the car around to take her to the store. "We are going to Manny's," she said, "Everything is always fresh and neat, from the produce down to the meat. Mother always said that Manny's is a good place to shop.

"Good morning, Mr. Manny." Breana said walking happily into the store.

"Good morning, young lady! How's your father?"

"He's just fine, Sir!"

"I'm happy to see you're okay after that terrible thing them kids done to you. Your daddy must be proud to see you following in your mama's footsteps."

"I could never fill her shoes but I'm doing the best I can."

"You're doing just fine. Your order is over here!" said Manny, pointing to several boxes stacked over the counter. "It's a rare thing to find someone your age taking interest in matters such as this."

"Thank you Sir," Breana started checking the contents of the boxes with her list, and Briggs started loading the boxes in the car. He only had time to load a couple of boxes before Rita Ives walked in. She looked at the boxes. She wasted no time to make her comment. "My-my, look at all this. It's no wonder there's not much tithe coming to the church. Who's going to eat all this?"

"This is for filling baskets for the needy, Mrs. Ives. It's not for us; excuse me please." Breana replied.

"Baskets for the poor?" Rita exclaimed, "In case you don't know, Jesus said, the poor you will have with you always. Your first duty is to the church, Missy. The poor is nothing but a bottomless pit. They can't be filled."

Mrs. Ives you are forgetting the part where Jesus said, I was hungry and you gave me no meat. I was naked, and you did not clothe me."

"I don't blame you; you probably know a lot about being hungry yourself.

Breana's back was turned to Rita. She turned around to face her.

"Mrs. Ives, before you preach to others, I suggest you read the bible and understand it for yourself."

"How dare you speak to me in such a manner? I have been reading the bible before you were born!"

"Yes, indeed you may read, but do you understand what you read?"

"Do I what? Of course I understand what I read, you insolent little waif! Where are your manners! I'll teach you to respect your superior, since no one else is willing to do it!"

Rita lifted her hand and attempted to strike Breana. Breana flinched and quickly put her arms up to cover her face. Briggs stepped in. He grabbed Rita's arm and forced it back to her side.

"Take your nasty paws off me you filthy beast!" Rita snapped,

"Then keep yours off Miss Breana, Ma'am. Do we understand each other?" Briggs intoned, as he let go of her hand. Her face was red with fury. She looked at him and spouted,

"Well! I never thought I'd see the day when the likes of you would dare to lay a hand on me! You haven't heard the last of this!" She left the store in a huff.

Two stock boys stood by and saw the whole episode. They looked at each other. The tall skinny one, with shaggy brown hair and to-bacco-stained teeth asked, "Jim-Bob, did you see that?"

"Yeah, I seen it, but I don't b'lieve it. Thangs like dis here gits me nostalgic for strange fruit. Somebody ought to teach dat boy a lesson," replied Jim-Bob as he removed his thick glasses from his face, wiped his brow and sat on a crate. His dingy green shirt was wrinkled, and his stomach generously flushed over the waist of his faded jeans.

"What is dis here whorl' cumin' to when a nigger thinks he can act uppity like gyat, puttin' his hands on a white woman!" said Jim-Bob as he ranted on.

Breana and Briggs finished their business and went home. "How was shopping? Did you get everything you needed?"

"Yes we did, but you would never guess who we saw," Said Breana.

"I'm afraid I can't. Who was it?"

"We ran into Mrs. Ives at Manny's. Couldn't believe it, but there she was, just as mean and hateful as ever."

"Rita was there? I'm not surprised at her behavior," Henry answered, "Nonetheless; I'm surprised she was at the store. That's not a place she would normally go. I wonder what she was doing there."

"Father, you know I wouldn't be surprised if she only stopped in because she saw our car parked outside. She probably just wanted to be nosy, as she always is." Breana told her father the details of the incident.

"Try to put that woman out of your mind. Someone must have given her a nasty pill when she was a child and she grew up nasty. I'm glad Briggs defended you, but I have a feeling we haven't heard the last of this incident."

Henry was right. It was a scorching night in Georgia. The night was still except for the crickets chirping in the distance. The waxen moon funneled a stream of light threw the open window of Briggs' bedroom. A warm breeze gently blew between the branches of a magnolia tree nearby, and a small branch from the tree scraped against the side of the cottage; the sound startled Briggs, and he was awakened from a sound sleep.

His deeply tanned skin glistened from perspiration. He lay almost bare on his single bed. Deep into the night, he was half awakened by the sound of the rustling wind against the tree branches. Then he became fully awake by what sounded like horse hoofs galloping toward his cottage. He sat up suddenly...leaving a sweaty impression on the dark blue bed sheets. He pushed the top sheet aside and sprang to his feet as the sounds got closer. He quickly moved to the open window to assess the situation. By the light of the moon, he could make out the presence of four riders heading toward the front of his cottage. Their faces were hidden under white hoods. Suddenly they were at the door.

The trespassers succeeded in kicking the door in. Two of them entered the cottage.

They pounced on Briggs, and he wrestled with them fiercely. He would have won, but, one of them, a short, burly man cast a rope around him and bound his arms to his side. He dragged Briggs outside, jumped on his horse's back, and dragged him to the nearby magnolia tree.

As his body went bouncing and scraping along behind the horse, they pulled their bull whips and proceeded to beat him. Just as they started to throw the rope over a branch of the magnolia tree, Breana was awakened by the uproar and witnessed what was happening through the window.

She ran to her father's room screaming, "Father! Father! They're killing him! They're killing him!"

Without question, Henry grabbed his shotgun and ran downstairs. Thelma awoke just in time to hold Breana back from running outside bare-footed and in a flimsy nightgown. Henry ran outside in his pajamas and started firing the gun in the air. One horse reared up, and the rider fell to the ground and started fumbling around. Henry ran to Briggs and untied the rope that bound him. Three horse men galloped away, but the fallen rider was still fumbling on the ground, looking for his eyeglasses. Henry grabbed him up and pulled the hood from his head. He looked up at Henry like a deer caught in headlights.

"What are you doing on my property?" shouted Henry, "I'll see that you get the full length of the law for this!"

Briggs lay curled up on the ground in pain, mainly from his torso and legs where he was beaten the worst. As Henry was interrogating the man, Briggs looked on and began to recognize his face and the faded green shirt he was wearing. He was one of the box boys from Manuel's store, Jim-Bob. By now, Henry had his shot gun pointed at Jim-Bob as he remained on the ground pleading for his life

Henry picked up the bull whip. "Briggs!" He shouted. Briggs looked up at Henry as Henry threw the whip to him and said, "Whip that Ass!"

The anger Briggs felt...fueled the strength of ten mules in him. He caught the whip from Henry, and he rose to his feet, and he WHIPPED - that - Ass. Enraged and hollering like a mad man, he dropped the whip and jumped on top of Jim-Bob. He straddled his body, and he began to beat Jim with his fist.

"Lick him! Lick him Briggs! Thelma shouted, as her patois kicked into full dear, "Beat the hell out-a him!" No one had even noticed that Thelma had come outside.

Briggs would have given Jim a few more punches, except, Henry rushed over to them. He grabbed Briggs' arm and said, "The police are on their way Briggs; let them handle it now!"

Then he moved closer to Jim, the fallen horseman—now cowering on the ground. Henry passed his eyes over Jim's body. "Just look at you; let this be a lesson to you," he said, as he wagged his finger to Jim's face and shouted, "If you ever bother me or mine again, I will not be this merciful!"

* * *

The police came and arrested Jim-Bob. During interrogation, he revealed that both box boys from Manuel's store, and two other men that worked for Rita Ives, made up the four horsemen. Thelma and Henry tended to Briggs' wounds until Dr. Lloyd was able to see him early the next morning. With the proper treatment, Briggs' wounds would eventually heal, leaving an inch long scar on his right temple. He would never forget the incident and he would struggle with anger for the remainder of his life. Thelma was still angry even after the police took Jim-Bob into custody. "I know a place where they wouldn't get off so easy. They would need a shovel to scrape themselves off the ground after they've been introduced to the machete. Bles-sed land of wood, water, and sunshine."

Rita's husband, Hank, had been staying somewhere in Europe. He was not around to witness any of the incidences between the

Nobles and his wife. Tuesday morning, three days after her latest scheme, Henry received a phone call.

"Hey, Henry old boy! Top o' the day to you old chum!"

"Hank Ives, is that you?" Henry asked.

"In the flesh my boy! In the flesh! How are you?"

"I'll be alright when I see you Hank! Come on over as soon as you can! We have so much to catch up on!"

"I'll be there shortly. It's been too long since we've seen each other old friend."

Henry hung up the phone and took long strides through the house. "Thelma!" He called out "Thelma! You'll never guess who was on the phone."

"Who was it, Sir?"

"Go ahead! Take a guess!"

"My guess would be Rita, Sir. And I hope I'm wrong."

"You are wrong, but close! That was her husband!"

"Mr. Ives is back Sir?"

Henry spoke with excitement. "Oh yes he is, and I can't wait to see the old rascal! It's been so long. I didn't realize how much I missed him until I heard his voice!"

"Oh boy! That man must be a glutton for punishment! Although it will be nice to see him again, I can't say I'm happy for him. Being home with that woman must be a living hell!"

"He's coming over you know. He should be here shortly."

"I think I'll make some of that coffee he likes so much. That poor man, I wonder how long he'll stay this time."

"I don't know, but I'll have to tell him about Rita. She has gone too far this time."

* * *

Hank drove the short distance to Henry's house. Thelma answered the door.

"Hello Mr. Ives, how nice to see you again," She said.

At fifty-five, Hank Ives was a dashing man. His light brown hair was neatly cut. His face was clean shaven except for a swallow wing mustache. His brown tailored suit was a perfect fit. He stood about six feet tall with a muscular physique.

"It's good to see you too, Thelma!" He said with a twinkle in his smiling hazel eyes.

He stepped inside. "Is that my favorite coffee I smell?" He asked as he handed Thelma his hat and cane.

"Yes Sir, it is! I remember how much you like hazel nut, so I have it ready for you!"

"No one makes a brew like you do, Thelma, and I've tasted many. Yours is the best by far!"

"Thanks for the compliment, Mr. Ives," she said as her cheeks turned pink.

"Take me to your leader. I can't wait to see that old rascal; where's he hiding?"

"That's funny. He said the same thing about you. Come this way, Sir. Mr. Noble is waiting in the study."

As Hank approached the study, Henry met him at the door. They both simultaneously grabbed each other and passed what might have been a fraternal hand shake as Thelma looked on and thought... *Two grown men acting like kids.*

"Come in! Come in! It's good to see you! You are a sight for sore eyes!"

"I can't tell you how good it is to be here Henry. It's been too long!" Hank said.

"You said it! I was beginning to think you would never come back to this side of the globe," Henry's eyes were beaming with excitement.

They talked at length about Hank's life overseas. Hank took a sip of his coffee and put the cup down on the table.

"Enough about me, Henry. You sounded as if you had something on your mind. What's going on?"

Henry's countenance changed. "I hate to burden you with this when you're barely home, Hank. However, it's a problem that has to be dealt with. Have you any idea what your wife has been up to lately?"

"No, she hasn't said anything to me, although she has been acting kind of strange, even for Rita. What has she done now?" He asked with a sigh of exasperation.

"Hank, you have no idea what that woman has been doing to my family. Her behavior has been intolerable. First of all, I want you to meet my daughter. Excuse me a moment."

Henry stepped out of the room and came back with Breana.

"Hank, this is Breana."

"Breana, it's a pleasure to finally meet my goddaughter. Henry told me you were beautiful and I can see the old boy was right," said Hank.

"I'm happy to meet you, Sir."

"So are you enjoying the summer? It goes by fast you know, better enjoy it while it's here."

"Oh yes, I'm having an enjoyable summer, getting to meet people and trying to make a small difference in the lives of people who are less fortunate."

"Well, that's refreshing to hear from someone your age. So what are you doing exactly?"

"I deliver baskets of groceries to some people in Summer Hill on weekends. I get to meet and talk with them. Some have interesting stories to tell. They make me more grateful for the life I have."

"As I remember, your mother used to do the same thing. You're doing a very good thing, keep up the good work."

"Thank you uncle Hank. May I be excused Father? Thelma was teaching me how to cook so..."

"That's quite alright dear, go ahead," said Henry, waving his hand.

As soon as Breana left, Henry told Hank of all the shenanigans he encountered with Rita. Hank listened in disbelief. He apologized for his wife's behavior.

"Now you have an idea why I spend most of my time overseas. I'm so sorry I wasn't here for you when Penny died. I should have been here, but I had my own hell to work through with Rita.

Hank had had his fill of Rita's reign of terror. "Henry the next time when I leave…I won't be coming back," he said, "The truth is, I don't know what to say to Rita anymore. I'm going home, and she won't be able to worm her way out of this one. Please convey my sincere apologies to Thelma and Breana. Henry, I just can't take this anymore."

He got to his feet and was ready to leave, Henry walked to the door with him. Thelma saw that he was ready to leave, so she brought his hat and cane. Henry watched him walk to his car, and his heart ached for the sorrowful look on the face of his dear friend. He almost wished he hadn't told him about Rita's behavior. *I had to do it. Rita is spinning out of control,* he thought as he watched Hank drive away from the curb.

* * *

Rita was waiting for Hank in the living room, already on the defensive.

"I know you went over to Henry's house. I'm anxious to hear what pack of lies they fed you about me, so go ahead; let me hear it." She ordered expectantly.

Hank walked by her without saying a word, and he went into their bedroom. She followed behind him shrieking, "Hank Ives… don't you walk away from me. I want to know what Henry said to you!"

Hank pointed to a chair, "Sit down Rita!" He said resolutely.

Rita gasped, placing her hand on her chest. She was shocked by Hank's stern command. She sat down on the chair, bewildered by his change of temperament.

"You have done some terrible things in the past, Rita, but the things that Henry has told me are unforgivable. How could you behave that way to Henry and Penny of all people?"

"Hank, don't you care that they took in that half-breed and expect Savannah to mix company with her?"

"I know no such thing; all I saw is Henry's daughter and *MY* goddaughter!"

"Your, what did you say?" she shouted moving closer to him.

"*My* goddaughter; that's a promise Henry and I made years ago...to be godfather to each other's child."

Rita's face turned red as the dress she had on. "And am *I* supposed to be a part of that package too?" she screamed, "Never mind. I'll go over there and settle this right now!"

She stormed out of the house and into her car. She drove to Henry's house and haphazardly parked the car in the driveway. She swung the car door open, and she stepped out of the car and slammed it shut. As she reached the front door, she started pounding on it as if the neighborhood was on fire.

* * *

"Who in heavens name could be knocking at the door like that?" Thelma said, while walking toward the door. She opened the door, and Rita pushed her way in.

"Don't bother inviting me to stay. I only came to say one—!" Henry heard the ruckus and went out to see what was happening. Before Rita could finish her sentence, Henry interrupted, "I suggest you leave my house, or save it for the police!"

"Police, indeed! Go ahead if you dare to take me on in court on behalf of your niggers. Justice may be blind, but the judge won't be! He will see behind the façade. I just came to tell you that if you expect me to play godmother to that half-breed reject daughter of yours, you're delusional! Hank may not care what company he keeps, but I do, and I will see to it that Savannah does too!"

She went back to her car and sped away from the curb muttering, "Police indeed, let him go ahead and call!"

* * *

Meanwhile, Hank was at his house pacing the floor. "Everyone warned me; did I listen? No! She baited her trap, and I walked right into it. She got me in a chokehold, and I've been wriggling with pain ever since. Well, no more; I've had it! I gave eighteen years and eight months of my life for Savannah's sake. I'm now fifty five years old. I've had all I can take!"

He walked over to the bar and poured himself a drink. He tuned the radio to his favorite country station. The music was blaring throughout the house as he thought of his life with Rita while his song played.

'Slowly, surely I'm slipping away, though I'd promised you that I would stay. You should know that anyone will roam when there's no love at the place called home....'

"Perfect song for an imperfect end." he muttered, sitting at the desk. He puts his drink down and took a writing tablet and pen from his briefcase. He wrote his feelings out on paper. When he finished the letter, he took one last gulp of his drink and folded the letter. He then walked to the bedroom where he and Rita had not slept together in years, and he started to pack a suitcase.

In the meantime, Rita was on her way from the Noble's house. The top of her red Chrysler 300 Convertible was down, and her long red hair was flying in the wind. She couldn't wait to get home to unload all that had happened at the Noble's house.

"Surely he will understand and agree that socializing with people like the Nobles would be detrimental to our good name. He has to listen to me now. After all, I'm his WIFE!"

Rita's thoughts were expressed loudly into the wind as she drove even faster. Blinded by rage, she was out of control. She sped past a parked police car, and was unaware of how fast she was going until she saw the flashing lights in her rearview mirror. The speeding ticket angered her further, and she placed the blame for it on the Nobles. She continued her ranting as she made her way home.

* * *

After packing his clothes, Hank returned to the living room and poured himself another drink. He looked over at the fireplace, took one last drink from his glass, and then threw it against the grate of the fire place.

As Rita's car drew closer to home, Hank was ready to walk out the house. He was leaving Rita for the last time. The chauffeur, on Hank's order, was waiting in the car in front of the house. Hank picked up his belongings and walked through the front door, leaving it wide open. The music continued to play as he got into the car; he said, "Take me to the airport."

The sky was getting dark. In the distance, the rumbling of thunder could be heard. As the car pulled out from the curb, a few drops of rain started falling on the windshield; then the downpour came. Hank did not look back.

The red convertible came barreling down the street, "Wait until I tell Hank that his best friend threatened me with the police!" Rita said as she entered the driveway. She heard the loud music as she stepped out of the car. She hurried up to the door trying to escape the rain. When she saw the open door, she was glad that Hank had opened it for her, so she thought; she was puzzled by the scene, but was more interested in telling Hank her news. She went over to the radio and turned it off.

"Hank! Hank where are you? You're never going to believe this!" She shouted as she walked through the house. She looked around the room, she saw Hank's note and picked it up. She walked over to the couch and sat down. She started to read the note; while the thunder rolled, and the rain poured.

Rita,

It has come to this at last! I'm leaving you for good this time. Savannah is now eighteen years old, it's time that I move on. She will be living with my sister, while she is away at college. I have arranged for your belongings to be taken to an apartment in Atlanta. I will be back in three months, and I do not want to find you on the premises when I get back. My lawyers will work out the details and they will get in touch with you. There is no reason for you to contact me. I've had enough hell from you to last the rest of my life. It's time I have some peace, and I wish the same for you. Goodbye'

Hank

She read the note over and over as if the contents would change. It was suddenly clear to her that Hank was gone, this time, for good. After reading the note for the last time, she slumped down on the couch, and she stared into space. The afternoon went by unnoticed. She sat motionless in the dark, on the verge of escaping reality.

Then, her expression changed. She looked as if she didn't recognize her surroundings. She got up from the couch, and she walked through the front door as if she was in a trance.

Virginia, the maid, came back from visiting relatives in the city that night. She made it home in the heavy down pour of rain. When she approached the house, she found the front door open, and the house was in darkness. She closed the door, and she turned the lights on. She called out for Mrs. Ives; there was no answer. She searched the house, but she did not find her. She walked by the couch, and she saw the note on the floor. She picked it up, and read it. She sat on the couch, and waited to see if Rita would come home. She fell asleep, awaking hours later to an empty house.

* * *

Daylight came and there was still no sign of Rita. Virginia was now convinced that something was definitely wrong. She started inquiring to the neighbors, but no one claimed to have seen her. The Noble's residence was the last place she thought Rita would be. However, she called just to be sure, but they knew nothing of Rita's whereabouts.

Finally, she called the police and reported Rita missing. The police went to the house, but found no clues. Virginia called Savannah at her aunt's home in West Port, Connecticut, but Savannah had not heard from her mother. She had no idea where she may have gone.

When Savannah hung up the phone, she started talking to herself. "I'm sure she didn't leave with Father. He would have to be out of his mind first before taking mother with him. She's probably gone somewhere to sulk because Father has left, and I'm here for the summer. She has no one to annoy," said Savannah, as she picked up a picture of her and Hank.

She walked around the room; then she stood by the window admiring the beautiful antique rose bush below. It was her mother's favorite flower.

"And it's just like her not to give any consideration to the people that might be worried about her." Disgusted by the whole idea, she flopped herself across the bed. "Oh well! She'll show up when she's ready," she said.

'If I worried every time mother got irate and did silly things, I'd die. I've never seen anyone so selfish in all my life. How could she do this? Gone off like that without a word to anyone. I guess she's just trying to punish Daddy,' all this ran through her mind.

The police questioned Virginia. As far as she knew, Rita took nothing of value with her. Her car and all of her clothes were there, and her purse was sitting on the couch. There was no sign of a struggle. Except for the broken glass, there was no sign of violence. Virginia thought it was strange, since Rita had always kept her purse in her bedroom.

The police asked Virginia about Hank's whereabouts. She told them that he was in town, but he left to go back overseas. The chauffeur told the police that Hank and Rita had been arguing that night and Rita left the house, and he drove Hank to the airport sometime later. The Noble's household told their story, but it lead to no firm conclusions. The search continued for many days, but it seemed as if Rita had vanished without a trace.

Chapter Six

Breana's mission of feeding the poor had been very successful. On Friday evenings, Briggs drove her from Stone Mountain to Summer Hill. The residents got to know and love her as they did her mother. She treated them with respect, in spite of their circumstances, especially Percy, a man who lived in a broken down shack. He seemed very intelligent. He was always dressed in worn-out clothes, but they were clean, and the holes mended to the best of his ability.

His gray hair shone beneath a tattered straw hat, and his skin, already dark, was savagely tanned by the hot Georgia Sun. His back was bent with age and he walked with a cane.

One Friday evening, he came to collect his basket. He was too happy to worry about his missing front teeth as he smiled at Breana.

"Miss Breana, you think I could have a lil' extra today? I have a friend staying with me that needs help like I do."

"Sure Percy, I'm so glad you're not alone anymore. I hope I'll get to meet your new friend?"

"Yes miss; maybe next week we'll come together. She's gonna like you, how could she not? You've been so kind an' all!"

The next Friday, Percy came alone with his bag to collect his food. When he approached Breana, he started opening up his bag for her to put the food in.

"Good morning' Miss Breana," he said in a dismal tone…which was unusual for him.

"Hi, Percy, why the long face this morning and where is your friend?"

"I'm a bit worried about her Miss. She was moaning all night, and she's a bit poorly this morning."

"I'm so sorry to hear that. I hope she feels better soon. If she doesn't maybe you should try getting her to the clinic or something. I put some carrots and potatoes in your bag, and..." she reached into her purse and pulled out a five dollar bill. "Here's five dollars. Go to the store and buy some meat to make her some soup."

He reached out and took the money. "Yes Miss, God bless you! I'm sure she would thank you too if she was here. I'm going to do what I can to help her feel better. I'm sure by next week she'll feel better, so she can thank you herself."

When Breana went back the next week, Percy did not show up. Breana asked the others about him, and she was told he would be there. While Breana handed out the food she was careful to save his portion. "I'll find him and give it to him myself if he doesn't come." She said.

While she was thinking of taking the food to him, Percy arrived. "Good morning, Miss Breana," he said, as he puts on a half-smile.

"Good morning, Percy! What happened? I was just thinking of coming to find you myself. You're always early to get your basket. What happened?"

"Bell's not feeling any better Miss Breana. Matter of fact; I think she's getting worse."

"Bell?"

"Yes, Bell, you know, my friend I told you about before."

"Oh, no Percy, I'm so sorry. Is there anything I can do?"

"I don't think so, but if you could bring some cough medicine when you come again, I would appreciate it?"

"Okay, Percy. I'll try to bring some for you next week."

"Thank you, Miss. God bless you for what you're doing for us.

Not everybody goes out of their way like you do, no mam, you really take after your mama."

"Thank you, Percy, that's the nicest thing you could say to me."

Breana finished her distribution, and on her way home...she started thinking of the situation with Percy and his friend. She sat quietly in the car on the way to Stone Mountain.

"What's the matter Miss Breana?" Briggs asked, "You've been so quiet, that's not like you."

"It's Percy, it's not like him to be so depressed. He might have a genuine concern for his friend and rightly so. She should be feeling better by now if it was just a simple bug."

"I know what you mean. She may need more attention than Percy can give her, but what can you do?"

"I don't know, but if she still isn't better next week, I'll have to think of something."

At home, Breana sat on the Lanai and stared into space, not uttering a word out loud.

'How can she wait until next week for cough medicine? She needs it now. Why did I say that to him? That was so stupid. I can't wait until next week.'

"What's on your mind, Pumpkin? Why are you so quiet this evening?" asked Henry.

"One of the men that always come to collect care packages said he has a friend with a terrible cough. He seemed very concerned. I told him I would bring him some cough medicine next week, but I'm having second thoughts. That was so silly of me to say that."

"Why do you think it was silly?"

"Father, you should see the living condition of those poor people, it's deplorable. No wonder they're getting sick. She needs help now, not next week."

The following morning, Henry and Breana sat at the breakfast table. Henry had the newspaper opened in front of his face.

"Father, may I have the A & E section," Breana asked. Henry gave no response.

"Father, still he did not respond. Breana got nervous. Her first thought was, *Oh no, not you, too.*

She panicked, and in a split second, she got out of her chair and rushed to Henry's side. She took the paper from his face. He sat with his eyes closed and his head bowed.

"Father!" she started slapping him repeatedly across the face in panic. Henry grabbed at her hands to make her stop.

"My goodness, I must have fallen asleep."

"You scared me half to death!" Breana said with relief "Why are you so sleepy this morning?" She sat down next to him.

"I didn't sleep very well last night. I kept thinking of the conversation we had yesterday evening about that fellow with his sick friend. I have some free time this morning. Maybe we should bring some cold medicine over there. The way you described the condition, it might take a bit more than cough medicine to help them out."

"Would you, Father? That would be great! Friday seems like such a long time to wait." Thelma came in and started clearing the table.

"Thelma, Father and I are going back to Summer Hill this morning. Do you need anything in Atlanta while we're there?"

"No thanks. I have everything I need. I went shopping yesterday."

"Then will you tell Briggs we're going and we'd like to leave around ten o'clock?"

"Sure will, sugar."

On the way to Summer Hill, Henry said, "Briggs when we get into Atlanta, we'll stop at Piggly Wiggly's and pick up some first aid medicine."

"Yes Sir, If they have some good old fashioned chicken soup in stock, the way my mama use to make it, that would do the trick," Briggs said chuckling, "She used to put in so much garlic, it scared away the bugs you got, and warn the others not to come."

"I did mention chicken soup to Percy yesterday. I'm sure he

made some. He looked so distraught. I believe he was ready to try anything?" said Breana.

When they got to Summer Hill, some of the people recognized the car, and started gathering around. "Has anyone seen Percy today?" Breana asked. His neighbors told her that he had been staying with his friend, whose cough seemed to be getting worse. When they got to Percy's house, it was so rundown that from the outside, they could see him wiping the brow of his friend.

"Percy, it's me, Breana! I brought the medicine you needed!"

Percy opened the door, and Breana handed him the medicine. "Percy, this is Mr. Noble, my father."

"I'm very pleased to meet you Mr. Noble. Your daughter is one of the best people I know. Thank you both for bringing the medicine."

While they were still standing at the door, Henry's eye caught a glimpse of a dress hanging in a corner of the room. He took a second look and called Percy outside.

"Percy, where did you get that dress that's hanging in your house?"

"It belongs to Bell, Sir. She was wearing it when she got off the bus on Sunset Ave over in Hapeville. Looked like she'd been wearing it for a few days so I cleaned it up for her. It's sure taking a long time to dry though." He answered, shaking his head.

Henry had a puzzled look on his face. '*This can't be possible. What would she be doing here of all places,*' he thought.

"Percy, would you mind if I take a look at your friend? I think I recognize that dress, and if I'm right, we've been searching for this woman for over a month."

"Oh my God! Well, come on in Sir. I calls her Bell on account, she don't know who she is."

Henry and Breana went inside. On a wooden cot a woman laid covered under a dingy white sheet made from flour sacks. There was rattling deep inside her throat with each breath she took; it sounded like someone slurping milk through a straw. Henry moved closer to the cot and looked on the woman's face. Although it was pale and gaunt, and the lips were dry and cracked, and around the eyes were dry and crusty; he was able to recognize that it was an emaciated version of Rita.

"Oh dear God, how is this possible?" he exclaimed, "Briggs! Get in here quickly!"

"You mean you really know who she is, Sir? Percy asked,

"I'm afraid I do Percy."

"Oh sweet Jesus, I'm so sorry Sir! I only tried to help her. I didn't mean no harm!"

"That's alright Percy. You may have saved her life."

Briggs ran inside the shack, "What's wrong, Sir?"

"Go quickly get Breana, and go to the nearest phone! Call an ambulance, and call the Sheriff; tell him Rita Ives has been found in Summer Hill.

"Mrs. Ives, Sir?" Briggs asked, standing aghast with wide open eyes and gaping mouth.

"Yes Briggs. It's Rita. Hurry!" said Henry, as Briggs ran off to the car.

Briggs drove to the nearest phone. He called the police, and then drove back to join Henry. The ambulance drove up first and the police shortly after. The emergency team applied oxygen and transported her to the nearest hospital Emergency Room.

Henry rode in the ambulance with her, and Briggs and Breana followed behind in their car. They waited for hours in the waiting room, before a doctor came out to speak with them.

"Is there anyone here for Mrs. Ives?"

"We are doctor. How is she?" asked Henry. Breana drew closer to hear the answer while Briggs stood back.

"Well, she is a very sick woman. She has Bacterial Pneumonia, and we suspect tuberculosis. However, we cannot be sure until the results are back from the lab. We started treatment for pneumonia. We'll have to wait and see how well she responds to the treatment."

"Doctor, is there anything we can do? We are not her relatives, but we have known her a long time."

"Find her relatives if you can," the doctor replied.

"Breana, you go on home and try to get in touch with Savannah maybe she knows where her father is."

On the way home, Breana said, "Briggs, let's drive back to Summer Hill, and tell Percy we'll take him to the hospital later."

When they arrived at his house, Percy was leaving to go to the hospital.

"Percy we came back to tell you that we'll take you to the hospital later."

"That's mighty nice of you Miss Breana, but I was on my way there now."

Breana looked at her watch. "There won't be a bus for another half hour. Why don't you come with us, have a hot meal, and then we can all go together?"

"You're very kind, I think I'll do that;" he said, "This is nobody but God."

Thelma waited in anticipation for them to arrive. The car drove up, and she met Breana at the door.

"Child, what is this I'm hearing: Rita Ives found in Summer Hill… doing what?" Thelma asked.

Just then Breana made the introduction. "Percy, this is Thelma. Thelma, meet Percy. He can tell you more about it than I can."

"I'm pleased to meet you, too Miss Thelma. I appreciate the goodies you sent us. Those cookies are wonderful."

"I'm pleased to meet you too, Percy. I'm dying to hear the story. Where did you find Rita Ives? People have been looking for her for months…"

"There's not much to tell, Miss Thelma. I saw her get off the bus at Sunset Ave. in Hapeville. She looked a little confused. Her clothes was fancy, but it was dirty, and one heel was missing from her blue shoes. She stayed in one spot, looking around, like she was lost or sup'n. I asked her if she needed some help. She said she was hungry, so I took her home wit me. I gave her sup'n to eat."

Rita didn't have any money to buy anything. Percy said she asked if she could stay with him for a few days. Since she didn't have any place to go; he took her in.

"She was just coughing all the time," he said, "I asked her name; she said she didn't know, so I just call her Bell."

"Heavens to Betsy! When Breana told me what happened, I thought she was pulling my leg," Thelma spoke with an appalling look on her face.

"Thelma, we have to take some food to the hospital for Father. He hadn't eaten since breakfast, and would you please fix something for Percy, too?"

"Sure, come with me to the kitchen, Percy. You can munch on some cookies, while I fix something for you."

Briggs drove them all to the hospital and they shortly joined Henry in the waiting room. Soon a doctor walked in and asked, "Are you all here for Rita Ives?"

"Yes doctor," answered Henry.

"She's unresponsive, but it's okay to go in now."

Henry and Breana went in, while Thelma, Briggs and Percy waited outside. Rita was lying under an oxygen tent. Her face was as pale as the sheets she laid on.

She was receiving antibiotics by IV. They stood around the tent in amazement, at the sudden downfall of a once prominent member of their society. Her eyes were closed, and her breathing was shallow. She had reduced to a mere caricature of the woman they once knew.

Suddenly, Rita started to make gurgling noises. Breana hurried to the nurse's station, calling, "Nurse! Come quickly! Something is happening!"

"Room 325; send in Doctor Marsh, quickly!" The nurse said to the unit secretary as she rushed into the room with a crash-cart laden with emergency supplies. "Wait outside please," she said, speaking to Henry and Breana. She entered the room in a rush. She obtained access to the Tent, and started suctioning Rita. After working feverishly, laboring to save her for what seemed like hours, Rita became unresponsive. Doctor Marsh picked up his stethoscope and placed it around his neck. He mopped the sweat from his brow and walked out into the waiting area.

"Are you Rita Ives' next of kin?" he asked Henry.

"No, but for now, we are all she has."

"Well we did everything possible, but it was too late, she's gone." Breana's mouth fell open and her hand simultaneously covered it.

"Do any of you know where her family is?" Doctor Marsh asked.

"Not at the moment," said Henry.

"I'm so sorry. Please accept my condolences," he said as he walked away.

"Thank God we found her before it was too late. Breana, I'm so proud of you. If it weren't for your efforts, we may have never found her."

"God bless you, Miss Breana," said Percy.

Two days later, Thelma was dusting the furniture when the phone rang. She almost broke a vase trying to answer it. Savannah was on the phone.

"Where have you been?" Thelma asked,' we've been trying to reach you."

She called for Breana to pick up the phone and told her who it was. Breana quickly picked up the telephone receiver in her room. She told Savannah how frantically she and her father had been trying to reach her and her dad.

"Aunt Martha and I went to Paris to meet Dad. We just got back this morning, and Dad went back to London. We told him all about mother's disappearing act. Can you believe her?"

Savannah carried on fiercely about her mother's disappearing act. "She's obviously trying to get revenge against Dad. Man, how can she stoop so low? Has she returned yet? Not that I expect her to call you guys."

"Savannah..."Breana attempted to speak, but Savannah continued rambling.

"But has anyone at least seen her?"

"Savannah...."

"To think, it's almost been a month, really!"

"Savannah!" Breana shouted, "Listen to me!"

Savannah was stunned at the sense of urgency in Breana's voice. "Breana, what's wrong?" Breana began hesitantly, "Savannah, we did find your mother. We found her in Summer Hill. She—."

"Breana, what are you talking about?" Savannah interrupted. "Mother would not be caught dead in Summer Hill," she chuckled nervously, "With whom? What was she doing there?"

"Well...she was with this guy that said he saw her get of a bus in Hapeville."

"A bus? Why was she even on a bus?"

"No one knows. He said that she was wandering around as if she was lost. She didn't even know her own name."

"Oh my God, how could this have happened? I—I thought she was just being spiteful when she left! Where is she now? How's she doing?"

Breana took a deep breath. Her stomach felt sick. "When we found her she wasn't doing well, so we took her to the hospital."

"She's at the hospital?" Savannah began to cry.

"Breana, I'm going to call Dad, and I'll be on the first available flight home. Will you tell her that for me, please?" Breana paused for a while as she listened to her friend sobbing. Knowing what she had to tell Savannah, Breana began to cry. "Savannah, I wish I didn't have to tell you this, the doctors did everything they could, but she was so far gone when we found her."

Breana's voice started trembling, "I'm sorry, she didn't make it. Savannah, she's dead." Breana said reservedly. Breana heard the phone drop to the floor, and then silence.

"Savannah! Savannah! Are you there? Savannah! Breana kept saying, but there was no answer. There was nothing Breana could do for her friend. She helplessly hung up the phone.

Thelma fixed a tray of food and brought it up to Breana's room. Breana was sitting on her bed with her knees pulled up and her head down on her knees. As Thelma walked in, she saw Breana's tears.

"Good grief child, don't tell me you're grieving for that old woman, after the way she treated you?"

"It's not as simple as that Thelma. Just a few weeks ago she had a life, a home, and a family. And in such a short time she lost everything including her life, and worst of all, there was no family there for her. It all happened so fast. Just like that, she was gone."

"Well, you can take courage in knowing that you did all you could to help,"

Henry knocked on the door. Come in Mr. Noble. We were just talking about Mrs. Ives."

"I can't believe what happened to her. I should be saying 'Ding dong the witch is dead', but the situation is so tragic that I can't help feeling sorry for the way it happened," said Henry. "   The irony is that the people she despised the most, happened to be the people who were with her in her last moments to restore her dignity," said Thelma.

Breana could not contain her curiosity, she said, "I wonder how she could just lose herself like that."

"Maybe she was mentally unstable all this time, and that's why she was such a hateful person. That is why we should never change who we are because of someone else's behavior. We never know what made them the way they are," said Henry.

Hank was having a romantic interlude. He needed time to sort through what happened to his marriage of almost twenty years. On a beautiful evening in Portofino, Italy; he ran into an old friend.

They were sitting on the Alfresco Terrace at the Water Splendio Mare, sipping cocktails, while they enjoyed the view. They were in the midst of planning a stroll through the olive lined gardens on the hotel grounds; when they were suddenly interrupted. "Telegram for Mr. Hank Ives!" the Bell Boy shouted as he entered the Terrace. When Hank accepted the telegram, he saw that it came from his sister, Martha who lives in Connecticut. He opened it and read the contents. *'Hank, come quickly; Rita has died.'*

He explained to his friend that he needed to get back to the states right away, "It's a family emergency," he said.

Hank took the first available, connecting, flights back home. His first stop was Connecticut to see Martha.

"Savannah spoke to Breana today," said Martha, "They found Rita somewhere in Hapeville, or Summer Hill; she was half dead. By the time they took her to the hospital, it was too late. She died shortly after."

Hank was quiet; then he gave a big sigh. "Exactly how is Savannah taking the news?" he asked.

"Oh, Hank, she's in a bad way. She fainted when she heard. I had to revive her with smelling salts, poor girl. She's just curled up on her bed, not saying a word, just crying her eyes out."

"I don't know what to do to make up for all this. Rita causes Savannah pain whether she is dead or alive"

"Hank all you can do is love her, and make sure she knows that she is important to you. Beyond that, she is going to have to allow herself to heal, one day at a time"

Savannah, Hank, and Martha returned to Georgia to make funeral arrangements.

On the day of the funeral, the church was overflowing with aristocrats and upper middle class in attendance. A lone black man shuffled his way from the back of the pew toward the front where Rita's remains waited to be eulogized. His black and white shoes leaned to the side, but they were clean. His black suit was tattered, but it was neatly pressed. As he made his way down the aisle, two of the ushers took hold of him, one on each side. They demanded that leave. Henry stepped in. "You will do well to leave him alone," he commanded, "Had it not been for his kindness, we would not have found Rita. Let him be."

They let go of Percy. He shrugged his shoulder and walked up to the casket. He removed his worn out top hat, with a hole in the bottom, and he laid it on his chest and bowed his head. He stood and stared at Rita's lifeless body and reminisced in silence.

Poor—poor Ananka, so this is the end of the road fa you. Well, you're sleeping with your poor mama now, God rest her soul. Rest in peace now, poor, poor Ananka.

He shook his head as tears welled up in his eyes. He pulled a handkerchief from the breast pocket of his worn out jacket and wiped his eyes; then he walked out through the front door, still shaking his head. As he went through the door, everyone heard him saying, "Ananka, oh Ananka!" No one understood his tears. But there was something about Percy. He knew something no one else did.

"Who is he? Why is he calling her Ananka?" could be heard among the whispering congregants. "Well this is strange" Lee Ann leaned over and whispered to Randy.

"He is the one who found her; I guess that's why he came." Randy replied.

"I understand that, but getting up to the casket like he did looked kind-a personal; don't you think?" Lee Ann remarked.

Percy had his own reason, but that's another story for another time...

Anyhow, they buried Rita in the Ives' family plot. That evening after the funeral, Breana stayed in her room. She read her bible and she contemplated the fragility of man. She realized that when you leave this world all that is left, are the deeds that you have done. Rita's tragic demise encouraged Breana to continue her food delivery zealously. However, her plans came to a halt when Henry received the assignment he had been waiting for.

The Jamaica Labor Party had won the General Election on April 10th 1962 and gained independence from England on August 6, 1962. The transition went smoother than many had thought. On August 7, at 12:00 midnight, the British flag was lowered and the Jamaican flag was raised in its place. Many foreign dignitaries attended the celebration. Princess Margaret represented England.

The island was alive with music and dancing, instead of rioting as many had expected. Breana was in the kitchen working on her shopping list for the gift baskets. Henry was on the back porch reading the newspaper when the telephone rang. Breana picked it up. "Hello. Yes he is, please hold on just a moment." She walked out to the Lanai.

"Father, there is a phone call for you!" she plugged a phone into a jack on a wall on the lanai, and handed the receiver to Henry. Henry's side of the conversation was very audible.

"Hello, good morning Mr. President. Yes Sir, I have been following the news, and I spoke to Alexander last night. Yes Sir, I'm pleased that everything went smoothly. After the conversation went on for a while, Henry said, "Yes Mr. President; thank you goodbye, Mr. President." Henry hung up the telephone.

He was elated as he walked inside the house, "Breana!" he called out.

"Yes, Father!"

"Well, my little mermaid, it seems like you will have your wish after all. I just finished talking to the President, and our move to Jamaica is back on."

Breana laughed and clapped her hands and jumped up and down with excitement. "Really Father? When do we leave?"

"We'll leave as soon as I've tied up a few loose ends," he said with a wide grin, watching his daughter bubbling with excitement.

"Oh boy! Thelma will be so excited! I'll go tell her right now."
She said.

Thelma was outside talking to Briggs when Breana showed up.

"Thelma! Briggs! Father just told me we're going to Jamaica after
all! He was just on the phone working out the details!"

"For real this time? How soon will we leave?" asked Thelma.

"He said as soon as he ties up some loose ends."

Thelma's excitement was obvious. "I guess I have to find someone to come in and help me prepare the house for closing. Hot dog!
I'm going home!"

For the next few weeks, the house was buzzing. The moving crew
came in to help with the packing. Thelma covered the furniture that
would be left behind. Breana took all of the food from the house to
Summer Hill. This would be her last delivery.

As she said her goodbyes, Percy said, "Miss Breana, you're just
like your mama for sure; except for you and your' family, no one
ever cared about us." God moves in mysterious ways, for in helping
us, you helped one of your own. That poor Mrs. Ives, God rest her
soul. As Percy spoke, he quickly reflected on his connection to Rita
Ives, the woman he called Bell and personally knew as Ananka.
Returning from his reverie, he hastily said to Breana with a sad
smile. "We're sure going to miss you around these parts."

"Thanks for remembering my mother," said Breana. "I'm sorry I
have to leave, but I'll keep you all in my prayers, and you all do the
same for me," she said as she tried to hide her tears.

Moving day finally came. Briggs was putting the last shine on
the car before taking the family to the airport.

"Briggs I'm going to miss you. Thanks for everything."

"No thanks necessary Miss Breana."

"I still wish you could come with us. It won't be the same without you."

"I wish that too, but it'll be alright, you'll see."

They exchanged hugs. Then she went inside the house. She went up to her room and looked around one last time. "Well I guess I have everything." Then her thoughts trailed. '*Everything, except mother.*' She was standing at the threshold of the room. Her eyes welled up with tears. Thelma's voice startled her. "Come on Breana, it's time to go!" She closed the door behind her. Thelma looked at her face. "That look tells me who you're thinking of. I've been thinking of her too. You know, she died thinking about you. She was a good mother, and you were very important to her. When she saw that she was dying, she sent your father to get me. I will never forget. I was in the kitchen making pie crust when I heard Mr. Noble shouting for me. I went rushing up the stairs. When I got into the room, she held my hand and told me how much she loved you, and asked me to take care of you. I promised her that I would…Thelma's voice trailed off as the memory returned. She sighed. "…so now you know. I will always have a parental responsibility to you, and I will not take it lightly."

"You've never told me mother said that."

"I'm telling you now, because the time is right. Moving to a new place can be overwhelming, and I want you to know that you are going to be alright."

She put her arm around Breana's shoulders and they walked out the door.

At the Atlanta Airport, they said goodbye to Briggs.

Henry said, "Now Briggs, you keep those telephone numbers I gave you safely, just in case you need to use them."

"Yes Sir. I have them secured by the telephone, don't worry. I'll make sure everything's alright." Thelma chimed in. "And don't forget to keep the lights in the main house on at nights and put them out in the mornings." After a while, their flight number was called. "*PAN AM Flight * * * 201 to Kingston Jamaica is now boarding at gate * * *13.*"

"Well that's us," said Henry. They all picked up their hand luggage and proceeded to the gate. "Darling, I remember how much you like the view of the ocean, so I made sure you had a window seat."

"Thank you, Father," Breana said as she took her seat. Her smile was only on the outside. "*Oh mother. I miss you so much, I wish you were here. Why did you have to go so soon?* Father I feel as if a part of me has been left behind." Henry saw her tears. "I know sweet heart. You're thinking of your mother, aren't you? I am too." He reached over and patted the back of her hand as it rested on the arm rest between the seats. He fastened his seat belt, leaned back in his seat and closed his eyes. '*I'll just rest my eyes a while.*' He thought, the plane took off, and he soon fell asleep.

Breana shook Henry's shoulder just as the plane started descending toward the Palisades Airport. "Father, wake up; we're almost there." Henry slowly opened his eyes. He yawned and stretched, and looked out of the window at the island below.

"Did you enjoy the view from your window seat, Breana?" asked Thelma.

"Oh yes, the water looks so inviting; it's so beautiful. I've looked forward to this for so long. I can't believe we're here." She responded excitedly.

"I think you'll like it in Jamaica. Thelma said. "At the beach the water is such a rich turquoise color and the white sand stretches for miles. It's magnificent. I'm so happy to be home again. It's been too long!"

Everyone was directed across the airfield to go through customs. Noting the lack of overhead cover, they were happy that it wasn't raining.

A black Cadillac pulled into the pickup zone near them. A man wearing a chauffeur's uniform stepped out of the car. He appeared to be in his forties. "Sir, are you Ambassador Noble?" He asked, with a deep voice that sounded like he could be on the radio.

"Yes," Henry replied, "This is my daughter Breana, and this is Thelma."

"Nice to meet you, I'm Dudley, your chauffeur."

Dudley took the hand luggage they were carrying and loaded them in the car. The three travelers waited while he completed his task.

Henry was thinking of his new employment, and Breana was excited about the life ahead of her. Finally, Dudley walked around and opened the car door. Henry said, "After you, ladies."

Breana and Mr. Noble sat in the back and Thelma sat in front with Dudley.

"How long will it take to get to the American Embassy?" Breana asked.

While Dudley was explaining the route, Breana was distracted by a little girl wearing a yellow dress and eating a chocolate ice cream cone. The melting ice cream dripped down the front of her dress, and Breana immediately had a flash back of her yellow, chocolate stained, nightgown.

Then she noticed Dudley driving on the *left side* of the road, and she felt uneasy. *'I'll have to get used this,' she thought.'*

Chapter Seven

The grandfather clock down the hall struck 6:00 am. Breana rolled over and sleepily opened her eyes. She threw the covers back and sat up on the bed with both feet dangling over the side. This was her first morning in her new home.

She got to her feet and stretched, and then she slid her feet into her slippers and walked over to the window. She pulled the curtains open and looked outside.

The truck that carried their belongings had arrived during the night. The men were waiting for daylight to unload. Breana went to Thelma's door.

"Knock—Knock, Thelma! The truck is here with our things." She said.

"What are you talking about? Who's here with what things?" When the door opened, Breana stepped into the room.

"I just saw the movers outside. I don't know how long they've been out there."

"Oh no, they shouldn't be here. Why can't they just follow directions," growled Thelma.

"What do you mean they shouldn't be here? They have our stuff."

"I'll have to speak to your father. I'll be right back." Thelma went to get Henry.

She knocked on the door, "Who's there?" he answered.

"It's Thelma, Mr. Noble. Something has gone wrong, and I need to talk to you.

"What's going on?" he asked as he opened the door.

Thelma whispered. "Sir, didn't you make the arrangements for the movers to take the things to the house in Harbor View?"

"Yes, yes I did, what happened?"

"Well Sir, they're outside. They're waiting to unload the truck. Breana saw them."

"Oh no, now we'll just have to tell her the truth, we can't surprise her anymore. Let me go and talk to those men first."

He quickly grabbed his robe and slipped into it, adjusting it, as he walked outside toward the parked truck. When he got to the truck, there was no movement inside. He peeked through the window and saw three men sitting in the front of the truck sleeping. Henry knocked on the door. The noise startled them. The man seated behind the wheel started rubbing his eyes and winding down the window.

"Good morning Sir," he said, "We got here since four o'clock this morning, but we didn't want to disturb yu sleep, so we were waitin fa daylight to unload de truck."

"No-no, you won't be unloading the truck here. I made arrangements for you to take the things to Harbor View- St Andrews, Kingston 17. It's just inland from Knutsford Boulevard. Here is the house number. My staff is there to open the door."

"Oh! I'm sorry Boss. When deh told me dat the load was fa the Ambassida, I just believe seh dis is where I should tek it."

By this time, the other men woke up and joined in the apology. "We sarry Boss. No problem mon, we will tek it dere right now."

Breana was dressed and ready to help. When she heard the truck leaving, she ran to the door. Henry met her at the door.

"Father, where are they going with our things?"

"Come sit, I have to talk to you. I knew that you wanted to be close to the beach, so I arranged for us to have a house in Harbor

View, over St. Andrews. From there, you'll have a clear view of the Kingston Harbor. You'll be able to watch the ships come and go out right from your veranda."

Breana's joy was all over her face. "Oh Father, I didn't think it was possible for you to make me any happier," she said, embracing him.

"Thelma! You and Father are something else. You two managed to plan this whole thing, and I knew nothing about it."

"I knew nothing about it until it was all settled. He surprised me too. Now that you know, we better hurry up and get out of here. We'll have a light breakfast and then an early lunch. Mr. Noble said the fellows are already on their way to Harbor View."

Dudley had already put the luggage in the car. He drove the family to their new home. Breana was in awe of the scenery. The lush landscaping and the tropical plants were spectacular. In the back of the house, there was a tree that hung over the gazebo. It was covered with beautiful rose-colored flowers and shiny black berries. At the beach, the water was as blue as indigo, and coconut palms loomed out of fine white sand. Breana felt as if she had just stepped out of reality and into a land of fairy tales where dreams come true.

At Thelma's direction, everything at the house was set in place. Besides Dudley, the chauffeur, there was a maid and a gardener to help Thelma maintain the home. She became more like a nanny to Breana, but she was still the cook for the family, and she supervised the household.

Breana was basking in the glory of her new home. Lying on the beach became her favorite past-time. During those moments of solitude she would think of her past, but more importantly, her future. She dreamt of things she wanted to do with her life, places she wanted to go, and even thought of one day meeting "Mr. Right", whoever that would be…but that was far off. Right now, she was focusing more on going to college, something at one point in her life she thought she would never get to do. The family was finally settled and it was time to set her plans in motion. She reluctantly gathered her things from her favorite spot on the beach and went inside the house.

"There you are at last," said Henry as she entered the house, ".Well, young lady; you have to get over to the University to register for classes. I think Monday will be a good day to go. I'll have Dudley take you and Thelma over there."

"Father, I'm nineteen years old. I can go by myself. Besides, what if Thelma has her own stuff to do?"

"Nothing is more important than making sure that you are okay," Thelma replied.

On Monday morning, Dudley drove Henry to Oxford Street, and then drove Thelma and Breana to the University for Registration. On their way back, Thelma decided to take Breana into town. They ended up at "Coronation Market". Breana was spellbound by the activities of the hagglers peddling their wares.

Ackee … shilling a dozen! Buy you ripe banana! Hominy corn! Hot sarsaparillas…it cures whateva ails you; it good fo' the mada an' it good fo' the dauta, hot sarsaparillas! Buy you Tiger Balm; Tiger Balm root out de pain! They chimed as they walked around the market place, each selling something different. Thelma pulled Breana close to her side and said, "Stay close to me sweetheart, and hold on to your purse. This here is a pick-pocket convention."

They walked around until it was time to go back to where Dudley was waiting for them.

"So how did you like your first marketing experience Miss Breana?" asked Dudley.

"Well, I was mainly trying to stay out of the way of everyone. It was so crowded, and everyone was shouting at the same time. I couldn't understand what they were saying. I liked the crafts, though. I bought this straw hat. I think I'll send it to Briggs."

"Who's Briggs?"

"He's sort of man around the house back home. He's supposed to be the chauffeur, but he does a lot of other things too. Do you think he'll like this hat for when he works outside Thelma?"

"Sure honey. It's a very nice hat, and he likes to work outside. He'll appreciate it, I'm sure."

Two weeks had passed, since the move to Harbor View, and Breana had finished her first week at the University. She was enjoying it immensely. It was a drastic change for her. The acceptance from the other students and faculty was refreshing and long overdue. She made friends easily as her confidence soared.

"Father, I've made up my mind. I want to study Public Relations," Breana said with enthusiasm, interrupting her father who was reading the Daily Gleaner at the gazebo.

"Oh, I thought it was Political Science? When did that change?"

"It was, but I think I'd be better suited for Public Relations. I feel it in my gut."

"Well, you know I wouldn't force you to do anything against your will," said Henry,

"If that's what you want, go for it. You'll succeed in whatever you do."

"By the way, said Breana, my study buddy is coming here tomorrow. We have a project to work on. I told him to be here around ten o'clock."

"That's fine, dear," He looked up from his paper. "I'm glad you're making friends."

Breana nodded and walked towards him. "Well, I'm going down to the beach. I'll be back before supper."

"My little mermaid," Henry chuckled.

Saturday morning came, and a beautiful morning it was. The flowering trees swayed as the soft breeze blew gently by. At nine o'clock, Thelma had just finished serving an outdoor breakfast. In half an hour, she would be leaving for the Seventh Day Church of God in Mountain View. She hurried back to the house, while quickly removing her apron. As she walked in, there was a knock at the door; she answered it. She was approached by a brown skinned young man. The laces from his sneakers were untied; his green and yellow floral shirt hung outside his jeans; the buttons were undone... showing his bare chest. His auburn dread locks were tied in a bundle and hung down to the middle of his back. He stood next to a bicycle smoking a homemade cigar.

"What is this I smell out here? Don't tell me it's that *funny* kind of tobacco!" she said, looking at the young man.

"Good morning Ma'am. Is Breana home?" Thelma walked outside and closed the door behind her.

"Boy, let me tell you something, and you better listen good. Don't come to this house to see Breana while you're smoking your ganja cigar. Just who do you think you are? As I look at you I see that you're up to no good, so don't come back here again!"

The young man cast his eyes on her from head to toe; then he backed away slowly. He sucked his teeth.

"I'm sorry to bother you, but Breana didn't tell me she had a pit bull," he said, as he mounted his bicycle and rode away.

Thelma was fuming by now. She went back into the house. She was crossing the floor, and she met Breana coming toward her. "Who was that at the door, and why is your face so red?" Breana asked.

"This little drifter came to the door smoking his ganja cigar. He asked for you, but I sent him away. I don't want to see you with the likes of him."

Thelma marched to the kitchen the tale of her green pleated skirt flashing side to side by the swiftness of her strides...she was MA—AAD.

"Oh no, he's my study buddy! We have an important project to work on!"

"He's your study buddy? Well you have to find another buddy fa your study; because, that buddy ain't coming back here. I don't want any ganja in this house. If I have to go to UC to talk to your instructor myself, I will. Besides, he has no manners. The boy had the nerve to refer to me as a dog."

"Really! Oh Thelma, I had no idea he was like that. What did he say?"

"When I told him he couldn't see you, he looked at me and said, 'She didn't tell me she has a pit bull,' can you imagine?"

"Okay. I'll switch partners when I go to school on Monday. For now, I'll work on it myself, I guess."

"A very wise decision," Thelma said. She looked at the clock. "Oh my goodness...I'm standing here talking and look at the time. If I don't hurry, I'll be late for church."

"Father said we have to find a place of worship. He said we're going to a church on

Maxfield Avenue, tomorrow."

"Good, I hope you like it," Thelma said, as she was all busy around the house, looking for her purse.

"I'll like wherever I find the truth."

Breana worked on her project all morning and most of the afternoon. She finished just before dinner. She walked out triumphantly to the veranda and announced to her father, "The battle is over, and I'm the Victor."

"My daughter, the brave soldier! She has single handedly finished the work of an army, and not a moment too soon. Thelma just said dinner is ready. Let's go," Henry said, motioning her to the dining room.

Sunday morning Breana was up before the sun. She crept quietly out of the house to go have an early morning walk on the beach and watch the sunrise. Afterwards, she had breakfast with Henry.

"It'll be time for church soon, Pumpkin. I think we better get an early start."

"Ok. So, how did you find out about that church?" asked Breana.

"I was driving by and saw the building. I went inside and spoke to the secretary. She seemed nice. I think it's a good idea to worship there today."

Dudley was already waiting by the car when they both walked out the door. "Good morning Dudley."

"Good morning Boss, and a fine one it is Sir. Good morning Miss Breana." Breana said good morning and sat next to her father in the back seat

When they arrived at the church, Sunday school was over and the congregation was gathering in the sanctuary. Soon after, the usher showed them to their seats. Praise and worship began. The choir sang, *"Sailing we are sailing on, sailing we are sailing on, with Christ in the vessel, He'll smile at the storm we are sailing on."* Brother Sam strummed the guitar; Sister Doreen shook the tambourine, and Sister Morgan played the organ. They played and sang on one accord, and the church came alive at the sound.

At the end of the singing, shouting, and gathering the offering, the minister took his place at the podium.

"Brothers and sisters!" he said, "The Lord is here this morning! Today is your day to be blessed, for the Lord is in His house! This morning, I'm going to talk to you about the blessing of the Lord, and the curse of the Lord! Which will you choose? If you are blessed by the Lord, eternal life will be your reward! But if you are cursed by the Lord, you will face eternal damnation! What will it be this morning? You that have faithfully paid your tithes; rise up and claim your blessing! You have a right to shout when you obey God, and if anyone has anything to say about the way you shout, tell them to take it up with the higher power because the bible said it. 'Rejoice in the Lord, and again, I say rejoice!' Yes my brothers and sisters; clap your hands and praise him on your instruments of ten strings! Glory to God!"

Well, the faithful few got on their feet, with flailing hands high in the air. They leaped up and down and spoke in diverse tongues; while most of the congregation sat quietly in the pews. Some looked on, steeped in guilt and dismay. Sis Green hung her head with shame. "I didn't have any money to pay today; because, the Landlord would put me out if I didn't pay him," she said, "I feel bad, but I couldn't help it. I have to keep a roof over my children's heads," she whispered to the person sitting next to her. Breana overheard as she sat quietly and pondered all that she had seen. At the end of the service, some stayed behind to greet each other, and others walked away in despair. Breana stood and watched as the woman went on her way. Her shoes were leaned to the side; her green floral dress had seen better days. She carried one baby on her side as she walked along holding the hand of another child assumingly three or four years old. An older boy trailed behind carrying a bible that was old and tattered. Breana opened her purse, and all she found was twenty dollars.

"Hello!" she called out to the boy. "What's your name?"

"Mi name Pip Mam," replied the little boy, speaking in his native dialect.

"Hi Pip, how are you?" Breana asked.

"Mi haughty Mam." (Meaning I'm alright)

"Pip would you give this to your mommy; ask her to buy something for you and your sisters." she said as she handed the twenty dollars she found in her purse.

"T'ank yu miss," Pip said, looking down at the money in his hand and grinning from ear to ear.

"It was nice to meet you Pip!" Breana said. She smiled as she watched him run to his mother and hand her the money. The mother listened to the boy then she took the money and looked at it. She looked back at Breana, but Dudley had pulled up with the car, and Breana was getting in. The woman bowed her head toward Breana as if saying, "*Thank you.*" Breana nodded her head in understanding. A bus pulled up; the woman step aboard with her children…crying softly, smiling all the way.

"Father I have always believed that the duty of the church is to help the poor," she said as Dudley pulled the car away from the curb. "It didn't seem that way from what I heard today."

"What did you hear?"

"This lady was ashamed that she didn't have any money to give; because, she had to pay her rent. Because of what the Pastor said, she felt guilty for paying her rent instead of bringing the money to church."

"No sweetheart that is not the way it was in the early church. The poor was taken care of always. I saw you talking to her little boy."

"Yes, I gave him what I had in my purse. He was so grateful; he ran to his mother and gave it to her. I saw her smiling as she walked on to the bus."

"A good deed never goes unrewarded Pumpkin. You will be blessed for always thinking of others.

Chapter Eight

B reana spent most of her afternoons in the gazebo looking over the harbor. She enjoyed the scenery of the ships going out and coming in. Silently, she hoped to meet her prince charming and sail away into the sunset.

One evening, Dudley went to pick her up from school and she sulked all the way home. When the car drove up to the house, she dashed into the house. She plopped her books down on a table, and the heaviest book fell to the floor. Without turning around to see what fell or to pick it up, she marched into the kitchen.

"Thelma! Thelma where are you?"

"Goodness gracious child, what's the matter with you? Since when do you blow into the house like a hurricane and start hollering out my name like that? This better not be a new habit. It's not lady-like Missy."

"I'm sorry Thelma. I don't know what I was thinking. I'm just so frustrated."

"Okay, what's bothering my baby girl?" Thelma asked as she sliced up some avocados to add to the green salad she was making.

Irately, Breana plopped down on a chair and began to speak, "Thelma, why are boys so immature?"

"I don't know," Thelma chuckled, "What happened?"

"There's this boy in my class. Every time no one's looking, he always smiles at me.

But when he's with his friends, they call me a 'Stuck up princess' and he laughs right along with them. Does he expect me to smile back at him when he's not with his friends?"

Thelma turned around, wiping her hands with a dish towel. "You do what your heart tells you my dear. That's all that's expected of you."

"My heart says to kick him in the shin! Well, maybe a small kick, but a kick just the same."

"Hmm…hmm, so you like him, don't you?" Thelma grinned mischievously.

"I do not. I can't stand him!" She snarled as she stormed out the kitchen.

Thelma laughed. She shouted after Breana, "Who's being immature now?"

After dinner, Henry went to sit on the veranda, looking out at the harbor.

Thelma went out to him. "Mr. Noble, do you need anything before I go take a rest?"

"Not really, but if you could sit here for a minute, I'd like talk to you."

"Yes Sir. What can I do for you?" she asked as she took the seat on the opposite side facing him

"Did you notice how quiet Breana was at dinner?"

"Yes Sir, I did. She was not her usual cheerful self, and she didn't have much to say, or eat for that matter."

"Well do you have any idea what's bothering her? Or what I can do to help?"

"I have an idea Sir, but I don't think she would appreciate me telling you the details." Henry's brow wrinkled as he asked, "If I don't know what's bothering her, how can I help her?"

"Well, I could tell you how you could make it a little easier for her, Sir."

"Go ahead, I'm listening."

"She needs a mother, Sir. It's been almost three years since we lost Mrs. Noble and she misses having someone other than me, as a female person to relate to."

"My dear sweet, Penelope," said Henry. "God rest her soul. It seems like yesterday she was with us. Just the same, a new relationship would not be easy for me you know. I could never find another Penelope."

"Well maybe you should stop looking for another Penelope. If you spend the rest of your life looking for what you've lost, you may miss finding something else just as valuable. There has to be someone that can complete your life. You have been alone for too long, and now, Breana needs someone too. That child grew up most of her life without a mother, and now she's at that point in her life when she could use some motherly advice."

"Don't be silly, you're doing very well in that department already."

"Thank you for the compliment Sir, but it's not the same. I hope you'll think about it for both your sakes. Are you sure I can't get you anything before I go?"

"Yes, I'm quite sure. You go take your rest."

Thelma slowly stood up. "It's time for healing, Sir. You need to stop festering and start living again. I'm sure that's what Mrs. Noble would have wanted for you."

"Ah, go take your rest. Make sure that mouth of yours gets some rest too."

Thelma walked away laughing, while Henry took a stroll to the gazebo. He covered his face with both hands, and he cried as if he had just buried Penny all over again. He recalled all the memorable times he had with Penelope...laughing together and holding hands on their early morning walks. He suddenly felt at peace. After a while he thought about Thelma's advice; with a smile on his face and tears in his eyes, he muttered, "Well my love, Thelma is right. It's time I moved on." He sat there until it was almost dark. Then he got up and went inside.

* * *

Henry awoke the following morning with a new perspective which was quite evident to his co-workers. His secretary had never seen this side of him before. He walked into the office, "Good morning, Melissa!" he said, very cheerfully.

"Good morning, Mr. Noble. My goodness, you are jubilant this morning"

"Burdens have been lifted, Melissa! Burdens have been lifted. Mark this date, November 22, 1963. I, Henry Noble have decided to start living again!"

"Well, whatever that means, I'm happy for you Sir."

That evening after dinner he got up to leave the table. "Thelma, I'll have my Brandy down by the gazebo, please."

"Very well, Sir."

She placed his drink on a tray and carried it to the gazebo. As she sat the tray down and turned to walk away, he said, "Wait, Thelma."

"Yes Sir?" Thelma turned around to face him.

"I do realize how much I've been missing out on life. Do you know that since Penny passed, until last night I have never taken the time to come out here and enjoy the beauty of this place? It's so beautiful and peaceful. Just look at that sunset on the skyline. Have you ever seen a more beautiful sight? When I look around, it makes me feel like I'm sitting under a dome. God is so awesome."

"It's so good to see you come out of that shell, Sir. I missed the old Mr. Noble. Now, all I have to do is to wait for you to take the next step."

"What step is that?"

"The next step is to get a companion for you, and a mother for Breana, Sir."

"Oh, THAT step. Hmm, too bad you already have a position in my life, or you could've been a good candidate, don't you think?"

Thelma laughed. "Now, there's that Mr. Noble sense of humor that I've missed. You are back!" she said chuckling.

While Thelma was on her way back to the house, she met Breana walking to the gazebo. "What's so funny?" Breana asked,

"Your father has rejoined the living with his sense of humor intact."

"I've noticed that he's been strange. What happened?"

"Well, we had a long talk, and it seemed as if he was listening."

"Oh, thank God! You should have been the ambassador in this family.

You always know the right thing to say in every situation. I don't know what we would've done without you."

Breana went to the gazebo. Henry turned his head at the sound of her footsteps.

"Hi, Pumpkin. It's such a pleasant evening I thought I'd take advantage and relax a little."

"It's about time." She sat down next to her father and looked across the harbor.

"Isn't that beautiful, Father? Look at that ship over there; I don't recall it being in port yesterday."

"There are quite a few out there today, which one do you mean?"

"The "Bogain-Villa; I've always noticed what's coming and going, but I've never seen the "Bogain-Villa" before."

"You're right. It's a beauty."

"I think it's the largest one I've seen so far." Breana remarked.

They sat and enjoyed the view for a while. Then, Henry said, "Well, honey, I would love to sit and enjoy the view, but I have some work to go over."

"Okay Father, I'll see you inside."

Henry started toward the house as Thelma was on her way back to the gazebo. "Oh I was just coming to collect the tray and find out if you needed anything else, Sir."

"I'm fine, but Breana is still there. Why don't you sit down and enjoy that view with her?"

* * *

Henry went into the house, and turned the television on RJR news. As he looked at the TV screen, he was struck by the footage. In shock and dismay, he sat on his chair and proceeded to watch and listen. The scene was in Dallas, Texas. A convertible was driving with President Kennedy covered with blood, bleeding, and Jackie Kennedy in blood drenched clothes, sitting next to him. Henry stared at the television screen. He could not come to grips with what was happening. After he had watched for a while, he walked outside in a daze. As he approached the gazebo, Thelma looked up and saw him coming.

"Look Breana something's wrong," she said, touching Breana on the shoulder.

Breana jumped to her feet. "Father what's the matter! You're as pale as a ghost!"

She and, Thelma hurried up the path to meet Henry.

"You're not going to believe this."

"Believe what, Sir," asked Thelma anxiously.

"I just heard on the news that President Kennedy was shot in Dallas."

"Oh no!" Breana said. She gazed at her father whose face was now wet with tears.

"Oh my God! I'll go pack your suitcase, Sir," said Thelma.

The phones at the Noble's residence began to ring constantly from colleagues who had heard the news. Henry was on the phone all night, delegating duties to who was in charge at the embassy during his absence. All travel preparations were done. Thelma and Breana went back to the gazebo. The harbor was now lit with an array of colored lights creating a spectacle second to none. They saw a shooting star zoomed by.

"Quick, make a wish!" said Thelma, attempting to lighten up the somber mood.

"If I should wish right now, I would wish for the president and his family to be alright, or to end world hunger. But I don't believe in wishes," Breana answered.

"Well, if wishes don't work, prayer sure does, so maybe you could try that," said Thelma.

"Sometimes I feel guilty for being so privileged while there are so many people that are suffering."

"Well, since you have such a contrite heart about being privileged, maybe God will reward you for that. After all, HE knows what we need before we ask. Hey, maybe someday you'll get to sail away on the Bogain-Villa. Why are you so fascinated with that one anyway?"

"Because, before I was adopted, the happiest home I ever lived in was in Jamaica, New York. My foster mother, Mrs. White had a pine tree in front of her house right by my window. A Bougainvillea plant twined around it covered with flowers. It was my favorite place. When I saw the name Bogain-Villa, it brought that tree to mind. Mrs. White had told me that she would think of me every time she looked at the tree."

"Have you ever heard from Mrs. White?"

"No, we were not allowed to keep in touch, but I would sure love to see her someday." "Maybe you will. Anything is possible. Maybe you could pray for that too."

Breana folded her arms together in an effort to keep warm. "I'm ready to go in," she said, "It's getting chilly out here."

"I agree." Thelma picked up the tray, and they both walked up the path to the house.

The following morning, Dudley drove Breana and Henry to the airport.

After the funeral, Henry returned from the exhausting trip. He thought of the sadness he saw in Mrs. Kennedy's eyes, a sadness that he was familiar with. He went out to the gazebo with thoughts of Penny. Breana joined him. She saw a look of dismay on his face and tried to distract him from his thoughts. "Need some company?" she asked.

"Hi Sweetheart, I'm afraid your favorite ship is gone," he answered.

She looked across the harbor. The Bogain-Villa had sailed, and others of less interest to her had taken its place. They made conversations to pass the time. After a while they both got silent. Breana started daydreaming of the voyages she would like to take on the Bogain-Villa.

"What are you thinking, Pumpkin? I see you're deep in thought."

"I was thinking about what it would be like to sail on that ship."

"Oh, you really favor that ship, don't you? I tell you what. As soon as I can take a vacation, you and I will take a voyage on the Bogain-Villa to any place you want to go. How does that sound?"

"Do you mean it, Father?"

"Of course I do."

"Father, you're going to spoil me, you're the best." She said as she threw her arms around his neck. Thelma was on her way to join them. "Thelma! Father promised to take me on a cruise on the Bogain-Villa."

"Really! When?"

"As soon as I can arrange a vacation," Henry said.

"That sounds very vague, Mr. Noble. Could you narrow it down a little? I'd like to make some plans of my own while you're gone."

"Sure, I'll narrow it down for you. You're going with us on the same day, narrow enough?" He smiled smugly.

"Oh yes Sir, quite narrow." Then, she whispered, "Breana that means we're not going anytime soon."

"I heard that!" Henry interrupted, "And just for that remark, you two will be in a leaky canoe with two spoons for bailing water; while I watch you from the luxurious Bogain-Villa."

That night, Henry dreamed of his wife. She spoke to him in that honey-soft voice he remembered. He jerked himself awake with her name on his lips. "Penny! Penny, don't go!"

He looked at the clock. "Ten minutes past midnight," he mumbled. "What kind of crazy dream was that?"

He stayed awake for the rest of the night. As he tossed and turned in bed, morning was approaching fast. At the first light of dawn, he stumbled out of bed.

"I had a dream last night," he said at the breakfast table. "It was about Penny. We were at our house in Georgia. She was on a lounge chair on the lanai. It seemed so real. While she was lying there, she looked at me and said, *'Thelma is right. I have been gone a long time. Go on with your life, Henry. Be happy.'* I reached out to her, but she started to fade away. Then she was gone."

"Saints alive," said Thelma. "Mrs. Noble is dead and yet SHE'S even telling you to move on. Please, take heed Sir. It's a terrible thing not to heed the warning of the dead.

When my Aunt Betsy died, my Uncle Sam swore he wouldn't marry again. One night, Aunt Betsy went to him in a dream. She said, 'Sam, if you don't find a wife, you are going to die alone." Uncle Sam ignored the dream, and six months later, he died alone in his bed."

"How awful!" exclaimed Henry. "I think it's a terrible thing for someone to die with no one around. Who knows what he may have suffered."

"Oh no Sir, two people were with him, but they just sat there and watched. He was the only one that died. Just like Aunt Betsy said, he died alone."

Henry laughed, "Thelma, how you come up with those stories of yours is beyond me. I only had that dream because of the conversation we had yesterday. She's dead, and her soul has returned to

God. She has no control over anything. Besides, this household is doing fine as it is. Do you have any idea how hard it would be to find another person and start over at this point in my life?"

"Well, you could at least go out sometime, Sir. You may find it's not as hard as you think. You always go from home to work, to business meetings, and home again. You need to take the time to meet people, other than your employees and associates. You need a little spice in your life, Sir. At least, I go to the church socials, and sometimes I go out with friends. A change in your lifestyle might be very rewarding."

"Oh, alright, I'll think about it if for no other reason, but to keep you quiet."

Chapter Nine

O n Linden Blvd. in St Albans, New York...red neon lights flashed 'GO-GO Girls' on the front window of a popular night club. The red door opened to a smoke filled room and the air was thick with the stench of alcohol and tobacco.

In the center of the room, a platform was surrounded by foot lights, and in the middle of the platform...a pole stretched from the floor to the ceiling. A large muscular man with dark hair, walked out to the platform. His skin was tanned, and his dark brown eyes were piercing. From shoulder to shoulder his muscles rippled like the Atlas man; he was fit for holding up anything. He picked up the mike, and a hush came over the crowd as they looked on in anticipation.

"La—dies and Gentle-men! Put your hands together for the dancing machine, the one, the only- Lo-le-t-a-a-a!"

The music started, and out came a girl, strutting to the beat. Her long blonde hair twirled around her shoulders, as she swayed and swirled her slender body to the rhythm.

Her light complexion was enhanced by fire engine red lipstick, delicately applied to her full robust lips. Her long false lashes curled over her green eyes cradled in pink and blue eye shadow.

She moved so easily in her red high heel shoes, she looks as if she was striding barefooted on soft carpet. Her black fishnet stockings were revealing up to the hips where her red teddy, trimmed with black lace ended.

She kept on dancing, romancing, and seducing the crowd, never missing a beat!

She pranced around the platform, and the audience went wild. They reached their hands into their pockets and brought out fists full of dollar bills. They threw the cash one after another at the girl, and she collected some in her bosom. She started to remove her clothes from the top, down to the bottom, and then stopped at her waist.

The audience got in an uproar as they hollered, "More! More! More! Take it off! Take it off!"

Her teasing got the better of one drunken patron. He reached out his hand and grabbed a handful of her flesh. She slapped his face and ran to a room in the back.

A tall man with his black wavy hair slicked to the back, followed close behind, and the audience booed!

"What do you think you are doing?" He shouted, "You're ruining my business!"

"Then you should be glad I'm leaving Gunther! Now your business will stay intact!" She shouted back at him.

"That was one of my best clients!" shouted Gunther.

"Then find yourself a better class of clients, and let that smelly old ape keep his damn dirty paws off me. Did you see him! His teeth are brown from tobacco stains, and there's so much dirt under his fingernails, you could raise a crop of potatoes. He's nothing but a grease monkey. You keep him, since you like him so much. I'm tired of this Gunther! I'm leaving and I won't keep in touch! " She said throwing her belongings in a bag.

"The man works at a gas station for heaven's sakes Effiedra! He's a customer, and you're here to entertain the customers! Besides, you didn't have any problem with the money he threw at you."

Without saying another word, Effiedra grabbed her coat, picked up her purse, and hurried through the door.

"Where do you think you're going? You get back here! You tramp! I made you! You owe me!" Gunther yelled, but Effiedra kept walking and did not look back. At the front of the building, she hailed a cab. The driver pulled up to the curb, looking Effiedra up and down.

"Where to?" he asked, as she got inside the cab.

"2101 Linden Blvd."

The driver attempted to make casual conversation, but Effiedra would have none of it. She rudely ignored him throughout the entire ride, with the exception of an occasional huff or sigh. As they approached her destination, the driver said, "That will be five bucks." She threw him a twenty dollar bill.

"Take this from someone who's going to be a lady if it kills her."

He looked her over and with a laugh muttered under his breath, "May you rest in peace."

Back at the club, Gunther was steaming mad. "Billy Bob! Did you see that?" He said to his bouncer. "Who does that little harlot think she is? After all I did for her! If it wasn't for me, she would be in the gutter right now! You go down to that apartment that I'm paying for and tell her either she gets her ass back here, or I'll come down there and put her out with the trash where she belongs!"

Meanwhile Loleta, a.k.a Effiedra was on the phone in her apartment. She was making arrangements to get out of New York.

"Hello, I would like a ticket for the next available flight out of New York please. Any place will be alright as long as it's out of here. A flight leaving to Jamaica at 6:00 A.M? That's perfect. Kingston, yes, I'll need a hotel reservation too, please. My name is Effiedra Wilson. The Whitmore Hotel on Knutsford Boulevard? I'll be in by five to pick up my ticket. Thank you."

As soon as she hung up the phone, Billy Bob was knocking at the door.

"Effie, open up!" She ignored the knocking.

Effiedra walked into the bedroom and picked up her suitcase, placing it on the bed. She opened it up and began packing. All this while, the knocking persisted. Finally, she went to the door knowing full well who it was, she asked anyway. "Who is it?" she shouted in a perturbed manner.

"It's me, Billy! Open the door, Effie!"

She simply cracked the door and said, "It's late Billy and I'm tired, go home."

He pushed passed her and stepped inside. Billy was tall, thin, and awkward looking.

"Effie! What's goin' on wit'chu? After all Guntha done for you an' me, you have no bin'ness walkin' out on him like dat. Our own kin never treat us as good as Guntha did. Before I knew him, I was nothin', an' look at me now."

Effiedra smirked. "Yes! Look at you now!" She shouted with all the anger buried deep inside. "He dressed you up in that monkey suit, and used you as one of his goons, but what have you done for yourself? You were born and raised in an English speaking country, and you haven't even learned how to speak the language properly! You would have been better off staying in that pigeon hole we called home, than coming to New York!"

"Now wait a minute." Billy Bob tried to interrupt.

"No, you wait!" Her voice began to crack with rage. "Men groped my body when I was too young to defend myself! My own step-father among them! It seemed like every foster home I went to, somebody was waiting for me! Well! No more!" Her face was red with anger. Tears streamed down her cheeks as she spoke of her past.

"I ran away when I was sixteen years old to find a better life, and now, I'm twenty-five. I'm still being treated like a piece of meat. I'm through stripping for those perverts while that flesh peddler gets rich."

She paused for a moment and tried to calm down, lowering her tone as she looked at how progressively pathetic Billy looked as she continued to talk. She walked over to him and looked into his eyes.

"Billy, can't you see? I want something better. I'm tired of this life."

"An' what 'bout me Effie? You know what he'll do to me, if I fail on a job he sent me to do?"

"You just said he's better than your own kin, so how bad can it be?"

"Come on, Effie! You know da' deal! You can't cross da man!"

"Well I just did! And as God is my witness, he will never get me in his clutches again!

I don't care what I have to do to keep that from happening!"

"An' what 'bout me an' you, after all we been through togedda."

She tried to finish packing. "From this day forward Billy Bob, there's no more me and you. You're a millstone, and I don't need you around my neck."

"Effie! You cuttin' my heart out when you talk like 'dat. All my life people look down on me, an' call me white trash, but you was diff'rent. Now, every since you start to study dem books, I aint talkin' good nuff for you no more, nothin' I do is right. Well, you ain't goin' to walk away from me just like that. I lo-o-ve you. So if you leave, I leave wit'chu. Hey you got anythin' to drink 'round here? My throat is dry."

Effiedra stopped packing. She looked at Billy and said. "I will give you something to drink, but you're leaving right after that, and let me take care of my business. I don't have time for this."

She walked into the kitchen and opened the cabinet. There was a bottle of whiskey on the shelf. She picked up the bottle and she started pouring the whiskey. Then she noticed a pill bottle. She picked it up and read the label. She discovered that it was a bottle of sleeping pills that were prescribed for her. She thought, *if I just give him enough of these in this drink, he would sleep until I finished packing. Then I can get out of this hell hole.*

She opened the bottle, and she took two pills out. She thought, *they're so old; they're probably not strong enough, I'll just put all of them in.* She brought the drink to him.

He took the glass and started his first sip. She went back into the room and resumed packing. "Everything is, either up to the hip, or plunged to the navel," she murmured,

"They're all trashy. I'll get a new wardrobe, and when I'm finished, I'm going to look like the wife of a Baptist minister. I'm going to get respect if I have to kill for it."

She salvaged a few pieces from her wardrobe. She put them into the suitcase and walked out of the bedroom.

As soon as Billy Bob came in focus, she dropped the suitcase and ran over to the chair he was sitting on. His color was pallid and his eyes were closed. His mouth was opened and his tongue was rolled backward. His left arm was across his stomach, and his right arm hung down to the side of the chair. The empty glass lay on the carpet beneath him.

"Oh dear God!" she cried, as she rushed over to take a closer look. She shook him by the shoulder as she called, "Billy! Billy! Billy answer me, you jerk! How could you do this to me? Oh my God! Billy, I didn't mean it! Oh no! Oh God! What am I going to do now?"

She sat on the floor next to the chair, and she wept bitterly. Thoughts of her and Billy, living in foster homes went racing through her mind. The schemes they concocted to run away, and the day they were rummaging through a dumpster, behind a Busy Bee supermarket near Springfield Blvd. That was where Gunther found them and took them off the streets. Suddenly, she pulled herself together and got to her feet.

She mumbled to herself. "Sorry Billy. I never meant for it to end this way. Please forgive me!" She tilted the chair forward, and Billy's body fell to the floor.

Effiedra struggled as she rolled his body into the rug. She opened the door and looked up and down the hallway. There was no one in sight. She pushed and pulled the body out into the hallway and down to the stairwell entrance. Breathing heavily, she rested against the wall and wiped the sweat from her brow. It was a difficult feat, but she was able to push Billy's lifeless body down the stairs. It rolled and fell to the bottom like a useless heap of clay.

She stood at the top of the stairway and looked down at him. She made the sign of the cross and said, "May God have mercy on your soul, Billy Bob Jenkins. You were my only friend."

When she got back to the apartment, she immediately picked up the glass he drank from, and stuffed it in her suitcase. She scanned the room one last time and hastily left the building. She took the bus heading for the bus terminal on Jamaica Avenue and then took a taxi to LaGuardia Airport. She kept looking around as if she was being followed.

Her flight was announced at six o'clock in the morning. The loud speaker blared, "*PAN AM flight number, 234 to Kingston, Jamaica is now boarding at gate six.*" She picked up her hand luggage, and went to the gate as quickly as possible without drawing attention to herself.

When Effiedra finally landed in Jamaica, she picked up her rental car. She removed the map from the glove compartment and studied the directions to the Whitmore Hotel on Knutsford Boulevard. When she arrived at the hotel, she gave her key to the valet and went inside. She walked up to the receptionist. "Hi, I'm Effiedra Wilson. My travel agent made a reservation for me last night."

The receptionist found her reservation and handed her key to room 312.

"Enjoy your stay Miss Wilson. If you need anything, please let us know," the receptionist said, gawking at her as she walked away.

"Thank you kindly," she replied in a syrupy tone.

She took the key and walked to the elevator. On the third floor, she walked down the corridor to her room. She opened the door and went inside. She just flopped herself cross the bed thinking on what to do first. She decided to drive to Kingston, in search of conservative outfits. She got dressed in a black skirt with the hem just above her knees, a white, short sleeve blouse, a pair of black pumps and her hair pulled back in a bun. You would swear she was a teacher in a catholic school. She was 25, but she appeared to be 35. She looked in the mirror and commented triumphantly, "If they could only see me now; I'm through peddling my flesh."

* * *

At the Nobles residence, Henry was getting ready to go to Kingston for a meeting at the Whitmore Hotel. Thelma and Breana had shopping to do, so they went along. Dudley dropped Thelma and Breana off at the 'Pink and Black' store. He then took Henry to the hotel.

"When I'm finished with my meeting, I'll wait in the lobby for you, okay."

"Yes Sir," replied Dudley.

Meanwhile, Effiedra left her room, heading for the elevator. She got into the elevator and pushed the down button. As the door open on the Lobby, she walked off the elevator. She noticed a mirror nearby. *Let me see how different I look before I go out.* She stopped to check her hair and makeup. Henry was looking at a newspaper article while walking. Effiedra was now satisfied with her touch-up. She abruptly turned to leave. They both collided into each other. She gasped as her purse fell to the floor. Henry picked it up and handed it to her. "I'm so sorry," he said, "It's my fault. I wasn't paying attention." She replied

"Oh no! I should've been looking where I was going you know; it's my fault. I'm so sorry."

"Your accent sounds like a New Yorker. Am I right?" Henry said looking her over.

"That I am! I wasn't born there, but I've adopted it. I've been living there for some time!"

"Really? How is the 'Big Apple? It used to be my old hangout, but I haven't been there in a while!"

"Well, it's still big!" She said smiling. It still lights up at nights, and it's still a rat race."

"Henry laughed, "A beautiful lady with a sense of humor. This must be my lucky day!"

He reached out to shake her hand, "I'm Henry Noble. I'm delighted to meet you."

"I'm Effiedra Wilson. I'm pleased to meet you."

"I have a meeting I must attend upstairs, but it should be over in about half an hour.

May I interest you in a cup of coffee as my way of an apology?"

"Apology for what?"

"For almost knocking you down, of course," Henry said.

"That's the best offer I've had all day. Apology and coffee accepted."

"Okay, I'll meet you in the lobby right after my meeting."

Well, I guess I'll go shopping later. The stores will always be there, but this offer may not. Who knows what may happen before the morning is over. She thought as she made her way back to the elevator.

* * *

Henry's meeting was over on schedule. Effiedra was waiting in the lobby expectantly.

"My goodness, you are a punctual man."

"Well, I should be flogged if I kept a beautiful woman waiting. I hope it's okay to have our coffee here since I have no car at the moment."

"That's fine, the coffee here is delicious."

"So you've tasted the Blue Mountain brew."

"I have no idea what it's called. I only know it's the best I've ever tasted."

They chatted as they walked into the hotel restaurant. The

hostess seated them at a table for two, and the waiter took their order shortly after. Effiedra sat quietly for a moment.

"So what are you doing in these parts, Miss Wilson?"

"Just a little R&R. I've heard a lot about the island, so I thought I would visit. How about you?"

"I'm a diplomat. I work at the American Embassy."

"Oh, a diplomat. That's nice to know. If I get into trouble, I'll know who to contact."

They both laughed and continued to make polite conversation while they sipped their coffee.

"So are you traveling alone Miss Wilson?"

"Yes I am," she said nodding her head.

By this time, Thelma and Breana had returned from shopping. Breana went inside to find her father. She looked for him in the lobby, but he was not waiting there as planned. She went into the restaurant. As she scanned the room, she saw him sitting at the table with a very attractive young lady. They were laughing and looked as though they were enjoying each other's company. Breana walked over to them. Henry stood up immediately.

"Pumpkin!" he said. "Shopping finished already?"

"We didn't have much to pick up," Breana, answered, trying not to stare at Effiedra.

"Miss Wilson, this is my daughter, Breana. Breana, this is Miss Wilson. We literally ran into each other in the lobby."

"Nice to meet you Breana, you're a beautiful young lady."

"Thank you, Miss Wilson. It's nice to meet you, too. Thelma and Dudley are waiting in the car, Father," she said hinting to Henry that it's time to leave.

"Miss Wilson, I'm sorry I have to leave. Perhaps we could have dinner, if you don't have any plans."

Breana was shocked by the sudden invitation. *He just met her.*

"I think I would like a rain check on that... perhaps tomorrow?"

"Alright then, tomorrow it is. I'll send my car for you around five o'clock?"

"Five o'clock will be fine." Effiedra said as she stood up.

Henry pulled out her chair, and they both walked away from the table; Effiedra in front swinging her hips.

"Alright then, until tomorrow," Henry said as they smiled and shook hands. He and Breana walked out to the car. Henry was smiling as if he had discovered a lost gem. Breana however, was concerned about her father's date with a woman he barely knew. Thelma looked at Breana and knew something was up. She looked at Henry and his face was glowing.

"Thelma, I invited someone over for dinner tomorrow night."

"Oh, really Sir? Who is it?"

"A young lady I met in the hotel lobby. She's vacationing from New York."

"Well, anyone who can put a smile like that on your face is welcome to dinner any time."

"Now don't go reading too much into this. It's just a young lady traveling alone, and I offered her my hospitality."

"Yes Father, we know," said Breana.

Thelma's brow got wrinkled for a minute. "You say young lady'. How old do you think she is Sir?"

"I don't know. She didn't say. She seemed to be in her thirties."

"That's a good age then"

Henry looking puzzled. "Good for what?"

"Any age below mine is a good age Sir," she said, with a chuckle.

"Thelma stop, you're not even old. Dudley how old do you think she is?" Breana asked leaning forward in her seat.

Dudley shook his head, "I don't know yet, I wasn't paying attention."

"Don't know yet? When will you know?" Breana inquired.

"When I see her next, maybe; it's hard to tell people's age sometimes."

Back at the hotel, Effiedra had her own agenda. She reasoned with herself. *He's a little old, but I've had young, and where did it get me? The only obstacle that I foresee is that daughter of his. I'll just have to figure out a way to keep her out of my way. Anyway, tomorrow I'll see if it's even worth my time.*

Dudley arrived at the hotel the following evening to pick up Effiedra as planned

"Good evening," he said to the receptionist, "I'm Dudley More. I'm here to pick up Miss Effiedra Wilson."

While he was speaking, Effiedra was sitting in the lobby. She walked over to him. Her voice was as smooth as honey when she said, looking for me?"

Turning around, he answered, "Yes I am."

Meanwhile, everyone was busy at the Noble house. Henry was getting dressed for dinner, and Breana was helping Thelma set the Table.

"Thelma, what if Father liked her enough to marry her?"

Thelma hesitated a moment then she asked. "How would you feel about that?"

"I don't know. I never thought of the possibility before."

Thelma didn't have time to answer before Dudley opened the front door and announced,

"We're back!"

When Henry heard Dudley, he nearly tripped over his feet in haste to get downstairs, but slowed down just before he turned the corner to approach everyone. He tried hard to appear calm and collected.

"Good evening, Miss Wilson. Welcome to our home."

"Well, thank you, Mr. Noble, for the invitation"

Breana went out to meet her in the great hall. "It is nice to see you again, Miss Wilson. I'm glad you could come."

"It is nice to see you too, Breana. Thanks for having me over.

Thanks indeed. She thought as her eyes roved over the room. Thelma came from the kitchen with a tray of hors d'oeuvres.

"Hello Miss Wilson. It's nice to see you again," she said.

"Thank you, it's nice to see you. I'd be pleased if you called me Effiedra."

"Okay, Effiedra, would you care for something to drink?"

"Yes, thank you. Sherry would be nice."

"And what will you have, Mr. Noble."

"I'll take sherry as well please."

"I'll be right back," she said walking away- elated that Henry had that glimmer in his eyes again. Later, at the dinner table, Henry said, "So, Miss Wilson, why is a beautiful young lady like you traveling alone?"

"Well, I was hoping that a kind family would offer to feed me if I traveled alone," she said with a broad smile.

"There is that sense of humor again," said Henry chuckling.

Then, she sat back in the chair and said, "Okay, I'm an only child. I grew up on a farm in Kansas. I wanted to be a doctor, but during my second year in school, my father died. Soon after that my mother died from the flu. I couldn't afford to stay in school after that, so I got a job working in a medical office," she lied. The only time she had ever been inside a doctor's office was to get a shot for whatever was ailing her at the time. "Then I was engaged to one of the doctors who had his practice in the building," Effiedra paused to get her lie straight. "He was sent to Vietnam, and he ended up missing in action."

"Oh, no," Thelma said with empathy. She believed the whole story, but they were Lies, lies, lies!

Effiedra continued. "Somehow, I thought since he wasn't on the front line, he would be safe, but I never heard from him again."

"That is quite a story," said Henry, mesmerized, "You are very brave to rise above all of that."

"It wasn't easy" she said, while thinking. '*Wow I could sell them a bridge,'* while shoving a piece of carrot in her mouth. Then she continued to say, "But you know, one has to do what one has to do to survive. I don't believe I'm so brave. I just had to stop crying at some point and move on."

After dinner, everyone was leaving the dining room. Effiedra's eyes caught the piano in the parlor. She walked by and touched a key.

Henry turned his head toward her and smiled, "Do you play the piano Miss Wilson?"

"Just a little, it used to be a hobby of mine. I even considered making it a career at one time."

"Well, let's hear it!"

She sat down and played that piano like David played the harp. She played Beethoven, Chopin, Ballard, and Blues. By the time she was finished, everyone was impressed, except Breana.

"Well!" said Henry, "I thought you said you only played a little! Where did you study?"

"Just here and there." she said sweeping her fingers tips across the key board.

Henry and Thelma were pleased with Effiedra and how well the evening went. Effiedra knew that she had them wrapped around her little finger.

"I hate to end this evening, but I really must be going now."

"Oh, what a shame!" We love having you," Henry said. "Breana, will you get Dudley please? Tell him it's time to take Miss Wilson home,"

Dudley was sitting on the veranda, listening to a Cricket match between Jamaica and Barbados. "Dudley, Father said it's time to take Effiedra home," said Breana as she joined him, listening to the game.

Dudley, still listening to the game said, "Uh, huh... just one minute..." Then he jumped from his seat. "Yes! Yes..." He shouted for his winning team.

"What a game! Did you hear that Breana?" He looked back at her. Breana was sitting in the chair sulking.

"Hey, what's with the long face? Did something happen in there?"

"No, well, maybe; oh, I don't know. I just have this weird feeling about Effiedra. I'm not sure if I'm being paranoid, but something's not right."

"Oh, come on; give her a chance, Breana. This is new for everybody. Just give it some time, and then you'll see how things go."

"Yeah, I guess you're right."

"Of course I am." He said, as he started into the house to get Effiedra. They were all high spirited as they said their parting good night.

Back at the hotel, Effiedra fantasized of being Mrs. Henry Noble. She wrote it on paper. She pretended to introduce herself as Mrs. Henry Noble, or Effiedra Wilson- Noble. She rolled over on the bed as she laughed.

"When I'm finished with that old goat, he won't know what hit him. I'm going to make him pay for everything his kind did to me. Using me and throwing me aside like a piece of trash. This time, I'm going to do it to him before he does to me."

The next morning, she got on the phone and called the Noble residence.

"I'm calling to thank you and your family for a wonderful evening. I had a good time."

"So did we," answered Henry, "No one has ever played the piano for us since my wife passed away. I think the house came alive. We must do it again before you leave."

"I would love that," Effiedra said, sounding extra excited. It made Henry's heart glad that she was interested. On the other end of the line he was beaming.

For the next three weeks, Effiedra visited the Nobles home frequently. It was Friday, the day before she claimed she was scheduled to leave. Henry invited her to lunch.

"So, tomorrow is the day you go back to New York," he said.

"Yes, I'm afraid so. I could have arranged to stay longer; however I'm running low on funds, so I have to go back."

'Ok, Henry…you may never get this chance again, say it, say it. "Would you change your plans if I asked you to stay a while longer? You could stay with us." Henry said.

Effiedra pretended to be caught off guard. She put her hand to her chest in faux disbelief. "Are you sure that your family will be alright with that? I don't want to impose."

"Nonsense, we love your company at the house, and my guest house is empty. Why don't I send Dudley over to your hotel tomorrow to help you move your things? Who knows what may happen. You might like it and decide to stay for good." He said with a little laugh.

"Oh I love it already. I just don't know how I would accomplish staying here."

"That's where I may be able to help. I could help you stay if you want to."

"You would do that for me? I've only known you for what, less than a month?"

"Well, the earth was created in six days. Surely a lot could happen in three weeks."

Effiedra chuckled. "You're so funny."

"So, will you stay?" Henry asked.

"How can I say no, when you put it like that? I'll call my boss and arrange for the time.

It will be good for me as well. I'm really having a good time, and I enjoy your family very much."

Henry grinned. "We enjoy having you too. You can turn in your rented car. We have enough cars at the house. You can use one of them.

Dudley went to the hotel and picked up Effiedra's belongings. Thelma gathered linens, and took them to the guesthouse. She made up the bed, and put fresh flowers, fresh water, and a basket of fruits on the table. When Dudley finally arrived with Effiedra, he dropped her off at the main house and took her luggage to the guesthouse. When Thelma walked into the living room, she found Effiedra walking around the room. She looked as if she was taking inventory of everything.

"Hello!" said Thelma. "Mr. Noble said I'm to show you to the guesthouse." They chatted and laughed as they walked together, Effiedra pouring on the charm. Thelma opened up the door and they both went in. "If you need help getting settled, let me know. Dinner will be at 6:00 p.m."

"Thank you. I'll try not to be late."

No sooner, than Thelma left for the main house, Effiedra plopped herself on the bed.

"Yes, I got one foot in. Boy oh boy, is that old goat in for a surprise or what? Effiedra-you're good." She said, talking to herself and praising her deceitfulness.

Henry came home a little earlier than usual. He put his briefcase down and called for Thelma. "Thel—" He turned around, and she was standing behind him. "Oh there you are," he said with a nervous grin.

"Yes, Mr. Noble"

He walked away, and then quickly turned back. Thelma wondered why he was acting nervous.

"Ok, I'm a little nervous. This is all so, so…"

"New?" Thelma said.

"Yes, exactly…NEW! I'm getting 5'oclock shadow, and she told me she is 25 years old. I don't want to make a fool of myself. You know what I mean?"

"Sir, whatever will be, will be; remember that."

Henry was making his way to the guest house. Effiedra was unpacking the few things she had brought with her. She came across the drinking glass that she had stuffed in the suitcase the night she accidentally killed Billy. A look of panic came over her face. Just then, Henry called out her name. She quickly stuffed the glass back inside the suitcase and put it inside the closet.

"Yes, Henry, come on in."

"I came to see how you're settling in. If you need anything, just ask."

Henry glanced at the scant amount of clothing on the bed. It occurred to him that she probably needed some clothing.

"Since I'm the one who has asked you to stay, you cannot deny me this. I'll have Dudley drive you into town tomorrow so may buy some new clothes."

"Thank you, but it's really not necessary you know."

"I know, Henry insisted, but I'll do it just the same."

Breana came home from a long day at school. She had been burning the midnight oil for the past few weeks writing two research papers simultaneously. Her classes were becoming stressful, even for Breana. Her eyes were red and she looked like a zombie. Now that her work was turned in, she couldn't wait to catch up on things with her father and relax. She walked into the kitchen.

"Hi, Thelma," she said, wearily.

"Oh sweetheart, you look like you could use a good meal and a good long relaxing hot bath."

"You said it."

"Well, dinner is almost ready. Why don't you go freshen up, and I'll bring you a tray."

"Thanks. Where's Father?"

"Oh, he's at the guest house with Effiedra."

Breana paused. "With who!"

"You know, Miss Wilson." Noting the confused look on Breana's face, Thelma said,

"You mean he didn't tell you?

"Tell me what?"

"He invited Miss Wilson to stay with us."

"He what! Until when? I can't believe this!"

Henry came floating into the kitchen, back from visiting Effiedra at the guesthouse.

"Hello, Pumpkin. Can't believe what?" Henry asked.

Breana looked at her father for a moment in dismay. "Nothing Father...um, excuse me please."

Thelma watched as Breana marched out of the kitchen. Henry looked puzzled at Breana's abrupt departure.

"Sir, I had assumed that you discussed Miss Wilson's moving in with Breana already."

"Well, she's been so busy that we haven't had a chance to talk much. Besides, everything happened so fast. Do you suppose she's upset with me?"

"I'm not sure, Sir, but she's overtired. That poor girl has been working so hard. Maybe you should just let her rest tonight. Then talk to her in the morning."

After breakfast, the following morning, Dudley made his way to the guesthouse. Effiedra was not there. He found her sitting by the gazebo. "Good morning, Miss Wilson," he said.

She mumbled something that Dudley accepted as a like response.

"I'm just sitting here enjoying the view. This is such a beautiful place."

What kind of tree is this? The berries are so shiny," she asked.

"That's Belladonna." Dudley replied.

She asked him if the berries could be eaten as she reached out to pick it. "No!" shouted Dudley.

"Don't even touch it, and if you do, be sure to wash your hands really well. It can cause heart palpitations and you can die from it. It's good medicine if you know how to use it. That's why we haven't cut it down. It can kill just as easy as it cures."

"How interesting, it kills, and it cures." She repeated. *"Hmm, very interesting."*

Chapter Ten

Almost three months had passed since Effiedra joined the Nobles household. The experience thus far had been bitter-sweet. It was sweet for some, and bitter for one, in particular. Breana felt ill whenever she had to listen to Effiedra's stories at dinner, and watching her father enthralled by her every word. Breana became scarce around the house. She didn't want to rain on her Father's parade, but at the same time, she could not ignore her own feelings.

One evening, Henry came home from work. Effiedra was waiting for him at the guesthouse, sitting on a chair with her sad eyes drenched with tears. Henry couldn't walk fast enough to get to her. "What's the matter? Why are you crying?"

"Oh, I just have a lot to think about, but I'll deal with it."

Henry took a seat on the chair next to hers. "I wish you would let me help you, after all, I'm the one who invited you here."

She gave him a sweet smile and took his hand into hers. "You've been so kind to me, I don't want to burden you with my troubles."

"Troubleshooting is my specialty, but I have to know what the trouble is."

"I spoke to my boss today. He said, "Don't bother coming back. I've already replaced you." More crocodile tears flowed. "Now, when I get back, I'm going to have to find a job and start from the bottom all over again. This is just awful."

She turned her face away from Henry to conceal the huge smirk on her face.

"Well, now that you have no job to go back to, who says you have to go back?"

"How would I live? I don't have a job here either. I can't work here. Wouldn't I need some kind of work papers? I'm just a tourist."

"You could work for me."

In wide-eyed wonder, she looked at him. "Doing what? I have no experience in the kind of business that you're in."

"Indeed not, but I'm a diplomat. If you become my wife, you would be qualified for a visa. That would solve the problem. Please say you will think about it."

"You mean marry you?" Effiedra asked.

"Well, yes. This is the easiest way right now. Take some time to think it over." He said as he squeezed her hand. He stood up and walked away.

After supper that evening, Effiedra went to the gazebo with Henry and sat with him as he enjoyed his evening brandy. She looked at Henry and said, "I've thought about it and I think it's the only solution. The answer is yes."

Henry felt his heart beating faster, but *this would be totally business, of course*, he thought to himself.

"That's a wise decision," Henry said. "No one will question your status then. It'll be alright, you'll see."

Henry went to his room. He opened a chest, and brought out a jewelry box. Inside was a diamond ring. He went to the guest quarters where Effiedra was. He walked in and immediately showed her the ring.

He told her that it belonged to his grandmother. "If we're going to make this look convincing, I suggest you put it on. I'll talk to the family in the morning."

* * *

Henry left for work early the next morning. He did not tell the family of his plans. Effiedra went to the main house for breakfast, wearing the ring. Thelma had seen that ring often enough. She knew that it was never worn casually. Effiedra asked Thelma for a drink of water. She used her left hand to take the glass; hoping that Thelma saw the ring.

"That ring is very familiar. It belonged to Mr. Noble's grand-mother. What are you doing with it? Thelma asked.

"Oh, Henry didn't tell you? He said he would. He asked me to marry him last night and I said yes."

Thelma wanted to say, *'This is going way too fast.'* Instead, she said, "No, he always shares *important* information with the family. This must have slipped his mind."

Effiedra missed the connotation of Thelma's remark. She just kept smiling. She was in her moment of triumph.

Dudley had picked up Henry from work and Breana from school in one trip.

Henry was glowing, but Breana's demeanor was aloof. In the car, Henry said, "Pumpkin, you know you'll always be daddy's girl, right?"

"Yes, Father I know. Why are you saying that now?"

"Well, lately, you've been sort of distant. I want to make sure that you know how much I love you."

"I know that Father"

"Okay, I have something very important to say tonight at dinner."

"Well, what is it? Tell me now."

"No, no. Everyone will find out soon enough." Henry replied.

About the time that Effiedra knew Henry would be home, she took off the ring.

When she came to dinner, Thelma noticed she wasn't wearing the ring, but she said nothing. As soon as Henry and Breana reached home, he said, "I want you to hear this too Dudley, so come to the main house after you've parked the car."

At dinner, Henry was seated at the head of the table, Effiedra and Breana sat facing each other. Thelma and Dudley were also seated. Everyone was enjoying the delicious food that Thelma prepared.

"Well, family, I have noticed how this house has come alive since Miss Wilson has been staying with us," Henry said, "There is no other way to say what I have to say, but to come out and say it..."

Thelma's gut already told her what was coming. Dudley tried to listen while concentrating on a morsel of spice cake in his mouth, and Breana was drinking her milk.

"I've asked Effiedra to marry me."

The milk from Breana's mouth went spewing across the table, right into Effiedra's face.

"What? She's barely older than I am, Father!" said Breana as she looked at Effiedra, then back at Henry. She attempted to keep her composure. "Excuse me," she said as her voice quivered. She rushed to her room, and Henry went after her.

"Breana, it's not what you think, let me explain," he said, standing by Breana's door.

She opened the door. "Pumpkin, how could you behave like that without giving me a chance to explain?"

"I'm sorry Father. I was just taken by surprise, that's all. Everything is happening so fast. All these changes in such a short time; I don't really know how to respond."

"Everything will make sense when you hear what I have to say."

"Okay, I'm listening," she said guardedly, wiping her eyes as tears trickled down her cheeks.

"Well, you see, I'm very fond of Miss Wilson. I'm partly to blame for her losing her job in New York; because, I asked her to stay a while longer. She spoke to her employer yesterday, and he told her that her position has been filled. So I told her if she would like to stay, I would help her secure a Diplomatic Visa."

"And how long will this arrangement have to last? And what happens between now and then?" asked Breana.

"Well, suppose we take it one day at a time," Henry answered.

"Have you noticed that she is far younger than you are? Have you even discussed that at all?"

"I never thought that it was necessary, my dear, I'm just trying to help the poor girl."

"Well, trust me Father, 'the poor girl' will find it *necessary* some day; mark my words. However, I can't tell you what to do. I'll just have to do what I can to accept it,"

"Thank you Pumpkin. It will be alright, you'll see."

They both walked out of the room to rejoin the others. "I'm sorry I behaved like such a baby. It's just that everything happened so suddenly. Please forgive me Miss Wilson, and I'm sorry for the spilled milk on your face."

"That's quite alright Breana. It took me by surprise too. I just hope we can be friends."

"I guess we're all surprised," said Thelma. *'I was hoping that Mr. Noble's marriage would produce a mother for Breana. Instead, it will be a playmate,'* she thought.

Breana got up from her chair and walked over to Effiedra. She hugged her and said, "Welcome to the family."

Effiedra stood up and hugged Breana, "Thank you that means a lot."

After dinner, Henry decided to spend the rest of the evening with Effiedra down at the guesthouse.

"Thelma, he said, "I'm going to be at the guest house. I need to go over some things with Miss Wilson."

"Would you like me to bring your drink to the guest house later Sir?"

"That would be lovely, thank you."

At the guesthouse, Effiedra protested, "Now, Mr. Noble, I understand that this is just a business arrangement to help me out, so you don't have to make any fuss over this. All I need to know is if it's legal."

"Well, a lot can happen within the course of time. Who knows, we may find that we enjoy each other's company, you know." Henry said, jokingly.

"Not if your daughter and the maid have anything to say about it,"

"Thelma has always been loyal to this family. She is not just a maid; she's far more valuable to this family. And Breana is a sweetheart. You have nothing to fear from neither of them. They will treat you with respect, and I trust I can say the same for you?"

"Oh, I told you how much I love being with your family. I wouldn't have said that if I didn't respect them."

"Good, so how would you feel if we had a small ceremony here at the house? I could ask Judge Lewis to come and officiate for us. We can invite a few close friends; that will make it a little more authentic."

"Whatever you say is okay by me. It's so kind of you to be doing this for me anyway."

There was a knock at the door. Henry walked over and opened it.

"Oh, Thelma! Come on in."

"Thank you Sir; I thought I would bring down some refreshments for you."

"Thank you, Thelma. That's very thoughtful. Come, sit down. If you have a minute we would like to discuss something with you. We were just discussing the wedding. Given the circumstances, we agree not to make a big fuss. We're going to ask Judge Lewis to come to the house to officiate for us. However, we will invite a few friends. We would appreciate your input on the rest of the plans. We want Breana to be involved as well."

"Yes Sir, just let me know which day it will be and how many guests to expect."

Henry made arrangements with Judge Lewis and the ceremony was set for that Saturday which was three days away.

On Saturday morning, Thelma was making last minute preparations. Breana walked into the kitchen. "Thelma, I know Effiedra said she didn't want any fuss but, Father is well known. We have to announce the wedding, don't you think?"

Thelma thought for a moment. "I believe that's a good idea. He said he wants it to appear authentic anyway."

"Okay, I'm sending the announcement to the Atlanta News since Father has connections there. And to the Long Island Press, since Effiedra said she is from New York. I'll just go ahead and take care of it. They have other things to deal with right now."

* * *

In New York, the Go-Go Girls establishment was on the verge of bankruptcy. Since the sudden departure of Loleta/Effiedra, revenue had hit an all-time low. The dancers were mediocre; the liquor was watered down, and the creditors were pounding on the door. Then came the fateful night; the final straw that brought the demise of the proprietor and his establishment.

The night was hot and humid. The booze was cheap, and the patrons were few and outrageous. The entertainer took the stage and started dancing. Butch, the big burley man, who groped Effiedra some time ago, acted as leader of the pack. He cupped his hands, brought them up to his mouth, as he filled his lungs with air.

"Boooo!" he bellowed, releasing a sound as if it echoed from the belly of a whale.

Soon, the others joined in. They tasted their drinks and spat on the floor, as the curses rolled off their tongues. Then, one by one, they started walking out. The discouraged proprietor, half drunk, called out to the bouncer.

"Hey, Bruce, Lock up! And you can leave when you're done!"

Bruce started the closing routine, and then he walked over to the bar.

"Is there anything else I can do for you before I leave, Boss?"

With his drink in his hand, he turned around and looked at Bruce. "Yes! Go find that Jezebel. The bitch that left me high and dry, after all I did for her."

"Boss, that's a tall order. I had men looking for her in all the places I thought she might be. I combed the area myself, and it's like the girl fell off the face of the earth."

"Yeah, and she took a good man with her. I know she killed Billy! I told the police, and what did they do? What did they do! I'll tell you what they did! They sat on their blessed assurance that a girl of her stature couldn't move a man his size! Those DUMB ASSES!" said an angry Gunther as he threw the glass of liquor across the room. The glass hit the wall, and it shattered to the floor.

"Go on Bruce! Get out of here! I have things to do!"

"Okay boss, I'll see you in the morning, and take it easy on that stuff, will ya? You know how ya get when you've had one too many."

Meanwhile, near the club, a black car was parked at the curb.

Inside, two men sat in the back seats, and a third man in the driver's seat. They watched the activities around the club. As soon as Bruce left, they drove around the back of the club and parked next to Gunther's car. Inside the club, Gunther went to the back room and came out with a gasoline can. He opened up the can, and he poured the gasoline all over the floor with the liquid trailing behind him as he walked back into the kitchen. He hurried through the back door, taking the gas can with him. The men in the car watched as Gunther removed a lighter from his pocket and lit a cigarette. He took two puffs as if contemplating his actions; he threw the cigarette inside and quickly closed the door. As soon as he walked toward his car, the two men rushed out of the station wagon and grabbed him from behind. He dropped the gas can on the ground as he struggled franticly to free himself. They forced him into the trunk of the car.

They drove about two miles away to an abandoned building at the end of an alley in St. Albans.

They stopped the car in a dark ally, and pulled Gunther from the car. They beat him within an inch of his life. They would have finished the job, had it not been for a nearby resident who heard his cries from the alley and called the police. While the police were on their way to Gunther's rescue, fire trucks were on the way to the club. There had been an explosion at a building near Francis Lewis Blvd the caller said. At the sound of the Siren from the police car, the two men fled. The police called an ambulance and Gunther was taken to Queens General Hospital.

* * *

By the time the firefighters got to the building, it was totally destroyed. While they were doing the investigation, the chief walked to the back of the charred remains and accidentally kicked an object. He shone a flashlight on the ground and discovered the gas can.

He picked it up, and he put it in a bag. Then he saw a silver Cadillac with a gray vinyl top. When he checked inside of the car, he discovered that it belonged to the owner of the club. He suspected that he may have perished in the fire. However, they searched diligently and found no evidence to support that theory.

It was already the wee hours of the morning. When the police officers compared notes, they discovered that at the time of the fire, Gunther was being assaulted, in the alley, approximately two miles away. He had three broken ribs, two busted kneecaps; a damaged cornea in his right eye, and a broken jaw.

As soon as he was able to talk, the police went to the hospital to question him. In his statement, he said, "I closed the club and walked out through the back door. As I got outside, two men pushed me back inside. They spilled gasoline over the floor and set the place on fire. They drove me to some alley and beat me up, and that's all

I remember. I don't know who they were. I never saw their faces." His story was almost believable, but his fingerprints were all over the gas can.

"Mr. Gunther, said Chief Mc Loud, "I'm aware of the assault on you during the time of the fire; Still, I have one question. How did your fingerprints happen to be on a gas can, found at the scene?"

"The gas can belong to me, Sir. My gas gage in my car wasn't working, so I tried to keep extra gas in case of emergency."

"That may explain it," said Chief Mc Loud, looking at his partner.

There was no proof to connect Gunther to the fire, so he escaped going to jail.

However, his effort was in vain, since he did not receive payment for his claim to the insurance company. The insurance adjuster's report stated that he was negligent in keeping gasoline on the property. Therefore, he was largely responsible for the fire.

* * *

Back in Jamaica, at the Nobles Residence, the wedding ceremony was moving full steam ahead. While the photographer was taking pictures of the Bride and Groom, the X-ray technicians were taking pictures of Gunther's broken bones. Breana sent the pictures to the newspaper publishers in Atlanta and New York to have the wedding announcement published.

Bruce visited Gunther on a daily basis. One morning he was on his way to the hospital. He stopped at a news stand on Jamaica Avenue. And picked up a copy of the Long Island Press. He started turning the pages. He discovered the announcement. Effiedra Wilson married to the American Ambassador in Jamaica.

"Holy hell! Wait till the boss sees this shit. All hell gonna break loose."

Bruce folded the paper, put it under his arm and hurried to

the hospital. He took the elevator to the sixth floor. He got off and walked down the corridor to Room 625. As he entered the room, he said, "Man you're not going believe this shit!"

"Try me, after what happened to me, I may believe anything," Gunther said with minimum interest.

Bruce stepped closer to the side of the bed. He opened up the paper, and held it in front of Gunther.

"For heaven sakes, you want me to lose the one good eye? Read it to me!"

"Look at the picture man. Look at the girl. Don't you recognize her?"

Gunther took a good look with the available eye, "Loleta? He growled, there is a God! What does it say? Read it to me!"

"Well according to the paper, she married the American Ambassador in Kingston."

"Where's that?"

"Jamaica, West Indies, man. Do you see the rock on that girl's finger?"

"Yeah, her finger is not too small for a rock that size, but her whole body is too frail to move one dead man. Bruce, go find her and make me proud. I want you to take a picture of me, and I want you to carry it with you. I want you to show it to her, so that she will know why she has to pay for what she did. I want every cent she owes me, and then some. A good place to start is that Embassy in Kingston. If you find this man, she's not far behind."

"Don't worry boss, when I find that harlot, she is going to wish she was back in the gutter where you picked her up."

Bruce boarded the plane for Jamaica. The flight seemed to take hours. *I can't wait to wrap my hands around Effiedra's little neck, and besides… this food is horrible,* he thought. He finally landed at the Palisades Airport. As soon as he disembarked, he walked over to the car and hotel rental office. He rented a gray Austin Cambridge bearing the license plate A40. He rented a room at the Whitmore Hotel.

Bruce took the map from the glove compartment of the car, and he went inside the hotel to check in. He had the rest of his evening planned out. He sipped on brandy, studied the map, and planned his confrontation with Effiedra- until he dozed off.

* * *

Everyone in the Noble's household had an enjoyable evening except, Effiedra. She was smiling on the outside, but on the inside—she was like a spider weaving her web, and Henry was the fly. While everyone talked and laughed, she was consumed with her own private thoughts. *Poor Henry, the old sacrificial ram! Too bad he's got to pay for everything his kind did to me. When I'm finished with him, he won't be laughing. None of them will.*

Of course Henry couldn't hear her thinking. "Why are you so quiet Effiedra? Is something wrong?"

"Oh, quite the contrary; everything is just right, perfect. I was just counting my blessings." She said to him. After the wedding, she had moved out of the guesthouse and into a bedroom across from Henry's. Now, she was ready to go to the next phase of her plan. After supper one evening, she sat on a chair with her head down.

"Are you not feeling well my dear? You haven't been yourself all evening." Henry asked.

"I'm just a bit tired. I'm afraid I'll have to turn in early tonight." She got up and walked toward the sleeping quarters.

"Well, good night then," said Henry, "I'll just finish up some paperwork. I'll see you in the morning."

When Henry finished his work, he started down the corridor to his bedroom.

When he opened the door and walked into the room, he heard, "Hello darling, I thought you'd never get here."

He turned around and looked on the bed and there she was. Effiedra was lying on his bed, in an alluring position. She wore a black silk lace nightgown that shimmered and accentuated her curves in all the right places. In a seductive voice, she said. "I've been waiting for you. What took you so long?"

Henry looked at her. He moved closer to the bed, and his heart began pounding.

"I thought this was to be just an arrangement, my dear?" He asked.

"I also remembered someone saying, "We might make a go of it," she responded with a sly grin.

He hastily went through his bedtime routine and was in the bed in a flash. In Henry's eyes, this was a new beginning. It made him feel young again; while Effiedra felt as if she had just sold her soul to the devil.

He looked at her through eyes of passion. She pretended to respond, but in her mind, she raged. *I wonder if this old goat really thinks I could be attracted to him. I'm sick to my stomach. Ewe, I hope I can go through with this.*

The next day, Henry awoke with a smile that he hadn't worn in a long time.

"Good morning, I almost looked around to see if there's someone else in the room. I'll have to get used to being called anybody's *Mrs.*"

He kissed her gently on the cheek; then he picked up his robe that was hanging from the back of a chair. He put it on and walked into the bathroom. He sang in the shower; while Effiedra sulked in bed.

"I can't wait to jump into that shower and scrub myself," she whispered to herself. Henry chatted away happily to his new wife while he got dressed. She was just nonchalant. He leaned over on the bed and kissed her. She smiled at him seductively, but inside she cringed at the thought of his touch. Henry left the room whistling as he walked down the corridor.

He went into the breakfast room and sat at the table.

"Good morning, Thelma! Mrs. Noble will be a while, and I have an extra stop to make this morning, so I'll start without her."

"Yes Sir," said Thelma. "Has there been some kind of change, Sir. Am I expected to call her '*Mrs. Noble*'?"

"I'll leave that between you and her, but yes there has been a change. We might really make this a real relationship after all. I feel right about it, so I know you'll be happy for me, and support us."

Effiedra dragged herself out of the bedroom with her arms wrapped around herself, as if she had just been violated. She heard Henry talking to Thelma and stopped short of entering the room. "I'll just have coffee Thelma," he said, "I have to get an early start this morning, and I'm running behind. I've never done anything about my will since Penny died. I do have a new wife now, and I think it's time to do an update. There's no time like the present. We never know what tomorrow holds."

Unbeknownst to Thelma and Henry, Effiedra was eavesdropping on the conversation. Henry's declaration brought a spark to her eyes. *Yes! I guess the hell I went through last night was worth it after all,* she thought.

In astonishment, Thelma shook her head in disbelief, but said nothing. Henry finished his coffee and walked outside to the car. He told Dudley he wanted to go to Beaton Street before heading to Oxford Street. "I have some business to attend to there," he said.

They drove off with Henry looking back at the house, hoping Effiedra would be at some window or door, trying to see him off. Effiedra was too busy in the bathroom trying to scrub herself clean. "I hope I won't have to do this too often, or for too long."

* * *

Bruce had just finished breakfast at the hotel. He walked out of the lobby to pick up his car. He had studied the map thoroughly the night before and it paid off. Bruce drove to * * *2 Oxford St. at the Embassy building and parked his car. He waited and waited… making notes of who came in and out of the building. For a while, there was nothing to observe and he found himself drifting in and out of sleep.

It was now midday and Bruce felt hungry. He noticed a little shop close by that sold snacks and beverages. He got out of the car, stretched his legs, and then walked over to get something to eat, still keeping close watch of the embassy building.

At 6:00 p.m., Bruce saw the silver Mercedes pulled up to the curb. Henry finally walked out of the building and got into the car. As the car pulled away, Bruce had an adrenaline rush.

"It's show time, baby." He said enthusiastically. He began trailing behind Dudley at a safe distance. Finally, Dudley turned the car into the Nobles' driveway, and Bruce drove past to a nearby address. From there, he could observe the activities of the Nobles. As soon as they went inside, he made a U-turn and wrote down the house address.

Bruce went back to his hotel room and picked up the phone receiver before flopping on the bed. He let out a deep, morbid giggle as he dialed the number.

"Man, you're not going to believe the life our little pigeon is living down here!" he said, speaking to Gunther on the phone. "You should see the spread…beach front and all!"

Gunther listened in silence, then he said, "Good work, don't call me again. You know what to do, just handle it."

"I got cha' boss, don't worry."

Chapter Eleven

T he next morning, Bruce drove back and parked up the street from the Nobles. Dudley noticed a gray car parked just up the street from the Nobles house.

"I've never seen that car in this neighborhood before." He said to Breana,

"Maybe someone just bought it," Breana replied.

Dudley looked at the vehicle. "Well, maybe you're right." As they drove off, he made a mental note of the license plate anyway, *Austin - A4*.

Henry, being his own driver for the morning, left soon after. All the while, Bruce kept watching their every move. He waited for the perfect opportunity when everyone was gone from the house, hoping for Effiedra to be home alone. He got out of his car and went to the house, and looked around guardedly before he rang the doorbell. Effiedra walked over to the door and opened it. When she realized who it was, she immediately tried to slam the door shut, but her strength was no match for Bruce. He easily forced himself in, causing Effiedra to lose her balance and fall to the floor. Bruce laughed sardonically.

"Oh no! Oh no! How did you find me Bruce? What are you doing here?" She said trying to move away from Bruce; finally, she got herself up off the floor.

"Well. I brought you a present from Gunther," he said reaching into his breast pocket.

"Don't shoot me, please, oh God! I'll do anything you say!" She said clasping her hand and begging for him to spare her.

He laughed. "It amazes me how people suddenly get religious just when they think they're gonna die. He shook his head. "Calm down...why would I want to kill you, sweetheart? That would be like killing the goose that laid the golden egg. Gunther wanted me to show you this picture." She grabbed the picture and gasped as she looked at it.

"Who did this?"

"You did that! You left, and everything went downhill. After all he did for you, he believes you owe him."

Bruce put his face up close to hers as she stood trembling.

"He sent me to collect." He said in a menacing whisper.

If he didn't kill her, the stench of his garlic breath might have. Effiedra held her breath as long as she could; then she had to let go.

"But I don't have any money, and I'm not going back there." She swiftly moved away from him.

"Don't tell me your problems; I have my own." He continued, sneering at her. "My order is to deliver. I'm sure you can be creative, and you were always resourceful. Unless you want me to wait around for your hubby to come home, you better start coughing up some dough, *Mrs. Noble*, or maybe you would rather a few unexplainable bruises?" He grabbed her arm, and saw the ring that belonged to Henry's grandmother.

"I'll be damned! Is this the stone David used to slay Goliath? It's a shame for this little finger to carry a rock this size." He said, salivating at the sight of the ring.

She attempted to free herself from his grasp, but that made him hold her tighter.

"Ah, ah, ah, not so fast," Bruce said, he pulled the ring from her finger, and he put it in his pocket.

"Consider this a down payment," he said. He walked through the door and left her standing, bewildered in the middle of the room.

"How did he find me? What do I do now? He's going to ruin everything. I have to buy myself some time." She was so afraid; every nerve in her body was in high gear.

That evening when Henry came home, he immediately asked for the whereabouts of his wife. Thelma told him that she was in their bedroom. Henry passed up his usual habit of leaving his briefcase in the study and instead brought it into the bedroom, and he left it on the bed.

Effiedra darling, where are you? He said as he walked into the room

"I'm in the bathroom, dear. I'll be out in a bit."

"I'll be out at the gazebo. Please join me when you get the chance."

"Of course darling, I'll be right out."

As soon as he left, Effiedra quietly stepped out of the bathroom. She saw the briefcase on the bed, and she opened it. She removed the papers and examined them. She scowled and swiftly replaced the documents back inside the briefcase and left the room.

Thelma prepared Henry's drink and placed it on a tray along with a bell. As she started toward the back door to go to the gazebo, Effiedra approached her.

"Thelma," she said, "I'll take my husband's drink to him. I'm heading down there anyway."

"Thank you Effiedra, I'm sure he'll enjoy the company." Thelma rolled her eyes and shook her head as she watched Effiedra walk down to the gazebo, hips swaying seductively from side to side as she approached Henry. Thelma walked away in disgust muttering. "The more I see in this girl, the more I dislike her".

Henry was engrossed in the newspaper he never had a chance to read that morning. She quietly walked behind him and picked some of the berries from the belladonna tree. She squashed them in his drink and stirred it with her finger. She handed him the glass.

"Thank you, Thelma," he said. Then he looked up. "Oh, there you are. I thought you were Thelma; how nice of you to join me."

"You don't think I'm going to let my Mr. Wonderful spend a beautiful evening like this alone at the gazebo, do you?"

"Wonderful huh? It's you who are wonderful, especially last night. He playfully pulled her onto his lap and would have kissed her lips but Effiedra skillfully turned her head and he kissed her cheek. She handed him the beverage concoction. Effiedra watched as Henry took his first sip from the glass then, gradually drank it all. She took the chair next to her husband and talked to him about nothing important. She waited and rambled on until Henry said, "Darling, this is a bit unusual for me to be so sleepy at this hour." She glanced at her watch and couldn't believe it took less than an hour for the stuff to work. She was pleased.

"Oh sweetheart, I hope you're not coming down with something." Feigning concern, she stepped closer and felt his forehead. "You do feel a bit warm, but it could be the humidity that's causing it."

"Would you mind terribly, if I went inside for a little rest? I promise I'll make it up to you."

"Not at all my love. Go get your rest and be fresh by the time I get there."

"Thanks for understanding my dear, I feel terrible about this."

"Darling, you worry too much, I'm fine; you go rest, *in peace* she thought.

A little while later, Breana went to the gazebo. "Where's Father?" she asked.

"He went inside to get some rest. He said he was a bit tired."

"That's not like him to turn in this early," said Breana. "He must have had a hard day."

"Well, I should be joining him myself. Enjoy the view," Effiedra said, as she picked up the tray and left.

* * *

Effiedra continued adding the poison to Henry's brandy, and he unsuspectingly kept drinking her witches brew. One morning, at the breakfast table, he was feeling faint. His speech was slow and deliberate. "I have no idea what's been going on with me. For the past few evenings, I've been feeling drowsy and sweating excessively. It's as if all my energy has been drained."

"Father, I think you should get an appointment with the doctor. You may have the flu or something."

"You're right, Pumpkin. If I'm not feeling better by tomorrow, I'll definitely make an appointment. I was so sleepy yesterday evening. As he spoke Breana noticed his voice slurred a bit. I haven't gone to bed that early in years. He reached for his wife's hand. "I'm sorry darling, I didn't mean to abandon you at the gazebo," he said to Effiedra. "That's okay, dear. I came in right after you, but you were already asleep."

After breakfast, Henry insisted on going to work even though he wasn't feeling up to par. He didn't want to scare Breana. He had become good at hiding his true state of health. As soon as Dudley drove away with Henry and Breana, Thelma began cleaning up the breakfast dishes, when the doorbell rang.

"Good morning Ma'am." A man wearing a suit greeted Thelma as she opened the door.

"May I speak to the lady of the house?"

"And whom should I say is callin'?" Thelma asked.

"My name is Doug Gamboni. I'm a salesman for Mutual Life Insurance, and I'm hoping that I can interest her into buying a policy." The accent was unmistakable; *a New Yorker? What would he be doing in Jamaica selling life insurance?* Thelma thought to herself. She looked him up and down.

"Wait just a minute. I'll see if she's available."

Thelma walked away from the door. "Effiedra!" she called out, "Dere's a salesman at the door. He wants to speak with you!"

"I'll be right there!" she answered from behind the closed door of her bedroom, trying to stay calm. Effiedra had a suspicion of who the 'salesman' was. Ever since Bruce came into town, Effiedra had been an anxious mess, but she always put on a content facade for the family. She looked in the mirror to fix her lipstick, and walked out to the front door.

Her suspicion was accurate. She came face to face with Bruce.

"Good morning Ma'am! How are you this fine morning?" Bruce taunted.

"Very well, thank you," Effiedra said, looking around to see if Thelma was in ear shot, but Thelma already was hanging clothes outside.

She quickly stepped outside and closed the door behind her. "For heaven's sake, what are you doing here again?" She anxiously looked around. "You already have my ring that cost over a quarter of a million dollars. You can't be thinking that I owe him more," she said in a whisper.

"Yeah, you owe him your life. As long as you're free, and who knows how long that will be. After all, poor old Billy would expect somebody to see that justice is done."

"Billy, what does he have to do with this?" she asked.

"Well, at first, everybody thought Billy was drunk and had fallen down the stairs, *see.* Then, the Coroner said he had enough Halcion in him to croak a horse. That puts a spin on the situation…like why would Billy go out after he took the sleeping pills. The poor guy fell dead with his boots on? Who takes sleeping pills fully dressed and leaves the house. Then, a funny thing happened; the police found out that he didn't live anywhere near the building. So they started asking questions like, "Was he acquainted with anyone that lives here?" Effiedra got agitated.

"I had nothing to do with it! You hear me? Nothing!" she said crossly.

"Chill out, baby girl. Don't get your bloomers in a bundle. I don't mean any harm. I'm just bringing you news from home. And how come you didn't even ask about old Billy? He used to be your main squeeze. Now, that's another funny thing. You knew that Gunther sent him to get you, and he failed. You know how Gunther handles people who fail him. Yet, you didn't even ask about your best friend Billy? That's a funny thing, don't you think?" He said mockingly.

"Well, there you go. Gunther might have done him in for not bringing me back."

"The police thought so too," said Bruce, "but guess what, Gunther was with me at the club all night long. The police found out that Billy knew a Lolita who lived in the building. As a matter of fact, her door is the closest to the stairwell where he fell. So even if she didn't do it, she might have heard or seen *something*, right?" He said with a mischievous grin.

"And you think that has something to do with me? You're crazier than I thought!" Effiedra spouted at him.

"I might not be the crazy one, for the way I see it; people don't disappear because they heard or seen something, you know! Usually, they call the police, see. That's another funny thing. If you don't want them to find out who Lolita is, you better cooperate."

"I need more time," Effiedra answered, "You go back to New York, and tell him I'm working on something. Tell him I'll make him a rich man when it's over. He just has to give me more time."

"How about I stay here, and you make us both rich men? I like that deal better."

"If you stay, you can't keep coming around here. What if someone sees you? How would I explain you to them? Don't you see? Your staying will mess everything up. I've come too far to let you screw this up now."

As she was talking Bruce walked across the room and picked up a vase; he contemplated on how much it cost, and considered taking it. "Okay, here's the deal," Bruce answered as he slowly put down the vase. "I'm not leaving this Island without some type of compensation. I'll give the boss a call, but I can't promise anything. You know how he gets when he wants something. See ya later, honey buns." Effiedra didn't breathe comfortably until he was out the door.

"Effiedra, you're going to have to speed things up around here," she started mumbling to herself. "Even if he can stall Gunther, it won't be for long. That flesh peddling, sadistic, son of a bitch. God, how I hate him! I hope he rots in hell sometime soon."

Thelma fixed the tray for Henry's drink as usual. Effiedra went to the bar and said,

"Really Thelma, everyone takes such good care of things around here. I'm the only one who seems not to have a routine. I think this should be my job from now on to bring my husband his drinks."

Thelma was surprised by her generosity, but appeased her just the same. "By all means; as you've said often enough, he's *your* husband."

She walked down to the gazebo and stood behind Henry. She quietly reached for a bunch of berries she already had stashed in her pocket and crushed them into the glass. She poured the drink and handed the glass to Henry. He graciously accepted the drink from the hand of his "loving" young wife.

"Thank you my beloved, and thanks for coming to be with me," he said with a wink.

"You are most welcome Honey. There's no place I'd rather be than with you. However, I won't be staying with you this evening. I have some letters to write. So I'll catch up with you later. Enjoy your drink. " She watched him take a few sips from the glass before she walked away. By the time Henry took his third sip, he had an anxious look on his face. He grabbed on to his chest and he reached for the bell that was always on the tray in case he needed something.

He started to fall, and tried to grab on to the table, but his hand slipped and he fell to the ground. The bell fell onto the pavement next to him. Thelma heard the sound of the bell and started walking briskly to the gazebo. As she drew closer, she saw Henry lying on the ground. The front of his pale blue shirt was stained with brandy, and the empty glass lay broken on the ground.

"Mr. Noble!" She called out as she ran toward him. "Breana! Breana hurry, call the ambulance! Something is wrong with your father!" She shouted. She looked at Henry and he was getting paler by the minute. "Mr. Noble! Mr. Noble, speak to me! Speak to me!" she said frantically, as she tried to shake him out his of his stupor.

Breana heard the commotion and ran to the gazebo. She saw her Father on the ground and thought he was dead until Thelma yelled at her that he had a faint pulse but she needed to get help quickly. She immediately went back to the house to call for help. Her hands trembled as she dialed the operator. On her way back outside, Breana grabbed a pillow for her Father. Her heart raced as she thought of losing him; it made her stomach sick, but she knew she had to keep it together to help him. She knelt down next to Henry's side and gently put the pillow under his head.

"Father- Father, can you hear me? Hang in there, help is coming. God please, please help us."

"He's still breathing, thank God. Where is Effiedra?"

"I don't know. I thought she was still down here with Father," Breana answered.

"She must be in her room, go find her and Dudley!"

Breana got up and ran back to the house. Thelma kept touching Henry's face and saying, "Mr. Noble, Mr. Noble!" she called, over and over again, but there was no response.

Dudley came running to the scene, carrying a bottle of smelling salts. He looked at Henry and said, "Boss! Wake up! Open your eyes!"

Henry's skin was pale, sweaty and clammy. His breathing was

shallow and his pulse was weak and threaded. Dudley swiftly passed the smelling salts under his nose. Henry's head leaned to the side.

"Oh, where is that ambulance!" Thelma said in an irritable tone.

"Damn! Boss would be better off if I put him in the car and take him to the hospital myself!" Dudley remarked, in frustration.

"Don't be absurd! Effiedra shouted walking down the path to the gazebo. Why didn't someone wake me? What's happening to my husband? And why do you think he would be better off if *you* take him to the hospital? He is my husband and no one bothered to ask my opinion!"

Thelma couldn't take it anymore. She would not keep quiet a bit longer. She lashed out.

"Listen here, little girl," Thelma snapped. "This is not about you and your wounded ego! If you can't help, then stay out of the way!"

"Do you think Henry would appreciate the way you speak to me? I'm his wife!"

Thelma looked at her hard with narrowed eyes, "Let me tell you something…If you did know what I was *thinking*, you would run far from me right now!" Dudley watched Thelma's face. He knew that look very well. He recalled his own aunt's face was like that just before she whooped her neighbor for stealing from her shop. The beating was so bad the neighbor was in bed for two weeks and then walked with a limp there after. Everyone in the community knew not to cross Dudley's aunt, especially when it came to her family. That look meant Effiedra had gone too far. He had to stop things before it got worse.

"For heaven's sake Effiedra! If he doesn't get help soon, he won't be appreciating anything! Go call the ambulance again and find out what's keeping them!" Dudley shouted. Effiedra started to say something but changed her mind when she saw the apprehension on Dudley's face. She looked at Thelma who was still tending to Henry and decided now was not the time for a confrontation. She backed away. "I'll go call for an ambulance, again!" She headed toward the house but her gait didn't match the urgency in her voice.

* * *

When the ambulance finally arrived, Breana was waiting for them. "Please hurry, follow me!" she said. The Medics quickly administered first aid and then took Henry to University Hospital. To everyone's dismay, he entered into a coma. All sorts of test were ordered by the attending doctor. Hours had passed slowly. Now at 10:00 p.m., Effiedra pretended to be the concerned wife. Dudley anxiously paced the floor, and Thelma ignored her own fretful feelings to console Breana. As the night progressed, Breana laid down on two conjoined chairs with her head on Thelma's lap. Tears slowly trickled down her face as she anxiously nibbled on her fingernails. Dudley's head began to bob front to back from falling asleep.

At midnight, Effiedra claimed to be exhausted. "Dudley." She whispered while shaking him by the shoulders. "Dudley." She said jarringly this time.

"Yes, yes, I'm awake. What happened?" he responded in confusion.

"Will you take me home? I'd like to get some rest. Besides, there's nothing any of us can do here," she said, glancing at the others for confirmation. No one acknowledged her.

"I'll bring the car around, meet me in front of the lobby," Dudley said, yawning as he walked away.

Dudley and Effiedra drove the whole way home in silence. They both had Henry on their minds, each hoping for a different outcome. They finally pulled up to the front of the house. Dudley got out of the car and walked around to open the passenger door. Effiedra almost sang, "If anything changes, give me a ring," as she got out of the car.

Dudley just stood there with a confused look on his face,

watching her walk inside. On his way back to the hospital, he started thinking. *'Boss has always been a healthy man. All these changes started since this woman got here. And before the ambulance came to the house, she sure didn't seem in too much of a rush to call them. She's not even concerned about him now, not like I expect a wife should be. Something isn't right.'*

* * *

The results of Henry's blood tests showed a high level of atropine and other substances found in the Belladonna berry. Thelma informed the doctors that they indeed had a Belladonna plant in the backyard where Henry spent most of his evenings. They speculated that he may have somehow come in contact with the berries. Then Thelma began to wonder, *Mr. Noble has been having brandy by the gazebo all this while, and nothing ever happen to him until Effiedra started taking it to him,* Thelma thought. *In fact, he started complaining about drowsiness since the first evening she brought him his drink.*

Effiedra was back at the house, raging against herself. She went to the bar for a drink. *Why didn't I take that stupid bell off the tray? How could I have been so stupid?* She poured herself a glass of brandy, and then collapsed on the couch. Looking up at the ceiling, she thought of what she did and what she will do next when Henry dies. By the time she fell asleep, dawn was fast approaching.

At 6:30 in the morning, Effiedra was rudely awakened by a pounding on the front door. "What the..." She opened the door, and found Bruce was standing there donning a huge grin.

"Oh great! I don't need your shit today alright!" She swiftly turned around, leaving Bruce to invite himself in, "Didn't you promise to let me work this out my way?"

"Wow, you look absolutely terrible. What the hell ran you over? What's the problem? Somebody got you stressed?" He asked with a chuckle. "By the way, nice touch with the old man. I just came by to say congratulations. You really work fast. I have to hand it to you," Bruce taunted her and followed her as she made her way into the study.

"I don't know what you're talking about. I didn't do anything to my husband."

"That's right, that's your story, and you should stick to it," Bruce chuckled and popped some coated chewing gum into his mouth. She looked at him as he crunched away at the candies.

"And even if I did it, I had every right," she snarled, "I sacrificed my life to marry that old fool, and he made his will and left fifty percent of his estate to that daughter of his! Twenty five percent to the so called housekeeper, and he left ten percent to me, his wife! He gave *ten* percent to me! He thought more of his servant than he does me," she raged on.

"What, said Bruce—mocking her; after all the years you gave to that man? He left you, his long suffering wife, TEN percent? After all, it's not like he just married you a few weeks ago. Get 'da heck outta here!" he said, as he sat in Henry's chair and put his feet up on the desk. He dismissed her self-pity and just kept on laughing.

"You can mock me all you want, but I'm going to have it all. You just wait and see, she said as she pitched Bruce's feet off the desk "Screw them, and screw you! I'll have it all!"

"How do you plan to accomplish that? He already made his will!"

"You'll see! All I need is for you to stay away, and let me do what I have to do!"

"You plan to do them in one by one don't you?" He laughed contemptuously at her.

"I knew you were resourceful, but you're cleverer than I thought. So tell me, how do you plan to get away with it?"

"According to you, I got away with doing Billy in, so why should this be any different? All I need is a little creativity."

She started pacing as she fidgeted with her fingers. As she got more furious at Bruce, her nostrils flared. She seemed like any minute her head would spin around while she vomited something like green peas soup. Her voice went up two octaves higher as she raged on. With eyes bulging, she stood before Bruce.

"All my life, whenever I tried to count my blessings, I'm never able to move from zero to one. No one cares that my cup is upside down; as long as their cup is full and running over! Well, since I can't make it! I'm damn well gonna take it; so help me God! So Screw them! Screw Gunther! And screw you Bruce!"

Bruce remained calm as he responded to her fury. He said, "Whoa, wait a minute now! I can see that you've just lost your mind. I didn't say you got away with what you did to Billy, God rest his soul. I said you DISAPPEARED; there's a difference. As far as I'm concerned, the clock is ticking, and the only person who's on the way to being screwed is you, unless you deliver."

"You know something Bruce, if you think I'm capable of all that, why are you here bothering me? Aren't you putting your own life at risk?"

"No, I have no fear of my life where you're concerned."

"And why not?"

"Because, Billy and Henry, they love you; well, loved in Billy's case. They trusted you, and they wouldn't hurt you. I, on the other hand don't have those faults… I don't love you, and I wouldn't trust you with spit. I wouldn't have any problem snapping your scrawny little neck like a twig and not think twice about." Bruce said with a callous grin that quickly turned into looks that could kill. He took out a pack of cigarettes from the pocket of his blue floral shirt and reached into his Levi's jeans for a lighter, never once breaking eye contact with her. He attempted to light a cigarette.

As fearful as she was of him, she couldn't allowed him to spoil her plans. "What do you think you're doing," she asked," No one here smokes in this house! How would I explain the smell of tobacco!

Look Bruce, you've got to get out of here before they get back from the hospital!"

As she walked by the book shelf, she saw the copy of the Long Island Press. "What on earth is a copy of the Long Island Press doing here?"

"Oh-oh, you mean you don't know?" asked Bruce.

"Know what?"

"Look at the Art s & Entertainment page." She picked up the paper and turned to the page. She gasped. "No one, except that little half-wit could be responsible for this and I swear on her father's life, she is going to pay," she said.

A picture of Breana was sitting on Henry's desk. Effiedra picked it up and stared at it. Her face turned hot with hatred. She was about to throw the picture to the ground and smash it, but Bruce grabbed it from her hands. "Is this the girl," he asked.

"Yes! And I would love it if you would find her and just drop her off somewhere!"

"Why would you want to do that? I love this girl. If it wasn't for her, I wouldn't know where to find you. She's a genius. Don't you even think of hurting one hair on that pretty little head of hers... besides, you're my business not her."

"Don't pretend you have a heart, you swine. I know differently," said an angry Effiedra.

"Yeah, yeah, shut your trap. I'm outta here. Whatever you're planning, you better do it soon; my patience is waning,"

* * *

Dudley, Thelma and Breana were on their way from the hospital. They arrived in time to see the car drive away from their house. Dudley recognized the car.

"Thelma, something is going on, and I'm going to find out what it is," he said.

He drove the car up the driveway. Thelma and Breana got out and went inside the house. As they walked into the great hall, Effiedra was standing there, waiting. They thought she was waiting for news from the hospital. Breana began to speak.

"Effiedra, Father didn't—"

"Never mind that!" Effiedra snapped at her before she could finish the sentence. "How dare you go behind my back and put my picture in the paper? I'm the 'Mistress.' of this house now, and nothing must be done without my approval! The sooner all of you realize this the better!

Breana just stood there, her eyes red from a lack of sleep. She was infuriated, more so every minute as the rage from the past few months began to spew.

"You money hungry, ungrateful, tramp! You will never, ever be the 'Mistress' of this house, and you will never take the place of my mother! Not in this lifetime!"

Effiedra walked up to Breana with her fist raised. She was ready to strike her as she yelled, "How dare you!"

"The only way you are going to get to this child is through me!" Thelma said as she stepped between them. With eyebrows raised and fist clenched, she continued. "And if you ever touch one hair, or any place on my person, I will grind you into the pile of manure that you are! As long as you live in this house, you will never attempt to abuse this girl! She is *YOUR* superior!"

Effiedra stood in shock with Thelma's response. "We know what you're up to, and you won't get away with it! You'll be back in the gutter where you came from sooner than you think!" Thelma said. Effiedra stood there looking. She was speechless as Thelma continued. "You may fool some people, but you can't fool me! I knew Mr. Noble took in a snake when he brought you here! Penny Noble must be turning over in her grave! You're going to get what you deserve! I'll see to that!"

She took Breana by the hand. "C'mon honey." As they started to walk away, Effiedra shouted "Are you threatening me?"

Thelma slowly turned around; she raised her eyebrows, "Oh no, Miss Effiedra. I'm not threatening you; I'm promising you." Thelma stared her up and down and sucked her teeth.

"Your days here are numbered." she said as she led Breana away from the unpleasant confrontation.

"If I were you, I wouldn't talk about numbered days. My husband is probably dead and you are putting added stress on me? Do you think I'm going to keep you here after the way you've treated me? I'm gonna' bounce you out of here like a bad check!"

When Thelma heard her say that, she responded vehemently "Effiedra Wilson. You should know about bad checks; you *are* a bad check; you are a piece of work! And what's worse—you are delusional!" Then she slammed the door behind her.

"That's Noble! Effiedra Noble! Remember that!" Effiedra shouted back at Thelma.

Even though the door was already closed she continued to rant and rave. "I'm the head of this house while my husband is in the hospital! I have the right to fire you right now if I want! Don't tempt me."

Thelma was like a fire breathing dragon. She became like a lioness protecting her young. She opened the door and stuck her head into the room. "If you try to pull any of your antics with Breana OR me, I will be on you like white on rice; you gold digging tramp!" she said.

Later that afternoon, Thelma made Breana a cup of tea and brought it to her room. "Never mind dear, she said to Breana, that girl can't hurt you as long as I have breath, and if I'm dead and she hurts you, I'll haunt her to the grave." Breana smiled slightly.

"Anyway, she's played her trump card and we've seen her hand. Now that we know who she really is, I have a feeling she'll be out of here, and it can't be soon enough for me," said Thelma.

"I feel so bad for Father. He's never done anything to deserve this. He has no clue about her. When he finds out how deceiving she is, it'll break his heart."

"Well, he's still unconscious. Let's just focus on your father getting better and leave that girl alone with her foolishness. Let's pray about it and then you get some rest. We'll be going back to the hospital as soon as possible." She said as she adjusted Breana's sheets, encouraging her to go to sleep.

Downstairs, Effiedra went to her room contemplating what to do. She picked up the phone and started dialing. "Hi, it's me, I'm going to have to speed things up, and I need your help. Just bring the ring with you and come to the house. When you get here, ask for Thelma, when she comes to the door, just give her the ring, and tell her you couldn't sell it or something like that."

"Okay, I hope you know what you're doing because I'm not the fall guy type."

"Just do as I say, and be quick about it. I have to move *NOW!*"

Bruce drove to Harbor View and parked his car in front of the house. Dudley saw the car from his quarters and decided to go up to the main house. He walked up just in time to hear Thelma saying. "What...what are you talking about?" then she turned to face Effiedra and asked, "Isn't this the man that came here the other day and asked to speak to you? He claimed he was selling life insurance. I never had anything to do with this man or your ring. Not like you deserved it anyway." She said contemptuously.

"Oh, so that's why you took it. You didn't think I deserved it? Well, you listen to me! *I'm* the wife, and *you* are the servant! You don't get to decide what I deserve. When the police comes, we'll see who deserves what!"

She picked up the phone and dialed the police station. She identified herself as Mrs. Noble the American Ambassador's wife. She told the officer that there had been a robbery at her house. The police took the information, and were dispatched in minutes.

Bruce tried to leave. "No, you stay right where you are. I need you as a witness to this crime!" Effiedra said.

Breana came from her room to hear Effiedra accusing Thelma of taking something. She quickly joined them to see what was going on. "You're making a huge mistake right now, Effiedra." Dudley said to her. Effiedra ignored Dudley's warning.

Breana sat on the couch with Thelma, tears rolling down her cheeks. She began to pray aloud, "Oh God, please help us. The family that you gave me is falling apart. Lord, I know this is not your will. You would not have given me a family just to take it away like this. Please, Father God, help us through this."

As she prayed, Effiedra's face showed some remorse. However, the wheels were already in motion, she was trapped between Gunther and Bruce. Then, there was a knock at the door, and Effiedra answered it. It was the police.

"Good afternoon, Mrs. Noble. I'm Constable Ryan."

"Good afternoon. Thank you for your prompt response. As I told you on the phone, my ring had been stolen. I have no idea when. This man came here, and he asked for the maid. He said she gave him this ring to sell for her, but he was unable to find a buyer, so he's returning it. When I saw the ring, I couldn't believe my eyes. I recognized it right away. There is no question in my mind that this is my ring."

Bruce continued the innocent and confused act. He sat back and watched the show, with Effiedra as lead actress. Thelma looked at the Constable and said, "That ring has been in this family for as long as I can remember. Mr. Noble gave it to her not long ago. I never took it and I only saw this man once before. He came here asking for the lady of the house. He claimed to be some sort of salesman."

Constable Ryan took off his cap. He had a dark skin tone and his hair cut was so low, he appeared to be bald. The red band around his cap was saturated with sweat. He pulled a handkerchief from the pocket of his dark blue uniform pants and mopped his forehead.

"Boy, it's hot out there, whew..." he said. "Okay, let's get on with it," he said looking at Bruce.

Effiedra started acting inconsolable. She broke down in tears. "My husband is deathly ill in the hospital. They suspect he might have been poisoned, and now I just found that the ring he gave me had been stolen. "Did you say the Ambassador was poisoned?"

"Yes, Sir."

"And items are stolen from the house?"

"No, just one item, my engagement ring.

Constable Ryan turned to Bruce. "How did you get possession of the ring in question?"

"A woman gave it to me. I was supposed to sell it to repay her debt."

"And do you see the woman here now?"

"Yes Sir, she is standing right there." He glanced over in the direction of Effiedra who was standing near Thelma. Constable Ryan wrote down Bruce's statement.

"And what is your name and a number you can be reached at, Sir," asked the Constable.

"Uh, Doug, Doug Aragón and uh, I'm from out of town, so just call the Whitmore Hotel, Sir."

The Constable took his handcuffs, and he put them on Thelma. "Miss, I'm sorry but you have to come with me to straighten this thing out at the station,"

Breana quickly became hysterical. "Wait, I know Thelma didn't do anything wrong. Thelma is family! She would never do that!" Breana pleaded.

"Didn't you hear her say that I didn't deserve the ring? What other motive do you want? It came from the horse's mouth. It's almost like an admission if you ask me?"

"Well, nobody is asking you. Ever since you came here, my family is steadily falling apart, and you're not going to get away with it! By God, I will find a way to stop you," said Breana. She turned to

Thelma. "Don't worry Thelma, Dudley and I will fix this." Thelma remained still. Her angry eyes welled up with tears as she stared at Effiedra. With eyes full of fury, she said, "You just stepped into it girl! You are finished! You hear me? Finished! Dudley, look after Breana until I get back," she said as the police took her away.

"Don't worry, Thelma," Dudley said.

Breana began to sob. She wasn't sure of what could possibly happen next. Bruce walked out of the house and was getting ready to get into his car. Dudley stopped him at the curb. "Hold on man, not so fast. I want to ask you something."

Bruce was nervous. Dudley's stature was smaller than his but Dudley was packed with pure muscle. Bruce was not. He stood by his car with the door open.

"Have you ever been to this house before?"

"Ahh-no."

"So how did you know where to find Thelma to bring back the ring?"

"Well, she gave me the address. Look, I have some place to be. I gotta go."

As Bruce drove away Dudley muttered, "There's something rotten here, and I don't like the stench. I'm gonna find out what it is." He went back into the house. "Breana, pack a bag and let's go. You need to get out of here for a while."

"To go where?"

"Don't worry you'll be back before you know it." He drove her to the Whitmore Hotel, and rented a suite for her.

"Don't worry, you and Thelma will be back home before this night is over, or my name isn't Dudley More." As he got back into the car he said to no one in particular, "You just hang in there, Boss. I'm going to free you and Thelma.

* * *

Dudley drove to his old stomping grounds, 'Shanty Town'. He had plenty of friends who owed him favors. It was simple for him to pick up three of his most intimidating buddies to tag along. One of them had dread locks that hung down to his waist. The other two had their dread locks rolled up and tucked under knitted caps colored red, black, green and gold. Dudley and the men greeted each other. He explained the situation to them, and the role he wanted them to play in his plan. He also explained his suspicions to an acquaintance from the police force, who agreed to help. They all drove to Harbor View, the Noble's residence. Dudley opened up the door and escorted the men inside. He hurried to Effiedra's room and pounded on the door.

"What is it?" she asked in angrily.

Dudley signaled to the other men to wait by the door. Effiedra opened the door.

"Where the hell were you? I was looking all over the place. I need to go to the hospital to see my husband!"

"Not so fast, we have business to discuss.

What sort of business would I need to discuss with the likes of you. You're just the driver, so *drive* me to the hospital like I told you. Dudley ignored her disrespect and remained calm. He would let nothing she said derail his plan. "I want you to get your man on the phone and bring him here. We can't have this discussion without him."

"What man are you talking about?"

He scoffed. "You know who I'm talking about. He's been lurking around here for the past few weeks. The same man who you brought here to frame Thelma. Call him, or I swear, I'm going to sit here and let these men have whatever way they want with you. I will watch them tear you from limb to limb and split you from Stem to Stern."

"What m—"

Effiedra never got to finish the sentence. She sucked in her breath as the men showed themselves one by one. Dudley picked up the phone and forced it in her hand. "I would advise you to make the call now!" She knew she was in trouble; Dudley's expression said it all. Reluctantly, she took the phone and dialed. She became increasingly anxious with every ring as she waited on Bruce to answer. Finally, after what seemed like an eternity the line connected. She waited, "Hello-Hello…Bruce; are you there? …"Bruce, thank God. Could you come over here…please, it's important. You've got to come right now…I don't care about your stupid steak, just get over here!"

Bruce was so angry everyone in the surrounding hotel rooms could hear his response. "Why! Did you not tell me not to keep coming over? Now, suddenly you want me over there, pronto! What's going on, huh! You trying to set me up over there!"

"Bruce, if it wasn't important I wouldn't call you! Why would I try to set you up?"

Effiedra cringed at the sounds of Bruce's steak churning around in his mouth, followed by a monstrous burp.

"Okay—okay! I'll be there in a little while, but this better be good." He threatened.

Effiedra hung up the phone. "He-he's on his way."

"Very good," said Dudley. They all stared her down. Effiedra could not remember the last time she was so frightened. "May I use the bathroom, please? I promise not to try anything."

The men laughed. Then one said, "All like you couldn't be so stupid fi try sum'ting."

Effiedra looked to the floor and scurried to the bathroom. When she closed the door behind her, she took a deep breath and thought to herself, '*Think, Effiedra, think. How the hell do I get out of this one?'* She looked at the bathroom window. It was too small for her to climb through. She looked for weapons, "*Toothbrushes…the toilet bowl scrubber? Oh, what's the use! Those guys will kill me.*"

* * *

When Bruce arrived, Dudley instructed Effiedra to let him in. He was stunned when Dudley suddenly entered the room flank by three other men.

"What is this; what gives?" Bruce said nervously.

"Frisk him fellas," said Dudley.

Bruce tried to resist. "Now wait a minute…" One guy held Bruce's arms behind his back, while the other looked for weapons. It did not take long to find a handgun tucked in his pants.

"Take a seat, man. Make yourself comf'table," said Dudley. But Bruce was actually pushed into the chair when they were finished frisking him.

He looked around at the three men with dread locks, and then he looked at Dudley polishing his brass knuckles. Dudley moved closer and stood in front of his face.

"This afternoon, I asked if you had ever been to this house before, and you said no. I saw your car frequently in this neighborhood for the past two weeks. Your favorite parking spot is just up the street, so I know you are a liar, and people only lie when they have something to hide." Bruce was sweating. "Now, before I send you away in a body bag, you better start talking."

Bruce looked at Effiedra. "Don't look at her. She's got diplomatic immunity to fall on but you, you don't have a leg to stand on, so staat talkin, Mon."

"Look, Effiedra," Bruce spurted out, "I told you to make sure you knew what you were doing 'cause I'll never be no fall guy for you. Why'd you even call me over here? You want them to hear the truth or something?"

"That's why we're here, man - to hear the truth, so spill it!" Dudley said.

"Oh yeah? What's in it for me?" Bruce asked

"You get to keep your life! I could put you where no one will ever find you!" Dudley said through clenched teeth.

Bruce looked around and found that he was outnumbered, and

then he saw the police officer lurking in the doorway. *'All this for the sake of Effiedra, no way,'* he thought. "Effiedra gave me the ring. That lady didn't know anything about it." He spat out. Effiedra realized that her world was crumbling around her. "Shut up, you idiot!" she screamed at Bruce. "Don't you see? It's a trick!"

"You're calling me an idiot?" he replied angrily. "You've been married barely three weeks and you thought you could poison your Old Man and take all his money and get away with it? You stupid broad! Look, this basket case is not who you think she is. She's a fugitive from justice. She already killed one man in New York, and she gave me the ring to pay off a debt that she owes my boss."

The police officer standing in the doorway crossed the room saying, "Would you come down to the station and make that statement?"

"Yes Sir, I will, with pleasure."

"It makes my job much easier." He took both Bruce and Effiedra to the police station for further questioning. After Bruce's statement implicated Effiedra, she was arrested on suspicion of attempted murder and conspiracy to commit fraud. The charges against Thelma were dropped. She was released later in the day. "Dudley, where's Breana?" she asked as she was set free.

"I left her at the hotel until this whole mess got straightened out. We can get her now."

They picked up Breana and drove home discussing the rise and fall of Effiedra Wilson.

* * *

At the hospital, Henry finally regained consciousness. His family did not go back to the hospital until the following morning. When Thelma and Breana went to see him, he was out of intensive care. His motor skills were slowly returning, and he was fully alert. Breana ran to his bedside. "Father, thank God you're alright," she said, leaning over to kiss him on the cheek. "Losing you would be more than I could bear. I've never prayed so hard in all my life."

"Well it's good that you know the power of prayer, Sweetheart." His raspy voice began to clear the more he spoke.

"Where's Effiedra?" he asked.

"I'd rather have Thelma talk to you about her," she said, as the smile slowly vanished from her face.

Henry's brow wrinkled. He looked at Thelma. She looked to the heavens before she said anything. "Thelma, what's going on?" He asked.

Thelma looked at him and began to tell him of the havoc that Effiedra wreaked on the family. Besides what she did to us, she's wanted on suspicion of murder in New York, and she is the one who tried to kill you."

Henry lay back in the bed, bewildered. After he had digested the story, he said, "I can't believe I put our lives in jeopardy this way. How could I have given that calculating, evil woman the opportunity to destroy my family and me? What was I thinking?"

"You were just being the kind and generous man that you've always been, Sir. It's not your fault that the woman is the devil's spawn, and there's no way you could have known that she's a habitual criminal. She slithered into this family so smoothly like the snake that she is. But don't worry Sir, thanks to Dudley; she'll get everything she deserves."

"What did Dudley do?"

"People can say what they want about the 'Natty Dreadlocks', but they sure came through for us. They put the fear of God into that witch. Dudley brought three of them to the house. When she saw them she almost wet her pants. She and her accomplice had no choice but to come clean, but that's enough for now. You need your rest." Thelma said.

"When I think of how close I came to losing my family and

my life, I will never take anything for granted again, and I will not repeat the same mistake."

"Father, none of this is your fault. It's like Thelma said, you were just trying to help her."

"Will you tell Dudley thanks for me?" said Henry.

"We will. I think we should leave now so you could get your rest. We can talk more about it when you get home, Sir."

* * *

Henry spent five days in the hospital, and his family visited him daily. Upon his discharge, he spent many days at home. He used a cane until he regained full use of his left leg.

He sometimes would just stare into space, hardly requesting anything. The story of the scandal appeared in the *Daily Gleaner,* and the news shocked the country. Thelma made sure that Henry did not get the paper until the story died. Not that it mattered anyway. Henry was in his own world.

"Mr. Noble, you've been in this house since you came home from the hospital," Thelma said, "Don't you think you should go out some, look around and see what you've never had time to see when you had to go to work every day?"

Henry said nothing, but continued to look out of the window. Thelma looked over at the plate of food that she brought in hours ago, still on the tray untouched.

"Now I know that snapper with rice and peas is your favorite Jamaican dish. You haven't even touched it." Still, Henry had no remark. "You know, I can't stop you from blaming yourself. However, the Christian thing to do is to forgive yourself. As angry as we are at what Effiedra has done, we have to forgive her too. A person, who can't forgive, will be miserable every day of their life. You can't be at peace, if you harbor animosity. It seems hard to forgive, but if we love as Christ loves, it's possible." Thelma went to sit down next to him. "Sir, what is it? He turned to face her. "I need my wife," he held his head down. I need Penny."

"I wish she was here too Sir, but God rest her soul, she's gone. She's not coming back."

Chapter Twelve

It was the anniversary of Henry's encounter with Effiedra. He had been tossing and turning all night. As soon as dawn arrived, he felt the need for an early morning walk along the beach. The lights were still on across the harbor...allowing for one last view before they went out. Thelma was up making fresh squeezed orange juice. From the kitchen window, Henry's red jacket caught her eye. She watched as he returned and sat by the gazebo. She poured a glass of orange juice and brought it to him.

"Good morning Mr. Noble. I thought you might need some juice to refresh you from your walk."

"Oh, thank you Thelma, he said, "but do I dare accept a drink from a woman under this tree? I should be careful, you know," he said, smiling as he took the glass.

Thelma chuckled, "I wouldn't blame you one bit for being wary, Sir. I'm glad that you can at least joke about it now. I can't believe it has been a year since Hurricane Effiedra blew through here."

"I can't believe it myself, but it kept me tossing and turning all night long, just thinking of what she almost did."

"Anyway, enjoy your juice, Sir. I have to go finish making breakfast,"

Breana was now toward the end of her four year program in Public Relations. She was excited at the prospect of being through with studying and sacrificing fun times because of mid -terms, finals, and burning the midnight oil.

Thelma just started to brew the coffee. Suddenly, she looked at the clock on the wall. "I wonder if Breana is up," she mumbled. "I haven't heard her stirring around."

She was still in bed, asleep. The smell of the coffee slowly seeped into her room. She took a deep breath and the aroma enticed her enough to open her eyes. She turned her head to face the clock on her nightstand. "Half past seven! Oh my gosh!" she said realizing she had overslept.

She threw the covers back in a flash, and shot out of bed like a bullet. "Oh no, look at the time! I'm going to be so late, today of all days!"

She darted back and forth across the room as fast as lightening, trying to get ready in a hurry.

She breezed down the corridor and across to the kitchen. "Thelma! Finals are today, and I'm late! I stayed up late last night studying, a lot of good that will do me if I miss the test!"

"I'm so sorry, sweetie. I just realized that you were still sleeping. Here, I'll put your coffee in a thermos?"

"Thanks, Thelma." she said as she hurriedly gathered her things.

"Where's Dudley? I hope he realizes that I'm late. Bye Thelma. Tell Father I'll see him this evening," she said dashing out the door. .

"Bye, honey. Good luck!" she shouted after her.

Breana raced outside. Dudley was waiting patiently. "I thought you changed your mind about class this morning." Dudley commented. "What took you so long?"

"I overslept. Now I'm so late."

Dudley smiled. "No worries; I know a few short cuts."

They quickly arrived at the university. Dudley stopped the car in front of the building. Breana did not wait for him to open the door. She leaped out of the car and ran up the steps into the building.

The door to the examination room was closed. Mrs. Hammond, the Proctor, saw her peering through the glass in the upper portion of the door and opened the door half way. Miss Noble, I'm sorry I can't let you in, you're too late," she whispered.

"I'm so sorry. I stayed up last night, studying for the exam, and I over slept."

"I'm sorry too, but I can't let you in. The exam started ten minutes ago. The only thing you can do is ask the proctor in the next room if you could do your test in there, but you'll have to hurry because they are starting in the next five minutes. "Breana quickly thanked her and bolted for the room. She made it just in time to take a seat. She was the last to enter and the Proctor frowned at the interruption. "Ahem, as I was saying, you may bring your exam to the front and exit the class room as soon as you're finished. Any questions before we begin?" No one responded they were all anxious to get it over with. "Very well, you have three hours. You may begin…now.

Breana looked over the test she had been studying so hard for, and gave God thanks for all the preparation. She completed the exam in record time and confidently turned her paper in. As she exited the classroom, she heard a familiar voice call her name. Breana turned to see Keith. He was a nice looking young man. He had returned to school after dropping out, and was working full-time. They had taken some classes together and had even helped each other with studying.

"Hi Breana, I was looking for you in there." He said pointing to the room he was in earlier. "You missed the exam; what happened?" Breana smiled at him and gave him a quick hug.

"Hello Keith!" I didn't miss the exam. I was running late but thankfully the exam hadn't started in the other room so I was able to take it there."

"Oh, that's good. It would've been a shame after all that studying we did." He snickered.

"Yeah, I know. Breana said, "I don't know what I would've done, but thank God I don't need to think about that. I'm just ready to get home and relax."

"I know what you mean. I'm done too. I could give you a lift home if you'd like. As long as I don't have to go into the house; your maid doesn't like me at all."

"Thelma? She is the sweetest person I know. She was just mad because you were smoking that stuff *AND* you called her a pit bull."

"Well, I eventually apologized didn't I? Plus, I've never smoked around you."

"Yes, and I appreciate that but it will take more than an apology to get on good ground with Thelma. Anyway, Dudley is supposed to be picking me up. I just need to call and let him know that I'm ready since I finished earlier than expected. Besides you don't even have a car." She laughed humorously.

"Very funny Breana…ha-ha. A friend of mine is giving me a ride. Why wait for Dudley? By the time you call and he gets here, you would've been home, if you go with us. And for your information I'll be getting my own car real soon."

"Oh come on Keith, you know I'm just joking with you." Breana thought for a while.

"You're right. I'll be home even before Dudley leaves for my scheduled pick up time. Okay, *Mr. I'm getting my car real soon.* Let's go."

Chapter Thirteen

A woman stood in front of the mirror in her bedroom. She was dressed in khaki clam diggers and a white buttoned down shirt with elbow length sleeves. The outfit clung to her 145 pound, shapely body, like husk on a corn cob. In her fortyish years, Susan Dooley was still turning heads. Her jet black hair with just a hint of silvery gray shimmering through it was neatly combed. *'I'll have to start dyeing it soon,'* she thought. She fumbled inside her makeup kit, and she picked out a tube of red-wine lipstick and carefully passed it across her voluptuous lips. There was neither a line nor a wrinkle on her chocolate brown face.

She heard a key tumbling inside the lock of the front door, and she quickly dropped the lipstick back inside the kit. The door opened and the young man stepped in. He wore khaki pants and a brown turtle neck shirt with long sleeves. His pectoris, deltoids, and biceps were straining the fabric. His hair was trimmed low and his face was neatly shaved with a thin mustache. His lanky body was dark and fine. Upon his entrance, Susan's brown eyes lit up. She wrapped her arms around him.

"Keith! What are you doing home? Unless I slept through a couple of days, this isn't Friday evening!" she said.

"I finished my exam and I took some time off to take care of a little business," he said, hugging her back.

"Oh. What kind of business?"

"Come sit down let me talk to you," he replied.

He held Sue by the arm and they both walked over to the sofa and sat down. Sue looked at him intensely.

"You remember Bunny?" he asked.

"Bunny Samson? Of course I remember him. Who could forget Bunny? Didn't he leave to go to foreign a long time ago?"

"Yes, he was in America, but apparently he's not there anymore." Keith replied.

"How do you know he's not there anymore? From the time he left Jamaica he has never sent us a line. How do you know where he is?"

"They deported him back here."

"Deported!" She exclaimed, "Why?"

"I have no idea. I don't know the details. All I know is he's back."

Keith sat next to Susan on the sofa. He picked up his feet and rested them on the coffee table.

"Feet off the furniture please!" Sue said slapping him with a newspaper. "Whatever bad habit you picked up, leave it in the streets. So what does Bunny have to do with you taking off from work?" she asked.

"He asked me to help him with a little problem he's having. He wants me to keep something here for a day or two."

"Oh really! Now that he needs help, AGAIN, he knows where to find us…typical ingrate!

So what is it that he wants you to keep?"

"He's outside. I'll let him come in and tell you himself."

Sue raised her eyebrows "Outside! You didn't say he's already here! I'm not sure I want to keep anything for him. He is too *bloody* ungrateful!"

"Don't be so hard Sue, cha mon. I'm just trying to help out a friend!"

"I think you better tell me what the story is before I decide how hard I'm going to be."

"Sue, he can tell you better than I. Why don't you let him in?"

"Why, because, he left Jamaica to seek a better life; next thing I hear, he's sitting in front of my house…deported! If I.N.S. deported him from the good old U. S. of A., you can bet he was up to no good! He doesn't sound like the Bunny I used to know! It's beyond me how someone like him had the opportunity to improve himself and wasted it by coming home in disgrace. This is a crying shame before God! Um-Um-Um-Hey!"

"Well, this American man, who lives out here, has something that belongs to Bunny's boss in America. Since Bunny owes his boss some money, they have an agreement that if he gets what his boss is after, that it will clear up Bunny's debt. That's what he told me," said Keith

"You know what Keith, you're right. Let him tell me himself; because, you're not making any sense. Keith, you're my baby brother, and I've been taking care of you and keeping you out of trouble since Mama passed. If this is anything illegal, I'm not going to let this reject drag you down with him; this story sounds very shady to me."

"Sue, he promised to help me with the money to buy the car I told you about. You know how much I need this car. If you do this for me, I will never ask you for another thing."

Susan got up from the sofa and began pacing back and forth. "Now where did I hear those same words before? And from whom did I hear them? Oh, now I remember! It was right here in this house, and from you. Every time you wanted something from me is always the last time!"

"Good Lord! Sue work with me on this; it will pay off, I promise. Why you being so haaad? (Hard) This is different! The guy is counting on me. I can't let him down at the last minute!"

"It's only because I love you is why I'm doing this," said Sue, "Since he's already outside, tell him to come in."

Keith jumped up off the sofa and kissed her on the cheek. "Thanks Sue, you're the best," he said, as he ran outside to the van.

Bunny Samson was impatient. He got out of the van and stood

by the passenger side. As Keith got to the van, Bunny asked him, "What took you so long? I thought she would be awake before you got back out here."

"Relax man. No problem; every-ting irie. Sue said. It's ok."

Bunny walked to the back of the van and opened the doors. Breana was lying on the floor, bound, gagged and blindfolded. She made no sound. They rolled her up inside the rug again and carried her in the house, and the third guy drove the van away. When they entered the house, Sue met them at the door, laughing.

"I knew you were teasing me all along! You finally got some ambition and bought your sister a new rug!"

While she carried on about her new rug, Bunny and Keith put the rug down and started unrolling it.

"Jesus Christ, my God! Have mercy on this poor girl! What is this? Keith what have you done?" Breana was just emerging from the sleeplike state that they had induced on her.

"How on earth could you all do this? What have you gotten yourself into? You told me Bunny wanted you to keep some*thing*, not some*one*!"

"Bunny made me promise to let him tell you himself."

Sue very irately replied, "Bunny made *YOU* promise? *He* made *YOU* promise!" What do YOU owe this sad excuse for a human being that he made you promise him to deceive me? Huh! Tell me! What is it that you owe this creep that you would lie to me for him?"

"But I really didn't lie to you, Sue. I just didn't tell you about the girl!"

"SOMETHING is a major difference from SOMEONE! So you lied!

Bunny looked her up and down. He tilted his head to the side and snarled, "Nice to see you again, Miss Sue. After all these years, you haven't changed. You're still miserable."

"Don't confuse being stern with being miserable. If only someone was that *miserable* with you, you might have been a better man."

"Hmmph," Bunny grunted, "Whatever you say. I won't be here long anyway."

"Who said you're going to be here at all? You are not going to involve me in your schemes. I'm not like Keith; I won't let you push me around."

"Sue! It's no big deal! He's just trying to force the man to give him back something that was stolen from his boss! She won't be hurt, and she won't be here for long!" Keith interrupted.

"That's the story he gave you, and you believed him? She said incredulously. "She is already hurt! In case you haven't noticed, she's bound and gagged!"

Sue stepped toward the telephone and picked up the receiver. "I'm calling the police."

Bunny pulled a gun from the waist of his faded blue jeans. "Not a good idea at all, Sue…put it dung rite nung." (down right now)

Sue looked at the gun and slowly put the phone down. Keith was stunned. His face looked as if a freight train was coming right at him and his back was against a wall. He couldn't believe Bunny was acting this way. He was about to protest but Bunny wasn't having anymore interruptions. Bunny shouted "Shut the hell up, you don't want to start with me boy! This isn't a marble game or stick ball… like the way you always cried every time you lost. We're grown men now in the real world. I don't want to hurt you Sue, but I can't let you call the police and mess everything up."

Bunny pulled the phone cord from the wall, wrapped it around the phone and slammed it on the table. He looked at Keith and demanded, "Help me get her up."

They both picked Breana up and sat her on the couch. Bunny stooped down in front of her and patted her face until she stirred, "That's it, wakey-wakey. Miss, miss, listen to me. Are you listening?" Breana made a noise. "You're being held for ransom. As long as your father cooperates you won't get hurt. I'm gonna remove the gag from your mouth, so don't scream. If you do, I'll put it back, and it will be worse for you then. Do you understand?" Breana was confused. *'Who are these people? I'm being held for ransom?'*

"I said do you understand?"

Breana nodded her head. He cautiously removed the gag. "My mouth is dry. May I have some water, please?" Breana asked in a feeble voice.

Bunny looked at Keith. "Bring her some water."

She was not only parched, her belly told of her hunger. She ignored her stomach's request. They may have brought her water, but she was afraid to ask for anything more.

Keith filled the order and held the glass of water for Breana to drink.

"Thank you," she said, as she started gulping it down. Keith almost responded with, *you're welcome,* but he caught himself. So far he hadn't said anything, and if this all worked out Breana would never know that he was involved.

"Honey, don't waste your breath thanking these low lives for anything," Sue sneered.

"Shut up, woman before you cause a crisis in here!" Bunny snapped at Sue.

"Boy! I remember when my mother had to feed you because you didn't have food!" Sue replied, "She treated you like you were her own child, and this is how you repay her? You coerced her son in criminal behavior! Dishonor the house where she fed you, and hold us hostage at gunpoint! Where is your morality and sense of loyalty?" Sue said, trying to appeal to his conscience if he had one. "I never had nothing in my life! So this is how I have to get it!" said Bunny.

Sue's temper flared, and her voice echoed in every room in the house. In spite of Bunny being over six feet tall with a gun, she stood in front of him, 5 ft. 5 inches, in heels. She pointed her finger at his face and shouted, "Don't you dare blame your behavior on poverty! You can blame it on schemes to get rich quick! Blame it on covetousness! Blame it on laziness! But don't you *ever* blame it on poverty!

You're not the only one to be born poor! You even got the chance to go to America! The land of opportunity, and you blew it! It is people like you that go to foreign and create problems that give Jamaicans a black eye! Never mind the decent upstanding Jamaicans who work hard to improve themselves! You're a disgrace to the human race! Look at this poor young lady, ehh? What has she or her family ever done to you to deserve this?"

As Sue raged on, Keith was huddled in a corner of the room sweating and holding his stomach. He was nauseated as he faced the truth; he was in over his head.

Bunny looked up to the ceiling; this was not the soft spoken Sue he grew up with. He rolled his eyes. "Unbelievable." He said. "Ten thousand houses in this neighborhood, and I had to come to one with a woman who can't keep her trap shut. The only reason you get away with that attitude is the kindness of your mother. Auntie Iris was good to me. In fact, she was about the only one who ever cared anything about me."

"And her effort seems wasted on you. Instead of trying to make a difference in someone else's life, look what you're doing to an innocent person; she has never done anything to you!" Sue looked at Breana. The blindfold cloth was now wet with tears, Breana trembled and grew more terrified each minute. She heard voices but recognized none. '*Where is this place?*' She wondered. Amid the tears, she started whispering her prayer.

Oh Lord, every time I believed that my troubles are behind me, they only end to begin again. Lord, why am I being tested so violently? Is there a purpose for all of this?

If not for your mercy, in my earlier years, I would be dead. You kept me alive through your mercies. Lord, please show me the same mercy now and deliver me from these that are tormenting me; If not for my sake Lord, then for my father's. Lord you know his heart. He's been through so much pain. Lord, don't let him have to go through the pain of losing me too.

Bunny looked at Breana and saw her lips moving. "Hey! What are you whispering over there? If you're praying, you better pray that your father cooperates, so you can go home; the sooner the better so I can get out of this mad woman's house. She lucky her mother was kind to me, or I would shut that big mouth of hers for good."

"Don't even call Mama's name!" said Sue. She faced Keith. "And you! She grab Keith's arm and shoved him into the next room and shut the door. How could you allowed this boy to spin his web and rope you in like a fly; because you want what…money to buy a car! The same car that I told you I would help you to buy next month when I get paid! You just couldn't wait; you had to have it now! I work my fingers to the bones to send you to Mico College, and it's all for naught! I was the Principal of Red Hills Elementary School, working hard here in Jamaica and still, to make extra money took leave every summer to work in the States. "I cleaned people's houses. Yes, I cleaned floors and toilets just to make sure I had enough money to pay for your tuition and essentials. And this is my reward, a reprobate minded idiot for a brother!"

"Papa was a deacon in the church," she continued, "He was an upstanding man! His only encounter with the police was when he died, and he got a state funeral! He must be turning over in his grave right now!" While Sue quarreled in her West Indian dialect; Keith was sitting on a chair in the opposite side of the room. He realized he had bitten off more than he could chew. In his confusion, he began to speak. "But Sue—"

"Shut up! Sue interrupted, "but Sue' nothing! I don't want to hear anything from you! When you dropped out of college, I was so disappointed with you. You dropped out because of him, remember? The same no account dope in the next room. When you came to me saying you had started taking classes again so you could finish and get your degree, I have to admit that I was skeptical at first, but you really showed me that you were serious. I was so proud, and you were doing so well. Now look at you! This fool comes back in your life and here you go throwing away everything you worked so hard to accomplish. There is a difference between cabbages and kings! Bunny is definitely cabbage! Stop hanging out with him. Don't use your head for a hat rack!"

"I'm sorry. I was just trying to help him out. I didn't know it was going to be like this, or I wouldn't have anything to do with it. Bunny made it seem like a piece of cake."

Sue got more irate with each word that rolled off Keith's tongue. "It's a piece of cake for him; because, he is a seasoned criminal! You, on the other hand, are a new recruit! You're in over your head!" she bellowed.

Bunny who was listening through the door suddenly burst into the room yelling, "Shut up…Shut up! I don't want to hear another damn word out of you. If you say one more thing, I'll slap the taste out of your mouth! I mean it Sue! Bunny looked like a person possessed. To Keith's observation it was obvious Bunny had completely lost his mind.

"Bunny!" Keith shouted advancing toward him. "It seems like you come back from foreign as a mad man *to rawtid* (Patois-Jamaican Slang); you waving gun and threatenin' people? No wonder they deported your ass! Who would want you behaving like that in their Country?"

"You tink mi care. Shut you blasted mouth' b'fore mi shut it fi you. You mus' have peanuts for brains. I'm the one with the gun! If anyone o' you try fi leave dis room, I won't hesitate to use it."

* * *

Dudley was mystified. After arriving at the University, he learned that Breana had already left. He was leaving the building wondering why Breana hadn't called to tell of her change in plans. As he reached the parking area, he saw a man put something that looked like a ticket on his windshield. The man got into a white van and drove away. *'That can't be a ticket,'* he thought. *'Martials Home Decorating, it must be an ad, but it seems like I've seen that guy before,'* he thought.

After he read the note, he hurried into the car. He drove to the Embassy as fast as he could. Dudley parked the car and rushed into the building. The guards were alarmed and stopped him. "Listen", he said. "You already know I'm Mr. Noble's driver. This is an emergency." He briefly explained the urgent matter to them and he was allowed through to Mr. Noble's office. He didn't need to be announced. He passed the secretary and went in. "Mr. Noble! Mr. Noble!" he said almost out of breath.

"What is it, Dudley?"

"It's that no good bastard, Sir; Bruce…he's back, and he's got Breana. I saw him!"

Dudley handed the note to Henry. With trembling hands he fumbled to open the note. His face grew as pale as the shirt he was wearing when he read the contents.

'If you want to see your daughter alive again, follow my instructions. I want the ring or one million U.S. dollars in unmarked bills. I will contact you at the Embassy to arrange the drop off. I strongly suggest that you keep the police out of it.

"Oh dear God, not again, How did this happen?" Henry asked frantically. Dudley sat on a chair still breathing heavily.

"Sir, I dropped Breana off at the University, and she went inside. I figured, since the exam is going to be three hours, and you had planned to drive yourself to work this morning, it wouldn't make sense for me to drive home and back again to pick her up. So I went down to the diner to have a cup of coffee. Then I went down to the club house to shoot some billiards with the guys. The Proctor told me that she left with a friend after taking the exam."

Henry was distraught. What friend?

"No one knew for sure, but it was a male. Don't worry boss, we'll get Breana back. When I get finished with him, he's going to wish he had never set foot on Jamaican soil."

"Dudley, call Thelma; tell her we'll be late."

* * *

At Sue's house, confusion among the occupants prolonged. Although Sue was not the one with the gun, her mouth was her weapon. She didn't care what Bunny threatened. She believed God would intervene. She said a quick prayer under her breath.

"So, wait a minute!" she said, "You think I'm going to sit here and let you keep this poor young lady roped up and not offer her anything to eat or drink? I'm going into the kitchen to fix her something to eat. You can shoot me in the back if you're coward enough." She got up and walked toward the kitchen. Bunny turned his head swiftly in Sue's direction. "Dat's di first sensible ting you said all day. As a matta o' fact, why don't you fix us all someting? That should shut you up for a while." I'm going to make a call. Don't try anything while I'm gone or there'll be hell to pay! He strode into Sue's office to use the phone.

While they were arguing, Breana decided to make a move. She had heard enough now to realize that Keith was one of her captors. Ever since she was grabbed from behind, she wondered what had happened to him. At first she thought he was tied up and gagged just as she was, but she dismissed that when all she heard the abductors talk about was what they were going to do with *her*. With no mention of Keith, she had feared the worst. Then she heard his voice, muffled at first so she was uncertain, but now she had distinctly heard him call the other guy's name…Bunny. What she didn't understand was why he would call himself her friend and do something so despicable. *I have to get out of here somehow.* She thought. After what she heard, she thought maybe she could play on Keith's sympathy. Breana gathered up her courage. She was going to save herself or die trying.

She began speaking cautiously. "Keith…Keith, I can't see you, but I know you're there. I need go to the bathroom, please?" Keith went still and Sue glanced at him. "Wait a minute. You know this girl?"

"Uh…yeah, we took some classes together." He said guiltily. Sue threw her hands up. "Oh, this is just perfect. You have really sunk to an all-time low." For a while Keith couldn't react. He was already ashamed of his involvement and now Breana knew. "Well!" Sue said looking directly into Keith's eyes. "Do something, help her. *Help* her!" She stressed.

"Hey, what's going on here" said Benny walking back into the room. "She just asked to use the bathroom. I was just about to take her." Keith said eyeing Sue with understanding.

"Yes, Bunny, that's the least you can do, for heaven's sake," Sue chimed in.

Breana was grateful for that extra vote, and had the instinct that Sue would help her out.

Bunny got nervous about that request. "How you so sure she really wants to go to the baat—room?"

Sue lied, "Because every time I look at her, she is wriggling around, and I don't want any accident on my Queen Ann chair that Mama left me!"

"Okay, I'm going to loosen her feet, but not the blindfold nor her hands, so you got to help her in the baat—room."

Thanks to growing up with Thelma, Breana understood patois.

Sue looked at Keith and winked. Keith nodded to her. Then he said, "I'll go make us some tea and something to eat, while Sue helps her to the bathroom."

Keith walked out of the room and went towards the kitchen. He put a skillet on the stove and began looking for matches to light it. Then he quickly lit the fire, poured water inside the hot skillet, and he dropped in a piece of onion and garlic. He filled a pot of water and put it on the other burner for some tea. Keith hurried outside through the back door and went around the back of the house to the bathroom window. He quietly removed the jalousie panes from the window, and he hurried back to the kitchen.

Bunny untied the cord from Breana's ankles and helped her to her feet.

Sue went over and held Breana by the upper arm. She accompanied Breana to the bathroom, and she locked the door behind her. She removed the blindfold from Breana's face and the cord from her wrists.

Breana pleaded and whispered, "Please, help me get out of here, you're my only hope."

"Never mind child, I'm right with you. Now you just climb up on me. I'll help you up to the window, be quiet."

Sue helped Breana up through the window. Breana jumped to the ground. Sue managed to lift herself up and squeeze through the window; then she ran with Breana to the next house over.

Bunny was getting weary. He took a rest from pacing the floor, and sat on the sofa.

The front of his green and yellow floral shirt was open. Had it not been for his long black dreadlocks, one couldn't tell where the sofa stopped and his shirt began.

When the aroma from the garlic and onion passed his flaring nostrils, he took a good whiff. "Hmm...that boy always knew how to work the kitchen. Some tings neva change," he mumble to himself, that's all he's good for." He hollered in a down home Jamaican tone as he lay back on the couch. "Mek—haste wit di food Keith! I man starving!"

Keith quickly made the tea, a special concoction of various island herbs his grandmother taught him and Sue to make for when they needed to relax or suffered with insomnia. He brought it to Bunny saying in patois, "Here drink dis, it will sekkle you stomach until di food ready." Bunny accepted the drink and sipped it until it became cool, then quickly downed the entire contents of the cup and set it down on the table in front of him. He burped and yelled. "Hurry up wit di food no mon!"

* * *

Sue and Breana made it to a neighbor's house. Sue knocked on the door.

"Just a minute," came a strong female's voice from inside the house. A middle aged woman of dark complexion came to the door. "Good evening Aunt Dora! Please let us in quick, Sue said almost whispering. This is an emergency. We have to call the police!"

She quickly opened the door and let them in.

"Poolice! Why?"

"Shhhh, I will explain later."

While they were calling the police, Keith continued to simmer garlic and onions as he watched Bunny drift off to sleep. *Peanuts for brains, huh*? "Hmph!" Keith turned off the stove and continued to keep watch over Bunny as he slept. He watched the gun that Bunny still had a firm grasp on. Keith prayed that Bunny would drop the gun, or stay sleeping until the police came.

While Bruce was on the phone with Henry arranging the money drop off, the police were on their way to Waltham Park Road. Just as Henry hung the phone up, it rang again. It was Breana. She was able to make the call from Aunt Dora's home. Henry was relieved to hear her voice. He immediately left to meet her.

When Henry and Dudley arrived, Breana ran into her father's arms. "Father, I was so worried about you!"

Henry hugged her then turned her around to check if she was okay. Breana's lips were dry and white. Her hair smelled of sweat and was matted against her head. Her skin was streaked with lines from the blindfold and her eyes were red from crying.

"You were worried about me? You are the one that was kidnapped!

I was so afraid of what they might do to you. Did they hurt you in any way?"

"No, except for the blind fold, they didn't hurt me."

Aunt Dora was in her kitchen fixing snacks and drinks for everyone. She became a little overwhelmed by her company and all that she was hearing, but she was excited nonetheless. "Let's get this poor girl some-ting in her belly, yes?" She walked over to Breana and Henry with a tray of sliced hard dough bread, avocado, bulla cake and cheese, and ham sandwiches, typical quick Jamaican snacks served with lemonade. Dudley immediately dug in. Breana was too distracted to eat.

"Thank God you're alright. Bruce is responsible for this. He came back for the ring, and that's why he held you for ransom," Henry said.

"Sue, how can I ever thank you? You were so brave. I'm so grateful to you," Breana said as she reached out her hand to Sue.

"It's alright child. It's alright. All is well that ends well," Sue said with a smile.

Henry said, "I too, thank you for helping my daughter Sue."

Henry turned to Aunt Dora. "Miss Dora, is it?" He asked.

"Yes. Mr. Ambassador, Sir, replied Aunt Dora, but call me Aunt Dora. Everybody knows me by that name."

"We are so sorry for the imposition Aunt Dora."

"Oh no Sir. It is no imposition at all. It is a honna fi help yu in yu time a need. Yes Sir we Jamaicans are not all bad you know. Some o' di the rotten ones dem will make it seem so, but it no true."

Henry walked over to shake her hand. "Thank you so much for your kindness and hospitality." He then slipped her a $100 bill in U.S. currency.

Aunt Dora looked at Henry as if she had seen Jesus. "Oh, thank you, Sir," she said, smiling at Ben Franklin.

* * *

When the police arrived, both houses were surrounded. Constable Miller and three armed policemen strategically walked into Sue's house for they were told that Bunny was still there with Keith. Constable Miller led the way inside. With his gun pointed, he cautiously moved through the kitchen, the dining room, and into the living room. From where he stood, he saw Bunny Samson lying on the couch with Keith sitting in an arm chair watching him. When Keith saw them, he said, "Thank God."

"Shhh," Constable Miller signaled with his index finger over his lips. He motioned for Keith to move out and for the three other police officers to come closer. All four of them gathered inside the living room, looking in disbelief at Bunny.

He was lying on the couch with one leg stretched out on the couch, and the other leg on the floor. His right arm bent at the elbow and lay across his chest with his fingers curled loosely around the gun. Constable Miller quietly and with extreme caution, removed the gun from Keith's hand and handed it to the officer behind him. Then, he stood over Bunny and shouted, "Samson!" Bunny awoke suddenly. He was disoriented. He jumped into a standing position. "What's going on? Where am I?" he shouted.

Officer Miller grabbed him on the collar. "SAMSON! This Philistine is down on you, and he's going to break the jawbone of YOUR ASS!" He shouted. He slapped Bunny to the right of his face and straightened it with another slap to the left. Then he pushed him down on the couch. "Jesus Christ! This is police brutality! Murda hoi! Murda!" Bunny cried out, as he flailed his arms and bobbed his head in defense.

"In answer to your question, 'where am I?' You are on the verge of a PRISION SENTANCE! It's trash like you who gives law-abiding citizens a bad name abroad! Do you know that the girl you kidnapped is the American Ambassador's daughter? Are you trying to start an international incident?"

"I don' know what yo talkin''bout. Ah don't kidnap nobody," said Bunny as he sat on the couch, cowering.

"Shut up! You got the chance to make something of yourself in America! Yet, you neither got SALVATION nor EDUCATION! You're under arrest!"

He placed the cuffs on Bunny and pushed him in front. Bunny resisted all the way to the car. People on the streets watched the drama unfold as they made gestures and exchanged opinions of what they think happened.

Constable Miller went next door to question Aunt Dora. He first tried to question Breana about her ordeal, but she was too distraught. Henry said, "Officer, I know the man who is responsible for all of this. He expects to receive a ransom for my daughter. He gave me these instructions on the phone before I came here, Henry said, handing the note to the police. This is my chauffer; he has some information also.

"Your name, Sir?"

"Dudley More."

"Okay, what can you tell us?"

Dudley repeated the ordeal, and then he said, "I'm certain that the note came from a man called Bruce."

"Alright, Mr. More, thank you. If I need more information where can I reach you?"

Dudley said, the same address; the Nobles house."

Officer Miller turned to Sue and asked, "And what is your name, Ma'am?"

"Susana Dooley,"

"Okay, Susana, what can you add to this information?"

Susan's recollection of the minute to minute encounter was right on target.

"Very interesting, and vivid recollection" he said.

"Officer, if I live to be a hundred, I would never forget what happened here today." Sue replied. Keith was standing next to Susan. Officer Miller looked at him.

"You are Keith, I presume?"

"Yes Sir,"

"So what part did you play in all of this fiasco, Keith?"

"Well Sir, this fellow Bunny Samson. I knew him a long time, and he was never mixed up in anything illegal. He came to me at about seven o'clock this morning and asked me for a favor."

"Were you involved in taking Breana from the University?"

"Well, yes Sir that was part of the deal." Constable Miller shook his head.

"Mr. Noble, as I remember you had some trouble last year around this same time?"

"Yes Sir, we certainly did, and I thought it was all behind us."

"I'm very sorry for all the troubles you've been experiencing in our country, Sir, but we are going to make sure that you get justice. He's expecting you at 8 o'clock you say?"

"Yes. He said eight o'clock behind the Pink & Black Store."

"Okay, you get ready to keep the appointment. Your daughter is out of danger, so just go now." Constable Miller turned to Keith. "As for you young man, you're under arrest."

One of the policemen supplied handcuffs and put Keith's hands behind his back. Keith was terrified as he looked at his sister for help. Sue looked at him, overwhelmed by emotion until she felt numb. Breana watched as he was placed in the police car. She shook her head as she walked away.

* * *

Dudley drove Henry and Breana home. The grandfather clock down the hall had just struck six when they walked inside the house.

"Thelma," he called out.

"Mr. Noble, is Breana with you? Dudley hadn't brought her home since she went for her exam this morning."

"Yes, Thelma, she's with me."

Thelma noticed they were both exhausted. Breana briskly walked up to Thelma and hugged her as if she would not let go.

"Child, what is it?" Thelma asked, as she heard Breana whimpering on her shoulder. She looked to Henry and Dudley for answers.

"Thelma, do you remember Effiedra's accomplice who helped her frame you a year ago?"

"Yes Sir, I would never forget that."

"Well, he's back." said Henry. He relayed the event while Thelma listened in disbelief "I never thought that guy would have the gall to come back here." she replied.

Henry said, "This time he did, but I'm going to make sure he never set foot on this Island again."

Henry and Dudley were deep in their own thoughts as they drove to meet Bruce.

"Dudley, he said suddenly, "You have no way of knowing this, but this is not the first time Breana has been kidnapped. The first time she was beaten and left to die at the bottom of a ravine. We didn't find her until the next day."

Dudley's nose began to flare as he fumed in anger. "If they would just give me five minutes with him, just five minutes, so I could bounce him like a rubber ball. It's such a pity that he drove away this morning before I realized it was really him."

"Well, thank God for the way it turned out today."

"I'm glad too Sir, because if I had gotten my hands around his throat, there is no telling what would have happened."

* * *

It was 7:45 P.M., and they were in the vicinity of where to make the drop. They drove around to make sure all the policemen were in place. At 8:00 P.M., Henry got out of the car and walked behind the Pink & Black store. He had a big, brown shopping bag folded under his arm, with the decoy money inside. The money was skillfully wrapped to ward of any suspicion. He walked over toward the dumpster, and then glanced around. He placed the bag in the spot where Bruce had instructed, and left. Minutes later, Bruce walked out from the shadows and cautiously crept over to the dumpster. He started to grin as soon as his hand touched the bag. He picked it up and started to leave. But he was trapped.

"We've got you surrounded! Walk toward us with your hands up where we can see them!" Officer Miller said through his bullhorn as he shone the light on Bruce. When he heard the voice of the police, Bruce's first instinct was to run in the opposite direction. He started to do so, but quickly changed his mind when he saw that he was surrounded on all sides. He turned around and stood in the street. Officer Miller slowly walked up to him with handcuffs and cuffed him. When they reached the police station, the officer was about to let him out of the car. Bruce looked at him slyly, smirked.

"I guess you'll be letting me out real soon, if that Mr. Noble wants to see his pretty little girl alive again. If my guys don't hear from me by 10:00, she's as good as dead."

He started to laugh, but his haughtiness was cut short with the officer's response.

"Think again, idiot." said Officer Miller. The police brought out Keith and Bunny.

"Dammit!" said Bruce. He clenched his fist and bit his lips. 'Damn armatures, I should have known' he thought. His eyes were as cold as steel as shook his head in defeat.

"Is this the man you've been working with?" asked Officer Miller.

They both answered, "Yes officer."

They all went through arraignment, but Keith received special consideration because it was his first offence, and for helping Breana escape. He became a witness for the prosecutor.

When Henry returned home, he found Breana was lying on the couch with her head in Thelma's lap.

"Father, you're here! Are you okay?" Breana said in excitement when she saw him.

"I'm fine now, Pumpkin."

"So, how'd everything go?" Thelma asked, eagerly.

"Just know that Bruce won't be a problem on this island anymore."

"Thank God. Lord, every time I think of how this could have turned out," Thelma said, nervously twisting a handkerchief she was holding.

"Thelma, don't. It's not worth raising your pressure," Henry said in hope of calming her down, "He'll be getting his just desserts. He will never bother us again."

Breana said, "I can't believe how people rewrite other people's lives out of greed, even the ones who say they're your friend."

"What do you mean Pumpkin?" Henry asked.

I thought Keith was a friend. We even studied together. Thelma you may remember him; he met me here once and you made him leave."

Thelma thought for a moment. "You mean that knucklehead boy who came here smelling of ganja? "Yes", Breana affirmed. "Oh my Lord...I knew he was no good as soon as I set mi eyes pon him... had a nerve to called me a Pit-bull! He's lucky I wasn't there. Listen Breana, I never trusted that boy. All we can do is pray for him and just thank God you're safe now.

It had been a long day that finally came to an end. They all went to their rooms, attempting to reclaim normalcy. Henry walked over to his clothes closet and took a bathrobe from the hanger. Then suddenly, he dropped his robe. He turned back and walked towards the bed. There, he knelt down and began to pray.

Heavenly Father, I thank you for bringing victory to my family today. I thank you even for the troubles, lest we take serenity for granted. All I ask is that you help us through our troubled times. Keep us strong, keep us faithful, and keep us safe. In spite of my victory tonight Lord, my heart is heavy. I have a burden for those young men that kidnapped my daughter today. They are in jail tonight. I don't know what will become of them. Lord. I'm asking you to bring a change to their hearts, redemption to their souls, and protection to their bodies from all that may seek to harm them. Help them to see the error of their ways that they may be better citizens to themselves and their fellow man. I ask in the name of Jesus. Amen.

It seemed like morning came too soon. The sudden aroma of coffee, and fresh baked muffins filled the room. Thelma walked in with fresh squeezed orange juice. Henry saw her walk by. "Thelma," he said, "You're up to your old tricks again with those muffins. If you're planning to ask for a raise, forget it; not one cent, at least until I see how many muffins I'm allowed to have this morning."

Thelma chuckled, "Oh no Sir, this batch is free. After what this family went through yesterday, I believe a little treat is in order."

"Thelma you're an angel. May your halo never get dim," said Henry, jovially.

Chapter Fourteen

On June 13, 1965, the whole Island of Jamaica was buzzing with excitement of the news that the charismatic civil rights leader, who won the Nobel Peace Prize, would be giving the commencement address at the University of the West Indies. Jamaica had just become a new member of the United Nations Human Rights Commission, and Dr. Martin Luther King's visit was just what the new country needed. Everyone was looking forward to getting, even a glimpse of the civil rights icon.

Breana was just as excited as everyone else. "Father," she said, "I'm a wreck."

"Why, what is it?"

"Making my Valedictorian speech. Father, have you forgotten? I'm sweating bullets already. Look at my hands; they are shaky"

"No, I haven't forgotten, Pumpkin. I just know that you're going to do well, just calm down."

"Good, that makes one of us who believes that. Look at me, I'm shaking. After all, it's not every day I get to share the stage with one of the greatest orators of all time. I have every right to be nervous."

Thelma returned from the market. She walked into the kitchen with each arm curved around bags filled with groceries. She set the bags on the kitchen table.

"Boy, everyone I met today was talking about Dr. King's visit," she said while unloading the grocery bags.

"I imagine it's the same all over the island," said Henry.

"I never thought I would ever have the chance to meet a person that has done so much to make a difference in the world. Will I be able to even speak in his presence?" Breana said.

"He will be right there cheering for you. This is exactly the kind of opportunity he is fighting to make available to everyone, whoever they may be," Thelma said, as she paused with a loaf of bread in her hand.

"Yeah, you're right. I never thought of it that way. I'll think about that to calm my nerves."

"Just go out there and speak from your heart. He'll be proud of you. I'm certain that he knows how it feels to be nervous."

"Mr. Noble, will you be going to the civic reception for Dr. King at the stadium?"

"Of course, wild horses couldn't keep me away. I've always been an avid admirer of Dr. King's, but I have never seen him in person, so you bet I'll be there."

"Father, did you know Dr. King will be presented with the key to the city at the reception?"

"Yes, I heard when I went to the University with you."

"I'd better start on my speech. If anyone needs me, I'll be at the gazebo."

Thelma watched her walk away. "I couldn't be more proud of her if she was my own child. After all that she has been through, her spirit is never broken, at least not for long. She bounces back, right on time."

"I know. She's a remarkable young lady. In spite of her mother abandoning her, and no one knows anything of her biological father, there must have been something good about them. How else would they've been able to produce such a wonderful child! I wish I had the chance to thank them for their beautiful gift to me," said Henry.

Breana walked into the study. She picked up a pen and a writing pad and started through the back door that leads to the gazebo. She sat down and stared across the harbor.

'What should I say?' She thought. *'What can I say that could make a difference to someone, or even provoke someone's thought?'*

She opened the notebook and began to write. She wrote a sentence on the pad, and she scratched it out, repeating the process several times, but nothing she wrote seemed right. She leaned her head back and closed her eyes. She collected her thoughts, and she wrote what was finally acceptable to her. She spent the rest of the week proof reading and rewriting.

On June 20, graduation day, the morning progressed quite rapidly as everyone prepared to leave. "Breana, it's time to go now. We don't want to rush getting there." She walked into the hall.

"Thelma, have you seen my gown?" she asked, "I had it laid out on the sofa and now it's not there."

"Yes, it's already in the car. Everything is all set, let's go." They walked out the door and Henry locked it behind him.

"I'm glad we're getting an early start. The news of Dr. King being here will draw such a crowd, I imagine the streets will be jammed. We may have a hard time getting a place to park," said Henry, looking at Dudley.

"I went down to John Crook's garage to have the car serviced yesterday, and he was the topic of everybody's conversation," said Dudley.

When they reached the university, the streets were lined with trucks, vans, buses and cars. Several police officers were in the area. Some of them were on guard duty, and others were directing traffic. Dudley moved slowly ahead until they reached the parking lot. They got out of the car and walked into the building. "Break a leg, Pumpkin," said Henry as he kissed Breana on the cheek.

"I don't know about that, my legs are like jelly."

At three o'clock, everyone was seated, and the band played the last note that signaled the end of the interlude. They promptly began to play Pomp and Circumstance. As the Class of 1965 marched in, everyone rose in their honor. The ceremony began with the singing of the Jamaican National Anthem. The Deputy Prime Minister gave the welcome address. As the ceremony progressed, Breana was introduced as the Valedictorian for the class of 1965. The crowd applauded as she nervously got to her feet. She walked to the podium and Thelma noticed that Breana did not have her speech. *'Oh my God,'* Thelma thought—as she looked on.

"She's forgotten her papers; Mr. Noble was the last to get out and locked the door. He never makes last minute check."

She leaned over and whispered to Henry. "I hope her memory serves her well."

Breana gingerly picked up the mike. Nervously, she cleared her throat and began to speak.

To the highly esteemed, Dr. Martin Luther King, faculty, visitors and fellow graduates: It is such a privilege to be chosen to address you today as Valedictorian of the class of 1965. I want you to know that I stand in awe at the thought of sharing a podium with such honorable company as Dr. King, so if my tongue ties and my knees buckle, please forgive me and applaud anyway. The audience laughed and applauded.

First of all, I thank God without whom this day would not be possible.

I would like to thank the most important person in my life. My father, Henry Noble who has been my inspiration, and my champion who made me believe in me. A greater father no one could ever have or hope for.

I thank Thelma Atkins, who has been my surrogate mother since the untimely passing of my mother. She always encourages me to be the best that I can be. She always knows the right things to say, and she knows when to just listen. I thank Dudley More, for always defending me. Finally, yet most importantly, I thank our Dean, Rolf Peters of this magnificent establishment, who has prevailed in a situation that could have otherwise been chaotic.

If there is anyone I forgot to thank, please, forgive me and take your bow anyway.

The roaring applause was like wind to her sail. She held her head high, chest out, and shoulders back. She made eye contact, and she continued to speak with confidence.

"Three years ago, I enrolled in this University with a heart full of faith, and a head full of dreams. As I remember my mother, being alive; she said to me, 'Breana, your dreams will be realized, if you have faith and work hard. However, if you work and have no faith, you are defeated. But also, faith without work is dead.' This afternoon, I fully understand what she meant. Over the years, I have worked very hard. Although there were times when I felt like giving up, faith kept me going. Today, I'm standing here, a part of history in the making. This, dear friends, is the fruition of faith and work.

I'm a seeker, and by faith, I came to this university. I sought to be empowered with knowledge that I may impart to my fellow man. The faculty of this university is responsible for the end product.

My fellow graduates, as we leave through the walls of this building today, let us use our knowledge to light the pathway for other hungry minds that are seeking what we have found. Let us be mindful of each person's circumstance. Let us not judge one another by nation, creed, or color. If we must judge, let it be by moral conduct. Let us neither stand so tall that we may not be reached; nor stoop so low that we may be trampled; let us meet in the middle with grace, that we may enrich each other. There is something to be learned from everyone, and we will do well if we can be the student, as well as the teacher. God bless you, one and all.

At the end of her speech, the graduates chanted her name... whooping and hollering" Henry took a handkerchief from the breast pocket of his smoke colored jacket, and wiped his eyes. Thelma bit her quivering lips, trying to hold back the tears.

"I have never been more proud of my daughter than I am right now. I wish Penny was here to see this, Henry said."

Thelma, now sniffling, "Victory at last."

"Yes indeed," said Henry, "Look at her now! Against all odds, she has made her life a success, always thinking that tomorrow will be a better day."

Her speech ended in a blaze of glory and would stay on the tongues of many, for days.

Dr. King delivered the Commencement Speech, which was more like a sermon, and the reception was overwhelming. At the end of the program, people crowded around him asking questions and seeking his autograph. Patiently, he moved through the crowd, touching as many as he could.

Henry had made a reservation for a celebratory dinner, at the 'Bay-Shore Restaurant'. As they dined and enjoyed the evening, Breana was ecstatic as she triumphantly said, "Gone are the days of midnight studying. I can sleep late if I want to. I don't have to open a book, if I don't want to. I'm free!"

She thought about it all, and then she said, "I feel so liberated. This is the first day of the rest of my life as they say. I'm looking forward to the next phase."

"I have an idea of what the next phase is going to be, and I for one am not looking forward to it," said Henry. Breana looked at him curiously and asked, "Why on earth would you say that, Father?"

"Because, one day some wise guy is going to walk into my house and walk out with my daughter on his arm. Don't expect me to hand you over on a silver platter, either." He said sheepishly.

"How about holding off with the silver platter and just hand her over; because it's bound to happen," said Thelma, "After all, she has done everything she was supposed to do. Your duty is to let her go."

"I know that, but it's not my duty to like it, and no one is going to make me. I bet Dudley agrees with me, right Dudley?"

"I agree with you one hundred percent, Sir. A daughter is priceless," Dudley said as he twirled his glass of iced coconut water around.

"Men! You can't ask Dudley, Sir! Men are unanimous in that sort of thinking," said Thelma.

"Well, how else do you expect me to level the playing field?" Henry replied, "There are *two* of you."

"Never mind, Father. When I find someone, you are going to love him like the son you never had."

"I'm holding you to that promise, and you better keep it unless you want to become Rapunzel, the second," a statement that tickled all of them.

They finished dinner and they drove home jubilantly chattering about the events of the evening.

On this post-graduation morning, Thelma was bewildered with her dilemma.

"I wasn't sure what to fix for breakfast," she announced as she walked in and set coffee and orange juice on the table. "Since you both slept so late, I have some sweet rolls, you could start with those."

"Coffee and sweet rolls are fine for me," Henry said, "I feel like I'm still full from last night's dinner."

"Same for me, Thelma," Breana replied

"So what kind of day do you have planned my dear?" Henry asked Breana.

"I plan to have a leisurely day at the beach."

"Good for you. I know the beach has always been your passion. That's long overdue."

"Yes, it is, and now that I'm finished with school, I can return to my first love."

"Why do I get the feeling that you would be content to live in a mud hut as long as it's by the sea?"

"Maybe because it's true," she started to leave.

"Did you remember to bring suntan lotion, Breana?" Thelma asked.

"Oh no, I forgot."

"The idea is to be tanned, not scorched, young lady."

"Thanks for reminding me," she said returning to her room.

"Oh, Breana, before you go, have you given much thought to what we discussed?" asked Henry.

Breana had a decision to make. Would she be taking advantage of her father's offer to work for him, or would she go to work for the handsome Deputy Prime Minister Daniel Banister. They had met in November the previous year when he presided over the Conference of the Commonwealth Parliamentary Association. Breana read between the lines. She knew her father had his heart set on her working for him. She would like to work for Daniel who was quite taken with her, and she with him. Henry, aware of this fact, hardly appreciated it. She had wrestled with the option and had finally made her choice.

"Although the other offer seems challenging, I'd rather work for you. After all, you'll have to 'hand me over to some wise guy' soon enough," Breana said with a smirk.

"I'm very pleased with your decision, my dear. It's that last comment I could do without."

Breana smiled at him as she stated, "I'm just giving you a taste of your own medicine."

"Yes, but when you regurgitate medicine, it tastes bad twice, so if it's already swallowed, it's best to keep it down."

After Breana left, Henry sighed. "So, Thelma, just how long do you think I can keep those hounds away from her?"

Thelma chuckled as she sipped her tea. "Not for long, Sir, not long at all."

Chapter Fifteen

July of 1966, Breana had been working at the American Embassy for almost one year. She was now the Education Specialist for the Office of Public Affairs. She loved her new job. She loved that no day was the same and she was able to do what she loved the most, helping people.

She assisted young citizens of Jamaica to fulfill their dreams of attending colleges and universities in America. However, every job has its down side. The paperwork involved made her head spin and the phones rang off the hook.

One day, Breana left work around 4:00 pm and decided it was time for a little 'TLC'. She gathered her beach towel, water, suntan lotion and a book, and she headed for the beach. She spread her towel on the ground and lay down under the cabana. The Kingston Harbor was impacted with ships from different countries. She sat there for a while looking out at them. Her eyes popped with surprise as her favorite ship came into view.

There's the Bogain-Villa! I wonder where it's been all this time.

She wondered about the different places and all the travelers aboard as she lay down and started to read. Her eyes grew heavy, and she shoved the book aside. She untied the strings of her bikini top to ensure an even tan, and she drifted off to sleep. As the evening shade grew darker, a young man came walking along the beach holding the leash that belonged on a Labrador retriever. As he neared Breana's cabana, the dog ran inside and started barking.

"Get back here Roscoe!" shouted the young man. Breana was startled by the commotion, and she woke up disoriented. She jumped to a sitting position when she saw a man standing in front of her cabana. He stood about six feet tall, perfectly tanned, with thick dark curly hair. Breana sprang to her feet and got out from under the cabana. His crescent shaped eyebrows accentuated his perfectly shaped brow bones.

"Hi, I'm Mark Bogain." The resonance in his voice was deep and masculine, and at the same time warm and soothing. It was the voice that a girl would love to hear crooning to her last thing at night, and first thing in the morning, and leaves her hungry for more through the day.

"I'm sorry for the disturbance. I tried to stop the little mongrel, but he just kept on going," he said with a Latin accent. His smile was wide, and his teeth were so white they seemed to sparkle.

"Oh, that's alright. I'm Breana…Breana Noble. It's late anyway. I should be getting home." She turned away and started gathering her things: her book, her bag, her sunglasses and Bikini top? She looked down, and she discovered that her breasts were naked. She started to move faster to get away.

Mark tried to put her at ease. "Look, you don't have to run off, if it's any consolation, you're beautiful." Breana was not convinced. She kept going quickly as she left in humiliation.

"You're beautiful," Mark repeated quietly to himself, as he watched her walked away.

Breana avoided going to the beach for several days after "The Incident", her official label of the most embarrassing moment in her life.

Thelma suggested that they take a stroll on the beach one evening after dinner. Breana hesitantly accepted her invitation, as they walked and chatted along the water's edge, she started enjoying herself. She became relaxed as they talked girl-talk and admired the scenery.

"That cake you made for dessert tonight was delicious," she said to Thelma.

"Thank you sweetheart, oh my goodness the cake! I have one in the oven for Miss Ivy! I need to take it out before it spoils. Sorry, dear, I have to cut this walk short." She said as she rushed back to the house. Breana stayed to finish her walk.

Suddenly, there was Mark walking his dog not far from her. She wanted to run but did not want to alarm Thelma. Besides, where could she go, she was already a good distance from home. She started to walk in the opposite direction.

"Hello there Breana!" Mark called, as he started walking toward to her.

'Oh please, just leave me alone', Breana thought, as that feeling of shame was revived. She kept walking as if she didn't hear him.

As Mark got closer, he pleaded out of breath. "Hello! Breana! Wait, please!"

His dog, Roscoe, got to her before Mark did and began jumping around and licking her. Breana hesitantly stopped, then began petting the dog. She felt badly about ignoring its master, so she turned around with a pasted grin on her face. "Hello, uh, what was your name again?" She very well knew what his name was.

"Mark, Mark Bogain. Look, I'm sorry about what happened last time."

"Forget it, okay? Besides, it wasn't your fault."

They stood there awkwardly, Mark looking at her, Breana looking at the ground. Then Mark finally spoke.

"Look, Breana, if it's alright with you, can we start over?"

"Start *what* over," she said defensively.

Mark stuck his hand out, offering a hand shake. "My name is Mark Bogain." Breana looked at his hand. It was smooth yet strong. Her eyes trailed his forearm, up to his muscular biceps. His skin was glowing and tanned. Breana reached out for his hand.

"Breana Noble."

Mark flashed a smile at her that was fit for a tooth paste commercial. "It's nice to meet you, Miss Noble."

Roscoe started to bark as he jumped and ran circles around them. Mark said, "Sorry, Roscoe normally doesn't act this way."

"Don't worry about it." She began petting the dog's head, and he responded by sidling up closer to her. "He's a sweet dog," she added.

"He really seems to like you. Are you a pet owner?" They started walking together.

"No, I've always wanted one, but circumstances never allowed it. Do you live nearby?"

"Not exactly, I came here from Columbia to attend the opening of the National Arena."

"Oh! That's set for July 13th, isn't it?"

"Yes it is," Mark replied.

"I heard it's going to be huge. Athletes and spectators from thirty-five commonwealth countries are expected to attend," Breana said. Some English Monarchs will be there among the honored guests. That's exactly what the island needs to boost the economy."

"It seems like a lot of people are coming in early for the event. The whole city is preparing for the Royal Family. Many of my passengers came because the Royals will be here." said Mark.

"Passengers? You carried passengers for the event? *I can't believe I just asked him something he already said,"* she thought as they walked along.

"Yes, my cruise ship, "The Bogain-Villa is docked over there in the harbor."

"You own the Bogain-Villa?" Breana asked, attempting to contain her excitement.

"Yes."

"I've always admired that ship. Why did you give it that name?"

"Well, because my name is Bogain, and I live on the ship, so I thought it to be a fitting name."

"Hmm, that's understandable." *His accent is so cute,* she thought. "So is the ship your home all through the year?"

"It is, most of the time; there's nothing more soothing than the wide ocean."

Breana got more curious. "Wow, you'd rather live on a ship?"

"Oh yeah, I have always been a sea lover. My father was a captain in the Navy. As a child, a great part of my life was spent on the sea. Then after my dad died and my grandfather retired, I was left to run the family business, so I chose to live on one of the ships."

"That's very interesting. I've never met anyone that lives on the sea all the time. What's it like?"

"It's like nothing you can imagine. To a sea lover, it's indescribable."

Breana wanted to reveal her passion for the sea, but she wrestled with her thoughts. *'If I tell him how I feel about the sea, I wonder what he would think. Would he even believe that I'm sincere? He would probably think I'm just saying that because he's rich and gorgeous. I can't take that chance.'*

Breana was captivated. She hung on to every word Mark said. She said nothing of her own love for the sea. They were enthralled in conversation by the light of the gazebo. They didn't notice that night had fallen. The ships in the harbor were all lit, and the view was spectacular. Inside the house, Thelma had turned on the lights and suddenly realized that she had not seen Breana since she left her walking on the beach. "Mr. Noble, where's Breana?" she asked.

"Isn't she in her room?"

"I'm not sure. I left her on the beach, but I haven't seen her come back."

When she walked down the corridor, Breana's bedroom door was open and the room was dark. She turned the light on, and briskly walked back down the corridor. "Mr. Noble! She's not in her room, and she's not any place in the house. It's already dark outside. She wouldn't still be at the gazebo. Where could she be?"

"I'll go outside and look for her," said Henry, springing up from his chair already worried.

On the beach, Mark and Breana had just discovered that the evening was far spent. "My goodness," she said, "I didn't realize it was so late. My family must be worried about me. I should go."

"Ok. Well, may I see you again?"

"Okay, we could meet at my gazebo tomorrow evening around five o'clock?" she said

"Five o'clock is fine. I'll see you then. Good night," Mark said as they both started walking away in opposite directions.

"Good night, Mark. *I wonder if he's watching me walk away. I can't look back. I wish I had a rear view right now.'*

Meanwhile, Mark had stopped walking. He was watching her, and he was captivated. *If she looks back, I'll just pretend I wasn't looking.*

As Henry neared the gazebo, he met Breana. "For heaven's sake-Breana, you scared us half to death. Why have you stayed down here so late?"

"I'm sorry, Father. I should have let you know where I was. The most fantastic thing happened. You're not going to believe this. I met the guy who owns the Bogain-Villa."

"Here in our backyard? What was he doing here?"

"Not exactly, I was down at the beach, and he was walking his dog. We started talking, and I found out that we have so much in common. It's unbelievable."

They began walking back to the house. Breana was floating on air.

"I heard all that, but what was he doing on this portion of the beach?" Henry asked.

"We didn't talk about that, but we're going to see each other again tomorrow by the gazebo."

"Okay, what time do we meet him?"

Breana came crashing down from her cloud.

"We? Father! You're not suggesting that you're going to be there, are you?" she said in dismay.

"Oh no!"

"Thank God," said Breana, lifting her eyebrows as she breathed a sigh of relief.

"It's not a suggestion. It's a fact."

"What? Well now I've heard everything, when my own father would humiliate me like that."

"You didn't let me finish! Now, you listen to me. You know nothing of this person, where he comes from, or what he's doing here; except, what he tells you. Therefore, I forbade you to see him alone, you understand?"

"Well, are you *finished* now? Because *that's* what *I'm* going to be if you do that, Father, come on now! Have you any idea how embarrassing that would be for me?" Breana opened the door with such force as she stomped inside. "I could live with your embarrassment, but if anything should happen to you, I couldn't live with that or myself."

"I'm just going to be sick, that's all!" said Breana as she flopped herself on the sofa.

Thelma walked into the room. "What is all the shouting about?" she asked, looking from Henry to Breana, in anticipation.

"Father is being unreasonable. That's what! He doesn't think I should be in the back yard without someone watching me!"

"Thelma, allow me to tell you how unreasonable I am! Breana met some person down at the beach. He said he owns that ship, The Bogain-Villa. She doesn't know where he comes from, or why he ended up almost in our back yard. This is a private beach. Why was he walking a dog here? He's up to something, and that thing with the dog is the oldest trick in the book! They made plans to meet at the gazebo tomorrow. I said I should be there, and that's why I'm unreasonable! You've always been like a mother to her, so will you please talk some sense into her?"

Thelma was careful to think before she spoke. *Yeah, I maybe like a mother, but as an employee, not want to lose my job!* She took a deep breath.

"I think we all should give this a rest for tonight, and discuss it in the morning when everybody is calm and willing to listen."

"I'll drop the subject for tonight, but I'm not finished. I'm very adamant about this. Good night," Henry said, as he walked away.

"You see that Thelma. There's no use talking to him. He didn't even let me finish telling him about the guy. The moment he heard that we were going to meet at the gazebo, he stopped listening. I'm going to bed," she said as she ran to her room.

Thelma sat on the sofa and whispered to herself, "Thelma, take your Dramamine, the boat is about to rock." She sat on the couch for a while; then she decided to go to see Breana. She knocked on the door. "Breana, its Thelma, open the door please."

Breana was lying on the bed talking to Savannah on the phone. "Savvy, I've got to go Thelma is at the door.

"Okay, keep me posted," said Savvy, as they ended the conversation. She sighed deeply then walked over to the door and opened it. Her eyes were red, and her cheeks were wet.

"Come in Thelma, I was just talking to Savannah."

"Oh, how is Savvy doing?"

"She and her father are doing fine. She's a partner at the psychiatric office where she works now."

"Well good for her, and I'm sure she's busy too; so many people are in need of psychiatric help these days," said Thelma. Too bad it's too late to help her mother."

"I'm sure it's because her mom why she chose that profession. Well, whoever goes to her will have the best psychiatrist that money can buy."

Thelma started chuckling, "I can tell you of a few people who could use her help, like Mr. Fred down the street. He's as crazy as...." Thelma stopped talking as she noticed Breana's tears. She was sitting on the bed contemplating the argument with her father. Thelma quickly sat beside her, and she put her arm around her shoulder. Breana rested her head against Thelma's shoulder and her tears flowed freely.

"I feel so humiliated," she said, "I have never known Father to be so unyielding. He's treating me as if I did something wrong. All I did was speak to someone who seemed like a nice person. Just because he's not from around here doesn't mean he's an axe murderer. We're not from around here either."

"Calm down, he's just scared for you, and who can blame him? After all the things that have happened to you, he would not be human if he didn't show some concern for your safety."

"But I'm trying to tell him that there is no danger from this man, and he's not listening."

"Okay, I'm here to listen, why don't you tell me? Convince me that it's okay for you to see this man alone."

"Okay," she said between sniffles. Thelma handed her some tissue. She dried her eyes and blew her nose.

"Go ahead baby. I'm all ears."

"Well, I know that I just met him, but I feel like I already know him. His name is Mark Bogain. We talked about so many things, and his love for the ocean is as great as mine. We have so much in common. He told me he owns the Bogain-Villa."

"Wait a minute, you mean that ship we saw in the harbor, *that* Bogain-Villa?"

"Yes, he sailed with passengers from Colombia. They're here to attend the opening of the National Arena."

"Did he tell you how he came to be on our portion of beach?"

"No. but I'm sure that's something I would find out, if I ever get to talk to him again."

"So what else did he tell you?"

Breana started smiling. "Thelma, she said, he loves the sea just as much as I do."

"Get out of here!"

"Yes, his father was a captain in the Navy, so most of his childhood was spent at sea. His family business is shipping. His father died when he was young, and his grandfather is retired, so he's running the business now, and get this...even though he has several homes, he chose to live on the Bogain-Villa."

"Mr. Nobel cannot compete with that for sure," said Thelma, as she tried to lighten the moment.

"He said it reminds him of when he was young and used to be with his father. He feels close to him when he's at sea." Breana tilted her head to the side, and she let out a deep long sigh.

"Thelma isn't that the sweetest thing you've ever heard?" Thelma watched as Breana swooned over the guy right before her eyes.

"You've learned quite a bit about him in such a short time?"

"I know! I'd like to learn more; that's why I don't want Father to spoil it for me. Can you imagine how it would look if Father shows up at the gazebo? I would die; I would just die! I don't know why he's doing this to me! Honestly, I have never seen Father behave so unreasonable!"

"Because he had never felt threatened before," said Thelma. "He never had to rival for your attention before. You're his little girl. That's how fathers are."

"What do you mean *threatened*?"

"Well, your father is used to having his little girl all to himself and now she has grown up, and he has to face the possibility of sharing her with somebody else."

"You know, I never thought of it that way," She threw her face into her hands. "Now I feel bad."

Thelma slowly stood up and walked towards the door as she spoke. "No, don't feel bad. It's just the way life has always been and always will be between fathers and daughters.

She turned around to look at Breana. "You have a goodnight sleep. I can't promise anything, but I'll talk to your father for you."

"Thank you. If he's going to listen to anyone, it would be you.

"Don't thank me yet." Thelma smiled softly. "Good night."

The first ray of sunlight touched the window panes of Breana's bedroom. She opened up her eyes. Her heart raced and her anticipation escalated. She pondered the effect that her meeting with Mark may have on her future.

We've just met, and I found out we have so much in common already. What else will I find out if I see him again? It's like I've discovered myself in talking to him last night. I never felt this way about anyone before. I hope Thelma will be successful in talking to Father. I might as well get up and face the music.

She threw back the covers, stepped into her slippers, and walked into the bathroom.

"The way to a man's heart is through his stomach," she said as she planned to get on Henry's good side before she spoke to him that morning. "Was it the bible what said that? I don't think so, but it's worth a try this morning," she mumbled to herself as she made Henry's breakfast 'special.'

Freshly perked Blue Mountain Coffee with a hint of hazel nut, and fresh baked cinnamon rolls collectively formed an aroma that penetrated through the house. Henry rolled from one side to the next. He got out of bed and stretched as he put his robe on and walked into the bathroom. Breana and this newfound man preyed on his mind.

'What do I say to her, so she can understand that I'm concerned for her? That man, whoever he is, why was he on our private beach and supposedly walking a dog, no less. That's the oldest trick in the book, looking for an easy mark, some unsuspecting soul.'

He started brushing his teeth vigorously, as these thoughts went racing through his mind. *Well, my daughter will not be his prey!* "Not my daughter!" He said aloud, looking in the direction of the Bogain-Villa.

Henry showered and shaved, and he got dressed and went to

join Breana. She was already sitting at the table. He bent over and kissed her on the cheek.

"Good morning, Pumpkin," he said, while masking his anxiety.

"Good morning, Father. Did you sleep well?" she asked, masking *her* anxiety.

"Hardly," Henry replied.

Thelma brought in the eggs. Henry sat down and gave thanks for the food. He picked up his glass with the orange juice. He took a sip of the juice and sat the glass down.

"Breana, I hope you know that the last thing I would want to do is upset you," he said,

"Whatever I say, it's only in your best interest."

'Keep cool Breana'. "I know Father, but you're acting as if I'm running away with an assassin or something. He's just going to meet me at the gazebo. Father, really, how much harm can come to me in the backyard?"

"Thelma, what do you think of all this?" asked Henry.

'Lord, why me?' Thelma cleared her throat, and then began to speak courageously.

"Well, I spoke with Breana last night Sir, and I think she has learned a lot about him, even in such a short time. In my opinion, I don't think there's any harm in getting to know him. It seems like they even have some things in common from what I hear."

"And what is that, exactly?" he asked, a little perturbed by her response.

"I'd rather you hear it from Breana, Sir." She looked at Breana, as her eyes said, *'your turn.'*"

"Okay, I'm ready to listen, start from the top. What's his name?"

"His name is Mark. It's just like I told you last night; except, you didn't let me finish. He—"

"What's his last name?" Henry interrupted.

"Bogain...Anyway, he sailed here from Columbia to attend the opening of the National Arena."

"But that's not for two weeks. Will he be competing?"

"I don't know Father, please let me finish."

"So, if he is a real sea man, how am I supposed to compete with that?"

"Father, will you stop! There is no competition! I don't even know the man, and even if I did—who could compete with you for my affection? I only have *one* Father."

"Well, that's a very smart thing to say, and by the way, Thelma... the breakfast was a very smart thing to do. I knew that you were up to something—hmm, cinnamon rolls indeed. I think I'm going to become less predictable. People around here think they can bribe me. So, are there anymore rolls?"

"Yes Sir, coming right up," Thelma said, winking at Breana.

Breakfast ended on a happy note. On the way to work, Breana asked "Father, are you still thinking of going to the gazebo this evening?"

"I'm still not convinced that this man is genuine, but I don't want to embarrass you, so I won't go; however..."

"Oh, thank you Father, thank—"

"However, Dudley will be very busy in the back yard this evening, *right* Dudley?"

"Yes Sir, I have a few things that need my attention, so I'll be working back there this afternoon."

"I don't know what kind of work you would be doing at 5 o'clock, but it's better than stretching over my Father's lap to talk to the guy."

"Stretch?" said Henry "If anyone has stretching in mind, maybe I should go down to the gazebo myself."

"Father!"

"Just kidding."

All day at work, Breana was floating on air. She thought about all the things that she would like to know about Mark. She looked at her watch. It was half past twelve.

"My goodness, look at the time. I have to get Father to go to lunch."

She walked down the corridor to her father's office.

"Father its lunch time."

"I know, Dudley just brought us lunch."

"How sweet, thank you Dudley."

"You're welcome. Thelma thought you should have a good lunch. She said you need to feed the butterflies in your stomach. Whatever that means," said Dudley

"Don't *you* start, now" she said rolling her eyes in Dudley's direction.

"Hey, don't shoot the messenger," Dudley answered, grinning mischievously.

"Seems to me that Thelma is investing heavily in supporting a relationship between you and this man that no one, including you, knows anything about; except for what he said of course," said Henry.

"Father, I thought we had a truce."

"Okay, okay, I won't say another word."

"Thank you! You're all acting as if this man has already proposed to me. You need to stop."

After lunch was over, Breana packed away the dishes in the basket. "I'll be here at four o'clock sharp just in case anyone has an important appointment, Sir," Dudley said teasingly as he picked up the basket to leave.

Henry chuckled, "Not me, I'll be free all evening."

Breana threw her arms high in the air as she looked up to the heavens. She walked out of the office leaving them to their laughter.

Back in the safe haven of her office, she watched the clock as the day seemed to drag on. She finished reviewing one of the many files on her desk. When she looked at the clock again, only thirty minutes had passed. She sighed heavily, "Will this day ever end?"

"What did you say?" asked one of the office assistants, as she was passing by Breana's office.

"Oh nothing, I'm just looking forward to an important evening," Breana's smile was a dead giveaway.

The assistant smiled back, glancing at Breana knowingly, "Oh? So, who is he?

"Serina, can you keep a secret?" Breana whispered.

"Of course," said Serina, leaning in closer for what she expected to be juicy details.

"So can I." Breana replied with a wink. The smile never left her lips.

"Alright, alright, I can take a hint," said Serina, realizing she walked right into that one.

"Anyway, have a great time," she added as she exited Breana's office.

"Thanks!" Breana shouted after her.

The evening was pleasant. A soft breeze rustled against the miniature trees on the lush landscaping. The air was scented with the aroma of night-blooming Jasmine. Breana looked at her watch. It was five minutes to five o'clock. As much as she wanted to see Mark, she was a bundle of nerves. She had male friends while attending college but had never before been on a real date, and no boyfriend to speak of. It was highly unlikely that her father would have approved anyway. He was always so protective. Granted, he had plenty of reasons to be. She picked up a purple colored afghan that Penny had made for her. "Oh mother, I wish you were here. I could use some of your wisdom right now," she said softly.

She swung the afghan across her shoulder and started out the door. She walked down the garden path to the gazebo. She was hardly there before Mark showed up.

"Good evening Breana!" He said as he approached. At the mere sound of his voice, Breana felt small flutters in her stomach. She was lost in a fantasy at the sight of him. He was speaking again and all she could think about was how it would feel to kiss him.

"Hi Mark." She said; more nervous now than before. "*What's wrong with me? Get it together Breana."* She started fidgeting with the end of her afghan. She was just enthralled by his presence, and with him.

With a wide smile that's famous of Mark, he moved closer to her and looked into her eyes.

"Señorita, how nice of you to remember, I'm flattered that you came."

He took her hand he kissed it softly, Breana blushed and became warm all over.

"I promised you that I would be here." She said as her cheeks got more red by the second.

"Do you always keep your promises?"

"To the best of my ability, yes I do."

While Mark and Breana talked, Thelma sought to satisfy her curiosity. She went into the kitchen and started setting up a tray to take to the gazebo. Henry saw her walking out with the tray. "Good idea Thelma," he said, "a better idea would be to stay there and serve them refreshments."

Thelma caught on. "Sir, I believe Breana can handle it herself." *You'll not make a spy outta me,* she thought.

She walked out the door to the gazebo, "A-hem!" she said clearing her throat to announce her arrival.

"I didn't mean to disturb you. I thought you might be hungry, so I brought some refreshments."

"Thank you Thelma. I'd like to introduce you to Mark Bogain. He is the owner of the Bogain-Villa. Mark, this is Thelma, she's... Breana thought for a moment, everything to me, I guess." They all laughed.

"It's a pleasure meeting you, Señora!"

"It is nice meeting you, too, Mr.—!"

"Mark... Just Mark! Thank you for the food."

"You're welcome; it's just a little snack. I hope you enjoy it."

'Ooh-la-la, what a hunk! No wonder Breana is in a tizzy', Thelma

thought. She swiftly turned around so as not to make her approval of Mark's assets too obvious. She walked up the garden path back to the house, smiling. Breana lifted the cover from the tray.

"Would you like me to fix you something Mark?"

"Only if you let me help."

Breana fixed the plates and Mark poured the drinks. They sat at the table and ate while they talked. When they finished dining, Mark asked, "Would you like to go for a walk down on the beach?"

"I sure do, after all this food, I need the exercise, and Thelma called it a snack." She chuckled.

Actually, she had only nibbled on the food, but she welcomed the excuse to be alone with Mark away from peering eyes.

"Do you know anyone that lives in this area?" Breana asked as they walked along.

"Yes, my ship is being worked on, so I rented a house about four houses away from here. It's only for a month though."

"I know that house. It's kind of large for one person. A month is a long time to be away from your family. Aren't you lonely there all by yourself? She asked, while at the same time thinking, "*Please, please don't have a girlfriend.*"

Some of my crew is staying there with me. The work that's needed is going to take some time to complete, so that's why we docked here early."

"So, will you be competing in any of the games?" asked Breana.

Mark chuckled, "Thanks for the compliment, but I'm not an athlete."

"Well, you sure look like one."

As the last word rolled off her tongue, she wanted to crawl under a rock. Silently, she started berating herself, '*why did I say that? He probably thinks I've been drooling over him. Maybe I shouldn't take another step. I should just turn back right now. God knows what he must be thinking of me. How could I be so stupid?*

Mark was still talking, but she was so busy rebuking herself, mutely, that she stopped listening to him.

"I'm sorry, what did you say?" she asked

"I just asked you, where you came from originally?"

"Well, I was born and lived in New York until I was eleven; then I moved to Stone Mountain, Georgia. Have you ever been there?"

"No, maybe someday a young lady will do me the honor of showing me Georgia. As a matter of fact, I'd like to make that my new goal."

"Are you, inadvertently eliciting my escort around Georgia, Mr. Bogain?"

"Not at all, Miss Noble, I've just made a deliberate statement. I set my goals that way."

"Have you always attained your goals Mr. Bogain?"

"Oh yes, Miss Noble, but this one might be a bit more challenging."

"Oh really, and why is that?"

"Mark looked at her smiling, because I will have to depend on the cooperation of a beautiful, young lady." Again she started blushing. She quickly tried to change the subject.

"Do you have brothers and sisters?" she asked.

"I have one sister in Ecuador. She's married, and she has three children."

"Oh, and how about you, are you married with children too?" she said, paying attention to his eyes. *Father always said watch out for shifty eyes; there's always a lie somewhere,'* these thoughts played in her head.

"No, no family of my own yet; I'm too busy with other matters. I do hope to one day find that special person to share my life with." Breana was elated *"No girlfriend no wife, well, well, well…"*

Henry was inside the house, eager to know what was going on outside.

He had put a smoking jacket and was coming out of his bedroom when Thelma saw him.

"Mr. Noble, said Thelma." If you don't mind me asking, why are you wearing a smoking jacket when you haven't smoked in God knows when?"

"No Thelma, I do mind you asking," he replied and went on his way to sit on the veranda, leaving Thelma speechless and watching him walk away. He positioned his chair where the gazebo was in full view. He looked down at the gazebo and saw no one. He shouted, "Thelma, hurry, come out here a minute!"

Thelma hurried out to the veranda, "What is it, Mr. Noble?"

"Look, there's no one at the gazebo. Where do you think they might be?"

"Well, on a beautiful evening like this Sir, I would say that they are out walking on the beach."

"It's going to be dark soon you know."

Thelma sat down and started sipping her tea. "She'll be alright Sir, don't worry."

"I can't forget that last ordeal. When I think of all that she has been through, I have the right to be paranoid. What if this man is just another one of those scoundrels trying to harm her?"

The evening was fading fast. Henry's fear grew simultaneously with the darkness.

The harbor lights went on, and still, there was no sign of Breana.

Thelma joined him on the veranda, and soon, they heard voices and laughter getting closer. It was Mark and Breana coming back from their walk on the beach.

"See, I told you she would be alright."

"Are you trying to say you weren't worried at all?"

"I was worried just a little, but only after you reminded me of everything I should worry about."

As the couple came closer to the gazebo, Henry and Thelma dashed back inside the house.

When Breana and Mark returned to the gazebo, they sat and talked for a while.

"This was a wonderful evening." She couldn't stop smiling. "I really enjoyed your company Mark."

"The pleasure was mine Miss Noble. I can't remember spending an evening with such an intriguing young lady."

Mark's thoughts went into over drive. *I'd love to see you all day, every day, and all night every night. Hmm-hmm.'* He was eager for the next date. "How about dinner and a movie tomorrow?" he asked.

"Dinner and a movie sound wonderful. Yes, I'd like that." Breana said.

"Then it's a date. Should I pick you up at six?"

"Six will be fine."

Mark saw the figure of a person sitting on the sand not far away.

I can't believe that guy is still here," he whispered to Breana. "He's been trying to surf all evening."

"Oh really, I didn't notice anyone out there,"

"Well, reluctantly, Miss Breana, I'll say good night because I must."

"Yes. It's getting late, I should be going inside. Well, goodnight then…I'll see you tomorrow."

He took her hand and held it in both of his. He kissed her gently on the cheek; then he whispered in her ear, "Dream a little dream of me"

Breana gave a nervous giggle and said, "Good night, Mark."

Buenos notches, Breana!" he replied. As he watched her move up the pathway she turned and waved goodbye. She met Henry sitting on the veranda and sat next to him on a lounge chair.

"Enjoying the view Father?"

"Immensely my dear; it's a delightful evening! Did you have fun with your gentleman friend?"

"Yes we did. We sat on the gazebo for a while; then we took a long walk down the beach, and we talked... Father, he is such an intriguing person."

"Hmm- intriguing, eh? So what did you find out about him?"

"He is renting a house up the street. That's why he was on the beach yesterday."

"I thought you said he lives on his ship?"

"He does, but the ship is being repaired. He docked here early, before the opening of the Arena, so that he would have a chance to work on the ship. He and some of his crew are occupying the house. He has one sister, who is married and she lives in Ecuador. She has three children, two girls and a boy. He invited me to go out with him again."

"Oh he did, did he? I would like to hear more about this fellow."

"Okay Father, all in due time; I want to shower this sand off first," Breana said as she scurried inside

'She seems to really like this guy, I hope she doesn't end up getting hurt,' Henry watched his daughter, now blossoming into a woman; he wondered where did the time go.

While Breana was filling her Father in on the details of her date, Mark was walking down the beach with thoughts of her racing through his mind.

I never thought a girl like that really existed. She likes me...I can tell. She said I looked like an athlete, he thought, grinning from ear to ear. During his walk home, he watched as the tenacious surfer started walking away from the beach. *I'll have to admit one thing, that guy is relentless,* he thought.

He slowly walked along the beach thinking, and picking up shells from the sand, tossing them into the water. When he finally arrived at his temporary home, he took off his sandals, knocked the sand off and set them aside. He opened the door and went in. None of his crew was home. He went into the bathroom and turned the shower on. Merrily, he stepped into the shower and started humming.

Breana was glowing like fireflies on a dark night. Henry was sitting at his desk reading a copy of the *Daily Gleaner*. "Getting a dose of stale news, Father?" she asked.

"I'm just catching up on what I missed this morning."

"Yeah, while you wait to hear about what you missed this evening, right."

"Did I miss something this evening?"

She sat on the desk. "Only the most fantastic time a girl ever had. Oh Father, he is so charming, and such a gentleman."

"So tell me, what else did he say?"

"Oh, lots of things, but you wouldn't be interested in all of them." she said, knowing very well that he was.

"Try me." Henry replied inquisitively.

"Well, let's see," Breana was selective in what she wanted her father to know.

"Hmm… he's interested in art, and he loves all types of music. He graduated at the top of his class a few years ago. He has a Master's Degree."

"In what?" asked Henry?

"In Business." She replied.

"Okay, go on." Henry coaxed.

"There's not much more to tell. Oh yeah, did I tell you that he asked me out again, for dinner and a movie?"

"Yes, you did. He doesn't waste any time, does he? What did you say?"

"I accepted of course. How often do I get offers like that?" Breana gushed on.

"Father, he's so incredible. He's smart, funny, romantic, and he's so muscular. I thought he would be competing in the games at the opening of the Arena."

"Well Pumpkin, it seems that you are well taken by this man."

"He somewhat reminds me of you." Said Breana.

Henry cocked his head to the side and massaged his chin, a trait typical of him when he is thinking mischievously. "Hmm, he looks a little bit like me, does he?"

"Spitting image of you!" Breana said, trying to butter up her Dad.

"Well, you know what they say; girls are attracted to men who resemble their fathers."

Breana smiled. "Where's Thelma?"

"I saw her going to the linen closet before you came in. I haven't seen her since. I guess she is some place waiting for your report."

"I bet she is! Let me go find out."

"By the way, did you and your friend enjoy the refreshments?"

"Yes we did."

"It was a facade you know. We figured we should at least know what this man looks like."

"For heaven's sake, I don't know what I'm going to do with you two. Dudley is the only sane one around here."

"Who is the sane one? Did you say, Dudley?"

"You heard me."

"Oh yes, Dudley, very sane young man. That's why he spent all evening surfing on a calm sea." Henry said roaring with laughter.

"That was Dudley Father? Boy, I give up! I can't trust anybody around here!"

"On the contrary my dear, you can trust everybody around here to make sure that you're alright," Henry said still chuckling.

"I give up," she said, walking into the house. Thelma was in the laundry room folding the last few pieces of linen. Breana was just about to join her when Thelma walked out with a basket of towels. "Here comes the third party from the conspiracy team. Thelma, I'm surprised at you! You teamed up with Father and Dudley to spy on me!"

"We did no such thing. We teamed up to love you and protect you."

"Well, I guess I should be grateful that you guys care so much, but next time, I won't be needing you guys to baby sit me with my playmate."

Henry said, "Next time, huh?"

"That's right Father, I said next time!" Breana said smiling.

Far into the night, the house was silent and the lights were out. Everyone was fast asleep except for Breana. She tossed and turned and fluffed her pillow, but to no avail. A tiny beam of moonlight streaked through the window and shone on her bed. *How can I expect to sleep with the moonlight shining on me?* She got up and walked over to the window and pulled the curtains closer together. She got back in the bed and pulled the covers over herself and lay still for a while, but sleep evaded her just the same. She got out of bed again and turned the light on. She decided to see if Thelma was awake, she needed some to talk to. She walked quickly but quietly to Thelma's room. She hesitated for a minute, not wanting to bother her, but she could not resist and knocked anyway. She knocked softly a few times before Thelma finally woke up.

"Who is it?"

"It's me, Thelma. I'm sorry to bother you, but can you let me in?"

"Just a minute," Thelma said while she adjusted her robe and walked to the door.

"Breana, why are you still up?" She whispered.

"I can't sleep. All kinds of thoughts are going through my head."

Thelma motioned for her to come in. "What kind of thoughts, honey?"

"I've been thinking about this evening."

"Okay, it's obvious that you want to discuss what happened this evening, so go ahead." Thelma yawned.

"It's not so much what happened; it's about what I'm feeling." Breana replied.

"Uh-huh," Thelma mumbled, "I think I'll need some tea for this. I'll be right back."

She sat down on Thelma's bed and glanced around the room.

Wow, Thelma did a good decorating job in here. The window was open and a gentle breeze ruffled the sheer, lace curtains in the window. Little knick-knacks of animals and dolls were carefully displayed on shelving, and there wall hangings with reflections of Jamaica and Africa all around the room. The ambiance had a relaxing effect on Breana. She curled up in Thelma's bed, and then she noticed several pictures on the wall. Some she didn't remember seeing. *I wonder who they are*, she thought.

In the kitchen, Thelma was fixing a tray with teacups and tea biscuits while she waited for the kettle to boil. She finished and headed back to her room.

"Okay, here we are. The best tea your money can buy."

Breana started to ask Thelma about the pictures, but remembering her dilemma, she decided against it. Thelma served the tea and said, "Okay, let's use what's left of the night to see what we can iron out." Thelma began sipping her tea to stay awake.

"Thelma, how do you know when you're in love?"

Thelma choked on her tea and coughed frantically. "You really cut to the chase, didn't you?" She said between coughs, as Breana patted and rubbed her back for her.

"Okay, let me see, how I should put this. Well, it's that special feeling you get when you're around the object of your affection. The way you think about him when you are apart. He's the first thing on your mind in the morning. He occupies your mind through the day, and He's the last thing on your mind at night, and then you'll even find him in your dreams… sometimes very often. In short, you are totally consumed, and you get a warm fuzzy feeling inside."

"But no one can afford to be consumed like that for a lifetime. How do you manage that?"

"Wait a minute! Let me finish; that's only in the beginning… probably why the divorce rate is so high. You see, some people go into the relationship expecting that romantic feeling of love to rage on. They expect life to be total rhapsody, but that's not realistic. It's good for a start. That kind of passion gets the sparks going, but after a while, you'll find a middle ground.

"What do you mean by middle ground?" Breana asked.

"Listen honey, a new pony rails up on its hind legs and kicks and gallops out of control because it has not been broken in. When a good trainer gets hold of it, he uses a bit and a bridle to tame the pony and brings calm to the pasture without breaking the spirit of the pony. That love you're feeling is that crazy-horse- love galloping through your heart. Once you get to know this man, and you are confronted with his flaws, and trust me, every one of us has them; the likes and the dislikes will be the bit and the bridle that will tame that crazy-horse-love. When you are aware of his faults and love him in spite of them, you have achieved unconditional love, and you won't be as restless as you are now."

Breana looked at Thelma in awe. "Just how did you get to be so wise Thelma?"

"Because wisdom and I are almost the same age."

Breana giggled. "Will you stop? You're not even old."

"Well, you're supposed to say that, but every morning my body tells me something different."

"Well, I want to tell you that I know you all are just trying to protect me, but Thelma, Mark is so nice. He's like a prince in a story book. The way he kissed my hand and the way he talks to me. He has never once got out of line. He asked me to go out to dinner and a movie tomorrow."

"I heard, it sounds to me like he's quite smitten, too."

"Oh Thelma! He's so romantic. The things he says just makes me want to swoon, and trust me, he'd catch me before I fell."

"So you trust him already? That's good. Love and trust work well together. From listening to you, you've named some of the likable things that you have already found in him. I have a feeling that you're going to love this man long after the crazy-horse-love is tamed."

"Thelma, those faults that you talked about, how long does it takes to find out what they are?"

"There is no time limit. They just show up like a bad penny. Sometimes you get rid of them, and sometimes they just circulate. That's when you need patience. It's not enough just to love. You must have patience too. And remember this; love and obsession are two different things. When your husband cherishes you in spite of your faults, you are the object of his affection. On the other hand, if he abuses you in any way, for any reason, you are the object of his obsession. You must know the difference, and preserve yourself against it. It takes two to form a successful relationship, and both voices must be heard. Remember that."

Breana reached out to hug her. "What would I do without you? Life would be unbearable for Father and me since Mother died, but you've made it seem so easy for us."

"Thank you sweetheart, it's so nice of you to say that. You know you're like a daughter to me."

They talked until the wee hours of the morning. Breana yawned and stretched. The action was contagious and Thelma did the same. She looked at the clock.

"My goodness, look at the time. I can't believe it's almost morning. These old bones need all the rest they can get."

"Okay, I'm sorry to keep you up."

"That's alright sweetheart. I just hope that something I said helped you."

"Oh yes, thank you so much, and now I'm going to let you get some sleep. Thanks for the tea, and by the way, you're *not* old."

Breana went back to her room and into her bed. In a few minutes, she drifted off to sleep hoping to dream of Mark.

Chapter Sixteen

Breakfast was long past when the clock in the hall chimed half past ten. Breana heard the chime from her room and opened her eyes. She rolled around on the bed and stretched. Suddenly, she was aware that the morning was almost gone. "I wonder what time it is - it's half past something I know?"

She walked over to the window and pulled the curtain open. The glass from the window pane was heated by the sun. She turned around and looked at the clock on her dresser. "Oh no! It's almost eleven o'clock. I never stayed in bed this late." She hurriedly went through her morning ritual and darted downstairs searching for Thelma.

From the window, she saw Thelma and Dudley outside. She went through the back door of the kitchen to join them.

"If this was a work day, I'd be in huge trouble. The clock woke me up at half past ten, and I'm still sleepy."

"That's what happens when you burn the midnight oil," said Thelma.

"But you were up too, and I see you're wide awake, and you Dudley, I expected you to be water logged this morning. Father told me that you were the 'Olympic Champion Surfer' yesterday evening."

In his Jamaican dialect, Dudley answered, "No problem mon! I was jus' looking out fi' you. Can't be too careful, you know Miss Breana, especially after all that trouble we had before."

"I know, and you're right to be concerned, but he seems to be a very nice person. We'll be having dinner tonight, and then we're going to see a movie."

"Oh, that's nice. I hope you have a good time," said Dudley meanwhile wondering. *Wonder if di boss want me to follow them.*

"Let me go inside and fix you something to eat. I'll see you later Dudley," said Thelma.

"Will you need a Showfa tonight, Miss Breana?"

"No thanks Dudley; Mark is picking me up."

"Are you sure you won't need me to chaperone?"

Breana gave him a mean, but playful look. "Yes, I'm sure. We won't be on the beach, so you won't need your surf board tonight," said Breana, giggling. Dudley laughed at her remark.

The afternoon went by slowly. It seemed as if Breana waited days for the afternoon to pass. She started getting ready for her date. Mark would be there to pick her up at six. Breana washed her hair and spent most of the afternoon styling and restyling it. After looking through her clothes, she couldn't decide what to wear. Suddenly everything in her closet was old and too drab. *Maybe I need to go shopping.* She asked Thelma to help her pick out something to wear. Thelma laid out several outfits for her to choose from, and she started getting dressed. She was just putting on the last touches of make up when Mark came to the door. Thelma answered it.

"Good evening Mr. Bogain, it's nice seeing you again," she said.

"Good evening, Señora. I came to pick up Miss Noble."

"She is expecting you, come on in." Thelma stepped aside to let Mark in. Then Mark extended a beautiful bouquet of white roses.

"Oh, these are lovely, Breana will love them. I'll just put these in some water-"

"Actually, they are for you Miss Thelma."

"For me?"

"It's for all you do for Breana."

"Thank you, they are beautiful!" Thelma was so touched. She

wanted to hug him, but instead, she graciously thanked him. She beckoned to him, and he followed her into the great hall.

"Sit here, while I let Breana know you're here."

Thelma went to Breana's room and knocked on the door. "Just a minute" said Breana. She put the compact down on the dressing table and looked at herself in the mirror.

"Breana," Thelma called through the door, "Mark is here."

"Okay, I'm almost ready. You can come in, the door is open."

"What's taking you so long? I thought you were ready a half hour ago," Thelma questioned as she entered the room.

"I know, but my make-up was all wrong and I had to fix it. What do you think, too much, not enough, what?"

"You look fine," Thelma responded.

"You think so...maybe some more mascara, or lipstick. Or maybe—"

"Maybe, you can just go on your date. You look beautiful just as you are."

"I can't believe he's here already," Breana said, while fussing with her hair.

"He's here, all six feet of him. He's looking suave, as smooth as honey and smelling good too," said Thelma. "He did say six o'clock."

Breana pulled Thelma closer and said, "Ok, are you sure I look good?"

"Oh my princess, the mirror doesn't lie. You are beautiful beyond description and alluring beyond measure; any man would be proud to have you on his arm. You have nothing to worry about; now go for heaven's sake."

"Thanks Thelma, I don't want to seem too anxious, so will you please tell him I'll be right down." Thelma rolled her eyes and shook her head as she chuckled. "Kids," she said under her breath as she walked out of the room.

"She'll be out shortly, Mr. Bogain."

Breana stayed in the room just a few more minutes, and then walked out.

As soon as Mark saw Breana coming down the stairs, he rose to his feet. He would not blink his eyes for fear that she might disappear. Breana walked toward him, and they met in the middle of the room. He instinctively took her right hand, brought them up to his lips and kissed it. He said, "Truly, I never imagined my eyes would behold such beauty, Senorita," he said.

"Thank you. You look pretty dashing yourself." *There ae those tingles again.* Her entire body was so excited just to be near him.

"Come, I want you to meet my father. He's around here somewhere," She said taking Mark by the hand. As soon as their hands touched, it seemed electricity passed through them. Their eyes met, silently asking, *did you feel that?* They walked through the house with Breana calling out to Henry. "Father…Father!" She called out. "Where are you?"

"I'm in the study, Pumpkin."

She walked ahead and Mark followed closely behind her. "Father, this is Mark Bogain. Mark, this is my father, Henry Noble."

Henry gave that suspicious *don't mess with my daughter* look, hoping it would keep Mark in check. "Nice to meet you Mark," he said as they extended hands to each other. Henry gave a more than firm hand shake that Mark accepted with a knowing smile.

"Likewise Sir, I've heard a lot about you."

"Is that so?" Henry replied.

"Yes Sir, I have. Breana just happens to think you are the world's greatest father."

"Good answer young man. You should have been a diplomat." Henry smiled cordially.

"You will have her home at a reasonable hour, won't you?"

"Yes Sir, I certainly will. We will be back no later than eleven o'clock, Sir."

Henry nodded his head to show his approval, and Mark turned

to leave, Breana kissed Henry goodbye. Mark took her arm, and they both went through the door. As soon as Henry thought they were at a safe distance, he hurried out to the window to see what was transpiring between them. He smiled when Mark walked around the passenger side of the car, and opened the door. He guided Breana to her seat. After he took his seat behind the wheel he said, "I'm glad I had the chance to meet your father. He seemed easy to be around. I wonder what he thinks of me. No one is ever good enough to take out daddy's little girl you know. Do you think he likes me?"

"Mark calm down. He has only seen you all of five minutes. He only had time to say hello, how much can he like or dislike?"

"Will you tell me as soon as you know that he likes me, assuming that he will?"

"Why is it so important that he likes you?"

"Because someday I may have to ask him a favor, and if he doesn't like me, he may say no."

"Okay, I'll tell you as soon as I know, I promise."

Mark drove to Knutsford Boulevard to Maxine's Elegant Dining. He drove the car up to the door and handed the car key to the valet, and they proceeded inside the building.

"Do you have a reservation, Sir?" asked the hostess.

"Yes, I'm Mark Bogain,"

"Oh yes Mr. Bogain, your table is ready. Come this way please," she beckoned Mark, and Breana followed. As they were seated, the hostess handed them the menu. "Your waiter will be with you shortly. Have a pleasant evening."

As the hostess walked away, Breana watched slyly to see if Mark had any *preoccupations* with other women. She was relieved to find that Mark only had eyes for her. They chatted constantly, only stopping to order. The service was impeccable and appetizers were soon served.

"Mmm, this is really good!" said Breana, after tasting the delightful dish set before her.

"Very savory, it's exquisite," said Mark.

"This is delicious," Breana agreed. She was anxious to know more about him, so she delved right in. She asked about his mother and her life after the death of his father

"She grieved my father's death for a longtime, but she eventually remarried. She lives in Ecuador. My sister and I stayed with our grandparents, but we spent some holidays with her."

"What's her name?"

"Anastasia Peron-Bogain, at least that's what she's calling herself now that she's divorced..."

"Oh, I'm sorry. Was it hard for her after the divorce?

"No, it was hard for her when my father died. She never really got over his death, and her new husband had no patience for that. She did not mislead him. He knew how she felt before he married her. I can't say I blame him, though. Anyway, after the divorce, she just filled her life with my sister and me, charity and shopping, although she has many admirers."

"So what's she like?"

He paused with a half-smile on his face. He patted his mouth with a napkin, and then he put both hands under his chin as he thought of his mother. "Oh God, how do I explain my mother?"

"Is she that bad or that good?" Breana asked, leaning backward in her seat, smiling.

"She is that good! She is free spirited; she's lighthearted, and she is stern all at the same time. She has nerves of steel. And even though we were not under the same roof all the time, we were in each other's lives constantly."

"So what does she look like?"

"She has a beautiful olive complexion. Dark, wavy hair like mine, she has light brown eyes, and a straight face with high cheek bones. She is tall and very shapely."

"How old were you when your father died?"

"I was ten. My sister was twelve."

"Where did you go to college?"

"I went to Princeton for two years. Then, my grandfather wanted me to have hands on experience in the family business. The headquarters is in Bogotá, Columbia, so I transferred to Bogotá University. I had a good time there. There was a bed and breakfast twenty minutes away from the University. They used to serve great food. My friends and I, we use to leave the dorm and go there to sleep, just to have our breakfast there; and that's a twenty minute ride back to the university, but it was twenty minutes well spent."

He noticed how Breana listened attentively, hanging on to every word, "But that's enough about my life," he said, "I want to know about Breana Noble."

"After listening to you, I'm not sure I should talk about me."

"Are you kidding…after I bare my soul to you, you're going to hold out on me?"

Breana took a sip of her ginger beer. Then she looked at him with a nervous grin. "Okay, but remember you asked for it."

"Go ahead, dish it up, I can take it," he said, as he looked at her with an impish grin.

"Okay, my father is not my biological father; I was adopted. My adopted mother died a year after my adoption, so Thelma helped my father raise me. Before we came here, I attended DeVry University in Georgia. After my father accepted the job as Ambassador to Jamaica, I transferred to UWI. I graduated three years later. Oh, it was the most exciting day of my life. I was the Valedictorian."

"I knew it!" Mark interrupted, "I could have told you that."

"Did you also know that my knees were like rubber when I stood at the podium?" she said as she gave account of the event. "Dr. Martin Luther King gave the commencement address that day. People from all over came to hear him. It was such a large crowd. All the graduates were dressed in red gowns, and we marched over to the Assembly Hall. It was so packed that many people had to stand. Even though Dr. King spoke for almost forty minutes, the people were so patient. I believe that speech will stay in the memory of everyone who heard it that day. His speech was motivating to us all. Breana began to recite the speech.

'If it falls to our luck to be street-sweepers, sweep the streets like Raphael painted pictures; like Michelangelo carved marble; like Shakespeare wrote poetry, and like Beethoven composed music. Sweep the street so well that all the host of heaven and earth would have to pause to say, here lived a great street sweeper.'

At the end, he shook hands with a lot of people. They were just reaching out to him.

It was a moving experience."

"And you said you had nothing to tell. I've never met Dr. King. I hope I have the pleasure someday," said Mark.

"He is *awesome.* I hope you get to meet him, too."

"If I was the Valedictorian at my graduation and he showed up, he would have to give my speech. There's no way I would be able to speak. The man is a legend in his time. Did you get his autograph?"

"I wish I had, but no such luck. Can you imagine people wading their way through the crowd to get to him? He showed so much patience with everyone. He displayed such gentleness. There was an aura of humility about him."

While they dined and strolled down memory lane, recapturing the essence of their past, and sharing it with each other, the evening was slowly ebbing away.

"Mark, would you mind if we go to see 'Life in Hopeful Village' instead of the movie. I think you might like it."

"What's 'Life in Hopeful Village'?"

"It's a play. I find it very funny. It starts the same time as the movie."

"Well, if you think it's funny, then by all means let's go see it." He looked at his watch.

"If we're going to make it to the show, we better leave now."

"I agree. I don't want to miss any of it."

Mark beckoned to the waiter, "Check please!" He paid the bill, tipped the waiter, and he and Breana walked out. The valet was already at the front with their car, he handed Mark the key. Mark gave him a handsome tip. They got to the theater just in time.

The show was spectacular. Even though Mark understood most of what was being said, Breana had to do some translation from Patois to English for him. He enjoyed the show, mostly because he liked hearing Breana's voice whispering in his ear, and the fact that she sat so close to him. At the end, Mark begrudged the idea of parting company with Breana. 'Any hour of the night would be too early to take her home,' he thought.

"How would you like a quick walk on the beach before turning in? We could let your father know we're back first."

"Sounds wonderful, it's a lovely night for a walk on the beach.

When they reached Harbor View, Mark took her key and opened the door for her. Breana stepped into the foyer and there was Henry, sitting in the Parlor, reading a book.

"Hi Pumpkin, you're home. Did you have a nice evening?"

"Yes, I had a lovely evening and no, I'm not really home yet. I just want you to know that we're back, but we're going for a walk on the beach."

"Well thank you for being considerate and for keeping your promise to be home at a reasonable time."

"Well, I know how you worry. Mark is waiting for me, I won't be long."

The skies were lit by bountiful clusters of bright glimmering stars, and the water shimmered by the shining light of the full moon. The air was filtered by the fragrance of night of wild flowers. As they walked along the beach, Mark told stories of the sea, and she finally told Mark of her fascination by the sea, even as a child. They gathered shells and played silly pranks on each other.

As the weeks passed, the dating continued. Mark took Breana to places that she never knew existed on the island. They frolicked in the warm Caribbean water and walked barefooted on white sand on different beaches.

One special night on the beach, Mark contemplated what he should say to her. He wondered how he could bring this date to a perfect end.

'Should *I tell her I love her, or should I wait? I know I love her, but should she know? Is it too soon to tell her? Maybe it is.*'

While he wrestled with his thoughts, Breana was experiencing her own turmoil.

'*What will I do when his ship sails? I love him, but I'll never say it first, and what good would it do? He'll be gone soon enough. Oh, God I wonder what he's thinking. Will he even remember me after he leaves?*'

They pondered as they walked hand in hand, in silence. Mark slipped his arm around her waist and pulled her closer to him. "This is such a wonderful night; I wish it would go on forever," he said.

"It sure is. The stars are so beautiful, it's like I could just reach out and touch them." She said.

"I wish that were so. I would have plucked the brightest one for you. Look over there; see that one that outshines the others in that cluster to the left?" he asked as he pointed to the star.

"Yeah, I see it; that's a bright one!" she replied.

"That's just how you are; my bright and beautiful star."

Mark gently pulled Breana towards him, preventing her from walking further. Her mind raced with the prospect of what was to come as her body tried to catch up. She felt her blood grow warm in her body, and her lips swelled as she anticipated Marks touch. He looked into her eyes as if he were studying her soul, deathly careful of what he was about to do. He cupped her face with his hands, brought her closer and kissed her passionately. It sent Breana's heart racing, as she felt the earth move under her feet.

Oh God, where is this going? She thought. Mark broke their embrace.

"I didn't plan this, but you're so beautiful in the moonlight, I just couldn't help myself, forgive me."

"There's nothing to forgive."

"Now you're being kind, if your father saw me kissing you like that, there *would* be a problem."

They strolled slowly towards Breana's house. "May I take you to see the Bogain-Villa tomorrow evening? We could have dinner on board."

Finally, I thought you'd never ask, she thought. "That would be fabulous. I'd love to see it."

They started walking back to the house. He lifted her chin and kissed her lips.

"I had a delightful evening, Breana." he said smiling at her. "I'll see you tomorrow?"

"Yes. I had a beautiful evening." She replied.

"Until tomorrow then, Hasta mañana mi amor" He waited for her to get inside the house.

Breana walked into the house. It was quiet. She assumed everyone was asleep, so she went to her room. Entering the room, she kicked off her shoes and threw herself across the bed. "Oh! What a lo-ve-ly night!"

"Yeah, I've been waiting to hear about the lo-ve ly night," said the voice coming from a corner of the room. Breana screamed as she jumped to her feet, then she started laughing. She saw Thelma sitting in an arm-chair in the corner.

"Thelma, you scared me half to death. Why did you do that? Why are you sitting so quietly in the corner?"

"I'm sorry love. I came to turn down your bed, and I decided to wait for you. I guess I dozed off. You woke me up when you kicked your shoes off. Now I'm so tired, I don't know if I can stay awake long enough to hear about your lo-ve-ly night, good night. See you in the morning." She yawned and walked out of the room.

Watching her leave, Breana chuckled, "Sleep tight,"

She went to bed savoring the memory of her date. She pictured them strolling hand in hand, barefooted along the shore as tiny waves dashed against their feet. Finally, she drifted off to sleep.

Mark couldn't sleep. He relived the evening he spent with Breana. He tossed and turned. He got out of bed and sat in a chair by the window in his room. He looked at the telephone as if he expected it to ring.

I wish I could call her, but I dare not. At this hour, her father would have my hide, no doubt. The sound of her voice played on his mind. He looked through the window at the moon. His thoughts of her were overwhelming.

I wonder if she is looking at the moon too, or is she asleep. If I could reach that star over there, that's the one I would give to her. It's as bright as she, and she is as beautiful as it. I want her, I need her. I've got to have her, but the time is so short until I leave. I don't want to rush her and take the chance of losing her. What do I do?

He sat by the window until the wee hours of the morning. His eyes got heavy, and he started nodding. He got into the bed and drifted off to sleep.

Thelma was up and bustling around the house. Breana slept late, and Henry had breakfast alone. He was just finishing his coffee when Breana walked into the room.

"Good morning Father," she said.

"Good morning, Pumpkin."

She sat at the table, and she reached for the pitcher of orange juice and poured herself a glass full. Thelma walked in carrying an assortment of breakfast treats. She placed them on the table.

"These breakfast pastries look so scrumptious," Breana said.

"You're welcome dear. But, it's more like brunch now. If you need anything else, I'll be in the kitchen."

"Mmmm…" she said, picking up a croissant, "What more could I need."

Henry looked away from the paper to Breana. "Indeed, what more could you need, so how was your date," he asked smiling.

"It was divine. Mark is a gentleman; I love spending time with him."

"Will you be seeing him again?"

"Yes, he asked me to go with him this evening to see the Bogain-Villa."

"Is that so? I know how much you've always admired that ship. That should be interesting to say the least."

"He said there won't be much to see because the men are still working on it. However, it will be finished in another week, and he would like me to see what it looks like before it's finished."

Mark was on the phone talking to the master chef on the Bogain-Villa. "Roberto," he said, "I'll be having a special guest on board for dinner tonight, so make dinner special. Alert the boys in the Band okay. We'll be on board at seven o'clock. I'll see you then."

At the Noble's house Henry was on his way out. "You'll probably leave before I get back this evening, so be careful." He said to Breana.

Thelma was entering the room. "Did you say you're going into town, Mr. Noble?"

"Yes Thelma...why, did you need something?"

"No Sir, I was just thinking about what to do for dinner."

"Don't hold dinner for me. I'll be at a business dinner this evening; have a nice day ladies."

"I won't be having dinner either Thelma. Mark and I will have dinner on the Bogain-Villa."

"No kidding! Ooh- la-la...!" Thelma said in her best French accent.

"So he has invited you to his house. Actually, I know all about it." She said, taking a seat in the chair across from Breana. "Mark called earlier. He said that he'll pick you up at about half past six this evening. I detect a note of love in the air." She sang the last statement, which made Breana blush.

"Now don't get carried away, he only wants me to see what the ship looks like before the repairs are finished."

"Yeah, that...*and* dinner, and lest we forget, the lo-ve-ly night which I have yet to hear of the details."

"That *is* the detail. It *was* a lovely night."

"Lovely is the sum of it. The detail is what makes it lovely, so start talking Missy," Thelma said, teasing her.

"Okay, remember when you told me that little things mean a lot, and they are the things that make you like a person?"

"Yes, I remember. So you *were* listening after all. I wasn't sure, since you had appeared so moonstruck."

"Of course I listened. It's good advice. He did all those little things and more." Breana paused. "I think he's the one Thelma."

Thelma narrowed her eyes, "The *one* what?"

"Okay, you want me to spell it out? I think I'm falling in love with him?"

"Oh, I knew that. I just wanted you to hear yourself say it child. I'm so happy for you sugar. Mark seems like a really nice man, and I hope he'll make a wonderful husband."

"I wouldn't go that far. I don't really know how he feels. I mean, oh, I don't know what I mean."

She picked up one of the apples from the dining table centerpiece, and began passing it back and forth from one hand to the other.

"Whenever we're together, he always says that he enjoys spending time with me, but he hasn't said he loves me. He did say mi amor in parting once, but I'm sure he meant it as just part of a saying."

Thelma watched her intently. "Well, if he isn't head over heels in love with you yet, he's heading that way like a bullet, or he wouldn't be spending so much time with you. Baby girl, you have to know how a man thinks. He has been spending all that time with you, and he keeps coming back for more. He has never gotten out of line or disrespected you in anyway. He came into this house as a respectable man and met your family. He brings you home, *always,* during hours when all decent young ladies should be home. That's the 'mark' of a good man, no pun intended," she giggled.

"Thelma, this is serious!"

"Okay, I'm sorry, keep talking."

"What do you think Father would say if he really falls in love with me?"

"I have no idea. The better question is what he'll say when he finds out *your* feelings. If I was you, I would be prepared to exercise patience; because, he has never had to let go of a daughter before.

"Thanks," Breana said, standing up and stretching. "I'll keep that in mind; meanwhile, I'm going back to my room. I'm a little tired, and I have some things to take care of too."

Thelma picked up the apple Breana was fingering. "Everything's going to work out," she said, smiling, as she replaced the apple in the bowl.

Mark spent the day *anxiously* preparing for Breana's visit. He checked and rechecked the smallest details. At half past five, he arrived at Breana's house. He was looking debonair, even casually dressed in khaki shorts and a green polo shirt. Breana answered the door.

"Mark, you're here, come in!"

Deep dimples graced his tanned cheeks when he smiled. "Thank you", he said as he stepped over the threshold "You look lovely as always. Are you ready to go?"

"Just a minute, I'll let Thelma know we're leaving."

"Say hello to her for me and your father too."

"I'll tell Thelma. Father isn't home."

Mark's eyes followed her until she was out of sight. Her pink floral dress clung to every curve. She said goodbye to Thelma and went back to join Mark. They walked to the car hand in hand, and he held the car door open for her. As they drove along in silence deep in their own thoughts, they both took turns stealing glances and smiling at each other. When they got to the ship, Mark took her by the arm and walked her on board. He walked her around the deck; then he gave her a tour of the interior. She had never been on a ship before; she was awestruck. However, there was one area that was off limits, the Majestic Suite. Mark had issued a new order to tear everything out of that suite and rebuild it. He took her to the Presidential Suite. It was beautifully decorated in purple and gold. He sat her down at a table and poured a drink from a bottle on ice.

"Here's to quenching your thirst," he said, handing her a glass and lifting his to her.

"Thank you."

"Thank you for coming to share it with me."

Breana tasted her drink. "I imagined that the inside of a ship was large, but I never thought it would be this large. This is gigantic."

"I can only take you to the places that aren't dangerous, due to ongoing repair. So there are still areas that you won't be able to see."

"I doubt that I would be able to see it all in one evening anyway. I can imagine how many times the passengers get lost."

"Sometimes they do, but it doesn't take long for them to learn their way."

"I feel as if I have just strolled through a whole neighborhood," she said, as they walked around.

"I think we better head back to the dining room. Roberto might be ready to serve dinner, and you don't want to keep 'The Roberto' waiting when he's ready to serve."

"Oh yeah, why is that?"

"I can't explain it. Let's just say I don't feel like buying new sets of pots and pans."

"Don't tell me he throws them."

"You got it."

"At you?" She started laughing, "I can just imagine you ducking flying objects from the kitchen."

Mark stopped in his tracks. "Thank you very much. Laugh at my expense, and for your information, he wouldn't dare throw anything at me; unless, I turned my back of course."

"I'm sorry, I didn't mean to laugh," Breana said, trying to tame her giggles.

"Apology accepted. Now let's go because, if he starts throwing things, I'm putting you in front."

"You wouldn't dare!"

"Are you kidding? After the way you laughed at me? I'd like to see how you would handle the situation," said Mark, heavy on the Columbian accent. "Actually, Philippe would be first in the line of fire."

"Who's Philippe?"

"He is the fellow who serves my table."

"Well, let's hurry then. I can't have Philippe's bodily harm on my conscience, and for you to be without a Butler. You probably wouldn't know what to do."

Mark raised his eyebrows, "You had no conscience when it was I who would be in the line of fire. Now you've grown one so fast to protect Philippe? He's fired. That kind of competition is not good for me." he said, turning to face Breana. "Besides, I know my way around the kitchen, the dining room…and I'm no slouch in some other rooms either."

They walked back to the Presidential Suite laughing, joking and giggling. Mark opened the door and ushered her inside.

Philippe was standing in the dining room, neatly dressed in a dark tuxedo. A white towel was draped over his left arm. His dark straight hair was styled in a crew cut and neatly combed. He saw Mark and Breana entering the dining area, and quickly moved to the table and waited.

"Breana, this is Philippe."

"Buenos noches, Señorita," he said, pulling the chair for Breana to sit.

"Thank you, Philippe."

Mark sat down and Philippe brought a delicate white wine to the table. He deftly poured some in Mark's glass. Breana watched with intrigue as Mark picked up the glass by the stem and proceeded to perform what she considered a ritual. He swirled the wine around, sniff it several times, and then took a sip and moved it around in his mouth.

"Very good," he said, nodding to Philippe.

Philippe attempted to pour some into Breana's glass, "None for me, thank you," she said—gesturing with her hand. "I'll have water or club soda if you have it."

"Yes Miss, I do have club soda, which would you prefer?"

"I'll have club soda with a twist of lime please."

"I'm sorry, I should have asked. I assumed that you would like the wine," Mark said. "I appreciate that you didn't pretend to like it for my sake. See how much I've learned about you already? And the night is still young."

"What exactly have you learned about me?"

"Well, you're a lady that makes up her own mind about what you want. I admire that."

"Thank you for the compliment and the admiration." She replied.

Philippe returned with Breana's beverage and began serving. The serving table was laden with a variety of foods, Chicken Cordon blue, grilled Portobello Mushroom steaks and vegetable couscous among other delectable dishes. "Will there be anything else, Sir?"

"No thank you Philippe. I'll handle it from here" he said.

"Very well Sir, enjoy your meal." Philippe left and closed the door behind him.

"Mmm, everything looks delicious," Breana said.

"Oh yes, Roberto is the best. He's been with the family for years." They began placing food on their plates.

"So what is it like living here in Jamaica, was it a difficult adjustment for you?" Mark asked.

"It might have been, if I didn't have Thelma. She's from here originally, and she helped me to adjust. She carried me around to different places, and she taught me the meaning of certain words, and the correct response to certain gestures. She has been a Godsend to me in every way since my mother passed."

"It's surprising that your father never remarried after your mother died."

"Oh please, don't mention that. He actually did, and it almost cost him his life. I'm still uncomfortable talking about it. Maybe someday I'll be over it enough, so I could discuss it without feeling like a dagger is being thrust in my heart."

"Oh, was it that bad?"

"Worse, my father was almost murdered, and Thelma was almost sent to jail for a crime she didn't commit, and I was supposed to be the next victim. She would have gotten away with it too, if it wasn't for Dudley." Breana's face began to turn red.

"Say no more. I can see it's disturbing you to talk about it. I'm sorry."

"It's okay, you couldn't have known". Breana said. Not knowing what else to say, she took a bite of her food. They both ate quietly for a moment. It was their first awkward moment.

Finally, Mark took a sip of wine. "Let's talk about something more pleasant."

"I agree."

"You know, the opening of the Arena is set for July thirtieth."

She swallowed. "Yes I do."

"Well, you seemed to know your way around pretty well, would you take pity on me and be my date?" She picked up her fork and started playing with her food. "I'll consider it on one condition."

"What's that?"

"August fifteenth will be the Commonwealth Paraplegic Games at the University. Will you be my date?"

"It's a deal! Let's shake on it?"

"Deal." they said concurrently, as they shook hands.

The smooth sound of rhythm and blues played on as their personal soundtrack to a romantic evening. While they took pleasure in dining in each other's company, the evening was ebbing away. Mark got up and walked to the back of Breana's chair. She stood up and he pulled her chair away. He took her hand and placed it on his arm. Her heart quickened.

"Shall we go on deck?" he asked.

"I'd like that." They walked outside, and she was immediately entranced by the amazing display of colors on the horizon where the ocean seemed to touch the sky. It was getting chilly, and he took his jacket off and laid it across her shoulders. "Breana, there's something I wanted to say to you." When he held her and said her name, she could have melted in his arms.

"What is it?" She looked up at him and waited. It seemed as if he was struggling for what to say. *That's not like him; he has no trouble with words,* she thought.

"I—ah, I think that dress looks beautiful on you." He exclaimed, recovering from his momentary loss of speech.

"Thank you, Thelma made it for me."

"Well, give her my compliments."

They arrived at his favorite spot on the deck. "I brought you out here, so you could see the last ray of sunlight on this side of the earth."

"Oh Mark, it's beautiful. It looks as if the ocean is being kissed goodnight by the sun."

"Yeah, the *Lucky Sun* gets kissed goodnight; then roams around heaven all day."

He held her from behind around the waist, and he leaned her head back against his chest. She could feel his heartbeat against her back.

Breana laughed nervously, "Well, Mark Bogain, are you jealous of the sun?"

"If I am, it's only because it kisses you every day as well."

"There's no need for you to be jealous. You're with me right now, and the sun is gone."

Although they had kissed the night before, he thought not to be presumptuous about his show of affection for her. He leaned forward and kissed the nape of her neck. Her response was beckoning for more, so he continued with kisses along the nape of her neck until he reached just behind her right ear. Her perfume engulfed him and provoked his mind. His thoughts raced ahead to what it would be like with her, feeling her softness against his body. The passion within him was overwhelming and he desired more of her. He kissed her ear, and it was all Breana could take. His breath was like fire against her skin. She began feeling as if she would melt. A soft whimper came from her lips. She closed her eyes as a warm sensation passed through her body, and she trembled with anticipation. Her heart was beating fast and her pulse was racing. She turned to face him and was met by his kiss.

"Oh Breana," Mark whispered, his eyes locked into hers, his heartbeat elevated, and his passion was intense. "You are so beautiful. Just let me hold you for a while."

"Mark, I—"

He kissed her breath away before she could finish her speech. The sweetness in her response to his kiss took him back to the first time he kissed her. Breana gingerly placed her hands on the back of his head and slid her fingers through his hair. Mark groaned with delight. They held each other as if they would become one body. Mark felt an urgent need to have more of her. *No*, he thought, *this isn't the right time*. He abruptly broke their embrace. Breana blushed as she looked at him. He leaned against the guard rail, just looking at her.

His eyes are so captivating. Why is he looking at me like that? What is he thinking?

"Mark, what's wrong?"

"Nothing's wrong. You're just so beautiful. I think I better take you home right now."

"I could stay a while longer, the night's still young."

"Oh no Miss Noble, he said, kissing her hand, your presence can be hard on a man at this stage in a relationship. I *want* you to stay, but its best that you go."

He took her hand, and they started walking toward the disembarking area. Mark guided her ashore and drove her home. When they arrived at Harbor View, he kissed her gently on her lips. "It was good being with you tonight." he said.

"For me, tonight is unforgettable, touring the ship was incredible." she replied.

"Oh, you liked that. Then we should do it again soon."

He took both of her hands into his and kissed them; then he walked her to the door. "Good night my princess," he said, as he turned to leave.

She half closed the door and watched as he drove away. *I better get used to saying goodbye. He'll be gone soon.*

Breana kept her promise to be Mark's date at the opening of the Arena. They hardly paid attention to the acting Prime Minister conducting the opening ceremony. In their minds, they were consumed with thoughts of each other.

The Duke of Edinburgh was presented and officially opened the Games. Breana and Mark had front row seats.

Being so close to royalty is not a big deal after all; I have my own prince sitting next to me. She thought, as the Duke read the Queen's message to a cheering crowd.

The Royal family stayed in Jamaica for two weeks. It was a time of jubilee on the island. For Mark and Breana, it was magical. They attended all the events together; they were inseparable. He would have gone anywhere to be near her.

The games came to a close, and the work on the Bogain-Villa was almost at its end. Mark was torn between extending his visit to have more time with Breana and fulfilling previous obligations. *I have to sail in two days. How do I say good-bye to her? When will I see her again? If I do see her again, will she still be available? I can't take that chance, but what can I do? The games are over, and the passengers need to go home. I wish the men hadn't worked so fast on the ship. At least I would have an excuse for staying.*

While Mark agonized over what decision to make, Breana's thoughts were no different.'

Mark will leave in a couple of days. I can't bear the thought of him leaving. What will my life be without him now? I can't even remember my life without him. Will he remember me after he leaves? Oh, I wish we had more time.'

Later, as Breana lay across her bed, waves of sadness swept through her heart. She was on the verge of tears when the phone rang. Thelma stopped vacuuming and ran to answer it.

"Hello, Noble's residence."

"Good morning, this is Mark Bogain. May I speak to Breana please?"

"Of course you may, Mr. Bogain. Hold on just a minute, Breana!" Thelma called out, it's for you!

Breana pick up the phone; "Hello, this is Breana."

"Hi there! Hope I'm not disturbing you, but I'm going crazy over here."

"Mark, what's wrong?"

He paused, still not sure about Breana's feelings for him. "I've been thinking about you.

I've been thinking about us, and what will happen after I leave the day after tomorrow."

Breana was so relieved that she was not alone in her thoughts. "I've been thinking the same thing. Wondering what it will be like when you leave."

"We have to find a solution. I can't lose you. Breana, I…I love you. I need to know if you feel the same way."

Breana felt a rush. "Yes Mark, I love you too."

They talked for a long time. After his conversation with Breana, Mark got his crew together. "There's going to be a gala. Decorations, meal planning and entertainment must be optimum. I want this to be the grandest gala that ever graced the seas!" he said.

Early the next morning, he went to the Nobles house. Thelma answered the door. "Hello Mr. Bogain, come on in."

"Thank you, Thelma. I'm sorry for being here so early. I wanted to speak to Mr. Noble, and I would rather Breana not know that I'm here."

Thelma raised an eyebrow. "Okay, wait here. I'll let Mr. Noble know you're here." She walked away thinking *Well he seems intense, wonder what he wants.*

Henry was in the den reading the morning paper. "Mr. Noble, Mr. Bogain is here to see you."

Mark's here to see me? "Send him in," he said, putting the paper aside.

Thelma went back to the parlor. "Follow me Mr. Bogain...

"Good morning Mr. Noble," Mark said, extending his hand to Henry.

They shook hands. "Hello Mark, how are you?" He gestured for Mark to sit down.

"I'm sorry to call on you so early, Mr. Noble, but there's an urgent matter that I need to discuss with you."

"Should I set a place for Mr. Bogain for breakfast, Sir?" asked Thelma.

Looking at Mark, Henry asked, "Will you stay for breakfast?"

"No thank you, Sir. I have a busy day today. Thank you, Thelma."

"Then may I offer you a cup of coffee," Thelma asked.

Mark said, "That I'll never turn down. I've heard about your coffee. I would love some."

"Okay, Mr. Sweet Talker. The coffee is already brewed, so I'll be back in a minute."

Thelma returned to the den with a tray of coffee and freshly baked croissants. She placed the tray on a table and poured the coffee. The gentlemen were laughing at some story Henry had just told. Thelma was pleased to see them getting along. "I figured you might like something with your coffee; especially for that busy day you said you'll be having."

"Thank you, Thelma. That was very thoughtful of you."

Henry looked on as Thelma fussed with the table. "You know, Thelma must have someone to feed, always. One way or the other, she will find a way to sneak the food in."

"Then she is a lady after my own heart," Mark said smiling approvingly.

"I told you he's a sweet talker, Thelma laughed, but I love it. Keep it coming honey." She said as she left the room and closed the door behind her.

"So, Mark, what can I do for you?"

"Sir, I hope this won't be a surprise to you, but it's regarding Breana. She and I have been spending a lot of time together since we've met. I've enjoyed her company very much, Sir. I have never met anyone quite like her." Mark paused to sense Henry's reaction to his statement. Henry was calm, sitting back in his chair with his arms folded across his chest.

"I want her in my life Sir, always. I'm in love with her, and if you will give me your blessing, I would like to ask her to marry me."

"Marry you? You've only known each other for how long? Less than two months? How much can you know about each other?"

"Yes Sir, I understand that, but I know the most important thing. I love her, and I want her in my life. If you give us your blessing Sir, I promise you, I'll spend the rest of my life cherishing her."

"How does she feel about you?"

"I know she loves me, Sir, she told me so."

"But aren't you supposed to be leaving tomorrow?"

Mark looked to the floor, then back at Henry. "I want to ask her to accept my ring, this way I know she will be here for me. I'll get back to her as soon as I can. You have my word from one gentleman to another Sir."

"So what you're saying is you want to keep my daughter locked down by giving her a ring."

"With all due respect Sir, it's not like that. If it were up to me, we would never be apart. Before I leave, I need her to know the extent of my love for her. *That* is why I'm giving her a ring."

Henry started massaging his chin as he always does when he's thinking. *Long distance courting, eh? Hmm, that's not a bad idea. He won't be anywhere near her, and it will keep everyone else at bay. Besides, we'll see if the relationship stands the test of time.* "Well if you feel that strongly about it, and she loves you as you've said, then you can go ahead and ask her. You have my blessing," he replied.

Marks' eyes bulged with excitement. He took a grip of Henry's hand and started shaking it vigorously. "I thank you very much Sir, thank you. You will never regret this. I will plan a party on board the ship tonight. It will be a formal affair. You, Thelma and Dudley are invited. The invitations will be delivered today. I should leave before Breana wakes up and finds me here. Thank you so much, Sir." He said backing away.

Just before he turned to leave, Henry said, "Just be good to my little girl and that will be thanks enough."

"I swear on my own life." He said as he started walking briskly away, grinning from ear to ear.

Henry walked Mark to the door. As soon as he got outside, he jumped up, and slapped his left fist in the palm of his right hand, "Yes, all is right with the world," he said.

"Thelma, I'll have breakfast now please." Henry said, as he sat at the table.

Thelma brought out fresh fruits, hot biscuits, ham and eggs. Henry sat and stared at the food. Thelma walked in with hot coffee, and he was still staring at the food.

"Is something wrong with the food Mr. Noble?" she asked.

"The food is fine, Thelma. Sit down. I have to tell you something."

Thelma sat on a chair on the opposite side. "Has Breana spoken to you about her relationship with Mark?"

"Yes Sir, I know she's in love with him. She told me weeks ago, and it seems every time they go out together she comes home fallen a little harder. We stayed up a whole night talking about it because she couldn't sleep."

"Then I guess it would be pointless for me to do or say anything to discourage the relationship."

"Without alienating her, I would say you're right. Why would you even want to? He seems like a nice young man."

"The point is he wants to marry her. He came this morning to ask my blessing. He's having a party on the ship tonight. He plans on asking her to marry him then."

Thelma smiled. "Well I'm not surprised Sir. They've been seeing a lot of each other, and he seemed quite smitten by her too. According to what she told me, they have a lot in common."

"I can imagine they do."

"It's the way he treats her; the way he adores her and makes her feel special when they're together. I've never seen her behave like this over anyone. I think she really loves him Sir."

"What do you really think about the fact that they have only known each other for such a short time?"

"I don't believe the length of time is as important as everyone thinks. I had a friend once. She met this man, and they dated for over a year. Then they moved in together, so that they could save enough money to buy a house. After two years, they saved up enough money for a down payment, and they bought a very comfortable house. They got married and moved into the house. In less than three years, they were divorced."

"Oh, what a shame!"

"It certainly was Sir. Then a cousin of mine got married to a man the same night they met at a black jack table in Las Vegas. He said she was his good luck charm. Anyway, they got drunk, and when they got sober the next morning, they found out they were married to each other. They enjoyed each other's company, so they decided to hold off on an annulment. I just sent them a card yesterday; wishing them happy anniversary, and congratulations on fifteen years of marriage. They started out not knowing each other at all. So you see, all we can do is trust in God and pray that he will keep his guiding hand on their life together."

"So you think I did the right thing in giving him my blessing?"

"There is nothing else you could do Sir."

"Not a word to her now. Mark wants it to be a surprise. I promised him I wouldn't say anything."

"Don't worry, Sir. My lips are sealed."

Breana walked into the room. "What did I miss?" she asked.

"Oh, we were just talking about Mark's ship. Now that the work is done he might be sailing soon." Thelma answered, watching for Breana's reaction.

"Don't remind me. He's such fun to be around, and he's such a gentleman. It's such a shame I may never see him again," she sighed sadly, and sat on a chair by the table.

Henry and Thelma looked at each other with knowing smirks on their faces.

"It seems as if he means a lot more to you than you're letting on, Pumpkin. I've never seen you lamenting over any one like this before."

"I just wish he didn't have to go so soon, that's all."

Henry winked at Thelma and they shared a secret smile. The doorbell rang and Thelma went to answer it. "May I help you?"

"I have a delivery for Mr. Henry Noble, Miss Breana Noble, Ms. Thelma Atkins, and Mr. Dudley More, Ma'am."

Thelma took the envelopes. "Wait just a minute," she said. She reached her hand into the pocket of her apron and brought up some change. She handed the money to him.

"Thank you very much Ma'am," he said, walking away from the door.

Thelma handed the envelopes to Henry and Breana. "This is from Mark," Breana said, opening the envelope. He has invited me to celebrate the completion of the Bogain-Villa. Oh, I can't go. I'd rather he just leave. Why drag out the inevitable? He'll be leaving soon, anyway. Going to this party won't make it any less painful," she said. She ran back to her room.

As soon as she got to her room, the doorbell rang again. "Good Morning, Ma'am. I'm delivering this package for Miss Breana Noble," said the courier to Thelma.

Thelma took the package and tipped the messenger. *I'll go broke giving tips by the time they get married.* She took the package to Breana's room and knocked on the door. "Breana, open up, I have a package for you!"

"A package?" She said as she made her way to the door. "I'm not expecting anything. Who would be sending me a package?"

"I don't know. You tell me, it has your name on it."

"It's a garment bag who could be sending me this?"

"Why don't you find out?"

She took the garment bag from Thelma, and she walked over to the bed. She laid it down and pulled the zipper open. She reached in and took out the contents. "*Ah,*" she gasped. "This is the most beautiful gown I have ever seen, look Thelma!"

Thelma moved closer to the bed. "Oh my goodness, I've never seen anything like this! And it looks like it's the right size too. Who sent it?"

"I don't know, I didn't order anything."

"Isn't there a card?"

Breana found an envelope pinned inside the bag. "Oh yes here's something." She removed the envelope from the bag and read the card.

"Oh my goodness, it is from Mark! Thelma, the dress is a gift from him; he wants me to wear it tonight. What am I going to do now? Father won't have me wear a dress that a man bought for me!"

"Why don't you make up your mind what you want to do, and let me talk to your Father?"

"I shouldn't go, but how could I not go now! He really wants me there. It would be rude if I didn't; don't you think?"

"Yes I do. Unless you're sick or something, it would be an insult."

"What am I going to do? I can't go and then say good bye at the end of the evening, not knowing if I'll ever see him again. I hate that he's leaving."

"Why don't you just do as he asks? Go to the gala, wear the gown, and see what happens. Love can make people do strange things."

"I don't think that's enough to keep him here. He's committed to taking the passengers to their destinations, as he should be. That ship sails tomorrow, and so is any chance I may have had with him."

Thelma picked up the gown and held it up in front of Breana. "This is absolutely gorgeous. Why don't you put it on and see how it fits."

"Who said anything about going? Haven't you been listening to a word I've said?"

Thelma was getting a bit frustrated, but had to convince Breana to go. "Look, I trust that wisdom will prevail. Try the dress on."

Breana took the gown to her dressing room. She opened up the zipper, and easily slid into the sequined midnight black gown. She gathered her long dark locks and held it up. "Thelma, would you zip me up please."

Thelma zipped the dress, and Breana stood in front of the mirror. "This is absolutely divine."

It tightly hugged her hips and flared in the back down to the hem imitating a peacock's tail. She picked up the sweeping tail from the floor and spun around like Cinderella at the ball.

"That gown fits you like a glove," said Thelma, "Any man who could pick out a gown and have it fit like that, has your figure indelibly etched on his mind. He has it in a bad way child. The way I see it, you're both lovesick. I suggest you go to the party this evening and let nature takes its course."

"But what will Father say? He wasn't too keen on the idea of me going out with him in the first place; now I'm supposed to wear a dress that he bought for me to his party?"

"Leave your father to me. Everything will be alright, you'll see."

"I'm going to show the gown to him, and if he says anything, I'm not going."

"For heaven sakes girl, you *are* going to that party and that's final! Have I ever steered you wrong yet?"

Breana looked at Thelma. "No, I guess you haven't. Alright, I'll go see what Father thinks of the dress, geez."

Henry was just getting off the phone. Breana stopped to compose herself, not wanting her father to sense her uneasiness.

"Look Father! A messenger brought this over from Mark. He wants me to wear it to the gala this evening. What do you think?"

"I think I've never seen a gown as complimenting to anybody as this one is to you. Mark has exquisite taste. He's a fine man."

She moved closer and placed her hand over his forehead. "What are you doing?" asked Henry.

"Are you feeling alright, Father?"

"Sure, why do you ask?"

"I'm trying to figure out why you aren't reacting over what I just said."

"There is no need to overreact. I just plainly stated the facts."

"Then you don't mind if I wear it."

"Certainly not, I just hope I won't look too shabby next to you."

Breana took a breath, "You couldn't look shabby on your worst day."

Chapter Seventeen

The atmosphere was filled with anticipation of the gala and the tour of the newly decorated ship. Thelma helped Breana with her hair and makeup. Dudley drove them over to the docks. Mark's attendant was waiting for their arrival and immediately escorted them on board.

Breana's shapely figure confirmed Mark's vision of how she would look in the dress. Her hair was in an upsweep with soft curls cascading down, and her makeup was flawless. A diamond necklace adorned her neck, and matching stud earrings caressed her earlobes. Mark was exquisite in his formal wear, and his eyes sparkled with excitement at the sight of Breana.

"You take my breath away," he whispered, for her ears only.

"Thank you," she said softly. *Gosh, he's handsome,* she thought, looking him over as he took her arm and escorted her inside. They were a beautiful couple, like high-fashion models walking down a runway.

A live band played the classics inside the ballroom. They began to play a waltz as Mark and Breana took to the dance floor. Photographers roamed around taking snapshots of everyone. An assortment of dishes prepared for the evening meal was mouth-watering. It had promised to be a joyous night. After their first dance, they hardly saw each other. Breana's dance card was filled and Mark had to compensate by dancing with other females. However, he was always close enough to cut in and Breana always wished that he would.

They danced with many; when all they wanted was to be in each other's arms. Breana watched as Mark danced with a silver haired woman, in her 70's, who flirted with him all night. Mark watched as Breana danced with her father; then she danced with a balding old gentleman who had his eyes on her ever since she entered the room. They had to communicate through sign language, facial expressions and body language, secretly sharing jokes from a distance.

Mark searched through the crowd for the woman who had captured his heart; the one he now knew for sure he loved dearly. It was time to change the course of the evening. When he found her, she was trapped in conversation by *'Mr. Texas Oil'* an oil tycoon from Dallas who had no trouble speaking of his business ventures, and recapping how he came into his riches with shrewd business tactics while inserting anecdotes. His yellow suit was glittering with rhinestones and sequined on the lapel. Breana's eyes rolled to the back of her head from boredom. Mark saw that she was cornered and laughed to himself, then finally went to rescue her. As he approached them, he heard the fortunate ending of *Texas Oil's* stale joke.

"Then the cow said, 'Boo-ooo', get it? The cow said, 'Bo—'"

"Mark!" Breana shouted in desperation.

Mark turned to the Texan and said, "I hope you don't mind if I steal her away." Not waiting for his answer, Mark and Breana danced off. At a safe distance away, they began to laugh.

"Thank God! I was dying back there." Breana said.

"*Your* problem is that you're too nice, you laughed at his boring jokes, so he kept telling them. He probably thinks you're sweet on him," Mark teased.

"Oh yeah, I saw you with great-grandma back there. For a minute, I thought she was your new Lady."

Mark laughed. "There goes that wicked sense of humor of yours. You had me laughing all night, just watching who you were dancing with," he said.

"Well, I haven't laughed so hard in a long time," said Breana.

Mark held her face and kissed her. He looked at his watch, *11:50.* "Come on," he said, taking her by the hand and leading her back to the party.

Mark nodded to the band and they started playing the Drifters classic, *"Save the Last Dance for Me."* The vocalist had an amazing voice that set the mood just right.

"May I have this dance," Mark asked. She felt warm and secure by the lovingness in his voice.

"I thought you'd never ask."

Everyone cleared the dance floor, while they danced and made it their song. At the end of the song, he kissed her in a way that no one would soon forget. The guests whistled and applauded. Then Mark led Breana to the platform. He picked up the microphone, and called for everyone's attention. A hush fell over the room.

"Ladies and gentlemen, I thank you for coming to share this very special night with me. They say there is a soulmate born for every man, but I have sailed the world over many times, and I've always came up empty. Nevertheless, this voyage has been the most fantastic of all, because I believe with all my heart that I have found my soulmate." Breana stood there, absorbing his words like a sponge.

"That's why I've invited you all here tonight. It's now one minute to midnight, and I will ask a favor of this amazing woman standing next to me. I hope to receive my answer before the clock strikes twelve." There was a wave of soft laughter throughout the room.

Mark turned to face Breana. In the audience, Henry and Thelma braced themselves. Dudley stared at Mark and Breana, blindly stuffing bread in his mouth as if he were waiting for the plot in a movie to thicken.

"Breana, I love you. I believed I've loved you from the moment we met." He reached into his breast pocket and took out a pear shaped diamond ring. He got down on one knee and took Breana's hand. The crowd stood silent in anticipation. Breana placed her other hand over her mouth in disbelief. He looked into her eyes, and asked, "Margaret Breana Noble, will you marry me?"

Breana was awestruck. She looked away from Mark and searched the audience for her father. Henry smiled and winked at her then nodded his head. She looked at Thelma, and Thelma gave her an approving smile. She turned her attention back to Mark, and looked into his eyes. Her eyes were now flooded with tears. It was exactly twelve o'clock midnight, when she softly said, "Yes, oh yes, Mark, I *will* marry you!"

Mark, now grinning from ear to ear, slipped the ring on her finger. He kissed her hand, and then he took her in his arms and kissed her passionately, lifting her off her feet. He pulled her closer and held her so tightly as if they were one. The guests cheered and the shipmates whistled. Some women began to cry. The photographers began snapping pictures of Mark and Breana. The captain blew the foghorn, and the musicians started playing the last waltz. The guests stepped off the dance floor and watched as they gracefully waltzed together. "Did my father and Thelma know about this?"

"They sure did."

"Oh my Gosh, how long have they known?"

"I was at your house early yesterday to talk with your father. I assumed he talked to Thelma."

"You are so amazing. It's no wonder why I love you so. I can't believe that I'm going to be your wife. Oh my gosh," she said as she held out her hand to admire her new ring"

As they danced, Mark steered her to the middle of the floor. Then, just before the musicians played the last bar, the co-host of the gala pulled a streamer hidden behind the curtains, and hundreds of purple, gold and white balloons and confetti showered down on them. Everyone cheered. Even the Texan stuck his fingers in his mouth and blew a piercing whistle that made everyone looked in his direction. Some were annoyed and others thought it was funny. It made no difference to Mark and Breana. They were lost in each other. It was a magical night. Near the end of the party, the photographer motioned to Mark. He wanted one last pose of the happy couple.

"This one will be for the announcements," Mark said. He took several poses of the whole family. When the gala was over, the guests gathered around congratulating them and saying goodnight. Those that would sail the next day retreated to their cabins, and the others moved down the gangway to leave the ship.

Mark was all set to sail at six o'clock in the morning. Breana's acceptance of his proposal made it even harder to leave.

"This is not the way I expected it to be," said Mark, "I thought if we got engaged and I was sure that you would be waiting for me when I returned, my heart would not be so broken up. But instead, I'm finding it even harder to leave. What will I do when you leave here tonight?"

"I wish I had the answer for both of us; because, I will be just as lost without you. You never said how long until you come back."

"I was pre-scheduled to be here by October 3. Falling in love was the last thing I would've expected to happen to me on this trip. I have Roscoe to thank for my good fortune. I wish I could just marry you and take you with me, but I know I don't have the right to ask you to do that. You deserve a proper wedding, and I'm not going to rob you of that because of my own selfishness." They shared a long lasting kiss and held each other.

"Oh Mark, I'm going to miss you so much. I'm going to write to you every day."

"You know, it just dawned on me, instead of waiting for me to get back to set the date for our wedding, why don't we set the date now; then while you're waiting for me to return, you can plan for it. You'll be so busy the time will go by faster."

"That's a great idea! Let me check my planner," she said fumbling in her purse.

It was 2:30 in the morning. While Breana and Mark talked in

the lounge, Henry, Thelma and Dudley waited. Thelma got weary, and she fell asleep. The crew was tying up all loose ends and getting ready for departure. Mark and his sweetheart would have to say goodbye. He took her in his arms and held her so closely that they felt each other's heartbeat. It was a tearful goodbye. He finally found the courage to stand back and said, "You have to go and join your family. They've been waiting a long time."

Breana was now satisfied in knowing that Mark loved her enough to make this engagement a success and to have her set the date for the wedding. In spite of the sadness his absence would inflict on her heart, at least she had the assurance that he would be back, and she would carry on with the wedding plans.

"I have an idea," said Mark, "What would you say if I let you keep Roscoe with you, this way you two can get acquainted. After all, Roscoe is responsible for bringing us together."

"Oh my gosh…I remember! Breana said excitedly. He ran under my cabana and didn't want to leave." Breana shook her head laughing at the memory.

Mark grinned, staring dreamily. "Oh yeah, I remember I was just returning home, and I saw you on the beach when you walked out to the cabana. I wanted to meet you so I told Roscoe what to do, and let's just say Roscoe was very convincing."

"You mean that you set the whole thing up?" Breana attempted to swat him, but Mark shrugged out of the way, laughing.

"Well, it worked, didn't it? I had to find a way to get your attention." He continued laughing. Breana started laughing too, until she remembered the *bikini top incident* and decided to change the subject.

"Honestly, do you think Roscoe would be happy staying away from you for such a long time?"

"I've never left him before," Mark replied, "so I'm really not sure how he'll react. He's a creature of the sea. I raised him on the ship since he was eight weeks old. He doesn't know any other way of life."

"You know what, as much as I would like to have him, I wouldn't want to keep him and have him fret after you. That could break his spirit, and I would hate to see that happen. You keep him and let him remind you of bringing us together." Mark and Breana concluded their plans with a prayer for their future. They asked God to bless their union, for in their hearts they were already joined as husband and wife.

Mark and Breana joined the family in the Muster Hall. Mark shook Dudley's hand, and he hugged Thelma. He then shook Henry's hand and took him aside.

"Sir, I want to thank you for believing in me, and allowing me the honor of having Breana as my wife. I know you have been taking care of her for all these years, but now it is my job to do so. It will be hard for me to accomplish that while I'm away. I believe it is my duty to ask you to keep on looking after her until I return. I promise I will not be away one day longer than I have to."

"That goes without saying son, but I appreciate your asking. You are a man of character." Mark walked back to Breana. He took her hand into his and said, "Well, shall we tell them?"

Breana blushed.

"Tell us what?" asked Thelma.

"Mark and I have set a date for our wedding."

"My goodness, Henry exclaimed, Mark, you really know how to keep the ball rolling, don't you!"

"Well, I thought it's best to roll it while it's in my court, Sir. After all, there's nothing to gain from a wasted opportunity, except remorse."

"That is very philosophical. So when is the big day?" asked Henry.

"Saturday, December 17."

Henry hugged Breana and said, "Congratulations my dear. I'm sure your mother would be pleased if she were here." He shook

Mark's hand. "Welcome to the family my son. Breana will be fine. Just concentrate on getting back to us safely. God be with you."

Thelma stepped closer to Breana. She embraced her and kissed her cheek. "Congratulations sweetheart. I wish you and Mark a long, happy and prosperous life together."

They walked along the gangway. Mark and Breana huddling together, side by side. The Captain sounded the horn to signal their departure was at hand. The family proceeded along the gangway. Mark and Breana stopped to savor the last few minutes.

The captain sounded the horn again. "Well, this is my signal to get off," She started walking down the gangway. Mark took Breana's hand and pulled her aside. He gave a signal to one of the crew members that swiftly disappeared. "I wish I knew how to make this temporary separation easier. I promise you, I won't be gone for long. You have my word on that."

"I know and I appreciate that." The crew member who had left returned, carrying with him a bouquet of yellow long stem roses. He handed them to Mark and then smiled at Breana. Mark thanked him, and to Breana he said, "These roses are the first of more to come. Expect a new bouquet every day that I'm away until we meet again."

"Oh, Mark thank you," Breana was so moved, she began to cry. "Each one looks so perfect. They're so beautiful."

"Yes, but they're not quite as beautiful as you my love. As the ship left the dock Breana felt the sting of sadness in her heart, and the tears began to flow. She silently prayed for God to protect and keep Mark safe. *Saying goodbye to the one you love is so hard.*

Chapter Eighteen

Mr. Noble, its 7 o'clock. I'm not sure what to do this morning. Do you want coffee, or should I prepare breakfast?" Thelma asked.

"Oh, nothing for me please after all I had on the ship, I don't want to see any food for now. Mark really knows how to put on a party,"

"Can I do anything for you Breana?"

"No thank you Thelma. I couldn't have anything right now. I'll just go to my room and try to get some rest."

"Okay then; I'm going to my room. If anyone needs me, just give a holler…as always. Although the way I feel, once I've fallen asleep you may have to sound a trumpet to get me up."

Henry fell asleep within minutes after getting into bed. Thelma was out like a light.

In Breana's room, the situation was different, her hormones were in overdrive. She thought of the events of the night. She picked up the roses she'd laid on her dresser when she first entered the room, and smelled their fragrance. She noticed an envelope inside. Her name was written on the front in Marks handwriting. She removed the note, and read the contents:

Breana,

All my life, it seems I've been looking for someone whom I could be myself with. Someone who makes me feel alive. I've prayed and waited for someone I believe would share life's ups and downs with me; someone who would even laugh at my corny jokes. Every moment I'm with you, I feel like my heart will explode. I ask myself how one person could make another feel like that.

It's sheer agony having to part from you even for a while. Breana, I love you. I knew it from the moment I saw you that first time on the beach. I've wanted to tell you so many times, but it seemed like every time I tried, I was tongue tied. If I had a genie and he gave me three wishes, my first wish would be for you to be here with me right now. My second wish would be for you to be in my arms, and my third wish would be for my genie to disappear.

I can't wait to return and make you Mrs. Mark Bogain. I love you dearly.

Till then...dream a little dream of me...

Mark

Breana sighed heavily and thought, *Mrs. Mark Bogain, Oh Mark, I miss you so much already and I 'will' dream of you tonight.* Thoughts of her upcoming nuptials flooded her mind. Then she thought of Savannah Ives. "Oh, Savvy will be so pleased to hear I will need her to be my maid of honor. I'll have to write to her. I do hope she can make it. It has been such a long time since I have seen her." She spoke in the mirror, as if there was someone listening to her. "Listen to me talking to myself,"

Breana couldn't rest, so she went to her desk and sat down. She took a writing pad and a pen and started to write. She wrote a few lines then she changed her mind.

'I think the best thing to do is to call her first. Then I will write her a

*letter after we have spoken. I will call her later this evening. There are so
many things racing through my mind right now. I just need to relax for a
while. I wonder what Mark is thinking right now. Lord please keep him
safe and let him return to me as healthy and strong as the way he left.'*

With her thoughts focused on Mark, her eyelids became heavy
and she soon drifted off to sleep.

The house was unusually quiet and stayed that way until noon.
Thelma was the first to emerge from her room at around twelve-
thirty. "Lunch would be futile now," she said.

Henry came out a while later. "Thelma, are you awake and
functioning?"

"Yes Sir, I've been up for some time. I was going to make lunch,
but thought better of it and decided to prepare an early dinner
instead."

Breana came in. "Good morning," she said.

"Pumpkin, are you feeling all right? Morning has been long
gone. I guess the all night escapade left you confused."

"I'm fine, Father," Breana responded as she sat on a chair next
to Henry. "I guess I'm a little disoriented. The sun was already up
when I drifted off to sleep. I was trying to write a letter to Savvy,
but I decided it would be better to call her first. How about you...
did you get any sleep?" she said turning to Thelma.

"No, I'm not a daytime sleeper. I'll have to make it up tonight."

Thelma put the finishing touches on their early meal and began
serving as they talked. Breana got up to help. "Thank you honey,"
Thelma said as Breana took the bowl of salad from her hand.

"I'll tell you one thing...Thelma said, while carrying the rolls to
the table, this night life is definitely not for me. My inner clock has
been thrown off balance. I've not stayed up all night in years. Even
still, I loved every minute of last night. I've never seen you so happy
until Mark asked you to marry him."

"I was really surprised. I never expected him to ask me so soon."

"I wasn't surprised. Mark came by earlier and asked for my blessing."

"If I had a clue he was going to ask me, I would've been nervous all afternoon."

"Well, I'm surprised that you set the date so fast, though."

"Well, Mark figured that if I have the wedding plans to keep me busy, the time wouldn't seem so long before he returned."

"That's true," Thelma said between bites of her salad.

"We should select a nice picture of you and Mark for the engagement announcement,"

Henry said. How soon will you get them?

"Mark gave the photographer this address, so I can choose the shots that I like," Breana replied.

"Did I hear you say you were going to give my god-daughter, Savannah a call?"

"Yes Father, I did. I'll call her now."

"When you do speak to her, give her my love, will you?"

"I will. Thelma, dinner was wonderful. It was just what I needed. There is so much to do now. I better get started."

"Okay, if I can help you in any way, let me know."

"Thanks, I'll take you up on that offer for sure." She got up from the table and went into the den. She sat at the desk, and dialed Savannah's phone number. "Hello, this is Breana Noble, may I speak to Miss Savannah Ives please."

"This is the housekeeper. Hold just a minute I'll get her for you."

Breana waited a few minutes, and then she heard a familiar voice, "Oh my Gosh, Breana? This is a welcome surprise. How are you?"

"I'm just fine. Oh Savvy, it's so good to hear your voice. How are you?"

"I'm doing well. I've thought about you a lot, but you know how it is, there's always something to keep me busy."

"I understand!" As the conversation went on, Breana said, "The reason for my call is to tell you that I'm getting married!"

"Did you say married?"

"Yes!"

"Wow! You and Mark? This is great!"

"A lot has happened since the last time we spoke. It's a long story. I'll give you details in my letter."

"I'm so excited for you! Congratulations! Margaret Breana Bogain. It has a nice ring to it."

"I agree," Breana said with a giggle. "The wedding is set for Saturday, December 17, and I would like you to be my Maid of Honor."

"Oh, Breana! Thank you so much. I'm honored that you asked me. You can count on my being there, and I can't wait to meet him. I want details before I come, though."

"I promise I'll send you a letter with pictures of Mark and me as soon as possible. Thanks Savannah, this means a lot to me that you will come."

"Don't give it a thought. So, how's the family?"

"They're great. Mark and Father get along great, and Thelma is in love with him.

They send their love."

"Well, let them know I said hello"

"Okay, I'll tell them. I love you, take care."

"Love you, too, *Mrs. Bogain.*" Breana liked the sound of that. She giggled every time she heard it.

"Alright then…bye Savannah."

Breana immediately started writing a letter to Savannah. When she began writing about the events that led up to the marriage proposal, and she fell in love all over again…

> *In explaining his love, he said the sweetest thing anyone has ever said to me. He said, "What I feel for you is like a consuming fire. It burns in all the chambers of*

*my heart." Oh Savannah, he's so romantic. Do you
remember when we used to talk about the ideal man
we would like to marry? Well, he's that and so much
more. I know you'll like him when you finally get to
meet him. Call me when you get this letter. And again,
thanks Savannah, for everything.*

Your dear friend,
Breana

Four days had passed since Mark left. Thelma was in the kitchen
preparing breakfast, and the doorbell rang. She looked at the clock.
Seven in the morning, who could be ringing the bell at this hour,
she wondered. She walked out from the kitchen. As she opened
front door, a uniformed gentleman said, "Special delivery for a Miss
Breana Noble."

"I'll take it." Thelma signed for the package and took it into the
study. She placed it on the desk next to the third bouquet of roses
Mark had sent. She started back to the kitchen when she saw Breana
walking across the hall carrying a pad and pen. "Goodness gracious,"
she said, "Girl, you're going to have writer's cramp. Every time I see you
these days, you have writing paraphernalia in your hands," she chuckled. "Put them down for a minute. You have a package in the study."

"Oh really! It's got to be from Mark!" she said excitedly.

Breana rushed into the study. She picked up the package and
read the label. The card read, "To Miss Breana Noble from your
secret admirer." Surprised, she timidly started opening the package
only to find a smaller one inside. She opened up the smaller package,
and there was yet another smaller package. "Oh come on!" she said
as she anxiously tore into the last package. It contained a jewelry box
and a note. At the bottom of the note, was the signature. *M A Bogain*
"Oh Mark! You devil!" she said as she laughed aloud. "Thelma, it's

from Mark!" She set the jewelry box aside, and proceeded to read the note.

My Darling Breana,

It's been less than a week since we parted, but it seems like four years. I have missed you so much, words cannot express. You have cast your spell on me. There is happiness on the horizon for us when this separation is over. It's such joy having you in my life.

I have sent you a cameo. It's been worn by the Bogain matriarchs for over a century. Now it's your turn to wear it my darling. I can't wait to see it on you. You are simply enchanting, and I adore you. Every fiber of my being aches for you when we are apart. I send you the Cameo so that you will have something that proves my sincerity in the relationship. There is no other person I would rather have wearing the token of my trust. I hope you will accept this gift as a token of my love and affection. I'm counting the days until we are together again my darling. You are the inhabitant of my heart, and you are my sole desire now and always.

Yours in love forever,
Mark

Breana removed the cameo from the box. She gasped and ran to the door. "Thelma! You have got to see this!" She was holding the cameo in the palm of her hand. "Isn't this beautiful? Mark sent it."

"This is the most exquisite cameo I have ever seen. This is an antique." Thelma replied.

"He said it's been in his family for over a century."

"I can see that it has character. Wear it gracefully my dear."

Breana wore the cameo all the time. "I feel bad wearing it casually, but I feel close to Mark when I'm wearing it." She decided to write him a letter in response to the note he sent, and in acknowledgement of the cameo.

Henry walked into the den and said, "Have you finished your letter? You've been writing for some time?"

"I just did. It's in the box with the outgoing mail."

"Good, there's something I want to talk to you about." He sat down on the sofa, and Breana followed.

"What is it Father?" she asked, sitting next to Henry."

"You know we have to make the announcement of your engagement. We need to have the pictures of you and Mark, so we can pick one to send along to the newspapers."

"Okay, the photographer will be here today with the proofs; I'll pick from those."

"Sounds good to me; the next thing is your gift. I want to give you an engagement present. I want it to be your choice, no surprises."

"You can give me anything you want, as long as it's a car," she answered jovially.

"A car? Why? Don't you like being chauffeured?"

She tilted her head to the side "I do, but I'd like to have a car of my own. I'll have errands to run sometimes."

"Alright then, do you want to shop for one or Dudley and I could do it?"

"Okay Father, I trust you and Dudley," she said, while getting to her feet. "Will that be all? I need to get dressed before the photographer gets here with the pictures. He should be here soon."

"That was all. You can go."

She hardly had time to get dressed when the doorbell rang. "Who's there?" Thelma asked.

"This is Russell, Ma'am, the photographer."

Thelma opened the door. "Good day Ma'am. Is Miss Breana in?"

"Yes she is, come on in. She's been expecting you." She offered him a seat in the living room. "I'll go get her."

"Your fiancée really knows how to throw a party. I think you'll be pleased with these pictures, Miss Breana." Russell said when Breana entered the room.

Breana greeted him. "I certainly hope so. Let me see what you have."

He opened up his portfolio and started showing her the pictures. "Oh my goodness," she said, "They're beautiful. I had no idea they would be so clear since they were taken at night."

"I had a good camera and the ship was well lit."

"Well, I think you did a wonderful job. Thank you so much. I'll see which ones I need for enlargement, and let you know."

"No problem Ma'am. It was my pleasure to work with you."

"Let me see you to the door. Thank you for doing such a wonderful job." She said.

"I like when my customers are happy, so I always try my best. Please tell your friends." He handed her his business card. Call me, I'll be happy to do your wedding and reception."

She walked back inside, "Father, Thelma, come see the pictures."

Henry and Thelma gathered around the table. They looked at the pictures and chose their favorites. Henry looked at Thelma and said, "Thelma, how come your favorites are all the ones that you're in?"

"Really? I didn't notice." Thelma replied.

Henry picked up one picture that included Mark, Breana and himself. He held it up and winked at Thelma, "Now here is a perfect picture for the announcement."

"Father, speaking of the announcement, will you be writing it or do you want me to do it?"

"That's my job. I'll start working on it right away so it will be in the papers tomorrow."

Henry walked into the study and sat behind his desk. He picked up a writing tablet and his favorite pen that had once belonged to Penny. He started scribbling, and his mind wandered on his beloved Penny.

Oh Penny, my dearest, our little girl is all grown up. She has found someone to share her life with, and to my dismay, you are not here to be happy for her. How I miss you, my beloved. Breana has occupied a big part of my life since you've been gone. Now, I have to face the fact that she's no longer my little girl. Soon she'll be Mark's wife, and now I'll be alone. How I wish you didn't have to go so soon, but God's plan is not ours to understand. I thank Him every day for the time He gave us. I'm praying that He gives Breana and Mark the happiness He gave you and me. God rest your soul.

Henry was so engulfed in his thoughts; he didn't hear Breana as she walked into the room.

She pulled up a chair and sat next to him. "Father, is there something on your mind? You seem preoccupied."

He looked at her. *She's so happy. Why bring up unpleasant memories of losing her mother. Let her remember Penny in her own way and in her own time,* "I'm thinking what I want the announcement to say. I'm thinking how time flies, and I'm thinking how fast my daughter has grown up. It seems like yesterday you were in school. And now, here we are today planning to announce your engagement. Now that you know what I've been thinking, leave me to my work!"

"Yes, Father dear," she kissed him on the cheek and walked away. Henry started writing.

Miss Margaret Breana Noble, daughter of Henry Hamilton Noble, and the late Penelope Margaret Noble, is engaged to be married to Mr. Mark Antonio Bogain This joyous occasion will take place on the seventeenth day of December, nineteen hundred and sixty-six..."

He proudly presented the paper to Breana. "I have finished my task, and I'm ready for inspection," he said handing the paper to Breana.

"Father, this is good work…approved! She said with a laugh.

"Okay, I'll send it by messenger to the *Gleaner* Company and have it run in tomorrow's paper."

"Oh good, I'll need a copy to send to Mark."

That night Breana thought of Penny. She remembered when they went walking in the woods and rested on the pine needles in Georgia, and just talked. She wondered if Penny would be proud of her; would she have loved Mark, and would she approve of the wedding. She wished Penny was alive to share her happiness. Then her thoughts turned to her birth mother. She pondered over the same questions she had been asking herself for years. *I wonder if my birth mother is alive. Does she even think about me? I guess I'll never know.* With a deep sigh, she finally, drifted off to sleep.

The morning after, Dudley had gone to the nearest newspaper stand to get multiple copies of the paper. He came back just as Breana came bouncing down the stairs. She could hardly wait to see how the announcement came out. She took a paper from Dudley, and she left the extra copies on the coffee table. After she saw the article, she went to her room to start a letter to Mark:

> *Dearest Mark,*
>
> *I hope you are well, darling. The announcement of our engagement was published in the Gleaner today. I'm sending a copy to you, if for no other reason, to let you see how handsome we are as a couple. You're very dashing you know. I wish I could see you now. I know you're blushing. I'm missing you terribly.*
>
> *I'm keeping busy with the wedding plans. What a good idea. When you come in October, we can spend more time together without the hassle. I'm sending you some pictures, so in case you get the chance to go to Ecuador,*

you'll have them to show your family. I can't wait to see
you my love. Until then, I'll keep thinking of you.

Yours always in love,
Breana

Thelma noticed the newspapers on the table and picked one up to leaf through it. Dudley came in for a cup of coffee. "Look Dudley! Don't they make a nice couple?" Thelma said holding the paper out to him.

While they discussed the picture, Henry joined them. "Good morning, Mr. Noble! How would you like your eggs this morning, Sir?"

"*Over easy* please, and a good morning to you too; morning, Dudley."

"Good morning, Sir! We were just admiring this fine picture here in the paper."

He, too, looked at the photo and grinned. "Now that's a handsome couple," He said.

"Breakfast will be ready in five minutes, Sir." Thelma said walking back to the kitchen.

Breana joined Henry. "Good morning Father, did you like the announcement?"

"It's beautiful. You chose the right picture." he replied "I'm sure Mark will feel the same way."

Thelma rang the bell to signal breakfast was ready. They went to the table and she started serving. "No need for that Thelma, sit down and have breakfast," said Henry, "We need to discuss some things."

"Alright then Sir." Thelma said.

"Thelma, your place is as mother of the bride," Breana said.

"I should be ushered in as mother of the bride?" Thelma asked, with eyebrows raised in surprise.

"Mother gave you that position before she died, so you will walk for her; unless Father has any objections."

"Objections to what? She's the only mother you've known since Penny died."

"I don't know what to say," Thelma said, as her eyes welled up with tears.

"Just say you will do it for me."

"How could I refuse an offer like that? It's an honor, of course I'll do it," she dried her eyes.

"Well, I know that I want a church wedding, so it should be at the Fellowship Hall, but I'll have to work on the reception and the catering though."

"Where ever you decide, be sure that it's the best. You are my only daughter. If this is the only wedding I'll have to pay for, I want it to be the very best."

Chapter Nineteen

At age 47, Henry was still a handsome man. He kept his sideburns neatly trimmed and connected to a low cut, rust colored beard he had recently grown out. A few gray hairs graced his temples, lending a distinguished appearance. The tropical climate had been generous to his complexion. His denim pants revealed the fruits of his early morning jogs. He had a lot on his mind and it showed on his face. As he sat at the gazebo, the cool breeze blew across his face and his neatly combed hair started flying in the wind.

"I thought you might want to quench your thirst, Sir, so I brought you a cold drink. Thelma filled a glass of the nectar and handed it to him. He took the glass and tasted the drink.

"Hmm—mm! This is very good. I like it, good job."

"Thank you Sir. I just thought I would try using some of the fruits before they all go bad, and I was sure you'd like it."

"Well, now you know what to do with them. But, you make fruit juice all the time and it's always delicious." Henry replied.

"Yes, but I made this one from mango, sweet sop and star apple. I've never tried it before, so I was hoping you'd like it."

Henry took another sip. "Hmm…this is so good…I don't like; I love it! You can make as much as you like."

"Yes Sir, except there will be less people to make it for now that Breana will be gone soon. It's going to be very lonesome around here when she gets married and leaves."

"Now Thelma, I know where you're going with that! But I don't mind telling you, after that last fiasco, I'd thank you to keep your opinions to yourself!"

"All I said was that it's going to be lonesome around here Sir! What's gotten into you today? Could it be that you were thinking the same thing?"

"Now there you go again; Dr. Freud, you're not paid to be my psychiatrist. Go do what you're being paid to do, or do whatever you want as long as you leave me alone!"

He picked up a newspaper and held it in front of his face. Thelma stood there, looking at him in disbelief. Mockingly, Thelma saluted and said, "Yes Sir," then in a huff, she briskly walked off toward the house.

"Well, he won't have the chance to talk to me like that again," she complained on her way to the house. "From now on I'll mind my own business until I get out of here."

Thelma was so upset; she did not realize that she passed Breana who was on her way to the gazebo. "What's wrong, Thelma?" she asked.

"Go ask your pig-headed father. I'm sure he'll have no problem laying it on you. His tongue is very loose today."

Breana proceeded to the gazebo. "Father! What have you done to Thelma?"

"What makes you think I did something to her? I did nothing to that woman! She just kept harping on things she knows nothing about. That's all! Don't make me the bad guy!"

"Well you must have said something! I've never seen her so upset!"

"I didn't say anything she shouldn't have heard! She's always butting into my business about women! I took her advice last time and look what happened! I damn near lost my life; God knows what the devil had planned for you, and *she* almost ended up in prison for a crime she didn't commit! I say she should mind her business!"

"Oh Father, you know Thelma is just worried about you. She knows I'll be leaving soon, and she just wants you to think about having somebody in your life. She's thinking about you. You can't fault her for that. I think you should apologize to her."

"She'll calm down soon enough and start nagging again."

"Thelma never nags Father. She shows concern. You know that's the truth."

"I don't think she's all that mad about it anyway."

"Oh really?" said Breana, "She almost knocked me down when I passed her on the way down here."

"Hmph," Henry grunted.

Thelma was fuming. She scattered and threw pots and pans as if she was looking for one special pot and none other would do. Dudley walked into the kitchen wearing khaki shorts. His red t-shirt was drenched with perspiration and pasted to his torso. Sweat dripped down his salt and pepper whiskers, and his chocolate brown complexion seemed to have gotten two shades darker. He took off his straw hat, and then he pulled a handkerchief from his hip pocket and mopped his forehead dry.

"Boy today is really a hot one," he said. Thelma paid no attention.

"What's wrong with you woman? And what have those pots and pans done to you?"

"I'll tell you what's wrong! Your boss has lost his mind! And as soon as Breana's wedding is over, I'm out-ta here!"

"I've never seen you and the boss at odds, but whatever it is, it can't be that bad to make you quit."

"It not di firss time. Mi juss don't talk 'bout it". Thelma replied in patois, still venting. There was an apple pie on the table. Dudley took a knife from the utensil drawer and attempted to cut a slice from it. Thelma slapped his hand.

"That's not for eatin'!"

Needless to say Dudley was really surprised. "So-rry! It looked like food to me, so I thought it was for eating."

She snapped at him, "You know what I mean! It's for later!"

"Ok, ok! I'm going back outside! The temperature is worse in here, and there are no knives out there, you got knives!" Dudley said as he tramped out through the back door carrying a glass of iced cold water. In his Jamaican dialect, he muttered under his breath. "De damn woman gawn stock steering mad to rawtid! A wanda what happen between she an' de bass nung?"

Down at the gazebo, Breana still argued her point with Henry. "Father, this is not like you to treat Thelma this way. No wonder she's upset. Is something bothering you?"

"Why is it every time I voice my opinion, something is bothering me? Oh, never mind! I'll go talk to her in a little while. If I go now, she'll most likely roast me for dinner."

Later, Thelma was in the kitchen cooking and sulking. Henry started on his way from the gazebo to the house. He stopped on the verandah, and took his white handkerchief from his pocket. Then he found a tiny stick in the yard and began to tie the handkerchief to it as he walked across the room to the kitchen door and stood behind the wall. He stretched his hand holding his makeshift 'surrendering' flag and waved it in front of the opened door.

"I see your blue long sleeve that I just replaced the button on. I know who you are. You might as well show your face," said Thelma.

Henry's attempt to reconcile was so pathetic that Thelma could not help but giggle. Henry walked into the kitchen and they were able to share a laugh. Then Henry's face grew solemn.

"Thelma, I'm so sorry I said those things to you. You were right. I was thinking about what this house will be like when Breana leaves. I've also been thinking about the two loves in my life. How they slipped away. At least I'll see Breana from time to time, but I'll never be with either of them again."

"But Sir, you know where Effiedra is! Locked up where she belongs, and well deserved, I might say, so why are you still pining over her anyway? After all she—"

"Come into the study Thelma." Henry interrupted. "I need to tell you something."

Once they entered the study, Henry began to speak. "You're mistaken," he said, "I would never refer to that poltergeist as the love of my life."

"Sir, I don't understand." Thelma said with a puzzled look on her face.

Henry took a deep breath, and then started speaking in a melancholy tone. "This is something I never speak about to anyone."

My Lord, what could this man be about to tell me? He sounds so heavy hearted. "Would you like something to drink, Sir?"

"Some cold water will do, thank you."

She got the pitcher of water from the refrigerator, and she filled the glass and sat it before Henry.

"Thank you very much," he said as he picked up the glass. She took her seat again, and he began to speak.

"Many years ago when I was a young lad, my family lived in Connecticut at that time. We had this beautiful home with a balcony in the back. Our maid had a daughter, Emily was her name. She had the most beautiful black hair. It hung down her back like a horse's mane, and when she turned her head swiftly, it swayed gently like it was going to wrap her around face. I used to hide and call her name just to see her hair move when she turned her head."

"Sounds like you admired her very much sir."

"You don't know the half of it. Her hazel colored, almond shaped eyes were as wide as saucers and full of splendor. When she looked at you, they sparkled… just so bright… His voice trailed off for a few seconds as he stared off looking at nothing in particular.

Thelma noticed how he held his head and smile as if he was recalling a fond memory. "Sir! She said snapping her finger, "You were saying…"

"Oh, yes where was I? Oh yes… when she smiled her teeth were like pearls. She was so beautiful. She had a little white poodle named

Cha-Chi. Emily was always running around and climbing into trees, pretending that Cha-Chi was a big bad tiger, and she'd climb up the trees to get away from it. I used to watch her from the balcony as she played her games. Then I went away to college. I hadn't been home for three years. My parents would either meet me at our house in Aspen, or sometimes we'd go on cruises. When my break was over, I went back to college.

One year we didn't go anywhere, so I went home to Connecticut. I remember like it was yesterday. The evening was beautiful, so I decided to enjoy it from the balcony. Out of the blue, I heard this voice coming from the servant's quarters. "Come back, Cha-Chi! Cha-Chi, come back!' Then I saw this beautiful young lady sprinting across the lawn after the little white poodle. Her hair danced around her shoulders as she bent to pick up the dog. She cradled it in her arms, and she stood there stroking the dog's hair. I'm seeing her now as if it was yesterday."

Henry's face grew softer as he spoke, looking as if he was seeing Emily's face. Thelma had never seen him so much at ease.

"She wore a blue and white floral dress down to her ankles. It had splits on both sides of the skirt. It was a little windy, so the skirt was doing a dance of its own and I saw LEGS! Her hair was gently blowing in the wind. It was like a serenade. From shoulder to waist that dress fitted like a glove on a lady's hand, and she was generously endowed."

"Wow, you remember that vividly, Sir?"

"I sure do." Henry sipped some water.

"She must have made a great impression on you."

"That she did. Anyway, I cleared my throat, and she looked up at me. You could've knocked me over with a feather when I saw that it was Emily. I couldn't believe the little girl I left three years earlier had blossomed into such a captivating young woman. She made a dash back to the servant's quarters. That picture of her stayed in my head all night. The next morning, I went outside. She was hanging clothes on the line. I stood there watching her quietly; she never saw me. Then she started singing this ballad...

'*There was magic abroad in the air; there were angels dining at the Ritz, and a nightingale sang—in Barkley's Square,*' she had such a melodious voice. I haven't been thrilled like that by any voice since then."

Henry paused for a while then he began again. "I walked over and I said, *Well, little Emily, all grown up.* She looked at me with those sparkling hazel eyes. Her smile was more dazzling than I remembered. Her skin was like burnt brass, smooth as silk. 'Henry! Is that you?' She said as she ran towards me. We hugged, and her hair smelled like eucalyptus. When we let go our eyes locked. Just then, I knew that something was happening. That night we talked about when we were growing up, and what we had done since we last saw each other. From then on we spent a lot of time together. Mother saw us kissing from the balcony one afternoon. I thought Emily would die. She was shy you know. She ran to the servant quarters, and I had to coax her to come out."

Woe, I can hear the old witch now, Thelma thought. Then she said, "I bet old Mrs. Noble had a lot to say about that Sir."

"She didn't say anything at the time. Anyway, Emily and I became much closer. I didn't want to go back to college. I wanted to transfer back to Connecticut instead. I spoke to my mother about it, and right away, she assumed it was because of Emily. She said I was infatuated with Emily, and she was wrong for me, but I didn't care what mother said. I loved Emily dearly. I went back to college and we kept in touch. I couldn't wait for spring break, so I could get back home. As soon as I got back, it was like I never left. We picked up right where we left off. Mother threatened to cut me off if I kept spending time with her. I can still hear her voice even now. *Do you understand the ramifications of getting involved with the servant's daughter?* She asked me that one day after see saw me walking towards where Emily lived. However, I didn't see her as anybody but Emily. I didn't care who her parents were, or even if she was a servant. I saw her beauty inside and out."

Thelma continued to listen attentively as Henry spoke. She watched the tenderness in his eyes as he strolled down memory lane.

"I remember the day I was leaving to go back to college. We hugged each other as if we were the last two people on a deserted island. We had no parting gifts for each other, except, she had a silver comb she wore in her hair to keep up her hair. I wanted to see her hair tumble around her shoulders, so I took the comb out. While I stood there admiring her beauty, she told me to keep the comb, so I would remember her. I still have that comb. Then it was my turn to give her a keepsake. All I had was the key chain that I got with my first car. It belonged to my grandfather, so I gave it to her. She promised to keep it safe until we met again. We wrote to each other often, and then out of the blue, she stopped writing me. When I asked mother about her, she told me that Emily had run off with some other guy, and her mother had left to work for another family. I was devastated. For a long time, I wouldn't get involved in any serious relationship. Penny was the one that got me over that hard spot in my life."

"Are you saying you only had two relationships in your life Sir?"

"Oh goodness, no! Those are the girls that managed to wrap themselves around my heart. Penny and I didn't start out as lovers. We were just friends. However, we grew to love each other more than life itself; needless to say, mother was pleased with that choice. Yet, a funny thing happened just before mother died," she had this strange look on her face as if she was trapped in another place and time."

"What was that, Sir?"

"The nurses said she kept calling for me. When I went to see her, she held my hand and said, 'Did you bring the baby? Bring the baby to me. I miss the baby." Then she kept saying Emily's name over and over. Emily and her mother were with us before Emily was born, so it seemed as if she was still remembering her as a baby. She wandered all over the house. She searched every room and believe me there were a lot of rooms. Whenever someone asked her what she was looking for, she'd ask, 'Have you seen Emily?' She would look at the nurses and call them Emily, and in the same breath, she'd start talking about the baby. Her mind wandered from one phase to the next in a matter of minutes."

Thelma listened patiently, as he poured his heart out. *'He has been burdened by this all this time'*, she thought.

"Mark and Breana remind me so much of Emily and me, and that's what got me on edge. However, that's no excuse to snap at you like I did. You've been a rock for Breana and me through all the bad times. I'm so sorry I hurt you."

"Well, to tell you the truth Sir, I was baffled by your reaction. I've never heard you speak like that to anyone. I thought maybe you had blamed me for the whole 'Effiedra' thing. After all, I was the one who encouraged you to open up your life to somebody, and when you did, look what happened."

"Nonsense, you've done nothing but good for this family. You did a good thing when you encouraged me to share my life with someone again. You didn't lead me to Effiedra.

I should have seen that the girl was a modern day Jezebel." Henry said, making a face that looked like he had just sucked on a lemon.

"For someone to be such a swindler at such a young age is beyond my comprehension." Thelma replied.

"I bought into her innocent act, and I would have done anything for her. Meanwhile, I was harboring a fugitive, one that would seal my own fate, and that of my family."

"Well, it's behind us now Sir, thank God."

"Not a word of this conversation to Breana, you hear? I don't want her to start thinking I'm going to fall apart the moment she leaves."

"Don't worry Sir. I won't say anything to her. I'm just glad you had the chance to clear your mind."

"Thank you for your patience and understanding. Well I, better go and take care of some business," said Henry, getting up from the chair.

"Yes Sir, I have some things to finish myself. I might as well get to work."

It took three weeks for Mark to receive the package Breana sent. He opened the wrapping and picked up the newspaper. He opened it up and Breana's letter fell out. He set the paper aside and picked up the letter. He walked over to a porthole and sat down on a chair to read. After he read the letter, he looked at the paper. "You're so right, my love, we have a purpose to be together," he said, reading the announcement and smiling.

He set the paper down and went into his office. He sat at his desk, and he picked up a pen and stationary and started writing.

My Darling Breana,

I woke up missing you so much this morning; then I received your package today. How did you know I needed to hear from you so badly? I can't wait to be back with you. When I read your letter, you said I should hurry home. It made me feel good all over because home to me, from now on, is where ever you are.

I'm rearranging my schedule, so when I get back I'll not have to leave before the wedding. I've enclosed a copy of my itinerary. We've left Panama, and we are on our way to Costa Rica. I did not get to go to Ecuador to see my sister and the children, but I spoke to her on the phone. I told her all about you, and she can't wait to meet you.

The children are pretty excited at the prospect of having an aunt. They're already asking if they'll be having cousins soon. Not to worry, I asked them to give us time.

Mother was in Bogotá. She said it was a shopping trip and also to see me. I guessed that it was to inquire about you. I was right. My sister spoke to her about our phone conversation, and she couldn't wait to hear it from me. She is anxious to meet you. You're going to love her.

I have arranged for the passengers to board one of the other ships from the fleet, so that the Bogain-Villa could remain in port until after the wedding. I can't wait to sail off into the sunset with you my love. I feel so lucky. I get to ride off into the sunset with the girl of my dreams. Roscoe misses you, too. I showed him the picture in the paper, and he barked, 'Yip, yip' so I took it to mean 'Yes, yes.' He was smart enough to help bring us together, so he should be smart enough to approve of the outcome, don't you think? I can't wait to have you in my arms. Give my love the family.

Yours forever,
Mark

Breana and Savannah corresponded frequently over the next months before the wedding.

Dear Breana,

How are you? So, my dearest friend is getting married. Well it's no surprise to me. It's just a wonder that it didn't happen sooner. Someone as beautiful as you is destined to be a bride. I hope your fiancé knows how special you are and how lucky he is to have found you. You are the best, Breana, and I mean it sincerely. I hope your husband will be good to you, and I hope he gives you the respect you deserve. I miss you. I can't wait to see you.

I spoke to Dad. Uncle Henry had already told him you're getting married.

He sends his love and congratulations. I'm hoping that he'll make it to the wedding.

He finally has a successful marriage. He and his wife just adore each other. I'm so happy for him. After all he's been through with mother, he deserves some happiness. She is the mother I wish I had when we were growing up. Life would have been so much simpler. I don't think I have ever thanked you enough for what you did for mother in her time of distress. It was such irony. You were the one person she despised the most, and you were the one responsible for bringing back some dignity to her life.

On a sadder note, I think you should know. I heard that Molly came out of Reformatory school, but she has lost an eye. I heard she was in a fight with another girl, and the girl scratched her eye out. She should have been out years ago, but she kept getting into trouble. Regardless of what happened in the past, with her trying to ruin our friendship, I still feel sorry for her. Evidently, incarceration has not improved her attitude, and her mother, Lee Ann, is still trying to clean up her daughter's messes. I'm sorry to be the bearer of such depressing news. I wish it were different, and I'm praying that someday it will. Anyway, give my love to Uncle Henry and Thelma. See you soon.

Love,
Savannah

Chapter Twenty

The Convent of St. Theresa, in St. Elizabeth, Jamaica, was a refuge for the sick, the battered, and the homeless. No one that sought sanctuary was ever turned away. Ozzie was a homeless man who found shelter at the convent. He showed up on the door steps one late afternoon. His dark skin could be seen through the multitude of holes in the rags he wore. He had no shoes on his feet and his head was covered with a tattered straw hat. His dark eyes exuded kindness and gratitude to anyone who assisted him.

In return for his keep, he worked around the convent. He tended the animals and ran errands for the sisters. One morning Ozzie was outside cleaning up the yard. The paperboy rode by on his bicycle. "Good morning, Uncle Ozzie!" as Ozzie was known to all the children in the neighborhood, "Here is your paper!" the boy shouted, as he threw the paper on the lawn. Ozzie got the paper and set it on a table that was reserved for newspapers and mail in the foyer.

A woman, looking about her early forties, walked over to the table. Her lustrous black hair streaked with strands of platinum, braided in two and hung down her back. A simple gray and white dress adorned by her radiant copper-tone complexion; she made the dress look good.

"Good morning Ozzie, how are you this morning?" she said with a faint smile, masking the sadness in her large green eyes.

Patois was the most comfortable dialect for Ozzie. It easily rolled off his tongue as he said, "Praise de Lawd Miss Emma! I'm no way worse! As we Jamaicans always seh, where dere is life, dere is hope!"

"You're so right Ozzie. That will be my thought for today. Where there is life, there is hope. She repeated. She picked up the newspaper and walked into the kitchen and sat down. She started turning the pages of the newspaper. She stopped when she saw the picture of a newly engaged couple, and read the announcement. An astounded look came upon her face as she read it a second time. *'Could this be possible? A man with the same name, who appears to about the same age, here in Jamaica? It can't be…Henry Noble!* She thought.

"How can I find out if this is real," she asked herself.

As she sat on the stool, lost in thought, the pot on the fire went unattended. Reverend Mother Isabelle came walking by the kitchen which was a separate building off the house. Inside the kitchen was a large wood burning stove. When Mother Isabelle went into the kitchen, steam and smoke mingled together and hovered over the stove, and the smell was pungent.

"Emma!" She called out.

"Oh my goodness, Reverend Mother, I'm so sorry. I didn't hear you. Oh my God, what have I done?"

Without hesitation, she grabbed the handle of the hot pot with her bare hands.

"A-a-ah!" she shrieked, as she dropped the pot. Red beans and hot water saturated the dirt floor.

"Holy Mother of God! For heaven sakes Emma, what is the matter with you today?"

Mother Isabelle said, reaching for a basin. She filled it with cold water and brought it to Emma.

"Here put your hand in this cold water."

"Oh Reverend Mother, I'm so sorry. I ruined the whole meal for today."

"Never mind about the food, child. It's only a pot of peas. The Lord has provided that. He'll provide more. Come sit and let me see your hand." Emma sat down on a chair and offered her hand. "Well, it's red but there is no blister, thank God. Come into the house. I'll put some Silvadene on it and wrap it with gauze."

Emma followed the Reverend Mother into the house and let her take care of her wound. After it was done, she buried her face in her hands and started sobbing uncontrollably, as Mother Isabelle tried to comfort her.

"Now—now dear, this is not like you. I've never seen you burn anything. Something is wrong. Tell me, what is it?"

"Oh Reverend Mother, maybe this is just a coincidence, but it is too much to ignore. I was reading the paper, and I saw this picture of two people engaged to be married."

"Ok, but why does it terrify you so?"

"The girl…the girl in the picture…if she is who I think she is, then I have to contact her. I recognized the name. This can't be such a coincidence. I think I may know that girl. Oh, it's a long story, Reverend Mother."

"I have all day, so start talking."

Mother Isabelle got Emma something to drink. "Here, take a sip of this water, and try to relax, she said, handing the glass to Emma, and let me see if I can help you with whatever is bothering you."

Emma took a sip of the water. She sat the glass down on the table, and she looked at Reverend Mother and said, "Many years ago, when my mother and I first came here to seek sanctuary, I never told anyone the reason." She broke down and started sobbing again. Mother Isabelle tried to comfort her, but the tears kept rolling down her copper brown cheeks. After a while, she gained some composure and told her story. Mother Isabelle was awestruck at the revelation of her deep secret and at the same time, her heart ached for the woman for what she had lived with on her mind for so many years.

"I can see that this is weighing heavy on your mind. I'm going to see what I can to do to find out who these people are. I hope we can get you some peace of mind. Don't worry about dinner. We'll think of something. Have faith, child. Maybe the Lord has just given you your miracle," Mother Isabelle said as she walked away.

It had been a week since the Reverend Mother had promised to help Emma. Since then, every messenger that came to the convent made her anxious. Emma kept her ears peeled to every conversation around the convent hoping to hear something, but it seemed hopeless. She had grown weary of waiting, and she cried each unsuccessful day. Then early one morning after weeks of despair, Emma had finished breakfast, and decided to do the laundry. She had just begun filling the washtub with water, when the Reverend Mother came to her.

"Emma!" she called, "Emma, where are you?"

"Yes, Reverend Mother! I'm in the wash room!"

"There you are. I've got good news. I have the information you needed. It's all here in this envelope."

Emma dried her hands and she stepped closer to the Reverend Mother and took the envelope. She held it in her hands and she looked at it. She hesitated to open it. She continued to staring at it as if afraid to find out what was inside.

"I will leave you to decide what you want to do," said the Reverend Mother, as she walked back to her office. Alone at last, Emma decided to open the envelope and read the contents.

Reverend Mother,

Greetings to you and your staff. We have some information on Breana Noble and Henry Noble, but we have none on Mark Bogain. Breana Noble is from America. She is the adopted daughter of the United States Ambassador, Henry Noble. He was born and raised in Connecticut. He and his wife lived in Georgia. However, she is deceased. He moved here with his daughter on assignment. That's all we could find out. Hope it helps.

As soon as Emma read the letter, her face went pale. She fell back onto the bench. *Could it be?* She thought, as she replayed the past in her mind.

Chapter Twenty-One

Breana stayed home from work. She had planned to go through her things to decide what to take with her when she moved, what to donate and what to throw away. Among her belongings, she found a book that Mrs. White had given her. She opened it to find a piece of a dried flower pressed between the pages.

"This is like finding a lost pearl… a piece of bougainvillea from Mrs. White's house."

I wonder how she is. I wonder if she's at the same place. I would love to see her again. I wish we were free to keep in touch when I left her. I would not have to be wondering about her now. I'll have to tell Mark about her. Maybe after the wedding we could go to New York and try to find her.

Henry got to work and went about his daily activities. A messenger walked into the building and delivered an envelope to the guard. "This delivery is for the Ambassador, Mr. Henry Noble." he said and promptly left the building.

When Henry received the note from the guard the guard stated, "The messenger said it's urgent Sir," Henry dropped what he was doing to read it. He folded it and he put it in his pocket. "I wonder what Father McCloud could want that he would summon me in this manner. I'm willing to bet it's probably some refugee's case he wants to talk to me about." He picked up the phone and called Dudley, and then he walked to Breana's office. He tapped his special beat on the door and opened it.

"Pumpkin!" he called. "I have an errand to run. Dudley will be here in a few minutes to pick me up. "It is two thirty now, and I don't know how long this errand will take. We'll come back for you later."

"Okay, Father. I'll just finish up some work I had been putting off while I wait for you guys."

When they arrived at St. Francis Rectory, Henry rang the door-bell. One of the nuns greeted him at the door. She guided him to Father McCloud's office, and he waited in the vestibule.

"Father McCloud!" said the woman in the black habit. "Mr. Henry Noble is here to see you!"

"Send him in, please."

The Nun walked out of the office. "Father McCloud will see you now, Sir."

She held the door open, and gestured for Henry to enter the office.

"Hello Father! Good evening! Your message said this was an urgent matter; I came as quickly as I could." Henry said, shaking Father McCloud's hand.

"Good evening to you too. I appreciate your promptness in coming to see me. I know you must be wondering about the urgency, but it is a very delicate matter, one that could change a lot of lives."

"Oh, how so?" asked Henry.

"It involves someone from your past." Father McCloud gestured for Henry to sit.

Henry stood there silent, not knowing who Father McCloud could be speaking of, but he was eager to find out. He slowly sat and watched Father McCloud's face expectantly. When he said nothing Father McCloud continued.

"I have a lady here that knew you, many years ago she said. She said you two shared a brief past, and there are things concerning the relationship that she never had the chance to tell you. She wanted me to prepare you."

As Father McCloud explained the situation, Henry's face grew ashen. He was dumbfounded as he listened. Father McCloud saw his distress and walked over to him. He placed his hand on his shoulder.

"Speak to me son." He picked up a pitcher of water and poured some in a glass. He handed it to Henry.

"Here," he said, "Drink this and try to stay calm, and then tell me how I can help you."

Henry took a sip of the water.

"Father, my mind is having a big problem processing what you just said. If this person is legitimate, this would truly be one of God's miracles."

"Well, our Heavenly Father is not short on miracles my son. It's just that sometimes we fail to recognize them. It's good that you realize that this could be your miracle.

Take your time. Get yourself together. I will let you see her when you are ready. "Meanwhile if you have anything you would like to talk about, I'll be here to listen."

"Thank you, Father? I would like to see her now, if I may."

"Certainly my son." Father McCloud walked out of the room.

Emma was sitting on a chair by a small table in the Reverend Mother's office. She was fidgety and her mind was scattered about, trying to understand how it was possible after all these many years of wondering how their lives could have been. Now soon she would be face to face with *Him*. She wondered what she would say when the saw Henry again. One of the nuns brought her a cup of tea.

"Drink this child, it will calm you down."

"Thank you sister, she said, reaching for the cup. Her hands trembled as she lifted the cup and took a sip. She placed the cup on the table and stared out the window. It had just started to rain. She watched the raindrops falling on the wide leaves of the banana plants. She got up from the chair and walked over to the window.

"Oh little raindrops, are you weeping for me? Or, are you bringing me blessings?" she said, as she stood by the window. She was captivated by the sound of the rain on the tin roof, and the water cascading to the ground. The sound of Father McCloud knocking on the door brought her back to reality. Startled, she turned around and said, "Come in."

Father McCloud opened the door and walked in. "Well Father, have you heard anything?"

"Yes, my child. He has been here for some time, but I thought it was best to speak with him first. I wanted to see what frame of mind he is in before you see each other. He is anxious to see you. It's all up to you to tell him the whole truth now."

Breana was getting anxious waiting on her father's return. She hadn't heard from him, and it was almost closing time. "Where is Father?" she wondered, "He should have been back by now. She tried to stay busy completing paperwork that had piled up." She walked over to a stack of files sitting on her desk she glanced at the clock above her door, and started working on them.

Emma paced the floor and fumbled with the long sleeves of the gray shirt she wore. She was getting increasingly nervous with each step. She looked at the priest and said, "Maybe this was a bad idea coming here after all. I don't know what to say to him. Father, this is a man I once loved more than life itself and God help me, I never stopped loving him. How do I face him? He will hate me, and I wouldn't blame him. Looking back, I could have handled the situation differently."

"Oh my child, we all get smarter with age, that's what it means to mature. I'm sure in the years to come your outlook on things will be different from what they are today. Then you'll probably ask yourself, "Why did I make such a fuss at the rectory that day? You see my dear, life is a learning experience, and no one gets it all in one lesson. Those circumstances were beyond your control. Now, you won't know what will happen until you go in there and speak to him. Just be honest and say what's in your heart, you might be surprised. He seems like a very understanding man to me. You've come all this way to see him, don't get cold feet now. I'll walk with you."

He opened the door and motioned for her to go through. Then he stepped out after her and closed the door. They walked together to the room where Henry waited. The door was open. Henry was standing by the window, looking outside. He was about to come face to face with his past

"Here we are," said the priest. At the sound of his voice, Henry turned around. "I don't believe a formal introduction is necessary since you two are old friends. I know you need to get reacquainted, so I'll be in the next office if you need me. God be with you, my children."

Henry and Emma did not respond. They just stood there staring at each other. Finally, Henry broke the silence. "Emily is this really you? I'm looking at you, but I can't believe my eyes." He walked over to her and touched her hand. *My God, her eyes are just as I remembered.* He made a gesture for her to sit. She sat on the chair, and he sat down next to her.

"The years have been very kind to you," he said. "You are as beautiful as the day I left for…" Henry paused and stared at her.

"Thanks for the compliment, but I think you are the one that time stood still for, save for the few gray hairs here and there, you look so much the same. Life has been good to you, I hope." She said, fiddling with the buttons on her shirt as she tried to choke back the tears. It had been so long since they sat together like this. Her attire was less by far, than what Henry was accustomed to seeing her wear. Her days of grandeur were long gone. *I must look a mess in his eyes. Why didn't I leave well enough alone? Why did I come here?'* she thought.

"With the exception of a few bumps in the road, I'll have to say yes." Henry answered.

"But never mind about me. I want to know about you. Emily what happened? Why did you leave? What are you doing in Jamaica?" Questions started rolling off Henry's tongue faster than Emma had time to answer.

"It's a long story. I hope when you hear it, you'll understand, and I hope you can forgive me. You know I wouldn't do anything to hurt you. I would do whatever I had to do to protect you."

The clock chimed, and Henry looked at his watch; it was five o'clock. "Do you live nearby?" he asked.

"No, I live at St. Elizabeth. I came here this morning, hoping to speak with you."

"Excuse me one moment," said Henry. He got up from his seat, and he opened the door. He walked across the corridor and knocked on the door.

"Just a moment" said Father McCloud. He opened the door. "Yes my son, what can I help you with?"

"I need to get a message to my chauffer. He has been waiting outside."

"By all means. What is the message my son?"

"I need him to go get my daughter and take her home, then come back here for me."

"Consider it done."

Henry went back to the room to join Emily. "Sorry for the interruption. I had to send my chauffer to take my daughter home." He returned to his seat without taking his eyes from her face. He drew a breath. It felt so surreal to be in the room with Emily after all these years. "So, you came to talk to me. Go ahead, talk." Henry said tightly. The hurt feels about her leaving him he thought long gone, were apparently just under the surface. He tried not to let it show.

"I'm afraid I don't know where to begin." She said, trying to gain composure.

"Okay, I know where to begin; because it has never left my mind," Henry said.

"The day I left for college, I thought we had an understanding. You didn't want me to defy my parents and go to a college closer to home. You disagreed when I said I would work my way through college if my mother cut me off. Nevertheless, we planned to correspond with each other. You promised you would wait for me until I got out of college. I wrote several letters, and you did not reply, not even once! I wrote my mother to find out what happened to you, she told me that you ran off with someone, and your mother no longer worked for us. Now, I'm asking you, what happened?"

Emily looked at him, her eyes now bulging with tears. "Is that what your mother told you? Oh my God!" she said, getting up from her chair. She looked around the room as if she were looking for her sanity, or maybe an escape.

"I knew she was hateful, but I never knew she would go that far." She turned her back to him, tears falling freely down hers cheeks.

"Are you telling me that was not the truth?" Henry asked. He stood up and walked towards her.

"Yes Henry, I am." She sobbed. "Your mother has done us all an injustice, more than you can imagine."

"Okay then, tell me what really happened. I have already spent half a lifetime wondering why. I have no problem spending a few hours hearing why." He said.

The memories of all that happened came flooding back. Suddenly she was angry. She turned around and faced him, still crying. "Then you better make yourself comfortable. It may be a long night. She had gone over and over how she would break the news to Henry ever since it was confirmed that he was the man in the newspaper photograph. Long before seeing the picture, she had even wondered if she would ever see him again, and here he was. Ready and waiting to hear what she had to say and she could not seem to find the words. She began anyway, hoping and praying the right words would come. She took a breath to calm herself.

"Do you have any idea how my mother and I came to live with your family?"

"No, you were there for as long as I could remember. It just seemed as if you belonged there. I never asked any questions, and no one ever said anything."

"Okay, before I was born, your parents visited Jamaica. My mother worked at the guest house where she stayed. When my mother met your parents, she and my father were married only three months. My father died in a car accident shortly after. Your parents took my mother back to America with them. About a month after she went to the States, she discovered that she was pregnant. Your parents liked her work, so they kept her on in spite of that. She had the baby…me, and I was raised on your parents' estate. I was a happy child. Your parents treated me well. Your father even got me a puppy."

"Yes, I remember. You named it Cha-Chi. I often wondered why you had a dog and I didn't."

Emily sat back down. "Yeah, you remember! Oh, how I loved that dog so," Emily said with yearning in her eyes.

"But what does that have to do with what happened between us?" he asked.

"I'm getting to that. Mother always said your father was 'the good one' and that your mother was being nice to us because of him, but even after he died—your mother continued to see that I wanted for nothing. Well, everything was fine until that summer you came home from college, and we started getting close."

Emily started pacing the floor as Henry looked on in amazement. "I saved your letters. I didn't want to make trouble for you, so I kept them hidden. Remember you came home again for spring break, and we were intimate, about a month later, I started feeling sick. Everything I tried to eat made me sick to my stomach. Mother and I thought it was the flu, but the sickness prolonged, and it was worse in the mornings. I could barely eat anything, and what I ate, I threw up. Mother suspected that something was wrong, and she took me to the doctor. We found out I was pregnant. Mother knew I wasn't seeing anyone, so she asked me if you and I had ever been together. I told her we had, once. I have never seen my mother so hurt and disappointed. She was certain that I had destroyed my life, and that you had only used me. I told her that you loved me and have been writing to me. She thought about it for a few days then she decided that she had to tell your mother. She thought if she took the letters that I saved to your mother, she could not deny what we meant to each other, and that it was indeed your baby.

My baby, my baby. Henry thought narrowing his eyes as her words penetrated his mind like a flying arrow. "Did you say my baby?"

"Yes I did."

"Are you telling me you and I have a child?"

"Yes I am."

Seeing the astounded look on Henry's face, Emily paused for a moment. "Are you alright?" she asked.

With eyebrows raised, he answered, "I can hardly wait to hear the rest, go on."

"Mother took me with her to speak to your mom. When she showed the letters to her, your mother read them. Then she looked at my mother and said, "Don't worry, I'll take care of this." Mama told her it was too late to do anything. She looked at Mama with crossed eyes, and in a very flat tone, she asked, "Why is that?' I felt so bad for Mama. She hesitated to answer. She couldn't find the words to tell her, and your mother yelled at her, 'Well, out with it Madeline. Whatever it is I already know it can't be good. It won't be any better no matter how long you stall.' I have never seen mother terrified of anyone before, and I started crying for putting her in that position. Then Mama told her I hadn't been well for the past weeks, so she took me to the doctor, and he confirmed that I was six weeks pregnant. Well, you have never seen your mother's anger, but I will NE-VER forget the way she looked at me that day! I felt cheap and dirty! I felt abandoned, and for the first time in my life—I felt inferior. She looked at me, and she said, 'I raised you in my home. You wanted for nothing, and this is the thanks I get? You want to ruin my son's life? I expect my son to marry a decent and proper girl from a suitable family. What decent and proper girl will marry him knowing that he bedded the Negro daughter of a servant and fathered her child?'

When I saw my mother hang her head, it was like a dagger to my heart, and I felt like I let her down in the worst way. Mama was always a proud woman, but there she stood, defeated, belittled, and ashamed. I died inside to see her like that."

Henry listened in dismay, as Emily spoke from trembling lips and a tear stained face. She sat on the chair in an attempt to quiet her trembling knees, as she continued to speak.

"Mama was never embarrassed of being a maid. She was never ashamed of who she was. She used to say, "One should only be embarrassed of what one does, if one is incapable of mastering what one does." But that day, when your mother spoke like that, my mother was too humiliated, too ashamed to be working for her. Your mother blamed me for seducing you; then she said to my mother, 'You make sure that she takes care of it right away.' And then she smiled in this-this strange way. My mother asked her what she meant by 'take care of it.' She said she would not have the grandchild of a servant call *her* grandmother, especially a half-breed, and that she would not have a thing like that follow her son for the rest of his life. She said to my mother 'You know what has to be done. It's nothing new to you people. You are not going to ruin my son.'

She arranged for mother and me to go to New York to see a doctor. His office was near the U.S. Navy Hospital in St. Albans. Mama did not believe in abortion, so she took the money that your mother gave her for the doctor. We packed as much clothes as we could carry, and we left for New York. I had to leave Cha-Chi behind, and I cried for days. When we got to New York, Mama had a little money saved up, so with what we got from your mother for the doctor and traveling expenses, we rented a one-bedroom apartment in St Albans.

Mama tried to find work as a housekeeper, but the only reference she had was your mother. She got a job working for a family in Jamaica estates. She worked there for four months, and her employer loved her work. Then one morning she went to work; they gave two weeks' pay, and they wished her luck in finding another job. She found another job, and after she had worked two months, she was let go; only this time, her employer was more honest. She told Mama that her work was good, but her reference was bad. Mama was devastated.

Henry listened patiently. His heart was breaking for the pain his beloved Emily had endured at the hands of his mother. Emily looked at him, and his tears moved her. Her own tears had waned a bit. She was getting stronger with each retelling of her story.

She said, "Shall I go on? We could talk another time you know. I hate to see what this is doing to you."

"Don't you dare stop now, you have carried this alone for too long, it's time you share it with me."

"Well, the situation got worse. Mama struggled to keep us fed and warm. She did the best she could. After I had the baby, I took her to the Public Health Clinic. The nurse asked me if I needed financial assistance. I told her yes. She did the paperwork, and I started receiving help through the system. Then, mother developed arthritis in her knees. It was difficult for her to work anymore. All three of us started living on public assistance.

One day in the fall of 1944, the weather had started to change. I went to the Mays department store on Jamaica Avenue, and I bought a snow suite for the baby. I had just returned home and was putting the packages down when I heard a knock at the door. I opened the door, and two men in dark suites were standing there. 'We're looking for Madeline Johnson,' one of them said. I told him that I was her daughter. I asked him what they want with her and he said, 'We're from the Immigration and Naturalization Services.' They stepped by me without saying another word and went into the house. One of them said to mother, "Are you Madeline Johnson?" Mama told them yes and asked them what they wanted. He looked at Mama and said, 'I'm sorry lady, but it has been reported that you have left your employer that brought you into this country. If you're no longer working for that employer, then you have no right to remain in the country. Unless you can show us some legal papers that say you have the right to be here, we will have to take you to detention, pending deportation.'

Mama didn't know what to do. She had no close relatives in Jamaica. My father died before I was born, and she had nothing over here. They had their orders to deport her, and she had no means of fighting them. She had to go. They took her, and they gave me the address where she would be. I was worried that once she got to Jamaica there would be no one there to take care of her. So the following morning..." she paused in mid-sentence "Oh God, this is so hard!"

She sobbed as she began to relive the past. Henry reached into his breast pocket. He took out his handkerchief, and he handed it to her. She took it and blotted her eyes. Finally, she pulled herself together and continued to speak.

"Early in the morning, I dressed my precious little baby in her little pink bunny suite. I fed her, and I filled a bottle with apple juice; I was afraid that milk would get sour and hurt her. I placed her, a bag with some clothes, and the bottle of juice in her carriage. I covered her with her little pink blanket, and I took the Q4 bus that ran on Linden Blvd from Jamaica to Cambria-Heights. I got off at 196th St. in St. Albans. After the bus drove away, I rolled the carriage to the side of the fire station. I was careful not to put it where the baby might be in danger from traffic. I wrote a note asking whoever found her to get her to a good home. I took away everything and anything that could connect her to me, except my heart. There was a King Kullen Super Market nearby. I hid by the side of the supermarket to see who would pick her up. I saw the firefighters come out and they eventually took it inside the fire station. Then I saw a police car drive up. By then, I was very nervous. I never thought the police would be involved. After a while, a white station wagon drove up. A lady got out, and she walked into the fire station. Not long after that, she came out with my baby, and she drove away. I was numb. I couldn't feel anything. I took the bus to Hillside Ave. and the train to the detention center. I told them I was a minor, and I wanted to be deported with my mother. Mother spent her life worrying about the baby, and I just went through the motions of living. My life was meaningless."

Henry managed to gain some composure. He said, "I cannot believe what I'm hearing. I have a child. I have been a father all this time?"

"Yes, you have. Many times my mother thought of your mother. She wondered if your mother had ever repented for the things that she did, or if she ever thought of that innocent baby that she had worked so hard to destroy."

"Oh no, oh my God!" cried Henry, "Yes she did!" Henry's tears were flowing now. He clenched his fists and shook them in the air, and he cried out loud, "How can I bear knowing that my own mother banished my child, after her plans to kill her failed? She did think about the child, Emily! No one understood what she was talking about. The nurses said she kept calling your name Emily and saying 'where is the baby?' I thought she was remembering you as a baby. One day I went to see her and she asked me if I brought the baby. She told me to go get the baby, but I dismissed it. I thought she was being senile. Right now, there are millions of dollars that she tied up in a trust fund. She named the biological child of Henry Hamilton Noble as the beneficiary. I thought of how my daughter could not claim it because, she is adopted. I just thought mother was eccentric. I had no idea she knew that I had a child, and she wanted me to go find 'the baby'."

* * *

While Henry and Emily talked, Dudley returned from driving Breana home. As he waited in the vestibule, he heard muffled voices coming from the room. He recognized his boss' voice; however, he could not hear clearly what was being said. He wondered what was keeping Henry so long. Whatever was going on must be serious because every once in a while one of the nuns would pass by with rosary beads in their hands mumbling some type of prayer.

"Henry, there is more." Emily said.

"I'm not sure I can take any more,"

"You have heard the worst." Emily said "this might help you heal. Before I left my baby, I put the only thing I had of value inside an envelope, and I placed it in the carriage with her." Emily took a deep breath. "I named our baby Breana, and I gave her the key chain that bears your initials, hoping that she may someday prove who she is…"

Chapter Twenty-Two

It was still raining outside the Rectory and it had long become dark outside. Inside, Henry sat staring in disbelief. Suddenly the information was overwhelming. The color drained from his face. He tried to sit down, but his knees buckled and he fell to the floor with a thump. Father McCloud heard the noise and ran to the room. From where he was waiting in the vestibule, Dudley heard the commotion and rushed to the door. He opened it and saw Henry kneeling on the floor. His shoulders were shaking. His head hung low as if he was sobbing, but, there were no sound. Emily was bending over him and shouting, "Henry! Henry, are you okay! Speak to me! Speak to me!"

Immediately, Dudley had flashbacks of Effiedra hurting his boss. Without hesitation, he rushed into the room. He grabbed Emily by the shoulder and pushed her away from Henry.

"Look lady!" he said, "I don't know who you are, and I don't know why you're here, but I'm telling you right now this is enough."

"Easy Dudley," he said, "I'm alright"

Emily wept, as she sat on the floor covering her face with her hands.

"I'm so sorry. I didn't mean to cause all this trouble. I should have never come here in the first place. I think I should leave," she said as the tears rolled down her cheeks.

"Nonsense," said Father McCloud, while helping her up from the floor. "You had a mission to accomplish; you must see it through."

Dudley helped Henry off the floor. What's going on boss? Are you sure you're okay Sir?"

"I'm alright. I just lost my balance, that's all. Don't worry about it, I'm fine,"

"Now, now, he had a bit of a shock, but he'll be fine," said Father McCloud.

He poured some brandy in a glass and handed it to Henry. Henry took a sip and set the glass down on the table. "Are you alright now Boss?" Dudley repeated.

"*Yes* Dudley, thank you."

"Alright then Sir, I'll be right outside if you need me." He left the room and headed back to the lobby. Father McCloud patted Henry on his shoulder and closed the door as he as he went back to his office.

Henry continued talking. "You know, there were so many signs that I should have picked up on. My mother kept talking about a baby, and she kept calling your name. Every time I went to see her, she would ask me if I had the child. I thought she was being senile. Then at the reading of her will, she left her estate to my 'natural born child'. We were all certain that she had lost her mind. Who on earth would believe that anything like this could happen? If I had known that you were pregnant, I would have never left you. You would have been with me no matter what."

"I was never allowed to let you know. Even after we were deported, we weren't sure if we were safe from her. Your mother was very influential. She did so much to hurt us. When mother used her name as reference, she told the potential employers that mother and I stole money from her and left without proper resignation. My mother couldn't even find a job to support us, and for the most part, I was still considered a minor.

We did not steal that money. She gave it to us to pay for an abortion that neither one of us thought was right. However, she saw it as stealing. We were branded as thieves. We had no one, or nowhere to go to. Mother was getting sicker, mostly from depression. She knew of a convent in Santa Cruz, so we went there and asked for sanctuary, and they accepted us.

Mother never recovered. We both stayed at the convent until she died. I had no place to go, so I stayed there. I worked around the convent, and I received food and clothing, and a roof over my head."

Except for the nights when I cried myself to sleep or stayed up wondering about my child, I did not allow myself to feel or think. I just stayed alive."

Henry was flabbergasted. "It makes me ill to think of what your mother, you, and our child have suffered as a result of bigotry. I cannot imagine that the woman I loved and adored as my mother is responsible for this, this TURMOIL!" Henry said, recognizing the agony on the face of his beloved Emily.

"Who made her God? Who made her God? Who gave her the authority to rewrite people's lives!" then in dismay he said, "You know, I never thought I could say this, but I'm glad that she's no longer with us. I don't know how I could ever look at her as I once did. The decent, caring human being that I thought she was did not exist. What do I say to my daughter? How do I explain to her that her grandmother is responsible for all the havoc that was wreaked on her life?"

Emily sat in silence; her heart ached for Henry. "If Breana would be willing to listen, I would like to tell her myself," She said, "You didn't do anything wrong, so why should you be the one to tell her?"

"Neither did you Emily, you did nothing wrong. You did what you had to do to survive. You played the hand that was dealt to you. My mother is the guilty party. Evidently, she thought her millions of dollars could free her guilty conscience, but she died calling for you and the baby. I think you had better stay on here until we get this thing straightened out."

"I'll do whatever you think is best." She replied.

"How can I even attempt to make up for what my mother has

put you through? Because of her, you don't know your daughter. Your daughter grew up not knowing you. In addition, she committed all those other unforgivable acts against you and your mother. How can anything make up for that?"

"Henry, you can't take responsibility for your mother's actions. She knew what she was doing. She was a grown woman, eccentric or not."

"Unfortunately, that doesn't make me feel any better," Henry answered, "I'm going to leave now, but think about what I said. I think it is best that you stay close, and give us a chance to work it out. Breana will need time, I'm sure of it, so please think about it, okay?"

"Alright Henry, whatever you think is best. I'll do it; that's the least I could do. I know I could never take back the decision I made in leaving her, but I would like her to understand why."

"All right then, I'll talk to her when I get home. Then we'll allow her the time she'll need to decide when she is ready to see you. Is that alright?"

"That is more than I could ask for, and if she doesn't want to see me, I won't blame her if she doesn't want to see me, much less get to know me."

"Nonsense, she is a very caring young lady, she'll see you. I know my…our, I know our daughter well. She has a forgiving heart. It may take her some time to process it all, but she'll come around eventually. I've just found out a few hours now and I'm still finding it hard to wrap my brain around it. I'll find a way to gently tell her. Just then the Rectory clock chimed, Henry glanced at his watch. My goodness, its 9:00 o'clock!" said Henry, "I'm afraid I must say good night."

"All right then, I look forward to hearing from you." said Emily.

"I promise I'll not keep you waiting." said Henry. They hugged awkwardly, and said good night.

Dudley was sitting on a chair in the vestibule. He heard the door open, and he looked up.

"Boss, are you okay?" He asked, "Are you ready to leave this place?" he said, getting up from the chair.

"Yes, we're leaving now. I'm sure Breana and Thelma must be anxious by now."

Breana kept looking out the window every five minutes, and every time she heard a car engine. She was waiting anxiously for her father to come home. Thelma walked into the room.

"Breana, did Dudley say anything of what the delay might be? Your father has never been this late getting home."

"No, he didn't. Father told me that he was leaving the office early to take care of some business, then he would come back to get me. Dudley came back alone and got me. He said Father was still in a meeting. He told me Father wanted him to take me home, and then go back to get him. That's all I know, but it's getting so late; I hope everything is alright." While they spoke, the light shone through the window as Henry's car turned into the driveway.

"Oh thank God," said Breana, "they're here." She got up from the chair and briskly walked to the door. While Henry was walking in; they met at the door. She ran into his arms.

"Father, I was so worried about you! What kept you?"

"A lot has happened tonight pumpkin. I'll tell you all about it inside."

They both walked back inside the house. Thelma stood up from her seat and moved closer.

"Is everything alright Mr. Noble? We were worried."

"Yes Thelma, everything is alright. I'll tell you about it later, but right now I need to talk to Breana."

"Then would you like me to fix you something to eat Sir?"

"Nothing right now. I'm not hungry."

"I don't know what's going on Sir, but I do know one thing. Starvation will not help. I'll bring you a little something" she said as she left.

Henry quietly headed toward the den. Breana walked quickly

behind him still wondering what was going on. "Father what's the matter. You look worried."

"I'm okay sweetheart, just a little drained that's all." He took her hands in his, and began the arduous task of telling her the news of her biological mother, knowing that there would be a multitude of questions during, and afterward. *I need some time to organize my thoughts.*

"Pumpkin, do you remember when you told me you had a key chain that you were saving to put your car keys on?"

"Yes. I have it in my room."

"Would you get it for me, darling?"

"Well, sure. I'll go get it right now." *This is odd,* Breana thought as she left the room.

Henry went into the den and sat down behind his desk. While he waited for Breana, Thelma brought in a tray with a light meal and set it in front of him.

"Here you go Sir. It's just soup and sandwich. Try to eat something."

"Thank you Thelma"

"You're most welcome Sir."

Thelma left the room as Breana was walking in with the key chain. "What's that?" she asked.

"Oh this is my key chain; I've been saving it to hold the keys to my new car."

"You don't say! Well, drive carefully," Thelma said, smiling.

"Here's the key chain, Father," Breana said.

As soon as Henry saw it, he knew right away it was the same one he had given Emily all those many years ago. He felt his heart quicken at the memory. *My love...* Henry took the key chain and rubbed his thumb over the Rolls-Royce logo. He held it in the palm of his hand and turned it over, and on the other side he saw the initials *H.H.N.* Scenes from the past flooded his mind as his memory unfolded. He swept his arm over the table, knocking the food across the room. Tomato soup, bread, ham lettuce and tomato went flying and plastered the dark mahogany wood floor. Thelma heard the crash and hurried to the den. She stepped on a piece of tomato and squashed it to the floor.

"Oh my God! What a mess!" She saw Breana's dress and in dismay she said. "Oh Breana! Your skirt is ruined. That tomato soup stain will never come out!"

Breana sat on a chair, stunned. In all of their years together, she had never seen her father behave that way. Henry had his face down on the desk, as he wept bitterly.

"What in God's name is going on?" Thelma asked, "What is wrong, Mr. Noble?" Henry gave no response. "Breana?" she said, looking at Breana hoping for answers.

"I don't know what's wrong," Breana answered. "Father asked me to bring him my key chain. When I gave it to him, he looked at it; then he got angry and knocked the tray off the desk and started crying." She turned to Henry. "Father, talk to me. Tell me what is wrong," she said as she walked over to her father's side. She too started to cry.

Thelma began to clean up the mess. Soup was still dripping from Breana's skirt. Thelma gave her a towel and she tried to wipe it away. She rested her hand on Henry's shoulder.

"Father, tell us what's wrong! Why are you acting…oh no; now I got tomato soup on your shirt," she said, removing her hand from his shoulder and trying to wipe the shirt with the towel.

"This makes it worse," she mumbled as she dropped the towel on the table.

"Child stop worrying about that shirt; your father has more shirts than he can wear. Boy, this is one strange evening," said Thelma.

Henry lifted his head. "Strange you said? You have no idea what strange is until I tell you a story that I heard today. Thelma, I promise I'll let you know what's going on. You deserve to know, but right now I have to speak to my daughter."

"I understand Sir. I'll be in the other room if you need me." She picked up the tray and the broken dishes, and left the room.

Before he could speak, he looked at Breana closely. It was like he was looking at his child for the very first time. He studied her eyes, her nose, and her mouth. *'Breana is my daughter, mine and Emily's. Heavenly Father, your Mercy and Grace amaze me...'*

"Father, what's wrong? Why are you looking at me that way?" Breana broke his trance.

"What I'm going to tell you will be very upsetting but please try to understand."

"Father? You are scaring me!"

"Pumpkin, I hardly know where to begin to tell you. I talked to someone this evening. She is someone from my past. Someone I was deeply in love with and she was in love with me. When my mother found out...." He continued to tell her the story of his separation from his beloved Emily.

"My heart was broken, but I thought she had made good on her promise to run away rather than cause a rift between my mother and me. I was withdrawn for a long time. Penny was my good friend; she helped me through that terrible time. We eventually fell in love, and we were married. I never heard from Emily again until this evening."

"You spoke to her?" Breana interrupted.

"Not only did I speak to her, I saw her. That's where I was this evening. She told a story that came as such a shock to me, and it will be to you as well. I have never experienced anything so incredible in my life. This has got to be one chance in ten million." He continued with the bizarre story of the child he didn't know he had

"Oh my God!" She said with much apprehension. "Father! This means you have a child somewhere out there?"

"I do have a child, but there is more to the story. Mother was not satisfied just to keep them from working. She had to take it one step further. Emily's mother became ill. She suffered from depression and eventually she just gave up." Gradually, Henry got to the part of the story where the child was abandoned.

"Oh my God," she exclaimed, "This is awful! Father, what are you going to do?"

"Let me finish the story. That summer when I was leaving to go back to college, we were saying good bye to each other. She had a silver hair comb in her hair. She gave it to me and she told me to keep it to remember her by. All I had to give her was a key chain."

"And my key chain reminds you of that? I'm sorry to upset you."

"You have nothing to apologize for my dear. You see, when Emily left, she left the key chain I gave her with the baby."

"Well, that's a coincidence."

"No, it's more than a coincidence. Emily named her baby Breana, and this is the key chain that I gave her. She left it with you. *You* are Emily's baby....You are *my* baby...*our* daughter."

Henry's lips started to tremble, and tears streamed down his face.

"These are my initials here on the key chain, *H. H. N*, Henry Hamilton Noble. You are indeed my daughter, Breana. You've made it home. You made it home years ago."

Breana sat motionless in her chair. "Please say something," Henry pleaded.

"How is this possible? I...uh, I don't know what to say...I don't feel so well. I'm going to my room." She got up from the chair, and in a daze, she made her way to her room. For a while, she sat on the bed and stared into space. *"How do I deal with this? Should I be happy, or should I be crying? Lord, how do I deal with this? I don't even know what to ask of you right now."*

She swung her feet up on the bed and laid down as Henry's voice echoed in her ears

She thought of all the pain and anguish she endured as a child, so many years of foster care and feelings of abandonment. *My mother cried for me just as much as I cried for her, all because of my grand-mother...* She buried her face in her pillow and cried herself to sleep.

Henry was still sitting in the den. He poured himself some brandy, and sat in the chair behind his desk. Thelma walked in. "Is there anything you would like Sir before I turn in?"

"No thank you Thelma. I've got everything right now, but could you sit and talk to me for a while?" he said as he gestured to the chair in front of him.

Oh boy, I know that look. It's a big deal, whatever it is. Thelma thought as she walked over to the chair.

"Sit down." He said, "So much has happened in this one day. A story that is so inconceivable came to my knowledge. It has taken Breana out of her wits and it has thrown me for a loop. Remember that story I told you about the girl I fell in love with when I was a young lad?"

"Yes Sir, you should've seen the look on your face when you said her name, Emily, wasn't it?"

"Yes, Emily...you better hold on to your seat because..." he sighed heavily "...that's who I was with this evening."

"Oh my sweet Lord! You've found her Sir? How? Where has she been all this time?"

"Right here in Jamaica. The circumstances surrounding her disappearance are very unnerving, and my mother is at the root of the whole ordeal."

"Your mother, how is that Sir? The woman is dead!"

"Well, remember I told you that she had found out that Emily and I had feelings for each other?"

"Yes Sir."

"Things had gotten, let's just say...out of hand, once, between Emily and me. Oh boy! When they say it only takes only one TIME, trust me, it's true. Anyway, I was gone, and Emily found out that she was pregnant."

Thelma sat slack jawed as Henry told the story in detail. "The baby that she left behind was Breana."

"I'm sorry Sir, but you're not making any sense now. You just said that the baby was Breana."

"That's what I said, and that's exactly what I mean. Breana is my biological daughter, Emily's and mine."

Thelma looked to the ceiling, "Oh my God! Have you told Breana this?"

"Yes I have."

"How did she take the news?"

"She has not said a word. She went to her room."

"That poor child, how much more must she deal with in her life? I don't even know how to help her through this one. Thank God she has Mark now. She can share whatever she feels with him too."

"My mother wreaked havoc and robbed me of the family I could have had. She rewrote my life. When we found out that Penny was unable to conceive after a miscarriage, we were devastated. It took us a long time to make up our minds to adopt. When we finally decided, my mother changed her will unbeknownst to me. She named the beneficiary of her trust to be my biological child. We didn't know until after her death and there was nothing anyone could do to change it. Therefore, she has millions of dollars waiting in the trust. No one had any idea she was talking about Breana. So all the time that Breana was going from one foster home to the next, enduring hardship, she was a multi-millionaire." Henry shook his head in disbelief.

"I think I'll go check on her before I turned in Sir; are you sure you're alright, you don't need anything?"

"No, you go ahead; I'll be fine."

"Sir, you look tired yourself, why don't you go to bed. Breana has already gone to her room."

"Perhaps you're right. I'm a little tired." he said getting to his feet. "You know, finding Emily again should have been a happy occasion. However, I'm concerned. I have no idea how Breana will react to her mother. I'm also thinking that Emily has suffered just as much. It would be a shame if she had to endure rejection from her daughter as well. I just hope that Breana can find it in her heart to understand what her mother went through, and why she had to leave her behind."

"I'm sure she will, Sir."

"Well, I'm off to bed…oh, I'm terribly sorry about that mess I made earlier."

"Oh never mind about that Sir, under these circumstances, that's the last thing you should be concerned about. You try to have a good night."

"Good night then and I'm sorry just the same."

"Okay Sir, I'll see you in the morning. A good night sleep will put things into perspective."

Thelma went into Breana's room and saw her lying across the bed. *You poor child, I wish I could turn back the clock for you.* She thought, as she covered Breana with a blanket. After Thelma left her room, Breana turned over onto her back and just laid there staring at the ceiling. *There's so much to process. It's all so fantastic.* As she lay there, she started praying for strength, and for God to help her understanding of how her life could be so capricious, more so than many people she knew. She slept fitfully, tossing and turning until she finally fell asleep in the wee hours of the morning.

Breana woke up early the next morning to find that she was fully dressed and lying on top of the bed covers. She was tired and disoriented. *What time is it? How long have I been sleeping?* She thought, pushing the blanket aside. She pulled herself into a sitting position and swung her feet over to the side of the bed.

"Was it a dream? Or did Father really say that my mother is here in Jamaica? It's so vivid, but how could this be real? This *had* to be a dream. There is no way I could find my biological parents without even looking for them. I know God has been at my side all my life. He has preserved me through tragedies. He has kept me all these years, but this?" She spoke softly to herself. She walked into her bathroom for a shower, and started removing her clothes when she noticed the huge reddish-orange spot on her skirt.

"Oh it's definitely real," she said as she cast it aside. She got into the shower and it felt good. She let the hot water run down her back trying to relieve the tension. She breathed in deeply and exhaled. Normally it would work, but not today. She finally gave up and finished her shower. She put on a knee length jeans skirt and a white sleeveless blouse. Her blue scarf completed the outfit; she tied it around her head and left the room. She walked into the kitchen.

"I guess it is okay to wear white since the food fight is over," Thelma said, smiling as she tried to lighten up the mood.

"So it *is* true. I wasn't sure whether I dreamed the whole thing, or not."

"I believe you already knew it was no dream darling. It's just a way for the mind to protect itself."

"So the story about my mother and grandmothers is real?"

"It is as real as these apple turnovers that you are looking at!"

"Any other morning my mouth would be watering, but this morning my stomach is in knots. I don't think I could eat."

"That's understandable. You have every right to bellyache this morning. But remember, it's not all bad. For now you know that *Noble* blood runs through your veins, and you have a chance to know your biological mother."

"You're right. I'm elated, confused, and heart-broken at the same time. Nothing can lessen the years of hurt and disappointment that abandonment had inflicted on me."

Thelma said, "Time heals all wounds my love. I can imagine what the poor woman lived through all these years. It had to be great desperation that would cause any woman to commit herself to living in a convent, and she is not a nun. She's not even Catholic from what I understand. That's got to be some heavy stuff."

"I can't imagine how she must have felt." Breana said, all the while playing with the pastry on her plate.

"I know she was a very young when she had you, and she is now what, probably in her forties? What young woman would choose to give up her secular life to live in a convent without the commitment to eventually become a nun?"

"She had no one else to turn to I guess."

Thelma tried to plead Emily's case. "That's something to take into consideration. Don't judge her harshly. That woman has some stories to tell. I hope you will give her a chance to tell them."

Henry came out and sat at the breakfast table. "Good morning Pumpkin, did you sleep well?"

"Good morning Father. It's hard to tell. I woke up and found myself fully dressed and lying on top of the bed covers. I couldn't tell if it was morning or afternoon."

"Who can blame you? After hearing the story of your life the way you did, I'm surprised you were able to sleep at all."

"A part of me wishes it was a dream."

"It's no dream. She is here, and in spite of everything she has been through, she is just as beautiful as I remember her. Sweetheart, I'm leaving it up to you to see her when you're ready. She is anxious to see you, but she won't push. In fact, she said if you don't want to see her, she would understand completely. I never knew that my own mother was such a cruel person. Everything Emily did, she did out of love for you and me, and by some miracle, her plan worked because here we are. We have found each other. You keep that in mind."

"Your mother never said anything about the situation, Father?"

"She said plenty, but no one paid attention. During the last years of her life, she made up a trust. She named the biological child of Henry Hamilton Noble as the sole beneficiary. Everyone, including me thought she was just being eccentric. She has left you a rich woman.

"What do mean Father?"

"She left you the mansion in Connecticut where I grew up, and its contents. It's been home to the Noble family for generations. We'll have to go to the trust company to make your claim. They will need proof of your paternity of course, but that's no problem we can arrange that. There are also stock holdings worth a lot of money. You are a multi-millionaire, my dear."

Breana was shocked at this news, "Multi-millionaire! Father this makes no sense. If your mother was as terrible to my mother as you say, why would she do such a thing? Why would she leave everything to me?"

"Well Pumpkin, she apparently did some checking on me once she found out I married Penny, Then later when she learned we had adopted, she wanted to take one last jibe at me. You see, I defied her by continuing to court Emily, and so treated her badly, to say the least. I think in the end she felt guilty about all she'd done, that and she must have wanted to make sure that only her blood related grand-daughter would receive the inheritance, thereby preventing any adopted child of mine from benefiting." Henry suddenly laughed in wonder. "You know, it's kind of ironic when you think about it."

"I guess so…but how did my mother find us?"

"She saw the engagement announcement in the Gleaner. She saw our names and started investigating. You know, she and her mother gave up their lives to save yours, for that, I'll be eternally grateful."

"I've been thinking the same thing. I'm grateful to her for making the choice to keep me alive…I want to see her Father, but I think I should wait for her here. She has stayed in convents long enough. Besides, I have so much I want to ask her. Meeting her here would be better."

"Good, I'm glad you've decided to see her. I'll go with Dudley to pick her up."

"I'll have one of the guest rooms ready for her," said Thelma as she left she room.

"I know she's anxious for news from you," Henry said, picking up his jacket from the back of the chair. "I won't keep her in suspense any longer." He kissed Breana on the cheek. "Tell Thelma we'll have an early lunch when I get back."

"Okay Father."

"You're going to love her. She's such a kind and patient person, you'll see. You'll not be able to resist her. Like mother, like daughter." Henry said as he was leaving.

Breana got up from the table to find Thelma. "How are you feeling honey? Thelma asked as Breana walked into the kitchen.

"I'm doing fine, I suppose. So much is happening all at once; it's a bit overwhelming."

"Well, I can't say that I understand what you're going through but I have keen ears and a soft shoulder whenever you need me, okay?

"Okay, thank you.

Lunch is just about ready and I know you didn't have breakfast; let me prepare a plate for you."

"Father asked me to tell you that we'll eat lunch as soon as they get here. I'll wait for them. I'm not really that hungry anyway."

"No problem, I'll keep everything warm." Thelma said, as she opened the oven to put in the makings of what would be a tasty dessert. "We can go get one of the guest rooms ready for her, while we wait. Everything is going to be alright."

"How do you know that? You haven't even met her yet." Breana said.

"No I have not, but I know your father, and he told me about her."

"Oh yeah? When did he have time to tell you so much about her?"

"Do you remember the day he was mad at me for saying that the house was going to be lonesome after you're gone?"

"Yes, he was so mad I had to talk to him about the way he acted."

"Well, you should have seen him. He was so funny. He tied his white handkerchief on a twig. Then he came to the kitchen door and started waving it, as if he had surrendered. Anyway we started talking and he eventually started telling me about her. Your mother was his first love. It's a miracle that they've found each other again."

"Let's not jump to conclusions. Just because she's coming here, doesn't mean they're going to pick up where they left off."

Thelma looked at Breana knowingly. "That's because you didn't see his face when he was telling me about her. Only a man with a longing in his heart could look like that. He is a free man, and as far as I understand, she has been living in a convent since she was deported. That means she too, is free. After all these years, they've found each other again. If that's not fate, then I don't know what fate is."

"After all these years that would be something, wouldn't it Thelma?"

"Well they may have a lot to work through, but it's not impossible. Especially since none of those things that tore 'em apart was their fault. I know old Lenora Noble was some character, but I had no idea she would go that far to preserve her blood-line."

"Did you know her well?"

"I wouldn't say I knew her well. She used to visit at the house in Georgia, but she never stayed there. One day she was visiting, and she said to Mr. Noble, *'Henry, if I live to be a hundred, I'll never understand why you treat those people as if they're your equal. You're such a liberal; I could never stay at your house. You were always like that. Even when you were growing up, you were always running around with that little nigger girl and her puppy.'* Of course I had no idea who she was talking about. Now I know; she meant your mother."

"And she said those things in your presence?" Breana asked.

"Of course she did! She didn't think I was capable of being hurt. Every time I saw her face, she looked like she had just finished sucking on a lime."

Breana laughed out loud. "So where did she stay when she visited Georgia?"

"She had friends, if you can call them that, over in Forsythe

County. She would stop by and visit with your parents then move on to stay with her friends. For the few times that I saw her, she never had a kind word to say to me. I guess since your mother and I are of the same nationality, I may have been a reminder of her to your grandmother. Hey, I just realized something. Do you know you're half Jamaican? Girl, you've been among your people all this time and you didn't even know it."

"Maybe that's why I feel so at home here Thelma; I wonder if my mother is anything like you."

"How do you mean?" Thelma asked.

"You're always so wise, so kind, and so thoughtful. You always know the right things to say in any situation. You have done such a good job straightening me out when I have my little mayhems. Remember the time I came home from school...thinking that I was so in love with this boy in my class. I acted like a raving lunatic, and you were so patient."

"Yes, I remember." Thelma chuckled. "Well, you've been easy to care for, but you and your mother will need time to build a relationship. You have to get to know each other. It will take time and patience, but you have to give her a chance to be the mother she might have been, if your grandmother's actions hadn't robbed her of the chance."

"Now you see what I mean; that's why I said you are incredible? You are the one who has held this family together all these years; yet you are willing to provide support for someone you don't even know."

"Well I know she has been wronged. There is no way to make up for those lost years, but we all can try to make things right."

"I'll certainly do what I can to make her comfortable, and I'll make every effort to get to know her as my mother."

"I know you will."

"I think we better get started on that guest room. I have a lot of my stuff in the closet. I better move them out so that she can have

the space. This reminds me, she may need some clothes right away."
Breana said.

"Yeah, living in a convent, her clothes maybe some '*Ba—ad Habits.*' Thelma said, trying to lighten things up.

Breana caught on to the pun. Ha-ha, she laughed, "I don't believe she was required to pick up those bad habits, since she wasn't a nun. Anyway, I think I'll take her shopping. That could be a start of us getting to know each other."

"I think you should take care of the guest room while I fix brunch. They must be on their way by now." said Thelma.

"Good idea, Father will be famished when he gets here. He didn't eat last night, and all he had this morning was juice and coffee."

"Well, he just got the surprise of his life; food was probably the last thing on his mind."

While Thelma and Breana chatted and made preparations at Harbor View, Dudley and Mr. Noble arrived at Saint Francis Rectory. Dudley drove the car up to the gate. He got out and opened the car door for Henry.

"Boss, he said, do you want me to come in? Or should I wait here?"

"I think you should wait here. If I need you, I'll call you." He started up the walkway to the front door and knocked. A plump lady dressed in dark clothes came to the door. Her face barely visible beneath the shawl covering her head, "May I help you?" she asked.

"Good morning sister. I'm Henry Noble. I came to see a friend of mine who is staying here, Emily is her name."

"Oh yes, you're Miss Emma's friend! I thought you looked familiar. You were here last night, come on in."

"Thank you," Henry said as he stepped inside.

"I'm Mary Louise. Please, sit down." she said directing Henry to a chair. "I'll let Emma know you're here."

Emily was sitting on a chair by the window when Sister Louise approached her.

"Emma! You have a visitor. It's your friend that was here last night."

"Is he alone Sister?"

"As far as I know, yes. If you'll come with me, the office across the hall is vacant. You could visit there if you like."

"Thank you sister, I'll just need a minute to get myself together."

"Okay, I'll have him wait in the office for you."

Emily got up from the chair and walked over to the mirror. Looking at her reflection, she brushed her hair away from her forehead. *So she didn't come after all. She doesn't want anything to do with me.* Suddenly there was a knock at the door. She quickly wiped way her tears with the back of her hands as she heard Mary Louise's muffled voice through the door.

"Emma, are you okay; are you ready?"

"Ready." She said, opening the door.

When Henry saw Emily again, he was stunned at the similarities she had with Breana and he wondered why he hadn't noticed it before.

"Come in Emily." Emily gingerly stepped into the room, glancing around. "Sit down; you're looking as lovely as always."

"And you are as kind as I remember, thank you."

Henry looked into her eyes. "You still have those big beautiful almond shaped eyes. You will always be beautiful."

Emily blushed at the compliment. "I see you came alone."

"Yes, I came alone. Breana didn't think it would be a good idea to come to see you here."

Emily stiffened her lips to keep from crying. "I don't blame her. What gave me the right to expect her to come here? Well, at least I did what I came to do. I have accomplished that much. You know that she is indeed your daughter, and now it's time for me to go."

She started getting up from the chair. "I have taken up enough of your time," she said.

"No-no, you don't understand. She wants to see you. In fact, she is looking forward to it. She just thought that you should be with your family. She wants me to bring you home, to Harbor View."

"Are you serious? She really wants to see me?"

"I've never been more serious about anything. She's at home waiting for you."

Henry took her in his arms. He lifted her chin, her face now wet with tears. He looked into her eyes and sympathized with her sorrow mingled with joy. His eyes exuded compassion as he wiped the tears from her cheeks. Holding her brought back those feelings of long ago. He held her closer and whispered in her ear. "Everything's going be alright, you'll see."

"Henry…I dreamed of this day for over twenty years, and now that it's here, I don't know what I'm going to say to her."

"Just be yourself, and whatever questions she may have, just answer candidly."

"Thanks for everything, Henry. I imagine you had to plead my case to our daughter."

Henry looked down at her and wiped away her tears. "I did no such thing. Don't underestimate our daughter. She is full of compassion."

"Then I should have known that you would raise her right."

"I had some good help, my late wife, who loved her as if she was born to her. After she died, my house keeper, Thelma, she took over as housekeeper/nanny. She did a super job with her and Breana adores her. I told her how it was between you and me."

Henry looked at his watch. "I think you better get your things, so we could leave now. We have delayed long enough." He said, finally letting her go.

"Just as well, before I lose my nerve. I only have a small suitcase." She went to the room to get her things. She started to return to where

Henry waited, then stopped and went back to the room. She knelt by the bed, clasped her hands and began to pray. "Lord, thank you for bringing me this far..." She finished praying, and got up from her knees. "Where there is life, there is hope," she said, as she walked out of the room, closing the door behind her. "Well Henry, let's go; it's time I meet my daughter."

Chapter Twenty-Three

I t was a quiet ride back to Harbor View. Dudley pulled the car into the driveway. He opened the car door, and Henry got out first; then he reached out his hand to Emily. She gently took hold of his hand and stepped out of the car. She took in the beauty of her surroundings, and then closed hers eyes at the wonder of all that was happening now after so many lonely years had passed. She thought, *Am I really ready for this?* They started up the walkway. Breana was sitting by the window watching for their arrival. *They're here; oh God I'm not ready for this,'* she thought. She got up from the chair.

"Thelma, they're here, I need a little time before I see her."

"Why don't you go to your room and wait. That will give her a chance to come in, and catch her breath before you see each other."

Henry opened the door, and Emily stepped inside first. He walked in behind her.

"We're home, Thelma!"

Thelma walked out to meet them. Henry made the introductions. Both ladies shook hands and greeted each other. Henry was holding the small suitcase that belonged to Emily.

"I'll take that to the room Mr. Noble," Thelma said smiling as she took the suitcase from Henry's hand. "Let me show you to your room Emily." Thelma led the way through the corridor. She stopped at the door nearest to Breana's bedroom. She opened the door and walked inside. She set the suitcase at the foot of the bed. She looked around and saw Emily still standing at the door. "Come on in; make yourself comfortable." Emily silently stepped into the room, but she was a long way from being comfortable. "The bathroom is this way, and the closet is over here."

She showed Emily around the room and the guest bathroom with all the toiletries she may need. "I'll let Breana know you're here."

"Thank you so much Thelma." she said, smiling.

"You're welcome. We're having an early lunch in about thirty minutes, I hope you're hungry."

"That's very kind of you. I'm sure I'll enjoy it," she said while looking around the room.

"Did you say thirty minutes?" She picked up her suitcase and put it on the bed.

"Yes I did. We postponed breakfast this morning."

"Okay, I'll be—"

Before she could finish the sentence, Breana walked up to the door, "Knock-knock", she said while softly knocking on the side of the open door. Emily, turning, looked toward the door. She saw Breana standing there. Suddenly, she couldn't move. Memories of the baby she left behind quickly flooded back like pictures in a slide-show. She looked at Breana and saw not a baby, but a lovely young lady with facial features and a smile that reminded her so much of her own. She moved slowly toward her daughter.

"Breana," she said softly, tears streaming down her cheeks. Not sure of how to make her approach, she laid both hands on her own chest.

"Yes, it's me," Breana answered. She was nervous.

Breana started walking toward her. Emily reached out her arms, and they embraced. She touched Breana's hair. She framed Breana's face with her hands as they both cried. Breana hugged her mother thinking, *twenty-two years, and now finally, she's here!*

"I've spent years dreaming of this day, but the girl in my dreams could not hold a candle to you," Emily said, she held her and closed her eyes, remembering the last time she held her baby at the fire station on that chilly autumn morning, so long ago.

"Oh, Breana! I know I can't make up for what I did, but I'm willing to spend the rest of my life trying. I'm so sorry," she said, sobbing and rocking Breana from side to side.

"Don't think about that now," Breana said, wiping tears from her own eyes. "Let's enjoy the moment. I'm willing to accept the past. I'm just happy for the present."

While Emily and Breana stood in the room talking, Thelma left quietly, wiping tears from her eyes. She closed the door behind her and walked down to the kitchen. She prepared lunch, and she brought a tray to Emily and Breana.

"I don't mean to intrude, but I thought you might need some time alone. I fixed this tray, so that you could have something to eat while you talk."

"Thank you, Thelma that was very thoughtful of you," said Breana.

"Yes, thank you, Thelma," said Emily. "I didn't mean to cause such a fuss."

"It was no bother at all, I'm happy to do it, enjoy. If you need anything just call," she said, closing the door behind her.

"Mr. Noble lunch is served," she said, as she approached the study.

As Henry entered the room, he noticed two place settings. What have we here? Not everyone is hungry?"

"Breana and Emily needed time alone Sir, so I fixed them a tray and brought it to the room."

"What a splendid idea. They do need time together. You are always one step ahead of us Thelma."

"Oh that's all in a day's work Sir. We can discuss the raise later," Thelma said in jest.

"Indeed, I suppose we should. After all, there'll be more of us living here now."

"Are you serious sir? Have you discussed Emily's living here permanently with her?"

"Well, not yet. But I will when the time is right and about that raise, don't give it another thought. You're worth it." Henry glanced towards the stairs. "So, how do you think it's going up there?"

"Beautifully, Sir."

Chapter Twenty-Four

The reunion between Breana and Emily continued. With tenderness in her beautiful hazel eyes, Emily looked at her daughter. "Sweetheart, ask me whatever you want, and I will answer you honestly."

"Okay…Father told me that my grandmother was responsible for what happened. What kind of a person was she? How could she do something like that?"

"Well, I have some responsibility too. She did not make me leave you at that fire station, *I* did that. I was afraid to take you to a country that I knew nothing about. My mother was apprehensive about coming back here because she had no idea how she would survive. My actions put her in that vulnerable position. She was sick, and could hardly walk. I had to go with her so I could look after her. There was too much uncertainty. I didn't want to take you into that situation. So I can't blame your grandmother for that part."

"But Father told me some of the things that she did to your mother because she supported you and prevented you from having an abortion. I'm her flesh and blood. She must have been a hateful person to do those things."

"Life with her was not always like that. I don't know if your father told you, but I was born on the Noble's Estate. They only had one child, your father before I arrived. She didn't have a daughter, so it seems like I filled that void. I have never lived in the mansion, my mother and I lived in a beautiful cottage on the grounds. It was nicely furnished. It even had a fireplace. Henry's father bought me a little puppy, and his mother bought me beautiful clothes, and she made sure I went to school.

Then Henry's father died, and the following year Henry went away to college. When he left, his mother, my mother, and the other servants and I were the only ones left on the estate. She treated me like her own daughter. I spent a lot of time in the main house with her, and she was always good to me, but I noticed that whenever Henry was home from college his mother never invited me to the mansion, not once."

"Father has never talked about his parents much. All I know is, his mother's name was Lenora, and his father's name was Hubert Hamilton Noble."

"Well, I'm sure if he had known the truth about the whole story, he would have talked more about them. I'm sure he will have more reasons to talk to you about them now."

"I hope so. There is so much that I don't know about my family; for instance, what was your mother like? I know even less about her than my other grandmother."

"Well, my mother's name was Madeline Johnson; her friends called her Maddie. She was beautiful inside and out. She was a Christian woman, and she walked in the fear of the Lord all of her life. She chose to walk away from a very comfortable position in life rather than compromise her faith. When I became pregnant out of wedlock, I felt so ashamed because she had not raised me to live carelessly. She used to tell me that my body is the Temple of the Lord, and I should fear the Lord and keep His commandments. When I got pregnant out of marriage, it served as proof that I had defiled the Lord's temple and put Mama to shame. But you know what? Mama never allowed me to feel sorry for myself. Even among her tears, she laid her pain aside to support me. She told me that just because I made a mistake, it didn't mean the end of my life. She did everything she could to help me see the good in myself. She never talked down to me, and she has never treated me badly.

That's why after she got sick, and Henry's mother got her deported, I had to go with her to make sure she was taken care of. When I was in trouble she poured out herself for me. I had to be there for her."

"That must have been hard for you too. You had to go to a place that you had never been before. You knew no one, and you had no means of survival."

"It was a difficult time. When we got to Jamaica, we were homeless, penniless, and we were clueless of how we would survive. But God was on our side. Mama knew of a convent that helped the poor. As the Lord would have it, two nuns traveled on the same plane with us. They were missionaries. When we got to the airport, we didn't have any transportation, and Mama was feeling really poorly. She kept coughing while we were at the airport. The nuns were also waiting for their ride and started talking to us. We told them we were going to Santa Cruz. Would you believe they were also from Santa Cruz? They were so nice, and Mama apparently felt comfortable with them that she eventually told them our story. During the conversation, we found out that they were from the same convent that Mama remembered.

They knew we didn't have a ride or any place to go, so they invited us to go to the convent with them. When their ride came, we all left together. At the convent, they helped me look after my mother. I'm telling you Breana, God provides for His own. Mama was heartbroken at the way her life had turned out, but she was grateful for the help. She died one year later. I was lost without her. I had no direction…I felt my life had no purpose. I didn't want to go on without Mama. I felt responsible for what happened to her. Although she kept telling me not to blame myself, I still did."

"Mom, you *shouldn't* blame yourself. I know that you didn't want to cause anyone pain. Whatever you did was out of love."

"You just called me 'Mom.' I never thought I would hear those words from you or anyone else. I'm going to tell you something that I have never told another living soul. Your father has been my only love, and when I lost him, I made up my mind that I would never love like that again, and that is why I stayed at the convent, even after mama died."

"Well, you are my mom, and that's what I'll call you. For years I've thought about what I would say to you if we ever met, and I've seriously been thinking about it since Father told me about his meeting with you. The healing has to start now. I promise you, we will make up for all those times that we missed." Breana said, as she tried to comfort Emily. Emily reached out and cradled Breana's face between the palms of her hands. "I used to think my whole life was a failure, but looking at you now, I can see that it was a success. Giving birth to you was a great accomplishment. God bless the ones responsible for raising you into such a fine young lady."

Breana's tears began again at the Emily's endearing words. She walked over to get some tissues off the dresser and dabbed at her face. She turned to Emily smiling happily. Emily's eyes followed her daughters every move.

"Mom, we've talked so much, we haven't even touched our lunch. We can't let Thelma's delicious meal go to waste. She is such a good cook. You're in for a treat."

"It would be nice to eat something I didn't cook for a change!" Emily answered with a smile.

"Did you have to cook a lot at the convent?"

"Oh yes, that was my job. I cooked three meals every day, but I didn't mind. I had no place to go, and I had nothing else to do, except helping with the laundry sometimes.

Sometimes I go to the market or to Mass. I could have left anytime I wanted, but I didn't feel like going anywhere."

"So, are you a Catholic?"

"No, I was raised a Baptist. It's not the same theological beliefs as Catholics. I never went to confessions or anything like that, but I went to other meetings, and no one had ever tried to force me into it."

"So how was it, I mean living there every day, all day?"

"Well, I have to admit, life was a bit tenuous at times, but I felt I had no other purpose, so it made no difference. I made up my mind that it was a safe haven for me."

"Mom, I'm glad you were able to find a way to preserve yourself against the horrible things that happened to you. The name of the church that you go to worship is not important. What is important is, believing on the Lord Jesus, keeping God's commandments, and being obedient to God's Holy Spirit. Wherever you find that combination, then it's a good place to worship. There are a lot of misconceptions that people have about denominations and serving God. They claim to believe in the same God, yet they use doctrine to separate themselves from each other. I know whom I believe, and He is able to keep me from falling, and I'm not going to play the superiority game. I will worship where I find the truth."

"Breana, you are wise beyond your years. How did I get to be so blessed? At your age, that's amazing. I'm so happy to know that you've been with your father. He taught you well. I knew he would be a good father. You should see the way he used to cuddle my little puppy, Cha-Chi."

"Mom, do you realize that our lives are similar? A little dog named Roscoe brought Mark and me together. I was on the beach, and I fell asleep under the cabana…"

Breana told her story, as Emily smiled…appreciating her first mother daughter talk.

"That is a fantastic story. I can't wait to meet Mark. Your father told me a little about him and your engagement on our way over here. When is he coming back to Jamaica?"

"He will be back in October. I'll have to write and tell him about you. Also, my best friend Savannah is in Connecticut. Wait until she finds out that I've found you mother. She'll be thrilled to death!"

Henry and Thelma had just finished lunch. Thelma started to clear the table. Henry took a mint from the dish on the table, and popped it into his mouth. He got up from the table and adjusted the chair. "What do you think is going on up there? He said, looking at Thelma.

"They've been in there for such a long time."

"I would think they're getting to know each other. They have a lot of catching up to do."

"Finding each other like this is a miracle. I'm going to do every-thing I can to help them build a relationship." said Henry.

"That is just like you Mr. Noble. You can count on me to do the same. They deserve all the support they can get."

"Thelma you are very kind to see it that way, especially, since you and Breana were always like mother and daughter."

Thelma thought about what he said for a moment, and then she replied, "Breana has a big heart, and it's filled with love. There's room for everybody, and the more people she has loving her, the better. She's like the daughter I never had, and that will never change."

"You have always been such an instrumental part of this family ever since you came to work for us. Have you ever regretted not getting remarried and having children of your own?"

"Charlie was such an honorable man," she said after giving thought to the question.

"He had principles. The four years that we were married were the best years of my life. When he died, a part of me died with him. However, I had our son to raise. I had to focus on that. He was a fine boy. He looked just like his father. When he was almost six years old he took sick. At first, I tried home remedies, but he just got weaker, so I took him to the doctor. He was diagnosed with polio. He died two weeks later, and the rest of me died with him. I shut myself off, because I felt that I was robbed. I had many admirers since Charlie, but none of them came close to measuring up to him. At least that's how I saw it. If I could not have Charlie and my son back, then I didn't want anybody. I was content just to look after other families."

"Did you work with other families before we met you?"

"Oh yes Sir! When I met you and Mrs. Noble, I had already worked for a few families. Some of them were alright. Some were so-so, and others were downright cruel."

"I can't imagine anyone being cruel to you, Thelma."

"I remember the Baileys; they were one of the first families I worked for after my son died. Their house was like a chamber of horrors. The yelling and the screaming were unbearable. Her husband used to come home drunk and smelling like a skunk. Cleaning that house was like cleaning up a pig sty. One day I was at a low point, thinking about Charlie and my son. I was sitting on the back steps of the house. I just couldn't stop crying. Mrs. Bailey was looking for me. Evidently she was calling me, but I was so caught up in my own thoughts, I didn't hear her. She walked around to the back of the house and she saw me sitting on the steps crying. She looked at me and said, *I'm crying because my husband is alive, and you are sitting on my time crying because yours is dead? You don't know how lucky you are.* She was very condescending. Well, by the time I got finished with her, she was crying for a whole other reason. I packed up and walked off the job that same day. The next day I got the job as head of housekeeping at the hotel...you know the rest."

"And that was a blessing for Penny and me, because, that was where we met you, and the love affair began. Penny thought you were the greatest. She loved you so much. She used to say that you are the realest person she ever met. I think she coined the word 'realest' just for you. She said words failed to describe you."

"I felt the same way about her sir. She was one of a kind. She never let me feel subordinate, and for that, I respected her even more. Some of my employers believed that the only way to be respected is to be aloof and treat the help like something that they brought home on the bottom of their shoes. You and Mrs. Noble were never like that. You both have always made me feel at home and as part of the family."

"And if I may interrupt, you have never respected us any less. I have to say it has always been a mutual admiration. Being privileged does not make one person better than the next person that is less fortunate. It's the character of a person that really counts, and money can't buy that. Think of Rita Ives. The woman was a rebel. She had no class, yet, she was one of the most privileged women in Atlanta."

Thelma shook her head. "Um-um-um, her evilness did not go unpunished. Although, the same people that she despised were the source of returning dignity to her before she died. God sees our souls, and not our positions in life."

"How true Thelma, very true. Well, not to cut the conversation short, but I have to take Breana to John Crook's Garage. Her car is being delivered today."

Henry went and knocked on the guest room door. Breana opened it.

"I don't mean to intrude, Pumpkin, but it's time to go to the garage."

"Oh, goodness, I forgot all about that."

"Do you need anything my dear," he said looking at Emily.

"No Henry, I'm fine; thank you for asking." Emily answered, smiling at her long lost love.

"Breana and I will be back as soon as we can. Meanwhile, you relax and get settled."

"Okay," she said.

Breana kissed Emily on the cheek. "I'll be back soon," she said as she walked out the room. If you need anything just ask Thelma.

"Thank you," Emily said, as she closed the door. She knelt down by the side of the bed, and she began to pray.

"Oh Father, I thank you. I thank you. Oh! I thank you. Blessed is your name in all the earth, Lord…"

Dudley had been waiting, so Henry and Breana went out to the car. Breana reached into her purse and pulled out the key chain.

"Father, maybe it would be a nice gesture to give Mom this key chain back."

"No, it would have been yours anyway. It's an heirloom. It's our family's custom to hand it down. It belonged to my father Hubert Hamilton, and his father before him, Harry Hamilton, and it was handed down to me, and now that I have it back, I'll give it to you."

"Thank, you Father," she said. She gave him a hug with a big squeeze and kissed him on the cheek.

"What was that for? Henry asked.

"I'm just so… happy today, I'm about to burst. Mom is back in my life and I'm about to finally get a car!" She laughed and Henry grinned at her as they got into the car.

"Was it intended that way…you all having the same initials, or did it just happen?"

"I have no idea; I think it just worked out that way."

"And being a girl, my initials are different. Maybe my name should be Hilda Harriet Noble or something like that," She quipped.

"Don't you dare! You have a beautiful name. You're named after two very special ladies, my beloved Penny and her dear mother."

"I'm only kidding Father, I love my name. I wouldn't change it for the world."

"Then let's go get your keys for your chain. When you have your child, you can find names that begin with H." He chuckled.

Chapter Twenty-Five

H enry was sitting in the den, reading, when he heard Breana said, "Last but not least, this is the den. It's Father's favorite room, as you can see. The proof is sitting right there in his favorite chair."

"Well, well! I was just getting ready to put a search team together," Henry said. "You ladies were missing in action for quite a while."

"Well Breana took me for a spin in her new car, and then she gave me a tour of the house."

"Don't worry Father; I left the outdoors for you to show. I know how much you enjoy the grounds yourself."

"Indeed, I do. I'll show her the most gorgeous landscaping this side of the Caribbean."

He got up from his chair. Then with that old familiar zest, he said, "Out of my way, Miss Noble! Your mother and I have a date."

All three laughed at Henry's make believe cockiness. He held out his arm for Emily, and she graciously accepted. "After you my dear." he said as he opened the door. They started walking down the garden path.

"Henry, this place is a tropical paradise. Everything looks so luxuriant. All the fruit trees are laden. Oh my goodness! Your gardener must have a green thumb." She said. "He certainly has. He could plant a dried up twig and before long, it becomes a flourishing plant."

From the kitchen, Breana could not control her curiosity as she asked Thelma.

"Do you think they'll get back together? After all, look at all that has happened.

They were separated all these years. Yet, look at them; they're getting along so well."

"Well my dear, anything is possible. There has to be a reason why those two were able to find each other after all these years, and they are both available. Not to mention you could be the tie that binds, in this case."

"Thelma, could I ask you something, honestly?"

"Of course baby! You could ask me anything, you know that!"

"How would you feel about it if they really got back together and got married?"

"I would be very happy. He's the kind of man that is happier when he's sharing his life completely. Oh, I remember him in the earlier years with Mrs. Noble. They reminded me of my Charlie and me, so in love. He came to life again for a little while; before that old serpent Effiedra revealed her true self. My blood runs cold every time I think of that woman."

"I know what you mean. I get this weird feeling every time I see Father sitting alone by the gazebo." Breana replied.

"Let us not allow our minds to visit that disaster area. I shouldn't have brought her up in the first place. Some things are better left alone, and Effiedra Wilson is definitely one of them. I hope your parents find their way back to each other. That would make up for the hell she put him through."

"Well, to say the least, I'd love to have my own parents together. The thought of it just warms my heart. You know, this entire story still amazes me. God is so good. I need to write Mark about this. Wait until he hears that I've found my mother, and Savvy, she'll be so thrilled when she hears. I'll be in my room if you need me."

"Okay dear, tell Mark I send him my love, Savannah, too."

"Will do." said Breana as she walked away.

Henry and Emily finished their walk, and they took a break by sitting inside the gazebo.

"It feels so right sitting here talking to you like this. It's just like old times. The only difference is I never thought we would be discussing our child. Life is full of surprises," said Henry, shaking his head. They continued catching up on their lives spent together, and apart. Thelma saw them from the kitchen window. Before long, she was on her way with refreshments.

"There you are. Are you enjoying the view of Kingston Harbor, Emily?" she asked.

"I am; it is truly beautiful."

Thelma set the tray down on the table. "I thought you both might need a cool drink. The salty air can make a person quite thirsty."

She attempted to pour the lemonade. "Wait Thelma, let me do that," Emily said.

Thelma let go of the pitcher into Emily's hands. "Certainly, I'll just leave you two and let you enjoy the view. If you need anything, I'll be inside." They thanked her for the drink, and Thelma went back to the house.

"Emily, do you remember the first real date we had?"

Emily looked at him, with a smirk on her face, "As if I could forget. You took me to the 'St. James Theatre' on Broadway to see the musical *Oklahoma*. I remember spending the rest of the week pretending to be Shirley Jones," she said with a giggle.

"I'm impressed that you remember! I never thought it meant that much to you."

"Are you kidding? That was the spring that changed my life. I loved the show, but the best part was being with you." She gushed.

"When I got home from college for the holiday, the cast had just left the 'Shubert Theatre' in New Haven to go to Broadway. All my friends that saw it were talking about it. Roger & Hammerstein's

Masterpiece they called it. When we went to see it, the moment Shirley Jones came out singing '*Oh What a Beautiful Morning*,' I saw what they meant. Speaking from their point of view, I mean, because, I only had eyes for you."

"You would have made an excellent Janitor, Henry Noble. You've cleaned that up really well!" Emily said, laughing. "Nice save."

"By the way" she said, "The original title to that musical was '*Away We Go*', did you know that?"

"No I didn't!"

"Oh yeah; *Oklahoma* was originally a duet for two of the cast members, but it was such a big hit that they used it for the title instead."

"I see! Agnes de Mille did a fantastic job on the choreography," said Henry.

"Yeah, she really made a name for herself on that one. Before that, she was an unknown. Can you *believe* that?" said Emily.

"How do you know so much about it?"

"I've done a lot of reading over the years. There's not much else to do at the convent. Whenever I thought about you, I would read more about the musical. I thought about you a lot." She looked at Henry, hoping he would say something similar, but he was quiet. He was turned from her so she couldn't see his facial expression and his lean body did not give anything away. She almost could not breath, waiting for him to respond. Henry finally turned to her and said.

"You know, if they ever show it again, I'm taking you to see it, no matter where it's playing. I want us to recapture everything."

Emily's heart sank but she tried not to show it; she held on to hope. She knew that she still loved him, even after all the many years without him. He was her one and only, the love of her life.

"I have everything I need to capture it right here. We don't have to visit the past. As a matter of fact, you didn't have to take me to Broadway to see it the first time. I would've been content anywhere as long as we were together."

"Now she tells me!" Henry said, lifting his arms, "I even bought you popcorn!"

"I loved being with you!" Emily replied, "Popcorn or no popcorn, couldn't you tell?"

"No, I was too busy trying to impress you."

"Well, the truth is, you impressed me just by being you. You're kind, thoughtful, and unpretentious."

"You know, Emily, when I went home for spring break in 1943, the place didn't seem the same without you. I went to see this movie, *'Going My Way'* with this girl that mother insisted I went out with, Isabelle was her name. Bing Crosby played an easy going priest, and he and this older priest at his parish were butting heads. Crosby was young and a little on the liberal side, and the old Priest was totally conservative. Even though I have always enjoyed Bing's acting, all I could think of was you and me being at the theatre the last time I was home. You stayed on my mind, and I couldn't enjoy the movie. I might have well gone home. I didn't hear a word Bing said."

A distinct sadness came over Emily's face. "Breana was born January 4, 1943. Mom got sick around that same time and we were at our lowest point." She looked so forlorn that it tore at Henry's heart. "I wish I had known then. I would have stopped at nothing to find you; you know that? I hope you know that. I would not care what mother tried to pull."

"Yes I do know that. That's why I couldn't contact you. Please say you do understand that." Emily pleaded.

"I'm trying to say that your mother and you would have never had to leave our child to go anywhere; if I only knew. You rest assure my dear, all that is behind us. I wish your mother was alive. It would've been a sweeter victory." Henry said, pulling her close to him. He held her in a rocking motion while rubbing her back. Emily savored the moment thinking, *even if he doesn't love me; at least I know he cares.*

As the week passed, Henry, Emily and Breana spent as much

time as they could with each other. Henry had taken a long overdue vacation, and Breana, after spending every waking moment with her mother, staying up until they both were falling asleep on the couch, suddenly began making herself scarce. Henry and Emily seemed not to notice as they became reacquainted with each other.

Breana came bounding down the stairs and was headed outside one beautiful sunny day. She stopped in her tracks and sniffed the air and made a turn for the kitchen instead. "Is that fresh bread I smell?" she asked as she entered the door.

"It sure is. I'm making your favorite dessert too."

"Peach Cobbler! Oh Thelma you're the best! Would you like some help with anything?"

"An extra pair of hands is always helpful, love. You could slice up those peaches over there. Don't slice them too thin; they're a little on the soft side. You can start making some green salad when you're finished."

Breana walked over to the kitchen sink and washed her hands. "Thelma I have a very strong feeling that Father has every intention of picking up where he left off with my mother, what do you think?"

"After all the times he told me to butt out, I refuse to speculate. Let them work it out on their own. If we say anything, it may just backfire, that's what *I* think. Why do you think so?"

"Oh, it's just that I saw them hugging each other the other day under the gazebo, and it looked really intimate. I've been giving them their space ever since. It would be so great if they were to get married. We could probably even have a double wedding!" Breana said excitedly.

"Now Breana, cool yourself. Don't get your hopes up. I would love for them to be together too, but you've got to let things happen the way they are supposed to. I'm still baffled about the whole thing. This only happens in fairytales, not in real life. I believe all three of you were meant to be a family in God's own time, and this is the time."

"Hmm, who's speculating now?"

"I'm speaking by faith and divine providence. You, on the other hand, spoke because of what you think you saw outside." Thelma said with a silly grin.

"In other words, it's not okay for me to speculate on what I saw with my own eyes, but it's okay for you to speculate by faith?"

"That's right, eyes can be deceiving, but in faith you have hope."

Breana laughed so hard, she said, "Thelma, have I ever told you how confusing you are?"

"No, and you better not!" said Thelma, humorously, as she remove a steaming pot from the stove to the counter.

Outside, Henry and Emily continued to fill in the blanks. "Henry, what led you to adopt Breana; I mean, how did you find her?"

"After Penny had a miscarriage, we found out that she would not be able to have any more children. For years, we contemplated adoption. Penny was such an amiable person; she would never do anything to offend anyone. She would even sacrifice her own happiness. She felt that we should consult my mother before we decided on adoption. Well, mother came up with all kinds of reasons why it was a bad idea. Penny said that since she would be the child's grandmother, if that's how she felt, it would not be fair to bring a child into that situation.

As the years went by, we kept it in mind. Then we finally went to an agency in New York to seek adoption. Everything had been cleared; we were just waiting for a baby to become available. We came close once, but the birth mother changed her mind. Then out of the blue one day, a social worker called and asked if we would be willing to adopt a teenager. Penny had read an article of the difficulty in finding placement for older children, so when she got the phone call, she was ready to make the commitment. We both decided that it was a good idea. We loved her from the moment we saw her, and we have been blessed by her presence in our lives. Penny loved her with all her heart; then she died about a year later."

Emily watched Henry closely, and marveled as his story unfolded. "I'm sitting here talking to you, and I can scarcely believe it, especially, being here in Jamaica."

"It is remarkable, I know...it was bittersweet moving here though...while we waited for the move to Jamaica, Penny died from pneumonia. It happened so quickly. I was a broken man, and I thought I would lose my mind." Emily touched his hand. "I'm so sorry Henry; it had to be hard on you both. I'm indebted to her for caring for Breana. I wish I had the chance to know her."

"She was wonderful, and she protected Breana like a lioness. Her absence had left a void in our lives for a long time."

"How did Breana cope with her dying so soon after the adoption?"

"She was devastated. Thelma kept a steady hand on her, and now you have made her life complete. She no longer has to wonder about her origin. You have provided the missing pieces of the puzzle for her, and I'm sure she is happy about that."

"It would be great joy to me if I bring some happiness to her life. She was such a happy baby. I've always wondered if my leaving her had changed her personality in any way."

"She had some rough-spots in her life, but that's all behind her now," said Henry.

Emily sat silent for a moment; then she said, "Do you have any concerns about the young man that she's engaged to?"

"No, from what I know of him, he's a fine young man and he's well able to support her.

You'll get to meet him soon. He'll be here in a few weeks. I believe Breana said October third."

Emily sighed. "I can't believe it. Our daughter, getting married; I'm still trying to get used to her being all grown up."

"It's not much different for me. She pretty much grew up in front of my eyes, and I have to admit I had trouble handling it at first." They were both quiet for a while, each contemplating Breana's nuptials in their own way. Emily decided to ask a question she had really been wondering about.

"Henry, what about you; do you have plans to remarry?" Henry sat and thought about the question and how best to answer it. He still had a bad taste in his mouth about the Effiedra debacle. However, the woman in front of him was not the conniving deceiver that Effiedra was. She was someone he had once loved dearly and seriously wanted to marry. By all accounts, they would be married today had his mother not interfered. Yet, he was remembering Emily as she was. It had been more than twenty years since they were together. What if she had changed? Could she be only showing her first face? These past days they spent together, some of the feelings he had for her seemed to have resurfaced. How did she really feel about him? Could he risk another disappointment? He watched her watching him with expectation and determined that they needed more time.

When he still had not answered her question, Emily said, "Maybe I shouldn't have asked you that. I'm sorry." She looked down at her hands and then started brushing at her skirt.

Henry began to explain. "Emily, you know I've been married twice already, and the last one almost killed me, literally. You already know about that. I'm trying my best not to think about it, it's such a sore spot for me. The idea of me getting married again is not something I had considered…until now!" Emily shot a surprised look at him. He stood up and walked over to sit by her.

"I would like for you to stay here stay here with us; this is where you belong. We are your family. You've lived in a convent without the benefit of being a nun long enough, and I don't think that was ever your intention."

"No, it wasn't. It's just that I was so depressed after all that had happened. The sisters and everyone in the parish did everything to help Mama. After she died they all were so very supportive, and I felt safe there. I might have been a nun if so much of my heart was not filled up with you and Breana, but it was impossible for me to commit to anyone or anything, let alone being a nun."

"Did you just say I fill up your heart?" asked Henry. He felt relieved, and he took her hands into his.

"Yes Henry, I've never stopped loving you. In fact I believe I love you more now than ever," she confessed.

"I feel the same way about you. I love you now as I did way back then, maybe more. Please say you'll stay and let us work this out."

"We have a chance to be a family with our daughter. It means a lot to me. How could I refuse," Emily said after a long pause.

"Then it's settled. We will tell Thelma and Breana the good news at dinner."

While they contemplated the future, Thelma and Breana were in the kitchen cooking up a special dinner in honor of Emily's homecoming. The aroma of all the home cooked food was tantalizing.

"If my olfactory is functioning right, said Henry, we're in for a treat. Thelma is working that magic that she does so well. I think it's time to get ready for dinner. Shall we go?"

Sometime later, the dinner bell rang. Everyone moved to the table. Henry said the prayer, blessing food, and gave thanks to God for the miracle that brought his family together. They dined in style and complimented the cook. During dinner Henry discussed the idea of Emily living with them. They were all excited about their future... together at last! Henry lifted his glass and proposed a toast. "Let us drink to the future of this family. May we grow in number and in grace?"

"Well hallelujah, and amen," Thelma said with a robust laugh, things are really taking shape around here, and it's about time!"

"Thelma," said Emily, "I hope you know I'll never encroach on your relationship with Breana. My being here will be of no threat to you in any way. I'll always be grateful to you."

"Thank you for saying that, although, I never thought it would." Thelma replied.

"Mom, I would like to take you shopping for whatever you need. I know you didn't come prepared to stay. We could go tomorrow if you'd like, and you can choose anything you want and twelve of each." She said as she laughed out loud.

"Your generosity is overwhelming my dear, but are you sure you have the time?"

"Mom, I will make the time if I could spend it with you. We have lost enough of it already. This is long overdue. We'll make up for all those mother daughter things we never did."

Breana never missed a chance to spend time with Emily and neither did Henry; although, she was careful not to ignore Thelma. She was included as much as she wanted to be.

It had been three weeks since Emily graced the threshold of the Nobles home, and everyone adored her. Late one balmy evening, Henry invited Emily for a walk on the beach. As they held hands and walked together, she looked across the harbor. "Those harbor lights are so beautiful. This is such an enchanting place. Living here feels like being on vacation. I can't remember when I've been so happy."

"I could be happier, and it's all in your hands," Henry answered.

"Oh, how is that possible?" She asked, looking at Henry as he stroked his chin, the way she remembered him doing when he's thinking. *I wonder what's on his mind,* she thought.

"How do I say this," Henry started.

"Just say it, whatever it is."

"Well, ever since you've came back in my life, everything's been wonderful. However…,"

The minute she heard however, her ears perked. *He looks so serious,* she thought, *is he going to ask me to leave?*

The gallop in her heart was like the hooves of a racing mare, as anxiety set in, Henry laid it to rest. "Breana is getting married on December seventeenth. It should not be that a child gets married before the parents."

Emily breathed a sigh of relief. Henry continued his speech. "I had no control over what happened in the past, but I want to make it right for us. This is our time."

He got down on one knee, and she looked down on him holding her left hand. "Say you'll marry me, and you'll make me a contented man. Let's seize the moment Emily, I do love you. So please say you'll marry me."

She placed her right hand over her mouth, and stared in disbelief. Inside she was screaming, *Yes! Yes! Yes!* Trembling with delight, as she quietly said, "Henry, I used to dream of hearing those words from you. Then I gave up on those dreams years ago. Now, here we are, on this lovely beach, and you're proposing to me. This is my miracle. Oh yes, Henry! Yes, I'll marry you!"

Henry reached into his pocket, and pulled out a ring box. He opened the box, and she drew in a breath with her mouth wide open. "Henry," she said, "I've never set eyes on anything more beautiful." It's was her birth stone surrounded by diamonds, and mounted on the finest white gold. "How did you find something so perfect?" she asked.

"I had it mounted especially for you."

"And you remembered that my birthstone is amethyst?"

"I have never forgotten anything about you. I chose your birthstone because I wanted it to be extra special for you."

"Oh Henry, I'm so sorry, my finger doesn't do justice to this ring. My hands are chopped, and my nails are all torn, I—"

"Shhh…," Henry whispered, putting his pointer finger over her lips. He held her close and kissed her tenderly. He wrapped his arms around her tightly, "Welcome home my beloved," he spoke softly in that seductive voice she remembered so well. She was thrilled. He lifted her off her feet, and her heart soared above them. She gazed up at him as he set her back on the ground.

"I'll treasure you for as long as we both shall live." She said.

Emily wept in silence as she stood there gazing at the ring. Henry reached into his pocket and pulled out a handkerchief and handed it to her. She dried her tears, and returned it to him. He took her by the hand, and he started leading her toward the house. "Let's go. I can't wait to see the look on Breana's face when we tell her!"

They hurriedly walked up to the house. Henry could not contain his enthusiasm. As they reached the house, he stepped onto the verandah. He pulled Emily along as she tried to keep in step with him.

"Breana! Thelma! Where is everybody?" He shouted, "I have got good news!"

Breana came rushing into the room. "Good heavens Father. Why are you shouting like the house is on fire?

"My news is hotter than a simple fire my dear, he said, looking at Emily, and this time no one can put it out. I want to shout it from the roof top!"

Thelma joined the group. "This has got to be good to have you so excited, Mr. Noble."

"It's better than good." he pulled Emily close to his side. "This angel has just agreed to be my wife. We are going to be wed! I'm going to marry my first love!"

"Oh my God, this calls for a celebration!" Thelma said.

Breana stood with her mouth gaping for a moment. Then all three of them looked in her direction. She looked at her parents and said, "Did I hear you say you are getting married to each other?"

"Yes Pumpkin, you heard right, both times, getting married, and to each other. I asked her to marry me, and she said YES, to ME, Henry Noble!"

She ran to them with arms wide open. She hugged them both, burying her face into her mother's shoulder. She was overwhelmed by the thought of her family finally being together. It was a powerful and intimate moment. The action of their embrace spoke volumes, as Thelma looked on wearing her smile of approval.

"My grandmother always said, 'It's never too late for a shower of rain' thank you Jesus," she mumbled to herself and quietly walked away.

I don't have to say welcome to the family; you were family before I was even a thought." Breana said, "Let me see the ring. Oh my, this is exquisite! She gasped.

Thelma, get in here!" Breana called out. "This is your victory too. You have borne sorrows with us, now you'll rejoice with us."

Thelma came back to join the group as they continue to rejoice. She walked in bearing champagne and glasses. "This calls for a toast, she said, handing out glasses of champagne, Oh, this ring is gorgeous indeed," she said as Emily reached out her hand.

"Thank you. Henry had it made on special order, to include my birth stone."

"No fooling! How did you get it back so fast Mr. Noble?"

"With much difficulty; at first, the jeweler said no way on such short notice. Then I explained my situation to him. He was still dragging his heels, but in the end, I dangled a few extra karats, and he did the Bunny Hop for me. He pushed everything aside and worked over time to help me."

Time was of the essence to plan the wedding for Emily and Henry. Emily decided not to have a large wedding so close to the approaching of Briana's own wedding date.

"This is Breana's time to shine. I don't want our plans to infringe on her wedding plans," she said.

"I agree my dear, but we shouldn't minimize your day either, so what do you suggest?" Emily said, "Let's just keep it small, immediate family only."

"Mark will be home in two weeks. He could be the best man, and I could be the maid of honor," said Breana.

"Fabulous, if it's alright with you Emily?" Henry said turning to look at her.

She fiddled with her new ring. "That's fine by me."

"That sounds like a plan, said Thelma. Just let me know what I can do to help."

"I have a great idea. Why don't we reserve the private dining room at the Whitmore for the ceremony, and the reception?" Breana suggested.

"Very well then," Emily agreed. "That's what we'll do, keep it simple and easy."

"I'll make a list of the things that we have to do, and then we can start with the arrangements," said Breana.

* * *

For the next two weeks, Breana, Thelma, and Emily were insep-arable, trying to prepare for both weddings.

"Mom, I think we should concentrate more on your needs. My dress is on order from New York, and I have already chosen my accessories. Thelma and I did the things that could be done without Mark, so we wouldn't have too much to do when he comes. He wanted me to wait until he gets back to work on my trousseau, so that we can do it together."

The ladies' joint venture was very successful. Purchases of cloth-ing for Emily, and everything necessary for her wedding were made; including a stunning Ivory colored A-line dress. It had a transparent embroidered lace Turtleneck and long sleeves. With some minor adjustments by Thelma, it fit Emily like it was made for her.

Chapter Twenty-Six

On October 2, 1965, a civil unrest erupted in Kingston. The city was being terrorized by political gang violence, and the Minister of Home Affairs had declared a State of Emergency in the area. Many were killed as a result of the outburst, and a curfew was set from dusk till dawn. Henry came home from work early, and Breana met him at the door.

"You are not going to believe this. I heard from Mark. His ship will be in port in two days. According to his message, he will definitely be in port on the third, which is tomorrow. Father I'm worried. With all this violence going on, Mark will be coming right in the middle of it all, and with this dusk till dawn curfew, who knows how long it's going to last. I do miss him, but I wish he wasn't coming in the middle of this. Oh Father, what am I going to do?"

"Now, now Sweetheart, don't fret about that. Mark will be all right. He knows how to conduct himself in matters such as this. He has sailed all over the world. These things are not foreign to him."

"I hope so. But what about the wedding, yours and Mom's, I mean. I would hate to see anything interfere with that. You both have waited so long for this."

"You bet nothing will interfere," said Henry, "If I have to perform the ceremony myself and have you and Thelma as witnesses, we are getting married on the said date." He went back to reading the most recent newspaper article about the political disturbance.

"I just hope they do whatever they have to do to return to

normal around here. People can't keep their lives on hold to accommodate tyranny for goodness sakes," said Breana.

"So which room will Mark be using when he gets here?" Henry asked, trying to sound nonchalant.

"Oh, uhmm…the one next to mine."

"Absolutely not, you'll put him in that room next to my office. I don't want anyone taking the wrong turn in finding their own room," he said, peeking from behind his newspaper."

"Father, nothing like that would happen!" Breana said.

The Bogain-Villa pulled into port, unfortunately no one could disembark. Due to the curfew, there would not be enough time to clear customs, and Mark's ship was fourth in line to disembark the following morning. The customs workers were reduced to two and the process slowed down. Breana went to the wharf, but she was denied entrance in regard to her safety. Reluctantly she went home by police escort.

* * *

Finally, Mark went through customs, and he immediately drove to Harbor View. From the window, Thelma saw him and quickly opened the door. "Oh praises be! Mark, you're a sight for sore eyes! Breana! Come quickly!" she said, grinning from ear to ear.

Breana heard the excitement. She rushed out of her room and down stairs. Seeing Mark, she shouted, "Mark, thank God!" while running towards him. Mark dropped his bag as they quickly embraced each other. "I'm glad you made it off the ship before today's curfew hours."

"I am too; you cannot imagine what it felt like being in port for the past couple of days and not being able to get off. After not seeing you for so long, it was no picnic I can tell you that."

"Well thank God you are here now. Let me show you to your room."

He picked up his bag, and they walked down the corridor. "Here we are. Your room is next to Father's office."

"So there is no room in the *inn* upstairs, huh," he said, with an impish smile, as he followed her down the corridor.

"Are you kidding?

Mark laughed aloud. "Yes, of course I am...I can't blame him. I would do the same thing concerning my daughter," he said, as they stood at the bedroom door. Breana opened the door, and Mark walked, and puts his bag down. The room was scented with the fragrance from freshly cut flowers.

"This room smells like a botanical garden. These flowers are beautiful." He said

"Thanks, I selected them from the garden myself. I wanted to welcome you home with fragrance and beauty."

"In that case my beauty, you could have left the flowers where they were. Their fragrance and beauty are pale in comparison to yours." He took her in his arms and kissed her passionately. "I do appreciate the flowers, but would I kiss them like that?"

Breana blushed, "I guess not. If you do, I would really wonder about you."

"Then there is the proof. Your beauty and fragrance surpasses that of flowers or anything else on earth."

He kissed her again. They held each other for a while; then Breana invited him to sit down. They sat and talked and relished just being alone...in their own little world.

"Mark," Breana said, reluctantly pulling away, "As much as I love being with you like this, I better leave now so you can get freshened up, dinner will be served soon. My mother can't wait to meet you, and Father has some news that I'd rather have him tell you."

"Oh, alright! If you must...give me another kiss before you leave." He planted a soft, tender kiss on her lips that she would not soon forget.

Mark, freshly showered and dressed impeccably, joined the

family in the dining. Emily was helping Thelma to set the table. Breana walked in from the kitchen holding a tray of water glasses she had just cleaned. Thelma, here are the glasswa—. She stopped in her tracks upon seeing Mark. Their eyes locked in mutual admiration. She quickly put the tray down and sauntered over to Mark and took him by the hand. Emily and Thelma looked up from what they were doing when Breana cleared her throat.

"Ahem. Mom, this is Mark, my fiancé. He's been dying to meet you ever since I told him you were here." Breana beamed. "Mark, this is my mother, Emily."

Mark took his future mother-in-law's hand and kissed it. "I'm so honored to finally meet you Senora!"

"I'm very pleased to meet you Mark, I've heard a lot about you!"

"Gracias Senora, but the pleasure is mine."

Henry walked in at the end of the introductions and clapped Mark on the shoulder. It's good to have you here young man."

"Thank you sir; it's great to finally be back."

Henry pulled the chair for Emily to sit at the table, and Mark pulled the chair for Breana. As dinner progressed, Henry picked up his glass. "I think this evening call for a toast; on behalf of the family being together, and the up-coming nuptials."

Mark was surprised to say the least. "Did you say nuptials sir?"

"Yes son, I did say nuptials as in two weddings. Emily and I are getting married. We waited for you to get home, so you could be my best man…that is if you will?"

"Of course I will sir, I'm honored that you asked. When will this be?"

"It will be on the twelfth, at 1 p.m. in the private dining room at the Whitmore Hotel.

We thought it would be a good idea for us to keep it small and have it done right away. This way we can give full attention to your and Breana's wedding."

Breana said, "Everything is already arranged. The catering and all will be done by the Whitmore staff."

"Well, it seems as if everything is set. All we have to do is be there. I'll do whatever you need me to do Sir. This is a wonderful surprise. Congratulations to both of you!" Mark said, as he lifted his glass.

"The real surprise is in finding each other again," Henry said, gazing at Emily, "Once we did, we both eventually realized that we couldn't take the chance of losing each other again. This kind of reunion has to be a once in a lifetime thing. No one could deserve such a blessing twice. I'm a God-blessed man."

Breana sat back in her chair appreciating the moment with her family. She reflected on Mrs. White and Mrs. Tucker. She thought of Penny who accepted her with such grace, and in her heart she gave thanks to God for placing them in her life. She was so deep in her thoughts that she didn't realize that she had stopped eating.

"Pumpkin, you've hardly touched your food. Is something wrong?" Henry asked, setting his fork down.

"Oh no Father, quite the opposite, everything seems so right," she paused, "Actually, I was just wondering about Mrs. White and Mrs. Tucker, whether or not they are still alive and well. "Well, that shouldn't be such a hard task. There must be a way we can find out. After all, you are grown now. You can contact whomever you please."

"I suppose you're right. It would be wonderful to see them again. There's got to be somebody who knows about Mrs. Tucker, and I at least have Mrs. White's old address. That might help."

"Life is full of surprises Breana, said Emily, look at us, who knew that anything like this could happen. This is what some people would call a bazaar story, but here we are, so miracles do happen."

The days hurried by, and the plan for Emily's and Henry's wedding were being finalized. Mark and Henry sat by the gazebo playing Dominoes. "Mr. Noble, have you given any thought about a honeymoon for you and Emily?" Mark asked, on the verge of slamming down the Ace blank on the table and yelled, "Six Love!"

"Where did you learn to play Dominoes like that?" asked Henry.

Mark laughed, "I had lots of practice while traveling with many players and attending tournaments on the ship."

"I see, well the next time we play…I'll choose the game, Chess it will be.

I'm pretty good at that game too, if I do say so myself. Mark responded.

Henry grunted in affected aggravation. "And as competitive as you are, I'm sure you play by a chess clock. Let's just change the subject shall we? Mark couldn't help laughing at his future father-in-law.

"We have discussed having our honeymoon after you and Breana are married," Henry said, as he began mixing up the domino pieces. "I have a better idea, said Mark, why don't you guys join us on the Bogain-Villa.

We could make it a honeymoon cruise, we have several honeymoon suites. We could be on board for months and never run into each other, unless we wanted to meet."

"And how long would we have to live in your world before we became land creatures again?"

"I promise it will be no longer than two weeks sir. I have to attend the United Nations convention on the Law of the Sea. You could fly back from New York if you like"

"Oh that's right. I forget that convention will be in a couple of weeks." Henry replied.

"Some of the countries have already extended their coastline from the original three miles from the cannon shot rule, and they're seeking to extend their national claims to include mineral resources, protecting fish stocks, and control pollution."

"I understand your neighbor Ecuador extended its rights to 200 miles."

"Yes they did. Good for them; that gives Ecuador coverage for their current fishing grounds."

"President Truman extended America's control to include natural resources. That is very clever," said Henry.

"I think that was one of his best moves. Many other nations jumped on the band wagon really fast and did the same thing," replied Mark. "I'm anxious to see what happens at the convention. Our Columbian coastline is being depleted by encroaching fishing boats. We need to extend our boundaries to preserve our resources. We're dealing with a larger population, and that archaic 'Freedom of the Seas' concept of the seventeenth century is not working anymore."

"I'm sure it will be alright Son. One by one each affected country is expressing the need for extension to their belt of water; soon they all will. However, not to change the subject, but there's one thing I'm concerned about," said Henry.

"What is that Sir?"

"Thelma. What will she do while we all sailed off merrily into the sunset?"

"I have taken her and Dudley into consideration sir. No one will be left behind, unless it's by choice. When the arrangements are final, I promise you will be pleased."

"Well you know my assignment here is finishing, and my replacement will be here soon, then I'll be a free man. I can go where ever I want, and stay as long as I want."

"I didn't know that, said Mark, will you be giving up the house to move back to the states?"

"No, I plan to keep the house. We can spend the winters here. However, we'll go back to Stone Mountain as soon as possible to open up that house since we haven't been there in a while."

"Well your shipmate is on board, and this is between us. Emily thinks we're postponing our honeymoon until after you and Breana are married, but she can't imagine how soon after it will be. Oh boy, will she be surprised!"

Later, Mark discussed the honeymoon cruise with Breana and they decided to share the information with Thelma.

"She might be making plans of her own. I want to make sure she is comfortable with the idea. Maybe we could tell her, and ask her not to tell Mom," she said.

After the discussion, Breana found Thelma hanging clothes on a line outside told her of the plans for the honeymoon cruise. Thelma dropped the end of the sheet she was hanging on the grass, while the other end still hung on the line. "What! Me...on a two weeks cruise? Oh Lord, life is sure having some turns around here." She said excitedly. Thelma returned to hanging the laundry, now with a little more pep. As she walked away, Breana laughed in amusement at the sight of Thelma who was humming and doing a little dance.

The household was buzzing in preparation for the wedding, and Emily was nervous.

"I wish we didn't have to be there so early. I need time to pull myself together. My hands are trembling so much. I'm having problems loosening my own hair, and my teeth are rattling like a bag of bones,"

"I'm sorry Mom, I really tried to get the latest appointment that was available for the ceremony; however, on account of the curfew, we have to get out as early as possible. That is why we have to be there by eleven o'clock. The ceremony will begin at twelve, and the reception follows immediately after that. We have to be out of there by four o'clock."

"I understand sweetheart. I'm not complaining. I appreciate everything you're doing. I'm just nervous."

"I understand, Mom."

"I can't believe they're still fighting and carrying on. It makes no sense to me. They expect everyone to put their lives on hold while they rant and rave and tear the place down."

Breana sensed her mother's anxiety. She walked over and sat

next to her, and she held her hand. "Don't worry Mom. Everything will be all right."

Henry had already left with Mark to go to the Whitmore and met with Judge Fitzgerald, a colleague and friend of Henry's who was officiating over the ceremony. The private dining room was lavishly decorated. Green and gold linen covered the tables and chairs. The array of fresh flowers was spectacular. Emily's tailored dress was made of the finest embroidered lace, gathered and sequined. The hem of the skirt ended at mid-calf. She wore it exceptionally well. Her hair was elegantly upswept with cascading tendrils. She wore a head dress adorned with antique pearls that was attached to a shoulder length veil. She wore light make up that allowed her naturally rosy cheeks to show through. Blue shadow enhanced her eyes and showcased her dark, lengthy lashes. Her lipstick enhanced her full lips and matched her bouquet of ruby red roses.

From her unique head dress to her antique satin shoes, she was altogether lovely. Henry was in awe as she walked to join him at his side. She was stunning and he couldn't believe that *finally* she would be his wife after all these years. He was overcome with emotion and fought to keep his tears from falling; they almost spilled over when he lifted Emily's veil to seal their vows and saw her cheeks were wet with tears. Their eyes met and there was so much love being spoken between them. He bent and tenderly kissed her lips and then he kissed away every tear from her cheeks. With everyone in attendance cheering, they both hugged and sighed with satisfaction.

They dined on an assortment of American and Caribbean dishes that whet everyone's appetite. Black cake with white icing was surrounded by a variety of sweet treats at the dessert table. While Emily dined, her thoughts drifted into the past. *Here I am at last, the long awaited, Emily Alberta Noble. Where there is life, there is hope.* She set her fork down, sat back in her seat and opened up a fan to gently cool her face. The music started and it was time they had their first dance as Mr. & Mrs. Noble. Henry led her to the floor and held her close; she didn't know where she ended and he began, *we are one*. The dance was intimate with a promise of things to come. Henry had to remind himself that they were not alone. As the dance concluded, they worked their way around the room, shaking hands, and thanking everybody for spending the afternoon with them and sharing their joyous occasion. The evening ended on a very happy note for the family. They tried to make it home before curfew. With everyone safely at home, Breana started reminiscing of the day's event.

"I can hardly believe my life. My parents are now married to each other. I have so much to be thankful for," said Breana to Thelma, as she admired the key-chain with the keys to her Rolls-Royce. "Someday, I will tell my children the story behind this key chain. And when I'm old, it will go to my firstborn. He or she will pass it on to the next generation. This will be part of my legacy to my children."

"I heard someone said legacy," said Henry, walking into the room. "Breana that's something I need to discuss with you."

"Okay Father, you heard legacy, and you're wondering what I'm giving you. Well, I'll make it very clear. It's lighter than air; you can take it everywhere. It grows on earth, and it flourishes in heaven."

Henry understood what she meant. However, being jovial, he looked at her and asked,

"Is it bigger than a bread box?"

Breana looked at him and cocked her head to one side, "Father! It grows on earth and flourishes in heaven. How could anything with a span like that be compared to a bread box? I'm giving you my love." She said with feigned exasperation.

"I'm only teasing; that item is at the top of my list for you too. That's the best legacy I could have received from anyone. It will be the most valued in my treasure chest." he said, smiling. "However, I want to talk to you about your grandmother's legacy. When I told you about it, you had no comment. How do you feel about?"

"That's because I haven't really digested the whole concept of being a millionaire. I think I better leave it on the back burner until after the wedding."

"Whatever is best for you my love, we'll discuss it when you're ready."

As Henry left the room, Breana had second thoughts. She went after him. She found Him sitting at his desk. "Father, do you still have time to talk?"

"Sure Pumpkin, what's on your mind?"

"I just have a question concerning the trust. Do the trustees know that I really exist?"

"Yes, I have contacted the trust company. I let them know that you've been located, and you will be contacting them sometime in the future. I received a reply that they are in receipt of my letter, and they are looking forward to meeting you. You will need to bring two forms of identification and proof of parentage to Hoffman, Hoffman & Goldstein."

"Will I need an attorney?"

"It wouldn't hurt to have one with us."

"The hardest part of our lives is behind us. We will get through it." said Breana.

"We certainly will. You know, I was talking to Mark, he told me he has to be in New York right after your honeymoon."

"Oh yeah, he said something about the 'Law of Sea' convention at the United Nations. He needs to be there because his fishing fleet will be affected by the outcome."

"I was thinking, if he has to be in New York, why don't we use the time to take care of your trust while you're there?"

Breana was silent for a moment; then she said, "We'll talk about that later? The designer is coming this evening for the second fitting of my gown. You and Mark are to meet with the tailor tomorrow afternoon. I had ordered Thelma's dress when I ordered mine. I need to have one made for Mom too. I'll speak to André when I see him this evening. Will you see that she is available?"

"Oh, *now* you need my expertise. I knew you couldn't pull this wedding off without me ha-ha!" Henry laughed.

"Yes Father, we know, you are the undisputable champ of organizers."

"Bless you my child. You are most observant."

Breana, laughing, shook her head as she left the room. She met Mark at the gazebo a few minutes later and handed him a glass of lemonade. Mark thanked her and took a sip. Breana stood watching him and waited for his reaction as he took a second sip.

"Mm! Best I have ever tasted, Mark said, as he licked his lips. It has a unique taste that I have never tasted before, a warm, zesty flavor."

"It's ginger. Thelma taught me how to make it like that for Father, and he loves it. Whenever he has a cold, he would drink it hot with a drop of rum, and he always claims that he is fine by morning."

"You made this? It's really delicious." He took another sip and smiled at her. He suddenly held up his glass to and said, "To my future wife, not only is she an heiress, she is also a good cook. What more can a guy ask for."

"Oh please! First of all, I only stirred some sugar in some water with lemon juice and ginger; that does not constitute cooking; and as far as being an heiress, as eccentric as my grandmother was, I'd have to see it to believe it. I hope she forgave herself for the things she did. I would hate to know that she died blaming herself instead of praying for forgiveness."

* * *

While Mark and Breana talked, the hours were swiftly passing. The designer arrived and Thelma let him in. Thelma opened the back door just as Breana was about to enter the house.

"Breana, I was just coming to get you. The designer is here, he is waiting in the hall."

"Thank you Thelma. I left Mark at the gazebo. I don't want him to get even a glimpse of my dress even though it's not the real one."

"You are right honey. It is bad luck. My Aunt Martha let her fiancé zip up her wedding dress the morning of her wedding. He left to go to the church before her, but he never showed up. When Aunt Martha walked into the church, the groom's space was empty, and she never saw him again. The poor woman bawled for a whole week. From that day on, she never trusted another man, and she died a spinster. Believe me when I tell you girl, it is b-a-ad luck!"

"Oh Thelma, where do you get all those stories! I'll talk to you later." Breana laughed and walked away.

"You can laugh all you want, but it is true just the same! So you better not try it. It's BAAAD LUCK!" Thelma shouted after her. Then she mumbled to herself. "These young people will not believe a word of anything until it happens to them."

"Hello André I'm sorry to keep you waiting." Breana said as she walked into the hall.

"Miss Noble! It is always a pleasure to see you." said André in his French accent, "The wait was quite all right, mademoiselle. I can see that you were enjoying yourself, yes? I like when the bride-to-be is happy. It makes my job easier."

"Thanks for being understanding, André. I know your time is limited and valuable, so shall we get started? Before we do, may I get you something?"

"Yes mademoiselle, a cold drink would be nice!"

"I just made some fresh lemonade, will that do?"

"That will do, mademoiselle, he said nodding his head.

Breana came back with the lemonade and handed him the glass. He took the glass and thanked her. He took a sip, "Ah, this is very refreshing." He put the glass down and set to work.

"First of all, Breana said, "I would like you to make another gown for my mother, identical to the one I picked for Thelma. Only, I want it in another shade. It can be darker or lighter, but I want them identical in fabric and style. Can you do the measurements today?"

"Sure, Miss Noble, as soon as we're finished with your fitting, I'll do the measurements."

Breana started putting the gown on. Her slender body slipped into it like a hand into a silk glove. "Oh! André! It's a perfect fit. It is beautiful. I wouldn't change a thing. It has such fine details. You have lived up to your reputation. I can't wait for everyone to see it. Are you flying back to New York tonight?"

"No, I have the first flight out in the morning. I wish I could stay and soak up some sun, but I'm too busy right now. It seems like there are many couples getting married next month. Yours was my last order for December. I've had to turn many clients away."

In that case, I'm glad I came when I did. Will you be able to do the extra gown?"

"I'll do my best. Can I see your mother now?

Breana left the room, and came back with Emily. "André, this is my mother, Mrs. Emily Noble. Mother, this is André, the renowned designer."

"It's a pleasure to meet you André. I've heard a lot about your work."

"The pleasure is all mine Madam Noble. I hope the work I'll do for you, will exceed whatever you've heard. If you're ready Madam, I must have your measurement for your new gown." In a short while, André had the measurement and he was on his way.

The curfew was lifted that same night. While some citizens were out celebrating, some were still apprehensive about leaving their homes after dark. The Nobles were included in the latter. They still carried on as if it was still in effect. "Be home on time, better safe than sorry," Thelma always said to everyone.

Although the days were sunny, the air was nippy. The North Wind delicately blew drizzling rain drops across the Island, and the poinsettias were in full bloom. This is typical of the Jamaican atmosphere when December arrives, and Christmas preparations are thrown in full gear.

"Hey Thelma, Dudley called out. "What about a tree? Would you like a blue mountain pine for the house?"

"Lord, I've been so busy I never gave a thought about putting up a tree. Go ahead, get a nice one."

"Will do!" said Dudley as he walked away, whistling a tune that sounded like *"Hark the Herald Angel Sing"*, the wind blowing gently against his green and yellow floral shirt.

Chapter Twenty-Seven

Mrs. White sat in a rocking chair. Her hair was now fully gray. She was sitting at the window inside her house and was looking out at the snow covered street. The first heavy snow had fallen in New York the night before and it was now stained with dirt and yellow coloring here and there. She saw her postman walk up to her door and ring the doorbell. She got up slowly and walked to the door.

"How are you today Mrs. White?"

"Oh, I just wish I could be any place but here right now. This arthritis is terrible in this cold weather, and that old furnace isn't helping the situation."

"I'm so sorry to hear that. I guess that's why I haven't seen you outside for the past few days"

"I'm just trying to stay warm. Since there isn't much I can do outside now, why should I bother?"

The post man handed her a clipboard. "I have a special delivery for you. It requires your signature right by the X."

While Mrs. White signed, the postman sifted through a handful of mail. "Nope, nothing else for you, take care of yourself," he said, as she handed the clipboard back to him. As he walked away, Mrs. White went inside and sat at the kitchen table. She opened the envelope and read the contents. Her face lit up, and she move to her phone as fast as her feet could carry her. As she waited for an answer, she reread the letter and smiled.

"Hello, may I speak to Elsie Tucker please?"

"This is Elsie, who is speaking please?"

"Elsie, this is Florence White, how are you?"

"I'm just wonderful, and you?"

Right then Mrs. White started rubbing her knees. "At the moment my knees are not so good, but I feel too good to let it get me down. I've just received the biggest surprise. Are you sitting down?"

"Go ahead Florence I'm sitting."

"I've been invited as a guest to a wedding in Jamaica, West Indies, all expenses paid!" She said excitedly.

Elsie started laughing. "An all-expenses paid invitation, by whom?" she asked.

Mrs. White read the invitation again. "Elsie do you remember Breana?"

"Breana! How could I forget her? She was living in Atlanta for a while but she and her adoptive parents were going to move to Jamaica." Elsie was sitting at the edge of her seat.

Mrs. White said, "She *did* move to Jamaica! The gentleman that she is marrying is the one that sent the invitation. He wants it to be a surprise for her as a wedding present."

"Florence! I got one, too! I tried to call you, but there was no answer. Oh, I'm so excited! Our little Breana didn't forget about us."

"Oh, I know. God bless her. Could you come over today or tomorrow, so we can discuss it further?"

"I sure can! I'll be there in an hour!"

"Oh my goodness, isn't that something" Mrs. White said to herself. "God sure is good. And mysterious too, yes, He works in mysterious ways." she said, shaking her head. She read the letter again. She went back to her chair by the window. She looked at the bougainvillea plant, and started smiling; thinking of the time Breana lived with her. *Well, my girl made it. I always knew she would.* She started rocking in her chair as she thought fondly of Breana. She proceeded to go through the package. It contained all she needed to get to Jamaica and reservations at the Whitmore Hotel, and transportation from the airport. Mrs. White read it out aloud in a proud manner.

Mr. & Mrs. Henry H. Noble
Request the honor of your presence
at the marriage of their daughter Margaret Breana Noble
to Mark Antonio Bogain,
Son of Anastasia Perrone Bogain and the late Captain Rolf Bogain
On December the seventeen, nineteen hundred and sixty six,
In the year of our Lord, at five o'clock in the evening at
Episcopal Fellowship Hall
Fourteen Mona Heights Boulevard, Saint Andrew.
Love eternally exists.

———

Reception follows immediately after the ceremony at the
Whitmore Hotel Ball Room
725 Knutsford Boulevard.
RSVP: 807-947-9427 by November 30th

"Well, well! You've done it again Lord, thank you. Imagine, I was just here feeling sorry for myself, and out of the blue you spread a little sunshine in my life. Lord, have mercy. It's going to be so good to see that child again. I bet she has grown into a stunning woman," she rambled on. Then she got up from the chair and put the tea kettle on the stove. She arranged some freshly baked cookies and coffee cake on a plate, while she waited for Elsie.

Preparations for the big day continued in Jamaica. "The days seem to slide by like butter on a hot knife, said Thelma, "I thought I was ready for this, but I'm going to miss her so much. This house will never be the same without her. It's like she breathes life into everything, and everything seems brighter in her presence."

"I feel as if I'm losing her just as I'm beginning to find her," said Emily. I thank God for what he gave us. It's just that wish we had more time to get to know each other before she has to leave." She sighed heavily.

"Oh, let's stop talking like this. She will always be our girl, no matter where she is.

On land, or on sea, our girl she'll always be," said Thelma.

"You sound like a poet Thelma! I can see what Breana means when she said you always know the right things to say in every occasion. First, you were there for her and Henry, and now I'm added to the list."

"No worries, we look after each other. I'm just glad you are finally here, so Breana can get to know you."

On Friday afternoon, Florence and Elsie arrived and were safely hidden away in their suite at the Whitmore Hotel.

Savannah arrived, and Breana spent the evening with her old friend giving details of the events of her life.

"That's incredible Breana. This story is unbelievable," she said, shaking her head in disbelief. "Who in a million years would believe that Uncle Henry would have turned out to be your biological father?"

"Tell me about it girl, I'm still pinching myself."

"And finding your mother here in Jamaica? Was that weird or what?" Savannah said nudging Breana with her elbow.

"That was the icing on the cake. I feel so blessed. The way it all happened is so surreal." Breana replied. "In my wildest dreams, I would never have thought this could've happened."

Savannah lowered her voice. "Is she really okay? Your mom I mean. I can't imagine what she must have gone through."

"You're right about that Savvy. She has been through a lot, but she seems to have put it behind her to start over. She and Father love each other even more than they did back then."

"I can see that," said Savannah, "Just looking at them together gives me something to look forward to."

Breana patted her on the shoulder. "Hey, enough about us, you haven't told me much about *your* Mr. Right. Are you holding out on me or something?"

"Oh no, I'm not, it just that this is your time," Savannah said with a wide grin on her face. "Besides, shouldn't we be thinking about the wedding rehearsal?"

After the rehearsal, they all drove to the Whitmore Hotel. Mark took Breana by the arm. "Darling, I have a surprise for you. I want you to have it before the wedding," he said, leading her toward the elevator. When they reached the fourth floor, Mark took her by the hand as they got off the elevator. Halfway down the hall, he said, "Close your eyes, and no peeking." He led her a few steps further and stood in front of a door. Breana was startled when Mark knocked on the door. As soon as the maid opened the door, Mark quickly placed his finger over his lips and motioned for her to remain silent. He then beckoned for the maid to leave the room. The maid, who already knew what was happening, covered her mouth to stifle a giggle and left the room.

"Open your eyes darling." Mark said.

Breana opened her eyes to find Elsie and Florence standing in front of her beaming.

"Oh, my God!" She said as she moved toward them for a long delayed embrace. Am I dreaming? Mrs. White and Mrs. Tucker, I have thought of you almost every day! Oh my goodness! Now my wedding will be perfect!" she said attempting to hug them simultaneously.

They held each other, and they cried tears of joy as they reminisced.

Breana turned to Mark, while dabbing tears from her eyes. "Mark, how did you manage to pull this off?"

Mark retrieved a box of tissues from the bathroom and handed it to Breana. He kissed her on her cheek. "I'll tell you all about it later. Take this time to catch up now."

Mrs. White looked at her and said, "He found a way to make

it possible because he loves you sugar, and as I always say, you're worth it."

As the three women gathered together chatting, Mark quietly left the room, smiling from ear to ear. He went back down stairs. Henry saw him as he entered the lobby in a rush. He got up from where he was sitting with Emily and quickly walked over to Mark. "How's Breana doing?"

"She's doing fine; she's still upstairs with Mrs. Tucker and Mrs. White."

"When you told me that you found them and had arranged for them to be here, I was glad because it's something I wanted to do for her as well. You're a good man Mark." Emily nodded in agreement.

"Thank you sir...could we talk later? I've got to make seating arrangements for them, and I still have some other last minute things I need to do."

"Okay son. I think we'll go up and see how things are going."

"That's good. They're getting reacquainted, and they are full of questions," Mark told them.

"Well, now that they're here, I have some questions of my own," Henry said, getting on the elevator with Emily.

* * *

Chapter Twenty-Eight

The reunion between Breana and her mentors was interrupted by a knock at the door. They ignored the first knock as Breana continued filling in the blanks of her life for Elsie and Florence. She had just finished telling how she met Mark and was in the middle of telling them about discovering that Henry was her real father when they heard another, more impatient knock on the door. "If it's housekeeping, ask them to come back. This is too juicy", said Mrs. White. They all laughed as Breana went to open the door.

"Oh, it's you. We thought it was housekeeping." She said over her shoulder as she walked back through the suite. "You're just in time. I was just telling Mrs. Tucker how she unknowingly placed me with you, my biological father. Come join us... Mrs. White, Mrs. Tucker, you remember my father Henry Noble.

They hugged and exchanged pleasantries. "It's good to see you two again", said Henry.

"And this is my biological, mother Emily Noble." Breana continued.

"I'm pleased to finally meet you both. Breana has told me so much about you.

Thank you so much for taking care of her." Emily said.

Every time Emily had to thank another person for playing a role in Breana's life, she felt uneasy, as if she was being judged. However, she hid her pain very well. She smiled even though her heart was breaking.

"I always said the Lord moves in mysterious ways," said, Elsie, as she shook Emily's hand.

"When Breana told us that you found her, it lifted my faith in miracles," said Florence.

"This whole story is a miracle. You placed her with her father without any knowledge of it, how often does that happen?"

Breana looked at her longtime acquaintance for answers. Mrs. Tucker looked to the ground, then back to them. Then she got uneasy as she began to speak.

"I don't know how else to say this, but to just come out and say it…," she hesitated. Everyone looked at her, hanging on her last word…waiting.

"I must confess. It was not by coincidence that I placed her, but I was sworn to secrecy.

Now that you have found each other, it doesn't matter much anymore."

Henry cast a suspicious look on Emily. *Has Emily been lying to me?*

Emily was astonished. She looked at Henry and shook her head in dismay. She still remembered his expressions and his face said it all. She felt accused and could have easily gone through the floor if it would have opened for her, as her life replayed among strangers.

Breana sat on the bed twirling her hair around her finger. She was close to tears, not focusing on anyone in particular.

"What do you mean by that, Elsie?" asked Henry, "What are you trying to say?"

"It was the eeriest thing, said Mrs. Tucker. "I remember it like it was yesterday; because, I've carried it with me all these years." She began to recount the events responsible for the reunion of this family.

Chapter Twenty-Nine

I t was *1957,* over thirteen years since Breana was found abandoned at the firehouse on 196th street. It was past nine o'clock in the morning. Elsie Tucker was sitting at her desk sipping on a steaming hot cup of coffee, and going over some paperwork. The door opened to an old man, bent with age. His hair was clean and white. His dark skinned face was chafed and dry, and his clothes, though clean, were wrinkled. He walked with a shuffled gait and a walking can. He moved to the front of Elsie's desk.

"Good morning, Ma'am," he said, almost out of breath and barely able to stand.

"Good morning, can I help you?" Elsie asked setting her cup down and looking up at the old man. He started coughing furiously, and then he swallowed hard. He took a dingy handkerchief from the pocket of his old faded dungarees and covered his mouth. When his bout of coughing subsided, he returned the bandana to the pocket of his long sleeved, plaid flannel shirt. He spoke in a raspy voice as if every word was an effort and his eyes were watery.

"Are you alright?" Elsie asked, walking swiftly around the desk. "Here, let me help you, she said guiding him to a chair. "I'll get you a drink of water," she said as she turned to walk away.

"Oh no miss, I'm alright. I just have to catch my breath."

"Who are you looking for Mr.—?

"My name is not important ma'am, but it's very important that

I speak to someone in charge o' this establishment," He said, almost gasping for every breath.

"Well, I'm Elsie Tucker, and I'm in charge, so you can talk to me."

He opened up a page of an old yellow newspaper and handed it to Elsie. "I know about this child in this here paper ma'am."

Elsie looked at the article in the paper. Her eyes widened and her jaws dropped.

"What do you know about this child, sir?" She asked in amazement.

"Well ma'am, what I'm going to tell you—. He started coughing again. —is the go-od honess truth, as the mama told it to me. I swear on my mama's grave, but before I tell you, you gots ta promise me that you will tell no one."

Seeing the old man's distress, Elsie said, "I promise, go ahead, tell me"

"The onliest reason I come is, I'm a dying man, and I can't carry this thing to my grave.

Elsie listened patiently as he spoke, between coughs."

"Okay, I give you my word. What do you know?" she said as she walk back to her seat and picked up a pen and paper.

"I don't know where the mother is. I never hear from them."

"You said them?"

"Yes ma'am. She and her mama lived in my building cross the hall from me. They took her mama away, an' that poor chile had to leave her baby behind. I never seen them again, but she tells me who the father is. As I said ma'am, you can't breathe it to a soul. The mother believes that it will put the chile' in danger."

"Put the child in danger, how?"

"On account that the grandma sees the chile as a blot on her family. I gots ta know that she is alright, 'cause its weighin' heavy on my mind."

"Who is the child's family?" Elsie asked, with frown lines etched between her eyes.

"He was supposed to live in Connecticut back then. He comes from a family of big shots. I don' know where he is now, but his name is Henry Noble."

Elsie dropped the pencil. "Who did you—!" before Elsie could finish the sentence, the old man suffered another coughing spell. She hurriedly got up from the desk to fetch a glass of water for him. When she came back with the water, the chair was empty.

She opened the door to her office and ran into the hallway only to see the doors of the elevator close and it began its decent. She took the stairs, but by the time she exited the building, the old man had disappeared on the crowded sidewalks of Manhattan.

Elsie returned to her seat and flopped in her chair, bewildered. *My God, Henry Noble has been trying to adopt all this time. What do I do now?* "I have to keep my word." she said out loud.

"Keep your word about what?" Connie asked, walking into the room.

"I'm just thinking out loud Connie. I'm just thinking aloud." Elsie answered limply.

Chapter Thirty

Henry was the first one to speak. Everyone else was still in shock at Elsie's disclosure.

"So, you knew all this time and didn't bother to notify me!" He said angrily.

I'm sorry Henry. You've got to understand. I had to keep my word. The man was dying. I had to keep my promise." Elsie pleaded. "Besides if I had made it known, your mother would have made life difficult for her…and you.

Henry's anger waned as he thought of how his mother was and what their life would have been like if she had known. He hung his head and sighed. "You're right, you know. I'm sorry."

"Henry, what are you sorry for? There's no need to apologize. I can understand your anger."

"Yes I do. I'm sorry that you had to hold this secret. I'm sorry that you are right about my mother, but mostly, I'm sorry that so much time was lost between Breana and Emily. He went over to his family and hugged them as if he would never let go. Dry eyes were scarce at that moment.

After they composed themselves, Breana asked, "Did you ever find the old man?

"No, I never found out who he was. To this day, I'm still baffled how anyone in his condition could have moved and gotten away so fast. He was possibly an angel of mercy! I believe he was. What happened to him? I don't know."

Henry took a big sigh of relief. He said, "Elsie, my family and I owe you a lifetime of thanks. I—"

"Dear God, I know who the man was, Emily interrupted. His name was Mr. Day. We lived across from each other in the same building. He was a kind man. He owned a small convenient store. That man may not have been an angel, but he definitely was sent by God; he helped us out many times with groceries."

"So we have solved the mystery, and all is well," said Breana. "I believe this was the last piece of the puzzle. Now we can put this all behind us and enjoy our time together."

At seven o'clock, the butler announced that dinner was served. They all filed into the dining room. Breana looked around the room at all the people that had been a part of her life at some point when she needed them most, and she fully realized that in spite of all that she had been through, she was blessed. She gave thanks that they had been a part of her life, mentioning every special thing that each person did for her. At the end of her thanks giving, every one needed a fresh handkerchief.

After dinner, everybody dispersed. Mark and Breana embraced each other.

"Good night fair princess. I shan't see you till the morrow," he said after kissing her and left her blushing. He went with his best man, who was his brother-in law, and his mother and sister to the ship.

"You've done well, Mark. Breana is a lovely girl. I like her. You must bring her over to Ecuador sometime. She and I could go shopping," said his mother, Anastasia."

"Mother, is that all you ever think of, shopping?

"At this point yes, and before you ask, yes I'm ashamed; all the more reason for you to bring her over. Maybe together we'll come up with something new and innovative to do dear."

"I agree with mother Mark, said his sister Val, she is a lovely girl. Finally I'll have a sister."

"It means a lot to know you feel that way Sis. Breana is an only child, and she always wanted siblings, so I'm sure she will feel the same."

As the day of the wedding unfolded, and breakfast was being served, Breana couldn't eat a bite. Mark on the other hand had a ravenous appetite.

"Another croissant please, Philippe. It's my last breakfast as a single man. I'm making the most of it."

"I don't blame you sir," Philippe replied as he served him the extra croissant.

* * *

Dudley arrived at Waltham Park. He was dressed in his black tuxedo with silver bow tie and cummerbund and white shirt. His hair was cut low and neatly shaven at the side; neat, sharp edges on the side burns. The fine outline of his moustache spread out like a swallow's wing. He was sharp. When Susan Dooley approached the car, Dudley opened the car door for her.

Sue looked him over. *Now, that's what I'm talking about- a hunk of dark delicious chocolate I could sink my teeth into,* she thought.

Dudley did not fail to notice her assets either. *She is gorgeous! I dare not make a move while on the job. But later on,* he thought, brainstorming on how to break the ice before the night was through.

"Thank you very much," she said as she got in the car. She continued to look him over very subtly. Her long black tresses were pinned back. Her flawless cocoa brown skin, further kissed by the Jamaica sun, had a delightfully healthy glow. Her make-up accentuated her high cheekbones and full lips. Her pill box hat with a short veil across her forehead was the perfect complement to her dress.

"Good evening, Sue. It's nice to see you again." Dudley said.

"Likewise Dudley, I'm glad it is under better circumstances."

"I know. How is your brother doing?"

"He's serving his time well. Since he helped the police with Bunny's arrest he did get a reduced sentence. He's been a model prisoner and may get out early for good behavior and all the good he's been doing."

"That's good. I'm glad to hear he's turned his life around."

They drove along in silence for a while; it was awkward. Finally, Dudley asked the burning question. "Have you ever been married Sue?"

"Oh yes, I have."

"So what happened, how come he's not around?"

"Well, he died years ago. My husband worked for the railroad. He was a conductor on the train. You remember the terrible train wreck at Kendal in 1957?"

"Yes, I do, a lot of people lost their lives in that crash."

"My husband was working on that train the day of the accident. He died later at the hospital, but I at least had an opportunity to say goodbye to him."

"Oh my goodness, I'm so sorry. I didn't mean to bring up bad memories."

"It's okay. I can talk about it now. There was a time when the mention of Kendal would evoke tears. It took me a long time to be able to talk about it. I've learned how to cope better now, but I'll never get over it."

"Did you have children?"

"Yes, we have one daughter. She is an exchange student in Canada."

Dudley looked at her and commented. "I bet she is as beautiful as you."

"Thank you. I'm not sure how beautiful I am, but she is a beautiful girl."

"Well your husband maybe gone, but he left you someone to be proud of."

"Yes, I am very proud of her."

They rode along in silence for a while then he asked, "So you've never consider getting married again?"

"No, the men I encounter are a different breed from what my husband was, so I'd rather be alone."

"Yes, but don't you get lonely sometimes?"

"A lot of people seem to think that a woman without a man is a fate worse than death, but as far as I'm concerned, a woman who thinks she can't make it on her own…considers herself a burden she can't bear. She'll cast herself on the first man that comes along, and she'll trade her dignity, her identity, and her self-respect for dependency on him. Before she realizes what's happening, she has no voice."

"There's truth in what you're saying," Dudley replied, "too many women suffer because they'll do anything to hang on to a man. In my opinion, a man who takes advantage of a woman in any way is a poor excuse for a human being."

"The first man I was engaged to…he carved out a mold for his ideal wife and tried to squeeze me into it, but there's no way I was going to cease being an individual to fit his mold. God made me an individual in his image. Just because after we married and became as one, doesn't mean I ceased to exist. So, I gave his ring back to him," said Sue.

"You know Sue, my dad used to say that marriage is a constant compromise. However, if compromising is one sided, there will always be turmoil. It's a foolish man who marries a woman and tries to change her into himself. Both cannot be the same, that's why opposites attract as they say." said Dudley.

"Hmm…you are so right." Sue replied. "I remember one day we were having a discussion, I told him the something similar to what you just said. He told me he couldn't compromise; because, it means he would have to accept what he doesn't believe in. That was the final nail that sealed the fate of our marriage and future relationship."

"Sounds like an idiot to me. Just because he believes it, doesn't make it right. You can't grow together by expecting change in the other person while you remain the same."

"That's my point exactly. The way he treated me, and the things he used to say to me; it made me believed that he didn't have the kind of love he should have had for me. He invited me in his life; then he treated me like something he brought home at the bottom of his shoe, yet he expected me to treat him like he was my king. Then I would hear from other people that he loves me," Sue said sullenly.

Dudley laughed out loud. "Nonsense, a man who really loves a woman makes it clear so she knows that he loves only her.

"That's what I'm talking about Dudley," said Sue, "I forgave the way he treated me, but there were some wounds that cut so deep that the damage was done. I never hated him. I'm blessed to be able to love everybody under any circumstances. However, I was determined to keep my identity, my sanity, and my integrity, so I just shut down, and I moved on."

Sue, listen to me. When a man loves a woman, nobody has to tell her. She feels it in his touch. She hears it in his voice; she sees it in his eyes; she tastes it in his kiss; he loves her with ALL of his senses. Anything less than that…is a shame before God.

Sue was drooling as Dudley talked about how to love a woman. She got quiet; then she changed the subject.

"Breana is such a nice girl. I hope she'll have a good life." She said.

"I hope so, too. She deserves the best."

"What do you think of her young man?"

"He seems like a nice guy, and he adores her. Anybody who has been around them can see that. I hope it stays that way. Well, here we are," said Dudley as he approached the gate to church.

"Here we are indeed," Sue replied, "you got us to the church on time, and we're not even the ones getting married."

"If it were, you would probably be late. As a matter of fact, I would challenge you on that." Dudley said, smiling at her.

"Sue giggled. "Very funny Dudley More! Ve-ry funny!""

He opened the door for her. As she exited the car, she pointed across the street.

"Oh look, there's another church right next door. "New Beginnings Assembly of Christ," boy the names they come up with for these congregations."

Dudley looked and replied, "Well, it doesn't matter what they call themselves, you know what they say, all roads lead to God."

"I beg to differ, said Sue. Who are "they"? Because *they* are wrong. Adams race had fallen away from God. Jesus the son came to lead us back on the straight path to the Father by teaching us how to love one another. What you call yourself doesn't matter, as long as your life is Christ-like and you follow in his footsteps. He is the way, the Truth and the Light. If all roads lead to God, tell me, what about the people who don't believe in God?"

"You sound just like Thelma, always preaching." Dudley said as he closed the car door.

"As long as she speaks the truth, I accept that as a compliment. Thank you." They walked inside the church arm in arm, smiling.

* * *

Before they were ready to leave for the ceremony, Henry took Emily aside. "I have something to show you," he said. She followed him to the bedroom. He walked over to the dresser and he took out a small trinket box and opened it. Emily gasped when she saw what it was. Inside the box was the comb that he took from her hair so many years ago.

"I believe on a day like this, you can find better use for this comb than to have it sitting in an old man's treasure chest among his souvenirs. Now that I have you, I can give it back."

"Oh Henry, you've kept it all these years! I'm so happy. Now I can give it to Breana."

Right away she went to Breana's room and knocked on the door. "It's open. Come on in."

Emily pushed the door open and walked in the room. Breana was sitting in front of the mirror brushing her hair. She turned to look at Emily.

"I have something for you. This comb belonged to your great-grandmother. I want you to have it as your 'something old'."

Breana got to her feet, "Is this the comb that you gave Father?"

"Yes, it is. He gave it back to me because on a special day like today, we both thought you should have it. Keep it as a token of the love your Father and I share, and as a symbol that no matter how far life takes us, we can find our way home and back with family."

"Thank you Mom, I shall cherish it. Someday I'll give it to my daughter. I'll tell my children of its significance to our family. Now I have both pieces to tell my children about."

"This is such a blessing for us. For all the times I prayed for your safety, I never imagined life would turn this way." Emily said, as she enjoyed being in the presence of the daughter she thought she would never see again. "God really moves in mysterious ways."

Breana placed the comb next to her key ring on the dresser thinking, "These are more precious to me than anything I could ever have. I will wear this comb with pride today, to hold up my hair."

* * *

André arrived on time. The bride maids were buzzing around. The limousines were already lined up, and the program director went around yelling to everyone who would listen.

"Places everyone, places...we will start on time!" He clapped his hands together to get their attention and started placing people where they should be.

Breana's limousine was the last to pull up. She turned heads while walking to get into the car. Her dress was made from wool knit and lined with Chinese silk. It was fully beaded with both white beads and iridescent sequins with diamond shape patterns throughout. The scooped neckline, front and back, was worn slightly off of her beautifully toned shoulders. Her long sleeves were fitted down to her wrists. The dress had a high waist, just below the bust and the A-line went down to an ankle skimming hemline. In the back, the train was made of organza and decorated with diamante beading. It fanned out like the shape of a peacock's tail, and it stretched six feet long. Her hair was pulled back in an up-do. The hair style complimented her veil, which had a beautiful lace trim with floor length tulle attached to a white beaded pillbox hat. Her shoes were of an elegant white silk. Pearl earrings and a single strand necklace pulled everything together. She carried a bouquet of white lilies of the valley...tied with a magenta colored ribbon.

Finally, everyone was seated in the limousines, and the motorcade started from Harbor-View to Mona Heights. Mark and his groomsmen were already at the church. The guests were being ushered to their seats. When the caravan arrived, musicians were signaled to begin playing. The harp was Breana's instrument of choice as the wedding party marched in. Then they changed the tune to signal that the bride was about to begin her march. Everyone rose and stood in her honor when the bride appeared on the arms of her father. She was radiant. Her steps were gingerly as she marched in. Her eyes searched for Mark. As she focused on him, she smiled nervously. *My knees feel as if they will buckle any minute.* She thought.

"Father, please hold me; don't let me fall." She whispered to Henry.

"I've got you Pumpkin. It's the jitters is all; you're doing alright." Henry whispered while he nodded to some of the guests as they marched to the tune of "Here Comes the Bride." When they reached the altar, the minister spoke about the true commitment to marriage and that it should not be taken lightly. Breana had more mothers weeping in the audience than any bride ever had-a biological mother, a foster mother, a surrogate mother, and Mrs. Tucker.

After repeating their vows and exchanging rings, the minister pronounced them man and wife.

"Mark, you may kiss your bride."

"About time!" One of the male guests was heard to say.

Everyone laughed and applauded as Mark lifted Breana's veil and kissed her with great passion. The musicians played as the wedding party marched out. It was a spectacular event. They went on their way to the Whitmore for the reception.

Florence and Elsie were seated at the family table. There were approximately 350 guests including family, close friends, co-workers, and acquaintances; including the Prime Minister of Jamaica. The reception hall was exquisitely decorated with a variety of fresh flowers and white and magenta colored balloons and streamers. With recommendations from Breana, the Whitmore chefs created an eclectic menu of Caribbean, American and Columbian cuisine. The cake was 3 feet tall. It was vanilla flavored, decorated with white icing and magenta flowers.

True happiness filled the air…an occasion that was long overdue. Breana and Mark danced to "The Way You Look Tonight." During the 'mother and son' dance, Mark's mother beamed with pride as she danced with her son. Breana watched them and found another reason why she loved Mark so much. *Mark cherishes and respects all of the women in his life. Look at how he dances with his mother, so gentle and protective at the same time. He adores her,* she thought. She grinned and felt so blessed to have found a man like him. Then Breana danced with her father. They laughed and cried together as they danced moving to the music beautifully played by the live band.

Emily sat at the table watching her new husband and her baby Breana dancing. She basked in the essence of Breana's joy. Instead of asking herself, "Is my baby happy?", as she had done for so many years, now she knew. Emily was in her own world thinking of Breana as a baby when suddenly she looked up and Henry and Breana were by her side.

"What are you two doing? The dance is only half way through; you should be up there dancing," Emily insisted.

Ignoring her statement, Henry took her by one hand, and Breana took the other hand. They both whisked her off to the dance floor. "This is your dance too, Mom and this is my wedding. If I want a 'father-daughter-mother dance', then that's what it will be. Now come on, let's dance the night away!" Breana said, laughing haughtily. "Listen to your daughter," Henry said as they scurried back on the dance floor.

Emily was speechless and teary-eyed as they all danced, huddled around each other. The guests applauded. The photographer went crazy, snapping away at what would be remembered as the highlight of the evening. By now, everyone knew of the family's story. There was not a dry eye in the room. Breana stated amid tears of joy, "Mom and Dad, WE HAVE COME FULL CIRCLE!"

Thelma enjoyed being served for a change. She was smiling and nodding at the servers,

"Thank you," she said to one of them as he poured her a second glass of wine. She cocked her pinky finger as she picked up her glass and took a sip of wine.

"You could get used to this, Thelma girl," she mumbled to herself.

"Is there anything else I could get you ma'am?" asked the waiter.

"Oh no, I'm fine, thank you." *Oh yes, I could sure get used to this,* she thought laughing to herself.

Everyone let loose and enjoyed themselves at the blissful affair, especially Dudley. He was making eyes at Sue all afternoon. They danced together most of the time. At the end of one dance, they went back to their table. Dudley asked for a fresh glass of champagne.

"You hardly touched that one," said Sue.

"Yea, but I've never finished a drink that I've walked away from. A lot can happen to that unattended drink."

The waiter came back with two drinks. Sue took her drink and thanked the waiter. Dudley leaned back and cocked his head to the side. He picked up his drink and took a sip, and started twirling around the liquid in his glass while he slyly studied Sue. He said, "So...Sue, do you think this might be the start of something big between us?"

Sue looked at him with a smirk. "Well, big things start from small things, and sometimes not, so who am I to say?"

"But is there a possibility in this case?" Dudley asked, taking another sip.

Sue hesitated for a bit, and then she said, "Anything is possible. You just never know."

The Bogain-Villa was set to sail at twelve o'clock the next day. All of their luggage, including, Dudley's were already on board. However, no one except Mark and Breana would be boarding until one hour before departure.

"Father I talked it over with Mark and we agreed to postpone seeing the Attorneys for now. I need time for Mark and me to bond and really get to know each other before I get occupied with a business of that magnitude. So we'll just continue the voyage after he's finished with his meetings."

"Oh, so how much time are we talking about?"

Breana tilted her head to the side with one eye closed and the other on Henry. She gave him sheepish smile as she said, "About a year', she said pensively." Henry was a little disappointed. He had wanted to resolve her inheritance so they could lay the memories of his mother's transgressions to rest-put everything behind them and keep moving forward.

"A year? Breana——." He started to protest, but Emily gave him an imperceptible nudge. He smiled. "Pumpkin, whenever you're ready."

The chauffer drove them to the Bogain-Villa, and they boarded the ship. When they reached the door of their suite, Mark picked her up and carried her over the threshold. When he put her down, she stood awe stricken, as her eyes roved around the room. The suite was lavishly decorated. There were fresh flowers on every table, a basket of fresh fruits, a tray of cocktail sandwiches, cubed cheese, and tea biscuits. There was wine on ice, caviar, and hot beverages. Green satin tapestry with gold trim covered the windows and walls. She slowly walked into the bedroom, taking in every detail that caught her eye. A Louis the XIV bed graced the center of the room. She ran her hands over the linen made from Egyptian cotton and plush pillows, and it reminded her of when she first came to live with the Nobles. All the woodwork in the suite was of dark mahogany with beautiful carvings. *This place is fit for royalty, it's a palace,* she thought.

"My goodness, I feel like Cinderella at the ball," she said as she drank everything in, amazed at the splendor.

Mark came up from behind. He slipped his arms around her waist and kissed her neck. "Welcome home, Mrs. Bogain."

"Never in my life have I ever seen anything like this place," she replied, "Its fit for a queen."

"Oh, but I've seen greater magnificence, darling," said Mark, "The first time I saw your face, although I never thought it possible. You are even more beautiful tonight. And as for being fit for a queen, that's why it was built for you 'Your Majesty' you are *my* queen. The servants have already unpacked your things. Your dressing room is over here," he said, taking her hand and walking across the room.

She walked with him to the open door, "Mark I can't imagine a dressing room of this size on a ship."

"Darling, this is our villa. The only difference is it is on water. If you ever get tired of being the seafaring wife, you have many homes to choose from. All you have to say is,

'I want to drop my anchor' and it will be done," Mark said, "I adore you darling you shall have anything your heart desires."

"Mark you're so thoughtful. I love you so much." She kissed him softly on his lips.

"Why don't I get more comfortable," she said as she pried herself from his embrace.

Mark poured two glasses of wine while he waited for Breana. She emerged from the dressing room wearing a lavender gown. It was fashioned around the bust with a pink ribbon hanging down the front. The gown flowed freely down to her toes. The bust was trimmed with costly lace that shimmered in the light, compliments of Andre's originals. She put on the matching robe and walked across the room; the hem of the robe trailed behind her. Mark removed the comb from her hair, and it tumbled down around her shoulders.

"Heaven is missing an angel, and I feel sorry for anyone who isn't me right now."

"Thank you for making my dreams come true," she said, as she gently brushed her hand across the side of his face, caressing him.

He kissed the back of her hand and pulled her closer to him. When Mark started singing the love song, "Just the Way You Look Tonight," the effort of the original artist grew pale in comparison. His baritone was faultless. He waltzed her across the floor. He looked into her eyes and softly said, "Mark and Breana, tonight and always."

He kissed her gently. Tear drops trickled down her cheeks, this time, for joy. He wiped her tears away and hugged her tightly. She rested her face on his chest. And for a moment, time stood still.

He took her hand, and he walked her over to the table, and sat her down, "I'm your genie," he said, "your wish is my command, and you have more than three wishes."

"Dear genie," she said, "I only have one wish, let's make this an unforgettable night."

"Granted." he said as he stood before her, enthralled in the moment. He picked up both glasses of wine, and he handed one to her. "Here's to life and love forever," he said.

They clicked their glasses and sipped the wine while looking at each other in adoration. Mark quickly set his glass down on the table and Breana followed his lead. Romantic love songs softly played in the background. At first, Mark kissed Breana's lips so tenderly, as if she would break. His touch was smooth as he slowly released the satin string of her robe. His kiss took Breana's breath away. He removed the gown from around her shoulders and let it fell to the floor. Then his kiss grew deeper in anticipation, and Breana grew dizzy with excitement. He pulled away only to take her hand and lead her to the bed. He placed soft kisses on her hands, her neck, and finally her full lips. He picked her up, and he placed her on the bed. As he laid her down, his body hovered over hers as if he had just created her and ready to breathe life into her. Breana waited intently; her heart beating passionately.

He started kissing her from her neck and then he moved south, pausing at her chest a while. He slowly moved from side to side on her chest lingering at the pinnacles of what seemed to be twin peaks of the blue mountain; then he started heading south again. Breana had never felt such bliss. She lovingly traced Mark's back with her fingertips. As eager as Mark was, he knew he would need to take his time. It was Breana's first time and he wanted to make it good for her. He turned out the lights, and he proceeded to fulfill his promise of an unforgettable night.

The next morning, Mark stretched in bed, "Oh my aching back," he said with a phony look of agony on his face. "I think I may need stitches."

"Before you'll need stitches," replied Breana, "There have to be broken skin and blood." Mark smiled and glanced at the sheets.

"That's not from you," she said, Race you to the shower," she said. She swung her legs over the side of the bed and moved fast, as Mark hurried to catch up with her. From fore-play to horse-play, they enjoyed becoming one with each other.

Chapter Thirty-One

J ust *before* dawn in the Kingston Harbor, on board the Bogain-
Villa, she laid motionless with her head resting on the bare
chest of her new husband. Her luminous, smoky grey eyes gazed
at his clean shaven and perfectly tanned face; while his tall and lanky
body lay sleeping close to her. The buttons on his sky blue pajama
shirt were all undone. Breana's eyes trailed from his rippling six-pack
stomach…straight down to the whole form of her Adonis.

She looked him over and counted her blessings to have found the
love of her life. *I can't believe it's almost one year already.* She swept her
hand across his brow; then she traced his lips with the tip of her pointer
finger. She pressed her lips against his and gently kissed him awake.

"Mmm," he moaned as he sheepishly opened his eyes. "Is it morning
already my darling, or have I died and awaken in the arms of an angel?"

Breana caught on to his dramatic dialogue and began to humor
him. "This is earth my darling, and morning is not yet," she said.

"It's impossible for earth to possess the joy I'm feeling," he said
hugging her closer, "How long have you been awake?"

"Quite some time," she smiled. "I was afraid if I slept for too
long, all of this would be a dream."

It became harder for them to keep a straight face as they continued
their theatrical performance. He lifted his arms and framed her face.
His strong manicured fingers gently caressed her cheeks. His brown
eyes were penetrating. He looked at her as if he could see her very soul.

"I'm the one that's dreaming, my darling, for no mere mortal deserves an angel in his bed to call his wife; yet here you are beside me. I want to see the sunrise with you, but it's still a while before daylight; which means, we have time on our hands, so how should we spend it?" He asked with a suggestive wink.

She ran her fingers through his dark curly locks, and flashed him an enchanting smile that revealed her pearly white teeth.

"I'll spend my time on expressions of love for my adoring husband."

"Well, in that case..."

Mark's response muffled as he showered her with kisses, heading south on her body; she giggled uncontrollably. As the horseplay ceased, Breana caught her breath.

"Mark Bogain, you have made me so happy. After all that I've been through, I never dreamed my life would be like this," She said, as her husband adored her.

They spent the morning searching and discovering each other.

As the first ray of sunlight crept over the horizon, Breana stood on the deck of the Bogain-Villa. Mark crept up behind her. Just as he moved closer, a gentle breeze blew her hair off her shoulders. He walked up behind her, and he slipped his arms around her waist. He kissed the nape of her neck as she tilted her head in responds to his touch. She discovered that ears were not just for hearing, and the lobes were not just for earrings. Mark's heart was full and overflowing with love for his alluring Bride. They held each other closely and at that moment, Breana felt as if she was born just to be in his arms. *I'm so blessed,* she thought, *my love is perfect for me in every way.*

"I'm a very blessed man." Mark said, as he gazed into her eyes. "When I came to Harbor View, I never thought I'd find my most precious jewel lying on the sand by the sea. As Mark said those words, they triggered her memory of her childhood song and her favorite book, only this time, she was happy. She thought; *I finally made it by the beautiful sea.*

* * *

Acknowledgments

For helping to bring Breana's Full Circle into the world, I would like to thank:

My daughters Cleo and Trina for being so supportive; you two are wind beneath my wings. My daughter Karrene for her constructive criticism that made me a better writer. Thanks to my sister, FDR, for her expert assistance in reading my work. A special thank you to all my family and friends for their understanding my limited attendance in family get-togethers, outings, and functions.

Author's Note

The harmful things that Breana went through, is not exclusive. We are all tested ad tried individually and collectively. Sometimes life takes us through some predicaments so difficult and worrisome, it seems we will never see our way through, and sometimes we feel like giving up. However, when we persevere through it all, at the end, we realize that all those obstacles, all those trials, were only stepping stones to get us where we need to be. That's why we must hold on and pray for strength and patience.

Oh yes! Breana's life began on the rough side of the mountain, lots of twists and turns. No one knew she was a diamond shining beneath the dust, an Heiress no less. I believe she went through all that to create an understanding of the plight of the poor and the down trodden. All that trouble served to build her character. The saga involving Breana, her family, her friends and her acquaintances continues in *"True Undertone"*.

"Do not be anxious about anything, but in every situation, by prayer and petition, with thanksgiving, present your requests to God. And the peace of God, which transcends all understanding, will guard your hearts and your minds in Christ Jesus." Philippians 4:6-7

"Weeping may endure for a night, but joy comes in the morning." Psalms 30:5